THE ROAD TO GESUALDO

GESUALDO

Erika Rummel

D. X. VAROS

Published by:
D. X. Varos, Ltd
7665 E. Eastman Ave. #B101
Denver, CO 80231

Book cover design:
SelfPubBookCovers.com/RLSather
Cover layout by:
D. X. Varos, Ltd.

ISBN: 978-1-941072-70-7

CHAPTER 1

Ferrara, 1594

Spring was in the air. The capes of the two ladies strolling in the ducal garden were fluttering in the warm breeze. Last night's rain had turned the lawns emerald green and swelled the stream crossing the park. It was a glorious day, but Livia was in a dark mood.

"Something is not right," she said to her mistress. "Every time I mention Prince Carlo's name, people lower their eyes and fall silent. What are they holding back?"

"I don't want to know," Leonora d'Este said and heaved a sigh that made the pearls in her hair quiver. "What's the use of chasing rumours? The contract is signed. I must marry the man my brother has chosen for me." Her skirt, densely embroidered with a floral motif of russet and gold, weighed her down and made her move ponderously. But it also gave her an air of dignity, and Leonora d'Este never forgot what she owed to her illustrious family. The House of Este had ruled Ferrara for the past three hundred years. "I must do my duty and marry Prince Carlo," she said.

Livia threw up her hands in frustration. "You must do your duty! You must do as your brother says! And what if it turns out that Prince Carlo is a monster?"

"He isn't," Leonora said and walked on stiffly. Beside her, Livia cut an insignificant figure. She was small and delicately put together, with a head of unruly hair and a voice as melodic as a poem.

"You have never laid eyes on Prince Carlo," she said to Leonora. "How can you be so sure that he isn't a monster?"

Leonora turned to her lady-in-waiting and held out a pendant dangling from a gold chain around her neck. "You may judge for yourself, my dear," she said. Carlo Gesualdo had sent her a locket with his portrait done in enamel. She opened it for Livia to see.

The man in the portrait was young and handsome. He had close-cropped hair, a narrow face with strongly marked crescent brows, a long straight nose, and a delicate mouth.

"He has sensitive lips, don't you think?" Leonora said.

"They look cruel to me. Beautifully cruel."

"Oh, Livia! I couldn't love and obey a man who is cruel," Leonora said with a breathless huff. The stomacher she wore was too tight, but loose clothes encouraged slumping, and Leonora was mindful of appearances.

Livia took her mistress' arm and patted it fondly. "I didn't mean to make you uneasy," she said, softening her voice. She was more than a lady-in-waiting to her mistress. She was her friend and confidante, the only person with whom Leonora could speak freely without fear of betrayal.

I should have kept my mouth shut, Livia thought. Leonora was right. Women had no say in marriage matters. They were not free to follow their heart. Livia herself was an independent spirit, but even so she could not escape the constraints of society. A woman's choice was limited. Leonora was obliged to marry a man she did not know and might not be able to love. Livia knew her admirer Pietro Paci very well and loved him dearly but was obliged to decline his attentions. There was no chance of a happy ending to the affair. She had no dowry, and Pietro had no money of his own. He could not afford to marry Livia. She thought of his handsome face, the feel of his lean hard body against hers, his strong arms, his hands with long fingers — the fingers of a man with a quick brain.

The two women walked on in thoughtful silence. They turned into the Padiglione, where the fruit trees were putting out the first buds.

Livia forced herself to stop thinking about Pietro and took up the conversation again. "What does your brother say about the Prince?"

"I asked him what Prince Carlo was like, and he gave me a look to pierce the soul," Leonora said.

"I doesn't take much to annoy Don Cesare, I know, but surely your brother cannot take it amiss if you express an interest in your intended husband," Livia said, "if you want to know his likes and dislikes, or his favourite pastime."

"I had only one question: Will I be able to love Carlo Gesualdo? But Cesare doesn't care about love. Wealth and standing are all that counts with him. The Prince is the descendant of an ancient family, he said. He commands great wealth and has important connections to the papal court. What more do you want? — That's all the information he gave me and that's all *he* cares about."

"Let me make inquiries," Livia said. "I'll ask Pietro Paci what kind of man Prince Carlo is. Pietro was present at the marriage negotiations and met him in person."

"Speak to him then," Leonora said, but her voice was hesitant as if she was afraid of what Livia might find out.

The two women turned into the path leading to the loggia and stopped by the pond to watch the goldfish paddle their delicate fins.

"There's another thing that puzzles me," Leonora said. "Prince Carlo will be welcomed here with great ceremony. I am told the Duke has arranged for a triumphal entry to rival the grandeur of the Roman emperors. It seems an extravagant gesture. The Duke has never paid attention to me before or favoured me in any way, even though I am his close kin. He must have an ulterior motive for making such grand preparations. And speaking of ulterior motives — Pietro Paci is as ready as ever to do you favours?"

Livia twisted the taffeta ribbons on her cape. "He is ready to do me favours, but nothing more —"

She was about to open her heart to Leonora and speak of her own troubles.

"Indeed, I cannot expect Pietro to do more," she began, but their tête à tête was interrupted by the clarion voice of a lady advancing toward them in great haste, her dress ballooning like a ship fully rigged. It was the Duchess Margherita. Her retinue struggled to keep up with her.

"Ah, there she is — the future Princess of Gesualdo," the Duchess trilled. She kissed Leonora on both cheeks. "My dear," she said holding on to her shoulders, "we cannot have you slip away like this and take your pleasure walking in the garden. The tailor is waiting for you, and the lace maker, and the perfumer. I have pledged myself to take the place of your late mother and see that every detail of your wedding is attended to and properly arranged. So don't make me run after you, my dear girl. For one thing, the ornamental sleeves have been delivered from Mantua and the silk brocades have arrived from Venice, and you must inspect them at once."

The Duchess took possession of Leonora's arm. Talk of the latest fashions silenced all other questions, and Livia joined in the discussion of the cut of sleeves, the shape of bodices, and the quality of Venetian brocade.

CHAPTER 2

The ducal archive, Pietro Paci's domain, was a narrow chamber with a vaulted ceiling. A row of small windows sat high above the bookcases which lined three walls. The shelves were stacked with bundles of papers and rows of ledgers, some bound in pigskin and secured with clasps, others covered in white parchment. They contained a hundred years or more of ducal correspondence and state papers. Pietro's desk was piled with books needed for his present task: writing a history of Ferrara and its distinguished rulers, the House of Este.

When his servant announced that Livia Prevera had come with a message from her mistress, Pietro's face lit up.

"Livia!" he said when she entered the room. "What a pleasant surprise."

He came around the desk and led her to an upholstered bench. It was short and served as a convenient excuse to draw close to her.

"I wish your mistress found more occasions to send me messages," he said, reaching for her hand.

She looked at him fondly and returned the pressure of his fingertips, then lowered her eyes.

"Since it concerns her future husband, I'm afraid it's a unique occasion," she said, "unless you expect Donna Leonora to take several husbands, like the Amazons."

"I believe the Amazons took lovers rather than husbands."

She slapped his hand playfully. "Don't be a stickler, Pietro."

"Very well. If you see no distinction between lovers and husbands, I won't quarrel with you, my sweet girl. I am willing to become your lover without insisting on marriage bonds."

"I quite believe you would," she said, "but I do make a distinction and am old-fashioned enough to insist on marriage bonds."

"Then I shall drop all talk of lovers," he said.

And of marriage, too, Livia thought, giving him a sober look.

"On to my present business then," she said. "Donna Leonora would like to learn more about her future husband, Prince Carlo. What is your impression of him? You were present at the marriage negotiations in Gesualdo."

"In the humble capacity of a scribe. I took the minutes of the meeting. It was considered my duty as the duke's historian to be present and record for posterity everything that is good and noble and will add to the glory of the House of Este."

"And off the historical record, what do you think of the bridegroom?"

"I had no occasion to engage the Prince in conversation — I'm not important enough to address a man of his rank, as you well know. I can only tell you what I saw and heard. People consider him a musical genius. He looks younger than his thirty years. He is fit, sits his horse well, and is a superb marksman." Pietro hesitated. Should he tell Livia about the incident he had witnessed? No, he could hardly make sense of it himself, and he had been cautioned not to talk about it, whatever it was — a spell of some sort? An ailment? No, it would do no good to tell Livia.

"And?" Livia gave him a searching look.

"That's all I can tell you, I'm afraid."

"But you haven't told me anything about the Prince's character. Donna Leonora and I studied the portrait he sent her. She liked his sensitive mouth. I thought it looked cruel. And there was something about his eyes, a brooding quality, that made me uncertain. What's your impression?"

"He looked melancholy to me, but I'm not sure what to make of him. He is hard to gauge except when it comes to music for which he shows unrestrained enthusiasm. It's a subject on which he talks happily and fluently for hours — too long for some people's taste."

"Not for Donna Leonora. She loves music and would never tire of hearing the Prince talk about that subject. But I have

6

another question for you. The ducal household is making grand preparations for the wedding. Donna Leonora is surprised at the marked interest the Duke takes in her marriage to the Prince."

"She is surprised?"

"You mean she shouldn't be, and there is a good reason for the Duke's unusual largesse? Then you must explain it to me."

"If I do, will you treat my answer with discretion?"

"It will be only for Donna Leonora's ears."

"Well, here is the story. You know the great misfortune of the Duke."

Everyone knew about it. After three marriages, Duke Alfonso was still childless. Ferrara was a papal fief and would revert to the pope if the Duke died without an heir.

"Naturally, Don Alfonso wishes to keep the duchy in his family and is negotiating about that point with the pope," Pietro said. "He would like to see the law of succession changed."

"But what room is there for negotiation?"

"The pope might benefit from granting Don Alfonso an exception and allowing the duchy to pass into the hands of his nearest male relative — Cesare."

"You mean, the Pope expects to be paid for granting that favour to the Duke."

"Handsomely paid—that goes without saying."

"I can see why he would want to ingratiate himself with the Pope, but what has that to do with Donna Leonora's marriage?"

"Obtaining the Pope's consent is not enough. The cardinals must support any change to the law of succession. A committee has been appointed to study the question. It is chaired by Cardinal Alfonso Gesualdo, who happens to be Prince Carlo's uncle and a very influential man in Rome."

Ah! Livia began to connect the dots.

"The Duke saw that he must have the Cardinal's support and came up with a splendid plan," Pietro said. "Leonora marries the Prince, linking the Este family with the Gesualdos. The Cardinal takes up the Duke's cause, since it would be in the interest of both families. The Pope alters the succession in Cesare's favour, and everyone lives happily ever after. There you have it, my dear Livia —I entrust the story to your discreet heart."

He took Livia's hands and kissed them devoutly and would have touched her discreet heart as well if she had not fended him off.

"Pietro," she whispered and pushed him away as his lips grazed her cheeks. "You'll get me into trouble. Your servant will see us. He is loitering near the door."

"Then let me ask you," he said. "Would you by any chance be taking a walk in the ducal garden this evening?" The park was a favourite trysting place for lovers and schemers alike.

Livia shot him a warning glance and briskly backed away. Her keen ears had heard footsteps, or perhaps it was just a shifting in the air that caught her attention. She barely managed to say "Thank you for the information, Signor Paci," when the servant entered the room followed by a man with dark curly hair and the neck of a bull — Leonora's brother.

Cesare had the solid step of a warrior on the march. He came to a halt when he saw Livia.

She curtsied to him. He nodded stiffly and shot her a hard, weathered look as she passed by him on her way out.

As soon as she had gone, he pounced on Pietro.

"What information did you give that woman, if I may ask?" He was a man who did not need to raise his voice to make faces blanch and hands tremble. A stare from his steely eyes could be unnerving, but Pietro knew better than to show fear to a bully.

He smiled amiably. "Donna Leonora sent her lady-in-waiting to inquire what the Prince looks like and what his interests are."

"And you said-?"

"I described his person and listed his interests — music and hunting. That seemed to satisfy her."

Cesare looked at him sharply. "I trust you said nothing about the prince's late wife."

No, Pietro had held back a great deal and said nothing about the strange scene he had witnessed or about the Prince's first wife. It was a scandalous story and sure to give offence, to innocent ears at any rate.

"Donna Livia did not ask, and I did not tell," he said. "But the story is making the rounds at court, and others may not be so prudent."

"Or worse, take malicious pleasure in fomenting a rebellion in the bride-to-be," Cesare said. "Seeing that Leonora is curious enough to hunt for information, I shall remove her at once and take her with me to Modena. It is better to err on the side of caution and keep her in seclusion until the Prince's entry into the city."

There goes my chance of meeting Livia in the park this evening, Pietro thought. She will leave the city with her mistress.

As if he could read his mind, Cesare said: "And a word of advice to you, Pietro. Keep your fingers from Livia Prevera if you know what's good for your career. That girl is too clever by half, and too inquisitive."

There was a menacing look in his eyes.

The warning was hardly necessary, yet it cut Pietro to the quick. He knew his love for Livia was a hopeless affair. She had no dowry, and he could not indulge his feelings if he wanted to make a career at court. Now that Cesare had expressed his disapproval, the barrier was raised another notch. Pietro could not afford to marry a poor woman, however noble her forefathers, but even if he could get around that impediment somehow, he certainly could not disregard the wishes of a man who might soon be Duke of Ferrara.

Pietro yearned for a place in the sun. He came from an old and distinguished family, but his father lacked the means to promote his ambitions. Pietro had the misfortune of being the youngest, by ten years, of four children, three of them girls and requiring a dowry. The two older girls were married by the time Pietro made his entry into the world, and their dowry had gone with them. The youngest was sent to a convent to save some money for Pietro's use. It did not amount to much, however, and the young man was expected to make his own way, to trade on his family name, to win the Duke's favour, and to find himself a wealthy wife.

A sigh rose up in Pietro's chest, but he suppressed it. To be successful, a man must keep his eyes firmly on his goals. He wanted to become a courtier and join the inner circle of the Duke's advisors. He should know better than sighing for Livia, even if she had the most enticing lips and her eyes had the lustre of stars!

CHAPTER 3

To the surprise of everyone except Pietro, Leonora d'Este departed for Modena with her brother.

"Why on earth would he take her away, two weeks before the wedding, when there is so much to arrange here?" Pietro overheard one lady say, as he made his way to the ducal garden that evening.

"Don Cesare has always been an unreasonable man," was the answer. "And to think that he may be the next duke."

Ah, the secret was out! People already knew about the Duke's maneuvers and Cesare's chances, however slim, to inherit the duchy. Pietro had counselled discretion when he told Livia of Duke Alfonso's negotiations with the Pope, but nothing remained a secret at court for very long. Rumours were everywhere, dark, malleable, taking shape in the whisperer's mouth as needed. It was surprising that Donna Leonora was still in the dark, but then again people would be careful in her presence. It wasn't politic to mention the subject to her. It might look like meddling. Cesare wouldn't like it. Nor could they speak in Leonora's presence about the "moods" of the Prince or the scandal involving his first wife. How to put it politely? It was distasteful. Of course, the Prince had to defend the honour of his family, that was understood — but did he have to go about it in such a beastly manner?

What was said or left unsaid at court depended on how useful a particular bit of gossip was to a man's career or a woman's scheme. Saying anything uncomplimentary about Prince Carlo or mentioning his late wife to Leonora was in no one's interest at this stage of the diplomatic game. In any case, the affair was old news. It happened four years ago and far away in Naples.

Nevertheless it was a blot on the Prince's reputation, Pietro thought, and that incident he had witnessed during the marriage negotiations at Gesualdo was another cause for concern. It was more than moodiness and would certainly have supplied welcome grist to the rumour mills in Ferrara! But he had kept the story to himself. It happened during the hunting party arranged by the Prince in honour of Cesare, his future brother-in-law. The courtiers spent the night in the forest surrounding Gesualdo, where a camp had been set up, or rather a city of tents, if the luxurious abodes of the Prince and Cesare d'Este could be called tents. The sides were hung with tapestries, the floors covered with carpets, and the beds as comfortable as any nobleman could wish to have in his palace. Pietro, who did not rank highly among the visitors, was obliged to do without such comforts, however. He slept in a plain canvas shelter on a straw pallet.

It was either the straw pricking his skin or the dampness of the early morning or the sound of a horse snorting that woke him. He parted the tent flap and in the gray light of dawn saw a solitary rider leaving the camp. The Prince! Pietro thought. But no, he must be mistaken. The Prince would not go anywhere without his attendants. Pietro sensed an adventure coming his way. He slung a coat over his shoulder, stuck a poniard into his belt for good measure, and followed the man on foot. The Prince, if it was him, rode at a leisurely pace. Pietro tried to orient himself. They were going in the direction of the river. Soon the forest gave way to a scruffy meadow. The rider stopped and dismounted. It was indeed Prince Carlo walking slowly forward toward the riverbank which dropped precipitously to the water's edge some twenty feet below. Pietro stopped as well and considered what to do next. It had been unwise to follow the Prince, he realized now. What justification did he have for trailing him? If he was discovered, his action might be ascribed to motives more sinister than idle curiosity. But if he made his presence known to the Prince now, it would be awkward, to say the least. Perhaps it was best to circle back to the camp and hope to escape notice. As he moved away, he saw that the Prince was standing at the very edge of the precipice. Dense brush covered and disguised the verge. Did he not realize how close he was to the brink, how close to taking a headlong fall and tumble into the river? The Prince was leaning forward now. Another step

12

— Pietro shouted a warning and set off at a run. Without stopping to think, he tackled the Prince bodily and pulled him back. Don Carlo hung in his rescuer's arms like a puppet, stiff, silent, insensate. Pietro lowered him gently to the ground and kneeled down beside him. The Prince's face was pale, his mouth contorted and moving strangely as if he was chewing his tongue. Pietro called his name, shook his shoulders, massaged his chest, all to no avail. He was at a loss what to do next, when the Prince fetched a deep breath like a sigh. His eyes fluttered open, and his gaze settled on Pietro. His lips moved, but without producing a sound.

"Let me summon help, my lord," Pietro said in reply to Don Carlo's silent plea. He took off his own cloak and rolled it up to make a cushion for the Prince's head. "I won't be long," he assured him.

As he rose and turned to go, he saw Giovanni di Grassi, the Prince's majordomo, riding briskly across the meadow, followed by a servant on a mule.

Pietro met them and informed Di Grassi that the Prince had fallen ill.

"Don Carlo," he started, pointing to the place where he had left the sick man, when he saw to his surprise that the Prince had rallied and was walking toward them with an uneasy gait.

The Majordomo dismounted and bowed to the Prince.

"My Lord," he said, "I see you have taken your morning exercise. I hope you found it refreshing."

The Prince raised his eyes with difficulty and nodded.

The servant meanwhile had brought up Don Carlo's horse which had strayed to the edge of the forest and helped the Prince into the saddle. Without saying a word or looking back, the Prince rode off in the direction of the camp. At Di Grassi's nod, the servant followed him.

The majordomo himself stayed behind and fixed Pietro with a hard stare. His face was an unhealthy colour, as if he spent too much time indoors, and his hair was prematurely gray as if he had taken on too many cares.

"What are you doing here at this early hour?" he asked without even a pretense of civility.

There was displeasure in his voice. Or perhaps something more than displeasure — suspicion.

"I had too much wine last night," Pietro said. "My head needed airing. I saw the Prince standing at the edge of the cliff. He did not seem well, and I was afraid for his safety."

"Your concern for the Prince does you credit, young man, but you are too easily alarmed. I suggest you keep your impressions to yourself. If you open your mouth, you will make a fool of yourself." He paused. A steep crease appeared between his contracted brows. "Or worse than a fool."

Pietro bowed. He understood that he had seen what he was not supposed to see. He had been in the wrong place at the wrong time. But what exactly had he seen? He could not make sense of the incident. Was the Prince suicidal? Was he possessed? Was he suffering from the "sacred disease" — the falling sickness?

Yes, the story would have pleased the gossips in Ferrara, Pietro thought as he recalled his adventure on his way to the ducal garden. But he knew: Discretion was a courtier's greatest virtue, and so he had kept his mouth shut. "Poor Leonora!" he thought as he turned into the path leading to the canal. "So young and shackled to a man in the grip of a horrible disease or under the influence of a sinister spell!" It did not bode well for a happy union. And then there was the unsavory story of the Prince's wife. What kind of man would do such a thing!

Taking out his boat and rowing the length of the canal that crossed the ducal garden was Pietro's way to relax and forget about ugly stories, tricky politics and unpleasant masters like Cesare.

The afternoon had been wet — unpredictable spring weather — but by the time Pietro reached the pier and cast off, the sky was clearing. He rowed leisurely at first, looking into the dark waters of the canal, a natural stream banked and shaped to satisfy the architect who designed the garden. Pietro's thoughts turned to Livia, her teasing eyes, her elfin smile, her full lips parting to kiss him — but what was the use of dreaming of a woman who could never be his? He began rowing more vigorously and concentrated on his strokes. Soon he was caught up in the spell of his own rhythmic movements and expected nothing less than the sight that greeted him as he rounded a bend: a woman walking along the path skirting the canal. She was wrapped in a voluminous coat, but the keen eye of a lover recognized her at once: Livia. She turned, caught sight of Pietro, and raised her hand in greeting.

He guided his boat to a landing, handed her in, and helped her to the seat facing his. She pulled the hood of her coat forward to conceal her face from curious onlookers. Fortunately for them, the evening was chilly and the pathways deserted. The clouds had begun to gather again, leaving the sky overcast and dull. There was no one to witness their rendezvous except another loving pair promenading in the distance, and they had eyes only for each other.

"Livia," he said warmly. "You didn't leave for Modena with your mistress?"

"I was told to stay behind and help the Duchess with the arrangement of Leonora's wardrobe. The truth is: Don Cesare wanted to get rid of me to keep a tighter rein on Leonora in these waning days of his power — before he hands her over to the Prince, I mean. I'm in his way. He believes that I have a corrosive influence on Donna Leonora."

"And on me, as he let me know! He told me to beware of you. —But how did you get on his bad side?"

"He always had misgivings about me, but the other day he caught me reading *Floridoro*."

"*Floridoro*! Not the kind of book he would want to come to his sister's attention, I imagine."

"Exactly. He took the book out of my hands and opened it to the title page. 'An epic written by a woman!' he said and read out the first lines in a mocking voice: *Women, by nature endowed with judgment, as apt as men to show great wisdom—*"

"Women who show wisdom would not be to Cesare's taste," Pietro said, laughing.

Livia nodded. "He wants us to be like chairs, decorative and bearing his weight without a squeak."

"Was he angry with you?"

"He scowled and wanted to know: Had I shown the book to Leonora? Of course I had shown her the book, but I didn't let on."

"And he believed you?"

"He gave me a dark look and said: 'Then keep this nonsense to yourself and don't go about putting ideas into your mistress' head.'"

"You'd better hide the book, Livia."

"I no longer have it. Don Cesare was about to hand it back to me, then changed his mind. 'I shall keep it for the time being,' he said, and stuck it into his jerkin. I doubt I'll see it again."

"Oh, he'll return the book once the danger is past, when Leonora is safely married to Prince Carlo and can no longer be corrupted by a chivalric romance."

The sun was now very low on the horizon. Pietro moored his boat below the overhanging branches of a tree. In the safety of this dark bower, he moved to Livia's side and put his arm around her.

"After you left the archive this afternoon, Don Cesare gave me a talking-to. He told me to keep my fingers from you if I knew what was good for my career, that you are too clever by half."

"Ah, then you are forewarned."

"But that's just what I admire in you, Livia: your quick mind. I like a clever woman who can think straight and has a capacity for facts." And what he liked even better was her fiery soul, revealed to him only in their private moments. Livia was prim and proper on the outside. She gave nothing away to the gossips. Only Pietro knew her passionate nature, her willingness to walk on the wild side and take risks. It was a secret the two of them shared, and yet Cesare seemed to have guessed it and saw Livia as a danger, a subversive force.

"Flatterer!" Livia said. "If it's my mind that attracts you, why can't you keep your fingers from my body?"

"Livia," he pleaded, "is it so wrong to love your body *and* your mind? The two are joined by nature after all."

"They may be joined by nature, but we have advanced beyond nature to civilization, and society commands us to keep our bodies separate until they are joined by the sacred bonds of marriage."

Her eyes were full of mischief and fun. If only she had a dowry! If only he was rich!

"Cesare is right," he said. "You are too clever for me, and I shall have to give you up and drown myself in sorrow."

"Poor man, even heaven is beginning to shed tears of pity for you, so I suggest you deliver me to the landing nearest to the palace that I may hurry home before the drizzle turns into a downpour."

He obeyed meekly and rowed back.

"When will I see you again?" he said when they reached the landing.

"At Leonora's wedding," she said quietly, thinking that soon afterwards she and Pietro would be parted for good. She was bound to follow Leonora to her new home in Gesualdo.

He had the same thought.

"I wish you wouldn't go away," he said.

"Remember Don Cesare's warning. I would only spoil your career." She gave him a half-smile, but her eyes remained serious.

He could think of no reply. At last he said:

"I love you, Livia, I do. It is the circumstances that are at fault. Fate is keeping us apart."

His eyes pleaded with her. He wanted to take her into his arms one more time, but she turned and quickly walked away.

The sun had almost slipped over the horizon, and darkness was descending on the ducal garden. It was only a short distance to the gate of the palace, but Pietro was uneasy about Livia walking home by herself. He decided to follow her at a discreet distance to make sure that she reached the gate safely. He tied up his boat, jumped onto the landing and went after Livia, expecting to see her receding figure, but the path before him was empty. He stopped mystified. Where had she gone? As he looked around, he heard the sound of a scuffle and a suppressed cry. Lovers, he thought, until he saw a man run from the bushes along the canal and dart across the road. A moment later, he reappeared mounted on a horse and galloped away.

Pietro stood for a moment, unsure what to make of the scene. What if the cry he had heard was a cry of distress rather than of amorous pleasure? He rushed to the edge of the canal. The water was running high after the spring rains. He parted the overhanging branches and there, in the gloom, saw a coat ballooning up from the water and a body drifting away, sucked into a whirling eddy — Livia! He kicked off his boots and dove into the frigid stream. Her coat was now only a shadow below the surface of the water. He grasped at the fabric, felt it slip away with the tug of the current, lunged after it and held it fast. One more stroke, and he had his arm around Livia's body. He pulled her toward him and, holding her head above water, paddled to the edge of the canal. Clods of earth came loose as he dug his fingers into the bank and hoisted himself and his sodden burden onto dry land. He knelt on the ground beside Livia, turned her limp body sideways and pounded her back. In a little while, he had the satisfaction of seeing her open her eyes. She coughed and spewed out a quantity of water, but she was alive.

Thank God I got to her in time, he thought as he helped Livia up.

She leaned on him, shuddering with cold.

He steadied her gently. "Are you hurt?" he asked.

She reached up to the crown of her head. Her hand came away wet with blood.

"The robber—" she said feebly.

"That was no robber," Pietro said. The man had struck Livia before pushing her into the water, leaving her to drown. He was an assassin.

Livia gave him a frightened look. "You mean-"

But there was no time to speculate. "We must get a doctor to look after you and dress your wound," he said.

17

He put his arm around Livia's waist to support her and, wet and bedraggled, they made their way to the gate to call for help.

Who would want Livia out of the way? Pietro asked himself, as he pressed his handkerchief against the side of her head to stem the flow of blood. He could think of only one man: Cesare.

CHAPTER 4

The ducal castle, where Livia was taken after the "accident" as she chose to call it, combined the safety of a fortress with the grace and luxury of a palace. The brick façade of the bulwark had been embellished with a grand stone portal, crowned by an elegant arch and flanked by noble pillars and balustrades. Deep in the bowels of the citadel, a dank and lightless dungeon awaited malefactors, its horrors unchanged through the centuries, but opulence greeted the visitor on the upper floors. The rooms were scented with musk kept in perforated balls of copper and silver. There was a show of precious objects in every room: crystal cups, astrological globes, carved corals on alabaster stands, gilt-framed mirrors, antique bronze statuettes, and curio cabinets displaying majolica plates, medallions and rare coins. Those were the public rooms shown to visitors. Guests who had the privilege of seeing the private apartments of the duke spoke with wonder of the luxurious furnishings and the splendid ceilings painted with Cupids and goddesses dancing with Bacchic frenzy.

Beyond those palatial halls was a warren of plain rooms with whitewashed walls and plank floors to accommodate the ducal household, the courtiers and ladies in waiting, the valets and footmen, and tucked away in the further reaches of the palace, the staff that looked after the chambers, the kitchen, the wardrobe, and the stables. The space was ample for the needs of the ducal family, but cramped at this time when extra help had been brought in to prepare for Leonora's wedding.

After her rescue from the frigid waters of the canal, Livia had been taken to the room of Giulia Morigi, one of the Duchess' ladies-in-waiting. The court physician came and asked a few polite questions. She had slipped and fallen into the water, she told him, and must have knocked her head against the rocky embankment. He said nothing, only nodded wisely, felt her pulse, and had the wound dressed by his assistant. Within two days, he declared her out of danger. The quilted hood of her cloak and her thick hair, which she wore braided and coiled around her head, had cushioned the assailant's blow. She sustained only a flesh wound, but the soaking gave her a chest cold, and she suffering more from the chill than from the pain caused by the wound. The Duchess kindly allowed her to stay at the palace until Leonora's return from Modena.

A bed had been set up for her on one side of Giulia Morigi's room. The arrangement could not have pleased the lady-in-waiting, but she was a good-natured young woman. She showed no annoyance at having her room cramped with a sickbed and a chest half blocking the window seat. Indeed, she gave Livia a warm welcome. The reason soon became clear: Giulia was a great talker and glad to have a captive audience.

The moment Livia opened her eyes in the morning, Giulia was by her side and nestled down on the edge of the bed. Her weight made the soft mattress sag as she bent over the patient, her round face rising above Livia like the sun. Giulia was all softness, full-lipped and rosy-cheeked, with dimpled hands and a well-padded body. She loved sweets and was rarely without a supply of sugar plums or honey-nuts — which explained the bulges at her stomach and hips, Livia thought.

"How is your poor head this morning?" Giulia said, planting a syrupy kiss on her forehead.

"Much better—"

Giulia settled herself comfortably. Livia saw that she was in for a lengthy talk.

"I'm glad you are better, my dear. Mind you, a headache is good insofar as it indicates that a healing process is taking place. Your body is working hard to get better, which in turn puts a strain on your head, thus causing it to ache. Now, dizziness — you aren't having any dizzy spells, are you, dear?"

"No dizzy spells, I'm glad to say—"

"Because dizziness is a bad sign. It means that the interior of your skull is disordered, or so they say, but opinions differ on what to do in such a case. Some doctors advise sufferers to lie very still and wait for the parts to compose themselves. Others say one should slowly bend forward and backward to help the parts find their place."

"You seem to take a great interest in the art of medicine, Giulia."

"That's what the doctor said to me yesterday. And I said: If I were a man and had my choice of professions, I'd practice medicine. Then he said: I'm sure you would do well, especially if you charged by the word. Wasn't that unkind of him when I only meant to be helpful? You'd think he would be pleased and thank me for describing your symptoms."

"You mean my coughing and sneezing? — I just hope I didn't keep you awake last night."

"Not at all. I expected a great deal of moaning and groaning, and would have put that on my list as well. I am keeping a record of all the symptoms I come across, you know. So far I have listed two hundred and forty-one phenomena, arranged in two chapters, one for injuries, the other for diseases. I'll show you what I have under 'blow to the head' — in case you can think of something I should add."

"I would rather forget about the whole unfortunate episode."

"Oh, of course you would. Poor thing! And you are so uncomplaining, so very brave, as I told the Duchess when she inquired after you." Giulia's glance went to a sheet of paper lying on Livia's nightstand. "I see she wrote you a note. On scented paper. It is Her Ladyship's hand, is it not? What a compliment for you." She eyed the letter. "The Duchess writes beautifully. May I have a closer look, dear?"

Livia indulged Giulia's curiosity. "Read it if you like. But I doubt she meant to pay me a compliment."

Giulia took up the note and eagerly perused it.

My dear Livia, I was sorry to hear of your misadventure. Donna Leonora will never forgive me for being so neglectful. I should not have allowed you to wander in the park, all by yourself. You must get well soon.

It was a thinly disguised reproof. Ladies did not walk in the park at dusk.

Giulia patted Livia's hand. Her chin gave a little wobble. "Oh well," she said. "It was not prudent to walk in the garden unaccompanied, even if it is walled and part of the ducal residence. How fortunate that Pietro Paci happened to come along—" She paused and gave Livia an inquiring look. "I wonder whether it was coincidence. Perhaps he was following you."

"Why should he follow me?"

"Because he admires you? At least that's what I've heard — that he has his eye on you."

Livia knew better than to take a gossip like Giulia into her confidence. Her love for Pietro was unwise, and now it seemed dangerous as well.

"Giulia," she said. "I'm sorry, but I'm not up to long conversations at present. Will you excuse me?"

"Of course you aren't up to it, poor lamb. And here I am talking away, when the most important thing for you is getting plenty of rest."

Livia had a strong constitution and soon recovered from her cold and from the wound her assailant had inflicted, but she thought it best to pretend weakness and keep to her room, even if it meant listening to Giulia's endless gossip and to suffer her treacle kisses. The attack in the garden had been the work of an enemy. "Beware," Pietro had whispered before leaving her in the care of the physician. He mentioned no name, but Livia understood what he left unsaid: Beware of Cesare d'Este, who considers you a troublemaker and an undesirable companion for his sister. She knew of course that Cesare did not approve of the fondness that had sprung up between her and Donna Leonora. But would he go as far as wanting Livia dead? She thought of the stories Leonora had told her about her brother. The pleasure Cesare took as a boy watching his pet snake eat live mice, the pleasure he took as a man in watching cockfights and bear-baiting. He was cruel and took a perverse pleasure in the pain of others. Would he be satisfied now that he had frightened her and made her suffer, or would he go after her again? She wondered whether other people knew of Cesare's enmity and his desire to keep her away from Leonora.

"I am surprised Don Cesare took his sister to Modena and asked me to stay behind," she said to Giulia the next day, testing the ground to discover what Giulia knew.

"I'm not surprised at all. He wants to prevent her from hearing the rumours circulating about the prince. At least that's what everybody says."

"What rumours?"

"That the Prince is unbalanced. Haven't you heard?"

Livia had heard nothing definite. She had seen the furtive glances people exchanged when the Prince's name came up, but she hadn't been able to discover the reason for their hesitance. "Unbalanced?" she said to Giulia. "What do you mean?"

"How shall I put it? It's too distressing for words. And really, we shouldn't talk about the Prince. The walls have ears! But you know about his first wife, don't you?"

"Only that she died young and that there is a son, a boy, nine years old."

Giulia gave her a strange look. "You don't know then. Well, now that I think of it, no one would tell you anything about the Prince's first wife, in case you told Donna Leonora and made her unhappy. If you ask me, Don Cesare was right to keep his sister in ignorance. The marriage contract is signed after all, so what's the use of worrying her? If I were Leonora, I wouldn't want to hear ugly rumours about my bridegroom on the eve of the wedding. Would you?"

"I can't say, unless you tell me what the rumours are."

"I shouldn't have mentioned them," Giulia said. "In fact, I'm keeping you from your needed rest, my dear. Rest is what the doctor ordered."

There it was again: the reticence she had noticed in others, the strange reluctance to talk about the Prince. Whatever the rumours, they must be dire if even Giulia, who loved gossip, refused to talk about them. Livia began to wiggle her toes — a bad habit of hers when she was uneasy. What was Giulia holding back? There was something in the Prince's past, she was sure, something so dreadful that it could turn Leonora against him and make her resist the marriage arrangement. But wouldn't Pietro have told her? Perhaps — if their conversation hadn't been cut short. They were interrupted by the arrival of Don Cesare. She remembered the grim look of disapproval on his face when he saw her at the archive. Did he suspect Pietro of giving her privileged information, the secret Giulia had been hinting at? Did he fear that she would tell Leonora next? If Cesare thought Livia knew too much and was obstructing his plans, he would have no scruples getting rid of her. Her only defense against Cesare's machinations was to lie low and keep out of his sight until the wedding was over.

In the circumstances, it was fortunate that she was sharing a room. The thought of Giulia sleeping in the bed next to hers gave her a sense of security. During the day when Giulia was not around, she locked and barred the door. And now she had to wait only a few more days for the danger to pass. Once Leonora was married, Livia no longer posed a threat to Cesare's plans. He would not give her a second thought then, or so she hoped. But how cheap the life of a woman was! Killing her had no more significance for Cesare than drowning a rat. Livia had no champion except Leonora. She was an orphan, the daughter of an eccentric nobleman who had never learned to play the game of politics and died in poverty. If Leonora had not chosen her as a playmate — for they were children when they first met — her prospects would have been bleak. But Leonora found her endearing and was charmed by the difference between them. Opposites attract, they say, and Leonora was, even as a child, unusually calm and deliberate, whereas Livia was as playful as a kitten and as temperamental. Playing together as children and, later on, sharing a tutor and a dance master, the two girls grew up and became fast friends. Even now that Livia was Lenora's lady-in-waiting, and court etiquette required them to observe certain formalities, she sometimes claimed the rights of friendship and dispensed with titles, calling her mistress Leonora, as she had in their childhood. It was never taken amiss. In their private moments, when the two young women shared the secrets of their hearts, they were once again just friends.

How sweet it was to have a friend. And who but Leonora cared whether Livia was alive or dead? Pietro? Yes, he cared for her, but not enough to sacrifice his career. Not enough even to write her letters. Out of sight, out of mind, Livia thought. He had promised to write every day when he set out with Count Fontanelli and a guard of honour to meet the Prince half-way and escort him to Ferrara. More than a week had gone by, and she had received only one letter. It was no more than a report, so sober, so devoid of affectionate words that she handed it to Giulia without a second thought.

Giulia read it with alacrity. It was fodder for her hunger for news and gossip.

"Don Carlo was three days late for the meeting!" she exclaimed after reading the first line. "You would think he'd be more impatient to be united with his noble bride."

She read on. The Prince traveled with a grand retinue — a hundred and fifty persons and three hundred pieces of luggage carried by a train of mules. In Venice, where the company stopped for two days, the Doge arranged for a visit to the shipyard, but the Prince showed little interest.

"How very odd!" Giulia said. "Perhaps that is what they mean when they call the Prince unbalanced. Why would he make a detour to Venice instead of coming straight to Ferrara? And once there, why wouldn't he want to see the shipyard? It is considered a great marvel by visitors."

"I suppose he is more interested in music than in shipbuilding," Livia said. "I have heard that he is a talented musician."

"And a composer, it seems, since Pietro mentions that the Prince brought along two books of scores, music he had composed himself." Giulia had reached the bottom of the page. *We have set out for Ferrara at last,* she read, *but the prince did not stir from his bed until extremely late in the day, so that we did not make much headway.* She looked up. "Is that the end of the letter? It seems rather abrupt. I would have expected a polite inquiry into your health at the very least. I thought Pietro was your admirer."

Livia did her best to look unmoved. "You keep saying that, but why would a young man in Pietro's position waste his time on me?"

Giulia said nothing more. Her eyes were full of sympathy. She saw that Julia was hurt. There was no greeting at the end of Pietro's letter, not even a proper signature, only a scrawled "P".

"Well, by now the Prince and his entourage have arrived in Gaibana," she said, changing the subject. "That's what they tell me. Tomorrow he will make his entry into the city. Donna Leonora returned from Modena yesterday. Have you had a chance to talk to her?"

"Only briefly," Livia said. She longed to talk to her friend and hear how she had passed her days in Modena, but the Duchess never left Leonora's side, acting more like a guardian than a family friend. Livia was allowed only a few minutes' conversation with her mistress. The two women embraced, and Leonora asked solicitously about the "mishap" in the ducal garden. Livia could not tell whether she understood the true nature of the incident, and there was no opportunity to speak in private. The Duchess kept her arm on Leonora's as if to keep her from escaping. She promised to make it her first business after the wedding festivities to introduce Livia to her husband. "I will tell him that I mean to keep you as my lady-in-waiting. I can't be without you. Already I miss our familiar talk," she said, before she was rushed away by the Duchess.

"We talked only for a minute," she told Giulia.

"Oh dear, only a minute! And what did she say?"

"She told me that the Prince will remain in Ferrara for three months. They will take up residence in the Palazzo dei Diamanti after the wedding, and if the Prince approves, I'll join them there."

"How wonderful!" Giulia said. "I envy you. The Palazzo dei Diamanti is charming."

CHAPTER 5

Pietro had expected more excitement from the journey. Escorting the Prince turned out to be tedious business. Don Carlo had brought along his academy, as he called it, a group of musicians who were permanent residents in his castle at Gesualdo. Every evening languorous music and yearning songs could be heard coming from the Prince's quarters. The concerts lasted until the early morning hours, keeping everyone from sleep. Even Count Fontanelli, that most diplomatic of diplomats, grumbled. "When I get home," he said, "I shall not listen to music for six months. And I won't be sorry if I never see or hear another lute."

Pietro did not find the music unpleasant, but it made him melancholic, reminding him of Livia's pure voice, which was so sweet it made his soul feel the joy of heaven. It was the thought of Livia rather than the princely concerts that kept him awake, and he spent the sleepless hours writing letters to her, pouring out his feelings in words inspired by the sounds that filled the air around him like so many love poems. He had promised Livia to write every day, and he was glad of the opportunity to share his day with her. If only he could share it with her in person!

The Prince's enthusiasm for music is sure to endear him to his future wife, Pietro thought. Donna Leonora, like Livia, had an ear for compositions and enjoyed musical performances. But the concerts were not welcome to Count Fontanelli because they upset his carefully planned schedule. The Prince was up all night and liked to sleep in. It was often noon before they got under way. Their journey to Ferrara made slow progress, and the Count worried that their arrival would be delayed and the plans for the Prince's reception ruined.

In every village they passed through, people had decorated their houses with embroidered cloth and flowers, and lined the roads to gawk at the Prince and his entourage. He barely lifted his hand to greet them and showed them a lethargic face, but that did not impair his popularity because he was prudent enough to know how to win their favour. He did not spare his purse and had his servants distribute the expected largesse among the people. Not surprisingly, he received a warm welcome everywhere.

At last Ferrara came into view, rising up from the plain of the Po River. They could see the imposing towers of the Duke's castle and the massive walls built by his forebears. The gate of the city was festooned with banners and garlands, and the Duke himself was on hand to greet his honoured guest and conduct him into the city.

It was a holiday for the people, but a working day for the Duke's historian. Pietro made a mental note of everything he saw. There was ample material for his chronicle of the House of Este. Trumpets blared and drums rolled as the Duke welcomed Leonora's bridegroom. A large and enthusiastic crowd awaited him, since this was another occasion for the Prince to show his generosity. He tipped the gate-keepers and the armed guards and the musicians one scudo each — that's twice the monthly salary of a stable boy, Pietro thought, but the lowly and the poor were not forgotten either. The prince saw to it that his footmen dispensed coins to blind men, cripples and old folk, and rewarded every itinerant musician and every little boy and girl who sang for him.

In the afternoon Leonora d'Este and Carlo Gesualdo, Prince of Venosa, were married by the Bishop of Ferrara in the private chapel of the palace, where the walls were clad in alabaster and marble quarried from ancient monuments. It was an exquisite room but too small to admit more than a dozen witnesses. The Prince had objected to a grand ceremony since this was his second marriage. Pietro guessed that he did not want to invite comparison between Leonora and his late wife who had died under unfortunate circumstances. There was no crowd to witness the union or see Leonora's splendid gown. It was up to the historian to commemorate the bride's dress, gloriously rich with jewels glittering along the hem and neckline, and a bodice trimmed with pearls. The bridegroom looked grave and dignified, dressed in black after the Spanish fashion. A narrow gold trim on his lace cuff was the only adornment he permitted, a discreet nod to the occasion.

That night, the Duke officially welcomed the newlyweds to the Castello and presented them to the court. There was a great deal of bowing and scraping, hand-kissing and embracing, and the requisite exchange of presents. No ceremonial detail was neglected, Pietro noted, and no effort spared to demonstrate the bonds uniting the Houses of Este and Gesualdo. At last the Prince and his bride were conducted to the dining hall, where they admired the splendid view of the Po Valley and the famous murals depicting hunting scenes and athletic games.

Pietro looked at the animated faces around him. And what was written on his own face — the man who observed others with a view of making them part of history? Before he became the Duke's archivist, Pietro had looked at his surroundings in a haphazard way. He saw the beauty of nature and listened to the song of birds when he was in a romantic mood, and he saw the grandeur of the court when he was dreaming of a diplomatic career for himself. Now he observed every detail all the time with a view of putting it into his book. The world around him had turned into a stage, and he studied the props and players until he recognized a pattern. Nothing was allowed to remain random. There were no accidents on that stage. He must discover the meaning of every action in the grand scheme of things. Once he understood it all, he thought — and then reined in his ambition. No, he would never understand it all! To understand life was divine, not human. He could only record what he saw and hope that it was to the liking of the Duke.

The banquet awaiting the Prince and his entourage consisted of twenty-three courses — oysters on the shell, sturgeon and eel, grilled fish with parsley and chives, stuffed quail, roast capon, venison, suckling pigs, veal steaks with morello cherry sauce — a steady stream of savory and sweet dishes with candied herbs, pine nuts, sugared raisins, and ricotta cheese tarts filled with quinces or medlars. In the interludes between the courses, the guests were entertained by musicians, jesters, jugglers, and dwarves turning somersaults and warbling in falsetto. Pietro recorded it all, for surely such splendor deserved a prominent place in his chronicle.

At midnight, the lower ranks were permitted to join the noble guests and watch the indoor tournament. The Great Hall was transformed into a jousting arena for the evening. Stands had been put up on each side to seat the audience. The floor was overlaid with paving stones and covered with sand to allow horses to gallop without risking injury to their legs. Among the men who entered the lists was Cesare d'Este himself, looking heroic in a magnificent suit of armor and a crested helmet with the family emblem, a white falcon. Yes, Cesare knew how to present himself, taking his cue from the cheers of the crowd, warming his pelt in the sun of their approval, and turning the light of his eyes on them, those twin beacons of power. Pietro wondered who Cesare was without an audience. Did that power fall away from him when he was left to himself in the grim morning light of his bed chamber? But the trumpets blared and recalled Pietro to his task — describing the tournament.

First, the men fought on foot with pikes and fencing blades. Then they mounted their horses and tilted lances at each other. As the riders pitched sideways and their weapons clashed, the men in the stands roared their approval and the ladies shrieked with excitement. Leonora's brother fought as fiercely as a boar, but his horse stumbled and so he missed out on the victory. The winner lifted his visor and accepted the prize ring from Leonora's hand. The young man did not realize that he had earned in addition to this guerdon the undying hatred of Cesare. But there was no place for that scene in Pietro's chronicle. Cesare's failure could not be mentioned in these annals of glory, and the young man's victory could not be allowed to cast a shadow over the brilliance of the House of Este.

The tournament was followed by a ball that lasted until dawn. Among the onlookers admiring the graceful dancers, Pietro discovered Livia. In an instant, the work of glorifying the House of Este was forgotten. He had eyes only for her. He made his way to her side, but left a prudent distance between them to avoid gossip.

"What a lovely sight," he said. His eyes were on Livia, although he gestured toward the ladies and cavaliers, who moved up and down the dance floor to the stately measure of a pavane.

Without turning to him, she said in a low voice:

"Ah, you are back. It must have been a hectic journey since you were too busy to write to me."

Pietro shot her a surprised glance.

"I wrote every day," he said.

They both realized at once what that meant.

"The only letter I received was written from Venice," she said quietly. "It consisted of one page and ended abruptly, signed with the letter P."

"I suspect the second page was lost," he said. He did not state the obvious, that someone had removed the page and intercepted the rest of his letters, perhaps to show them to a third party who was interested in Pietro's feelings for Livia. He had ended all his letters with endearments, calling Livia his rosebud, his turtledove, his doe-eyed beauty, and all the other silly flatteries and blandishments a young man in love was apt to use. Those words will come back to haunt me, he thought, or at any rate embarrass both me and Livia. I'll have to do better if I want a career as a diplomat. In future I will be on my guard against corrupt messengers and disloyal servants. But he dismissed those unpleasant thoughts to rest his eyes on Livia's sweet face.

"Will you be watching the ballet tomorrow evening?" he asked.

"I might," she said and could not help smiling, happy that he had not forgotten her after all, that he had kept his promise and written every day, even if someone had deprived her of the pleasure of reading Pietro's letters.

CHAPTER 6

What a fool I am, Livia thought when she woke up the next morning. In the sobering light of day it seemed unwise to talk to Pietro, or rather, to be seen talking to him. Why am I taking risks for the sake of love when I know that nothing can possibly come of it? It would be better not to attend tonight's ballet, not to see Pietro again, but when she thought of his radiant smile, she couldn't resist the tug of her heart. He had looked so handsome and elegant at the ball yesterday in his blue velvet jerkin and crisp white shirt, and her fancy was all too ready to put a romantic gloss on their meeting.

It did not take much for Giulia to persuade her that it was her duty to attend the ballet that evening.

"You cannot possibly miss it, Livia, you cannot!" she said. "The ballet has been organized by the Duchess, and she will perform in it herself, together with twelve of her ladies. I wish she had chosen me to take part in the performance, but I know my limitations." She cast a rueful glance in the mirror, which reflected her well-rounded figure. For once she regretted her sweet tooth, but she recovered quickly. "On the other hand," she said, "I'm not sure I'd want to wear the costume the Duchess designed. The ladies will be dressed as knights! That will cause a stir, I guarantee you." Cross-dressing was all the rage at court, at least in private performances, but the Church frowned on mixing up the genders. "It is immodest for a woman to dress like a man, don't you think?" Giulia said.

"And impractical as well. How can they dance wearing armor?"

"Oh, it's only cloth made to look like burnished metal. But still—"

In any case, Giulia said, the court would be in full attendance, and Livia must not miss the spectacle. What if the Duchess asked her how she had liked the performance? It would be very awkward to say she had missed it. And what reason could she possibly have for not going?

"I see I have no choice," Livia said, and smiled inwardly.

When she arrived, she saw that the Great Hall had been cleared and the floor restored to its original condition. The whole court had gathered to watch the ballet. A confused noise went up when the dancers entered. The costumes were daring, but after a little hesitation, the crowd broke into a welcoming applause. The noble troupe went through their carefully rehearsed steps with such grace and majesty that they quite won the hearts of the audience. A few old curmudgeons grumbled and harrumphed about the costumes, but their words were drowned out by the enthusiastic applause of the rest.

After the ballet, the guests regrouped for another night of dancing. In the commotion Pietro signaled to Livia, and they slipped away. They ducked down the hall and into Pietro's private kingdom, the archive that served as his office. The room was illuminated only by the thin light of the moon coming through the windows, and shadows enveloped the couch where they took their seat.

Pietro cradled Livia's face in his hands. "Are you quite recovered from that nasty attack, my love?"

"I am well again," she said. "It was only a surface wound. I was in greater danger of catching pleurisy from floating in the icy water than I was from the clout that man dealt me."

She could not deny her rescuer a kiss. Pietro immediately traded on his advantage and ran his hands over her back and down her sides, making her tingle and crowding out all reasonable thought. She yielded to his gentle pressure and sank back on the couch, her heart hammering with desire. Burying her fingers in his dark curls, she answered his caresses and opened her lips to receive his ardent kisses. She would have opened her thighs as well, had not the brawling voices of night revelers in the corridor broken into her rapture and brought her to her senses.

She tried to push Pietro away. He clung to her with passionate entreaties.

"Don't refuse me, sweet love. Have you no mercy?"

Her heart beat and her hands trembled as she broke free from his embrace and sat up. She rearranged her clothes and pinned up her hair, which had fallen over her shoulders in a silky cascade.

"Pietro," she said. "Do you really love me?"

"How can you ask? Have I not given you proof of my passion many times?"

"I am speaking of love, Pietro, not of passion."

"But passion is just love to a higher degree."

"Don't play the sophist with me, Pietro. Whatever you wish to call those feelings, do they include a willingness to marry me?"

He leaned back and passed his hand across his eyes as if he wanted to wipe away a cobweb, a dream perhaps, then sat up with a sigh and gave her a sober look.

"I have never made any pretenses to you, my darling. I love you, but the reality is that neither of us has any money, and we cannot afford the luxury of marriage."

"Not now and not ever?"

He lowered his gaze. "I see no chance of my situation changing in the near future. You will become a wizened old maid, waiting for me." He tried on a smile, but Livia's face remained solemn.

"This is no joking matter," she said. "True, you made no pretensions, but tempting me with embraces is not honourable when you have no intention to marry me. If you care for me at all — and I am not even saying 'if you love me at all' — you will respect my reputation and release me."

He hung his head and sighed. "I must be in love, for I do not have the courage to keep you back with fine words or by force. I release you, my darling, and may God and good fortune smile on you in everything you do."

They were both standing now. With their hands joined, they kissed sadly, knowing that this time it truly was farewell and the invisible thread connecting them must be broken.

CHAPTER 7

A price had to be paid for making a career — Pietro knew it, but his days were fraught with memories of Livia and the thoughts that remained unspoken pressed down on him like a hundredweight. It was best to bury his head in work. If his days were full, there was less time to feel the pain of separation and the stab of his qualms. Had he wronged Livia and been untrue to himself? Or had he done what he owed to his family, what he needed to do to succeed in life and be a credit to the Paci name?

The first step to banishing the gloom from his mind was to concentrate on the task at hand — writing the history of the House of Este. It was a pull in the right direction, but he must work harder, get past the pivotal point and create a momentum to carry him to success. Writing a chronicle was slow and plodding work. It would take a long time to bear fruit, too long for an ambitious young man like Pietro who was in a rush to get to the top. Alexander the Great was ruler of Greece when he was twenty-two and had conquered an empire by the time he was thirty! Pietro was almost twenty-five and had nothing to show for his work. What he needed was an opportunity to shine, to blaze like a comet rather than cast a modest light on the courtly scene. How could he bring himself to the attention of the Duke? There were no battles to be fought at present, and no empires to be conquered. The times called for diplomacy. The Duke was preoccupied with the question of succession, with convincing the pope to change the laws and allow Ferrara to pass into the hands of Cesare d'Este.

Pietro leaned back in his chair and looked up to the vaulted ceiling of the archive, looking for answers in its gray shadows. What could he do to turn the situation at hand to his advantage? An idea struck him. Why not support the Duke's diplomatic maneuver with a piece of research documenting Ferrara's loyal service to the pope, a demonstration that a change to the laws of succession in favour of Cesare d'Este was no more than a just reward, no, a richly deserved reward for services rendered by the House of Este? The duke might find an outline of that particular aspect of the family history a useful tool in his negotiations with the pope and reward the man who had come up with the ingenious idea. Well, perhaps not the idea, which was problematic since Ferrara's relations with the papal state had not always been smooth, but the execution of that idea, a rhetorical sleight of hand that would make it *appear* that those relations had always been cordial. The duke would certainly reward Pietro for this kind of practical demonstration of diplomatic skills. A treatise that tweaked and massaged the historical facts to suit the Duke's case would be just the thing.

Pietro set to work energetically. There was Bartolomeo Roverella, related to the Estes at any rate, who made himself so useful to the Pope that he was elevated to the cardinalate in 1445. Then there was the Council of Ferrara in 1438 — Pope Eugene wouldn't have held it in the city if he had not considered Ferrara an ally, right? The wars of the last century were more problematic, what with all the switching back and forth, but ultimately Ferrara ended up on the right side: the Pope's. On to the sixteenth century and Hippolito d'Este, whose cardinal's hat cost 40,000 scudi, enriching the papal coffers. The pope had certainly benefited from that transaction — perhaps there was a way of hinting politely that a change to the laws of succession might yield a similar benefit to the pope. Well then, with a bit of rhetoric, the relationship between the papacy and the House of Este could be made to look good. The emphasis would of course be placed on future relations, which could only improve if the Duke's wish was granted.

For some days Pietro scoured the chronicles and ledgers on the shelves of the archive and put what he found into a lengthy essay. He arranged the facts and rearranged them, he stuck in a phrase here and took out another there, mused on the choice of words and the cogency of his arguments until he was satisfied that it was a well-crafted piece. He read over his words once more and was pleased with the rhetorical flourish he had given them. The arguments were convincing, and he was all but certain that the the piece would make his fortune. The question was how best to bring it to the Duke's attention. After some hesitation, he made a copy in his neatest handwriting and sent it to Cesare d'Este with a plea to present it to Duke Alfonso on his behalf. It was a gamble. Cesare had never been forthcoming with favours. In fact, Pietro was not sure that he was still in his good graces. After all, he had defied Cesare's warning not to associate with Livia and had written to her every day during his journey escorting the Prince. He suspected that Cesare knew about this infraction, that it was on his orders that his letters to Livia had been intercepted. And if Cesare had been behind the attack on Livia in the ducal gardens, her rescuer would certainly be persona non grata. But all that was only speculation. He might be entirely wrong and his suspicions unfounded. It was difficult to read the tides and currents at court, to know who was friend and who was foe. But whatever Cesare's intentions were, Pietro had no choice but go through him. He knew no one else who had influence with the Duke and or could promote his career.

Success! The result exceeded Pietro's expectations. Within two days of asking Cesare to present his essay to the Duke, he received a summons to the palace. Cesare had shown him more good will than he had dared to hope for. Pietro had of course meant to impress Cesare with his rhetorical skills and win him over, but the victory seemed too easy. A stubborn kernel of doubt stuck in the back of his mind.

Cesare met him in the entrance hall of the palace and greeted him with a thin-lipped smile. His mien put Pietro on guard. One could always trust in the sincerity of Cesare's sneer. His smile was harder to interpret.

The two men ascended the grand staircase and turned into the gallery, where the Duke was sitting for a portrait. He was dressed in an elegant green velvet coat and matching jerkin that showed off his pleated ruff of Flemish lace. A round hose embroidered in gold completed his stylish outfit that might have suited a younger man. He looked fit at any rate — Cesare will have to bide his time as heir-in-waiting, Pietro thought.

The Duke raised his bejeweled hand in a salute to Cesare, then held it out for Pietro to kiss.

"Come in," he said. "I'm glad of a respite from this infernal posing."

The artist made apologetic noises. He was on his knees arranging the folds of the curtain which formed the background and draping them over the arm of the chair from which his noble sitter had risen.

The Duke shook his white-stockinged legs and stretched his neck, pulling at the starched ruff.

"Damned uncomfortable, this arrangement," he said. "Even Perseus has had enough." Perseus was the name of the hunting dog at his side, a fine deerhound panting and straining against the leash. "It was an idiotic idea to include him in the picture."

"If Your Highness prefers, I can paint in the animal later," the artist, said. "I have sketched him at any rate."

"Well, then, take him away, take him for a walk," the Duke said sharply. "He is getting restless. I don't want him to piss on the floor."

The artist bowed and, without another word, took the leash from the Duke's hand and led the animal out of the gallery.

Cesare inspected the half-finished painting.

"The man has talent," he said. "But what is it good for, that's the question, isn't it? An artist may give a woman a beautiful face on canvas — but does it make her beautiful in life? He can put a crown on a man's head, but does that make him a king?"

"So what's your point, Cesare?" the Duke said, giving him a petulant look. "You want to add to my irritation? I'm sitting for this portrait to please the Duchess. She has expressed a wish to have my likeness and that of Perseus — don't ask me whom she likes more, the dog or me. In fact, don't ask me anything right now, you hear?"

Cesare ignored the Duke's ill humour and continued his line of argument.

"My point, sir, is that some skills are more valuable than others. Now this young man — Pietro Paci —has a knack for making history serviceable, a very helpful thing just now."

Pietro had been waiting in the back of the room, afraid that they had not picked the best time to approach the Duke. He stepped forward when Cesare motioned to him.

"He is the author of that nice little conceit about Ferrara's loyalty to the papacy, which I showed Your Highness yesterday," Cesare said.

"Ah, a man who knows how to make himself useful," the Duke said and looked Pietro up and down.

"And even more to the point, a man who knows how to please," Cesare said.

40

"Turn around," the Duke said, as if Pietro had come for a dress rehearsal. As he followed the Duke's instructions, he remembered his mother's disapproval of fashionably short jerkins. Showing too much butt, she had said. The Duke was an older man. Would he take umbrage at the immodest length of his jerkin? Pietro's cheeks reddened.

"And blushes very handsomely," Cesare said.

The Duke laughed a mirthless laugh. "He will do."

"Oh, he'll do very well, I think," Cesare said. He seemed greatly amused for a reason Pietro could not fathom.

"His Highness has decided to give you an opportunity to deliver your work to the Pope in person," he said, turning to Pietro.

Pietro bowed deeply. This was more than he had expected in his wildest dreams.

"I am greatly honoured by the trust Your Highness places in me."

The Duke gave him a negligent wave of the hand. "Well, do your best, young man. Cesare will discuss the details of the assignment with you."

He turned his attention to the painter who had returned with the dog.

"What's the idea of bringing Perseus back?" he said to the cringing artist. "Take him away at once. Didn't you say you'd paint him in later? In fact, why don't you paint me in later as well!"

The painter backed out of the room with the animal in tow.

"A pox on that slowpoke of a painter," the Duke said. "He's kept me here for an hour!"

"And will keep you many more hours, if I know painters," Cesare said.

The Duke snorted. "We'll talk later," he said to Cesare, waving Pietro off and ending the audience.

"I'll walk back to the archive with you," Cesare said to Pietro. "It's on my way, and I can give you your instructions. First, make a fair copy of your essay on vellum. Soft lambskin looks more ceremonial than paper and preface it with a short letter to the Pope in the name of the Duke. — I know you are a practiced letter-writer."

A sarcastic smile was playing on his lips. Was this a sly hint that he knew of Pietro's letters to Livia? Had they been intercepted on his order, as Pietro suspected?

"And if His Holiness, the Pope, has no objection," Cesare continued, "your essay might be printed, thus making your name

41

known to the public and beyond our city where, they tell me, you are a hero already."

He paused and gave Pietro a sideways glance.

Pietro realized what he was getting at and decided to play the fool. "I am grateful to Your Lordship for advancing my cause," he said, "but I doubt I'm anyone's hero."

"I am referring to your rescue of the damsel in distress. Very courageous of you, especially in view of my advice to keep your hands off her."

"I have said my adieus to Livia Prevera," Pietro said, keeping his voice level.

"Have you now?" Cesare said. "In that case, you deserve my encouragement. I can only add: Stay the course, and we'll make a courtier of you yet, for that is your ambition, I understand, is it not?"

"I am indeed desirous of making a career at court, my lord, and I hope you will not withdraw your support and continue to act as my patron before the Duke."

Cesare nodded. His eyes were veiled, his face unreadable.

They arrived at the archive and stepped into the book-lined room.

Cesare leaned against Pietro's desk, moving a few manuscripts out of the way, not without giving them a casual glance first. "And now that you are about to begin your new life as courtier," he said in the voice of a professor lecturing a student, "let me teach you the first lesson. A courtier must be discreet, of course, but more importantly, he must be like an actor — handsome and pleasing. He must know his lines and adjust his face and gestures to give them life and a semblance of truth, although they may be only half-truths."

He paused, waiting to see if his words had sunk in.

"I will do my best," Pietro said, although Cesare's rules for the courtier seemed more like rules for a hypocrite.

"Well then," Cesare said, "now that I have made myself clear on the theoretical points, let's talk about practicalities. I will arrange for the necessary funds and letters of introduction. You will travel to Rome and present yourself to Cardinal Alfonso Gesualdo, the uncle of Prince Carlo, my respected brother-in-law. He will arrange for your audience with the Pope. This may take a few days or a few weeks or even a couple of months since we cannot take the risk of presenting your brief to the Holy Father at an inopportune moment. I expect you to keep you ear to the ground while you are in Rome and report your findings to me."

"Is there anything in particular that I should be listening for, if I may be so bold to ask?"

Cesare raised his brows in mock surprise. "A very apt question, young man. You have more talent than I gave you credit for. You will be listening first of all to the Cardinal, to what he says and what he leaves unsaid. And you will let me know whether his intentions toward us are as good as he wants us to believe they are. Secondly, listen to what others say about the Cardinal and let me know whether he is as powerful as we take him to be. And mainly, whether he is powerful enough to promote the Duke's cause. Flatter the old man, get to know him, entertain him, make yourself useful to him, in a word, ingratiate yourself with the Cardinal, and report back to me."

"And how will I let you know what I find out?" Pietro asked and could not stop himself from adding. "I would not want my letters to be intercepted."

Cesare's lips curled into a mocking smile. "Another apt question," he said. "You will send me letters through the banker Leonardo Cigi. He will also take your drafts of money — the travel bursary supplied by the Duke—and will convert them for you into ready coin. You can trust Cigi. He will make sure that your letters reach me. But to protect the content from curious eyes, you will refrain from naming names. Refer to the Cardinal as 'my friend', to the Pope as 'my patron', to the Duke as 'my father,' to myself as 'my uncle', and so forth. We'll draw up a list of names and words that are better not spelled out."

"Why not use cipher?"

"Using code would only attract notice and the interest of those who make it their business to poke into the packets entrusted to messengers. Besides, there is no code that can't be cracked. A little camouflage that makes a letter sound unimportant is the better way to go, believe me."

There was a great deal to be learned for an apprentice in the art of diplomacy.

"As for compensation: your travel expenses will be covered, of course, and you will receive a stipend to allow you to live in Rome in a style becoming to an emissary of the Duke. If you show yourself diligent and transact your business to the Duke's satisfaction, there might be a reward. Indeed, His Highness has enough confidence in you to offer you something in advance."

He paused significantly, and Pietro obliged him by asking what that something was.

"He has written on your behalf to a gentleman in Rome, Signor Tommaso Amosto, a man who has proved his mettle as courtier in the service of the Pope. Amosto has an unmarried daughter, and the Duke has put in a good word for you. I need not tell you that a connection with his family will be invaluable to you. Amosto, on the other hand, will not derive much benefit from an association with you and your family. That fact will no doubt be reflected in the dowry he is willing to give his daughter, but he will not reject your offer outright, as he would under ordinary circumstances. He will defer to the Duke's wishes, and if you yourself make a good impression, I don't see why the marriage shouldn't come off."

Pietro bowed deeply and asked Cesare to convey his thanks to the Duke for putting his trust in him. In his heart, however, he did not consider it a great reward. Although he knew nothing of Amosto and his daughter, he was convinced that she could not possibly measure up to Livia, but then what woman could? His heart contracted at the thought of his loss, but he was careful to show Cesare a contented face. He had embarked on the career of a courtier (or was it, a hypocrite?), and there was no turning back now.

"By the way-" Cesare said and pulled a small book from the folds of his coat. "May I ask you to return this to Livia Prevera for me. I felt obliged to confiscate it. Most unsuitable reading for a young lady, in my opinion. Just as Livia is a most unsuitable lady-in-waiting for Leonora. But that's Prince Carlo's business now."

"As I mentioned earlier, I am no longer in touch with Livia Prevera. I took your advice, my lord, and am keeping my distance from her."

"You did indeed mention it, but I am sure you will want to bid the young lady a formal farewell on the melancholy occasion of her departure for Gesualdo," Cesare said, stretching his lips into a malicious smile.

"As you wish, my lord," Pietro said, doing his best to sound unconcerned. What game was Cesare playing now? Was this a test of his resolve? No, more likely Cesare took a perverse pleasure in making Pietro suffer through a second farewell. He looked at the title of the little book. *Polidoro*.

"A notorious book," he said. "I've heard of it before."

"Read it," Cesare said. "It will serve you as a warning against clever women."

CHAPTER 8

"Travelling to Rome!" Pietro's mother said, taking hold of his hand and peering anxiously into his eyes. "How long will you be gone, my dear boy?"

The older Paci gave his wife an irritated look. "For Heaven's sake, Maddalena. Don't fuss over him like that."

She had sat down by her son's side, pressing him close, afraid of letting him go. Pietro looked at her with affection. Everything about his mother had a crispness about it — her white hair, the starched collar, the papery skin of her hands. The house itself was like its mistress, neat and sparingly adorned, the furnishings a little old-fashioned in appearance but of good taste and quality.

"It's an honour for Pietro to be sent on a mission to Rome," her husband said. "You should be congratulating him. Instead you are whining." He mimicked her tone. "How long will you be gone? When will you be back? — He isn't a little boy, you know."

Pietro felt sorry for his mother. The old man was getting more petulant each day.

Maddalena compressed her lips and lowered her eyes. She had the Christian virtue of patience.

"I know you mean well, mother," Pietro said and consoled her with a hug.

She smiled up at him gratefully. "Your father is right," she said. "I should be proud of you and glad that the Duke is taking an interest in your future."

"Except for that bit about arranging a marriage with Tommaso Amosto's daughter," Girolamo Paci said. The crosshatch of lines on his forehead deepened. It was clear that he didn't like the proposed family connection, however advantageous Cesare considered it.

"Do you have any reservations?" Maddalena asked, her voice not quite as meek as before. Choosing a good wife for her son was a mother's task. Even if the final decision rested with the men of the family, she ought to be consulted. A marriage contract wasn't like other business transactions. It concerned Pietro's happiness and the perpetuation of the Paci name. "What do you know about the Amostos, Girolamo?" she said.

Her husband threw up his hands. "Tommaso and I used to be friends when we were boys, but when his father became Master of the Wardrobe to the Archbishop, I was no longer good enough for him. And when the Archbishop acquired a cardinal's hat and moved to Rome, Amosto accompanied his employer and did very well for himself at the papal court."

"And his son — your friend Tommaso?"

"My erstwhile friend, you mean? He followed in his father's footsteps and has a lucrative post at the papal court. Ah, it's a wonderful thing if you can promote your son's career. I wish I could have done something for you, Pietro, but-"

Pietro knew where that "but" would lead. Next, his father would say something about how foolish it was to marry young, meaning how foolish he had been to marry Maddalena, a woman with a small dowry. Then tears would veil his mother's eyes, and a look of guilt spread over her face, although Pietro knew very well that his father's lack of success was not her fault. Girolamo Paci had no head for business. When all his investments failed, he was thrown back on the income from his estates, but even the running of his estates needed more business acumen than he had to offer. He was fortunate that his wife was frugal and understood human nature better than her husband. Maddalena kept up good relations with the families on the neighbouring estates, accepting and returning their invitations. She talked to the wives of the tenant farmers on their own estate, listened to their concerns and showed a friendly interest in their children. Working those invisible lines, she avoided a great deal of unpleasantness and ill will that might have damaged her husband's interests. As Pietro grew up, he came to appreciate his mother's skills and her understanding of human nature. In many ways, her judgment was better than his father's.

He certainly did not want to resurrect the old story of his father's foolish marriage and the money-grubbing men in whom he had placed his trust and who had cheated him out of his investment. He was in no mood to listen to a long lament from his father that he was a failure and could do nothing for his son.

"You have given me your good name, father," he said. "That is an invaluable gift. It's up to me to do the rest."

"Indeed, there is something to be said for a self-made man," Girolamo said, "but a little help does not come amiss, whether it's from a father, or a patron, or through an advantageous marriage."

"And how advantageous is this marriage to Amosto's daughter?" Maddalena said.

"I haven't seen Tommaso in many years. All I know is that he married into Roman nobility and has a daughter, Isolda. By my reckoning, she must be twenty-three years old, which makes me wonder—"

He paused and gave his wife a significant look. Twenty-three years old and still unmarried! How was it that a young woman of good family, and no doubt well-dowered, had not yet found a husband?

"There is bound to be something wrong with her," Maddalena said.

"That's what I suspect. Tommaso is rich and well-connected. Why should he give his daughter in marriage to Pietro Paci, a nobody and the son of a nobody?"

Maddalena drew herself up. "My dear! Pietro is a gentleman and the son of a gentleman and well respected everywhere. And a suitor who comes recommended by the Duke isn't a nobody."

Pietro spread his arms, trying to make peace between his parents. "You are both right to raise questions about this proposed marriage. It may not be the wonderful thing it appears to be. The bride may have personal deficiencies to match my financial shortcomings, but luckily I will be on the spot and in a position to judge the situation myself."

"I wish I could be there with you," the elder Paci said. "Just don't rush into anything. This is a grave decision and best made after carefully weighing all factors."

"Very well," Pietro said, "but if it is the Duke's will that I marry her?"

His father drew a deep breath. "If it is the Duke's will, of course—"

In that case, there was nothing more to say. Their hands were tied.

"In any case Amosto's daughter will be better than that penniless young woman you have been courting," he said.

Maddalena saw the blood rushing to her son's cheeks and said quickly:

"Never mind that now, Girolamo. When will you leave for Rome, my dear boy?"

Pietro saw the wisdom of her "never mind". He swallowed what he wanted to say to his father and answered his mother's question instead.

"Not until September. Rome is deserted during the summer months, they say. All the important people leave the city for their summer residences. So you needn't go into mourning for me yet, mother," he said, smiling, but he could tell she was not cheered by his jocular manner.

The question his father had raised about the prospective bride deepened Pietro's own feelings of unease about the Duke's unexpected patronage. The interview with him had been peculiar, and Cesare's purpose in arranging for it unclear. Pietro had the impression that he was being paraded before the Duke like a horse for sale. Was the inspection for the benefit of Amosto's daughter? Did the Duke want to assure himself that Pietro's appearance was pleasing? Or were looks and deportment of such importance in diplomacy that they constituted a factor in entrusting him with the Roman mission? Yes, that is what the famous author Castiglione said in his book about the ideal courtier: He must have grace. *A man's outward appearance is a token by which his soul can be recognized.* But Pietro was not unknown to the Duke. Why this renewed scrutiny?

He understood that sending him to Rome and keeping him there in style was an expensive proposition. The Duke wanted to know what he'd get for his money and for that reason perhaps looked him over carefully, but what exactly did the Duke get for his money? Apart from asking him to present his historical essay to the pope, Cesare's instructions had been vague. And the arrangement of his marriage to a woman of wealth and standing seemed almost too much of a reward for the service he hoped to render to the Duke. Then there was the strange turn the conversation had taken when Cesare asked him to give Livia the book he had confiscated. It was as if he wanted to tempt Pietro to renew an acquaintance of which he had explicitly disapproved. If it was a cruel test, Pietro was not sure he could pass it. He was afraid love would overcome reason.

He made up his mind not to return the book to the owner. That way he avoided all temptation. Instead he would keep it as a memento and take it along on his journey to Rome. It was an object Livia had touched. He thought of the book as a keepsake and a talisman to protect him against evil. In his eyes, it was a more valuable token of love than any favour — a satin heart or knotted ribbon — a woman could give her lover. It contained a tale of romance after all and was filled with words of love. Besides, what harm could it do to cherish Livia at a safe distance? If Cesare inquired about the book, Pietro would say he had no opportunity to return it. For all he knew that was the answer Cesare was looking for. Yes, that was the way to pass the test, he decided: declining another meeting with Livia to show that he respected Cesare's advice.

The book itself was an odd thing: a chivalric romance written by a woman. Pietro was curious enough to read the opening pages. *Tell of the cruel battles and the ardent flame,* the first canto began. How very appropriate! A cruel battle was raging in his own heart as well, when he thought of Livia.

CHAPTER 9

The boisterous celebrations to honor Leonora's wedding continued. The warm spring weather and the bright sun seemed to mock Livia's sadness. Her courage was failing. Her cheeks grew pale.

Giulia noticed it and brought out her book of symptoms.

"It's a relapse," she said. "Your cold is back. I can tell by the tone of your voice. It wouldn't be so languid if your lungs were sound. But let me check the symptoms." She ran her finger over the columns in her notebook. "Sighs, murmurs, heaving... night-tears. That's the giveaway. I have heard you crying in your sleep, Livia. You've gone from healthy back to invalid. Would you like me to call the doctor?"

"No, that's quite unnecessary," Livia said firmly. "It's something I ate yesterday. The mutton, I suspect."

Giulia was leafing through her booklet. "Let's see now. I have a section on food poisoning, you know."

"It isn't anything like food poisoning, Giulia. It was a passing thing. I'm well again, I assure you I am."

"If you are well, then you must come with me to the main square and watch the game of quintains." She wouldn't take no for an answer. "Everyone is going," she said. "We'll all sit together in the loggia. Come, the game will cheer you up."

The game did distract Livia. For a few hours she did not think of her troubles.

A wooden shield had been affixed to a pole. Rider after rider came forward and galloped over the course of packed clay, trying to strike the target with his lance and knock it down. Dust clouds swirled as the men spurred on their horses. The shield hanging from the poles rattled and turned under their blows. Lances got stuck in the wood or shivered and broke. Horses balked and tossed their riders down into the dusty road. When a young fellow finally succeeded in piercing the target and carrying it off, a wild cheer went up from the crowd. The winner was hoisted on the shoulders of his friends and carried off in triumph.

The next day brought more excitement. A parade was held on the Giovecca, the thoroughfare which was the pride of the city. Ferrara's most beautiful and luxurious palaces lined the broad avenue: the Palazzo Roverella with its terracotta ornaments and graceful arrangements of windows, Santa Anna famous for its exquisite cloister, the Palazzo Pareschi with its stately iron gates, and the Palazzina with its long low façade. The brick facades of the palaces and their garden walls had been freshly painted for the occasion and were festooned with banners displaying the Prince's coat of arms and the Este colours of red, white, and green.

Giulia pleaded with Livia to come and watch the parade, but this time she stood her ground. She had woken up with sad thoughts of lost love and was feeling dejected. It was impossible to put on a cheerful face. She begged off, but she knew she wouldn't get away scotfree. At the end of the day she had to listen to Giulia's report, recounting every detail. The procession was a mile long at least, she said. The townspeople lined the road, elbowing each other and struggling for the best places to see.

"It was a wonderful spectacle," she said. "All the balconies were decked out in embroidered cloth. And you should have seen the men in heraldic costumes twirling banners over their heads and the float pulled by horses disguised as stags and unicorns. I'm so glad the Pareschis asked me to sit with them and watch the parade, except that the girls aren't very friendly. I sat beside Anna and couldn't get as much as a peep out of her. Whatever I said, she just pressed her lips together and didn't say a word in reply. Once she even shushed me, can you believe it? When I asked her what was wrong, she said she had an earache, but that was just an excuse. If you ask me, she was in a rotten mood because she has her eye on Pietro Paci, and he ignored her and talked to me instead."

Livia gave a start when she heard Pietro's name.

"Yes, he was there and asked after you," Giulia said. "Now, aren't you sorry you didn't come along? I must say, he is very handsome. Anna doesn't stand a chance with him, what with her squint, the poor girl. I know she can't help the squint, but it isn't just her looks. She's so unpleasant. A regular sourpuss. Her parents despair of ever arranging a suitable match for her, I'm told. They are thinking of putting her into a convent."

Giulia went on and on until the candle spluttered and threatened to leave them in darkness.

"Goodness, it's late," she said. "I suppose we should go to bed. But I almost forgot to tell you: someone asked Pietro Paci if it was true that he was leaving for Rome. And he said yes, in September. No one dared to ask him about the other rumour floating around at court: that the Duke has arranged a marriage for him, with the daughter of a papal chamberlain. But it doesn't sound likely to me _"

She stopped when she saw tears glinting in Livia's eyes.

"Oh, my dear," she said, grasping Livia's hand. "Now I understand it all. Tears, pale cheeks, trembling lips, listlessness — I should have known. Those are the symptoms I have under 'broken heart'. I put it down under diseases because a broken heart can be quite as fatal as the quartan fever."

Livia smiled through tears. "And is there a remedy for this disease?"

Giulia reached into the pocket of her dress and pulled out a lace handkerchief. She unfolded it and revealed two squares of marzipan.

"Have one," she said. "It's the only remedy I know."

CHAPTER 10

"Well," Giulia said when she returned from her outing on Sunday, "the wedding celebrations are over, alas, and we shall have to content ourselves with the old routine."

She had accompanied the Duchess on a visit to the abbey of San Silvestro and listened to a concert of sacred music.

"Let me tell you all about it," she said, sitting down and filling her lungs with a deep breath.

Livia resigned herself to the inevitable: a long and detailed report about the astonishing nuns who played in an orchestra, like men. But as it turned out, Giulia had nothing to say about the musical performance. The Duchess, who was well known as a matchmaker, had taken her along to meet a certain gentleman who had asked for permission to court her.

"He is in the service of the Prince, and very eligible, but I won't name names — oh, never mind, I will tell you, Livia, I can't keep it to myself. His name is Giovanni di Grassi, and he is the Prince's majordomo. After the concert, the Duchess asked me what I thought of him. Well, for one thing, he is old, thirty-five at least, but I couldn't say that because the Duchess was sixteen when she married the Duke, and he was thirty-eight. So I said: 'He is pleasant enough, but I don't want to make my home in Gesualdo. I couldn't bear being separated from Your Highness.' Then the Duchess said: 'Your loyalty is commendable, my dear, but every little bird must leave its nest, and you will hardly sway your father with the argument that you don't want to leave Ferrara.' And I thought to myself 'Oh, but my tears will sway him.' Then Donna Leonora put in-"

Livia came alive. "Was she there?"

"Yes, she was there and thankfully put an end to that awkward conversation by asking after you and giving me this together with a note for you." She handed Livia a scroll. "It's a madrigal the Prince composed, she said."

Livia untied the string wrapped around the rolled-up sheet of music and eagerly read the enclosed note, while Giulia prattled on:

"I said to Donna Leonora: You will be so bored now that the festivities are over. But she said no, she was glad of a little peace and was looking forward to sitting in the courtyard of the Palazzo dei Diamanti and admire the flowering trees and rose beds and to spend her evenings quietly with the Prince, listening to chamber music-"

She stopped when she saw the anxious look on Livia's face.

"What does she say in her note? Not what you expected?"

Dearest Livia,

I have mentioned your name to Prince Carlo, asking him to allow you to continue in my service. I praised your beautiful singing voice — that caught his attention at once, for as you know, he loves music. And now I have the pleasure to convey to you an invitation from the Prince. He wishes you to perform for a select group of guests after dinner tomorrow. I enclose a madrigal he composed, which he would like you to sing for us.

"What is it?" Giulia said. "You look worried."

"Donna Leonora wants me to come to the Palazzo dei Diamanti tomorrow," she said. "I am to entertain Don Carlo's guests with a song, a madrigal he composed himself."

She trembled at the thought of performing before a noble audience and before the Prince himself. He was a connoisseur of music. She dreaded his judgment, but Giulia eyed her with envy.

"An invitation to sing before the Prince! What a wonderful chance to impress him! They say he is a generous patron, you know."

"But, Giulia, what if I don't impress him? This invitation is a double-edged sword. If I perform well, he will approve of my continued attendance on Donna Leonora. If I blunder, he will send me away, covered with shame."

"Oh, he won't send you away." Giulia patted her arm. "You'll carry it off. But if you stay with Donna Leonora, won't you have to go to Gesualdo with her?"

"Of course I will."

"You'll be ever so far away! Three hundred miles, they say. And think about it, Livia: you won't know anyone there!"

"Neither will Donna Leonora. We will comfort each other."

Giulia sighed. "Oh, Livia," she said. "I'll miss you."

"Who knows? If Giovanni di Grassi wins your heart after all, we may meet again in Gesualdo. In the meantime, you'll be glad to have your room to yourself again."

Giulia dug a hand into her pocket and brought out a handful of almonds. "Well, I don't know," she said, her eyes somber. "I didn't mind sharing with you." She popped the almonds into her mouth and brightened.

"So, what are you going to wear tomorrow when you sing for the Prince?"

Before Livia could answer, she was already lifting the lid of Livia's chest and peering in. "The green one suits you best," she said, eyeing the garment. "And if you want, you can borrow my pearl earrings. And you know what they say? That the Prince loathes bad smells. So, you'd better air out the dress and rub your arms and neck with scented oil."

There was no stopping the steady stream of good advice pouring from Giulia's mouth. She would not rest until every detail of Livia's outfit was settled.

CHAPTER 11

The Prince's guests were still at dinner when Livia arrived at the Palazzo dei Diamanti, so called because the stones making up the facade were hewn in the shape of diamonds. She was shown into a salon, where two dozen chairs had been set up for the audience. The musicians were there already. Some were pacing up and down, humming or playing their pieces, others were tuning their instruments. She was introduced to the bass-lutenist who was to accompany her, but there was time only to do one practice run before the servants threw open the doors of the salon. The guests entered and took their seats, and the musicians took up their places as well.

Leonora came into the room on the arm of the Prince, looking plump and rosy beside the gaunt figure of her husband. She was dressed in a gown of shimmering purple with dusty-rose sleeves, whereas the Prince observed the Spanish fashion as always — black breeches, black hose, black doublet. A wide ruff of organza covered his neck.

It was the first time Livia saw Don Carlo up close. The Prince looked much like the official portrait he had sent Leonora, except that his skin was sallower and, whereas he had been clean-shaven in the miniature, he now sported a small goatee. His face was handsome, and there was dignity and grace in his movements, but Livia looked with pity at Don Carlo's thin calves. A well-turned leg was a man's principal attraction, after all.

The princess gave Livia an encouraging smile and took her seat in the first row between her husband and Count Fontanelli. The placid expression on her face told Livia that she was a happy bride and well pleased with Don Carlo's company, his thin calves notwithstanding.

When everyone was seated, the music master stepped forward and with a deep bow welcomed the noble assembly and expressed the hope that they would find the performance enjoyable. The first piece was music for cembalo. The performance was greeted with polite applause.

Next, it was Livia's turn. The lutenist played the first chord, and she began to sing "Tirsi morir volea" in the style that had become fashionable at court, a mode halfway between singing and reciting. The score trembled in Livia's hands, but as her voice soared, so did her confidence. It was a strange and beautiful song evoking love and death, joy and grief. When she finished, there was silence.

Livia looked up and saw that the audience was waiting for the Prince to applaud.

He did not applaud. He got up from his chair and briskly walked to where she was standing, took the lute from the hands of the man beside her and said in a severe voice: "This lady deserves better accompaniment. We shall do an encore."

At his words, the audience broke into thunderous applause, while the lutenist's face reddening with embarrassment. He bowed deeply and made way for the Prince. Don Carlo nodded to Livia and started the piece over, playing the lute with admirable expertise. He signaled the tempo to her, raising his head sharply as he speeded up and compressing his lips when he slowed down, revealing to her the lights and shadows of his composition. She followed his lead and modulated her voice, allowing it to leap up in joy and exultation, or slow to a melancholy pace of infinite yearning. Keeping her eye on the Prince, she felt as if she was seeing him for the first time and discovering his true nature. His whole person was infused with the beauty of the music. He had endowed it with such deep emotion that it made the sentiments of every other song appear dry and artificial by comparison. Truly, his music was like a divine oracle, expressing what could not be said in words.

When the performance ended, there was no hesitation. The guests rose from their seats and gave the pair a standing ovation. For a moment Livia regretted that Pietro was not there to witness her moment of triumph, but she quickly suppressed the thought.

A painful twinge cut into her happiness when she thought of their last farewell.

The Prince led her to the first row and, at a word from him, the Count made room for Livia to sit down beside Donna Leonora.

The prince bowed to his wife.

"Madam," he said, "you have shown excellent judgment in choosing this lady as your attendant, and excellent judgment also in recommending her to me."

Leonora inclined her head in acknowledgement of Don Carlo's praise, then gave Livia a radiant smile and squeezed her hand.

Relief flooded her heart. Her place in the Prince's household was assured.

The next day she packed up her belongings to join her mistress at the Palazzo dei Diamanti.

CHAPTER 12

Livia was glad to rejoin her mistress, but she could see that the occasion was not entirely joyous to Giulia.

"My room will be so large and lonesome without you," she said, her eyes dull.

Livia had been apprehensive at first, thinking that Giulia would regard her as an intruder on her private space, but the two women had gotten along well, and Giulia had turned out to be good company even if she talked too much.

"I'm not that far away and will see you often," Livia said, taking her hands in hers.

Giulia only sighed. "But you will soon be off to Gesualdo. I understand of course: It is your duty. It is your livelihood. And I wish you well."

Her duty? Livia had never thought of her position as Leonora's lady-in-waiting as a duty. Every day spent in Leonora's company gave her pleasure, and once she had moved into the Palazzo dei Diamanti, the two women resumed their familiar routine. They shared the mundane and the sublime. Together they chose the dinner of the day. Together they selected Leonora's gown — was it to be the green taffeta dress with the gold trim or the deep burgundy with the lace edging, the amethyst earrings or the emerald pendants? They walked in the park or read in the loggia or practiced playing the dulcimer. Best of all were their heart-to-heart talks, when they shared their happiness and their sadness, their fears and anxieties— but would they be as close as before? Leonora was a married woman now. She had the loving company of a husband. Perhaps she no longer needed a confidante. The distance between us will grow, Livia thought, just when I am most in need of a friendly heart. There was no one whom she could tell about her break-up with Pietro. Even if Leonora was willing to lend an ear, it was hardly appropriate to speak of her sadness to a young bride and spoil this happiest of times with her own tale of woe. A few weeks ago, they had shared every breath of hope and fear, every rush of sentiment, but now she must get used to the idea of being second in Leonora's affections.

The weeks went by, and Livia could not overcome her sadness. The loss of Pietro's love wrung her soul. Her chest contracted whenever she thought of his handsome face and cheerful voice. She felt pangs of sorrow even at the sight of someone resembling Pietro in figure or gait. Loneliness threatened to overwhelm her. She thought her heart would burst if she could not speak to Leonora of her troubles, and one afternoon she did. Leonora herself raised the subject. The two women were sitting in the loggia overlooking the courtyard, sheltered from the sun and the eyes of servants by its broad roof.

"And now you must tell me what distresses you, Livia, for you can't deny that you are sadly out of spirits. I know you too well. I have never seen you so quiet, with your hands resting in your lap, and your feet as still as if you had never danced in your life, and your eyes as demure as an old lady's. Is it the thought of leaving Ferrara — and Pietro?"

Livia hesitated.

"What is it, Livia? You can tell me. You know I am your friend."

"I am glad you are keeping a little corner in your heart for me even now when it must be full to the brim with thoughts of your husband."

Leonora moved closer and planted an affectionate kiss on Livia's forehead. "Do you think my heart is not capacious enough to embrace both you and Carlo? Indeed, my happiness with the Prince is so great that my heart is overflowing. I need to share my happiness, I need to tell the world — no, not the world, which is treacherous, but you, the friend of my soul. How I longed to have you by my side again. I know the secrets of my heart are safe with you. You have always received my little worries with a sympathetic ear. You wept with me when my father died. You trembled with

64

me before Cesare. You comforted me when I turned nineteen — still unmarried, when I was afraid that he would pack me off to a convent."

"And now *I've* turned nineteen and fear I'll soon be an old maid."

"An old maid! Surely Pietro—" She stopped when she saw the pain in Livia's eyes. "Oh my dear, you've had a lover's quarrel!"

"No quarrel, only a sad reckoning that we are not meant for each other. Pietro has his career to think of, and I could see that our relationship had no future, that I must give him up." She took a deep breath as if to expel all thought of Pietro. "But how quickly he has forgotten me. I hear he will go to Rome and enter into a marriage the Duke has arranged for him. At least that is what Giulia Morigi told me, although she could give me no particulars."

"Giulia is a gossip and hardly a reliable source. She repeats indiscriminately whatever she hears. It may not be true."

"True or not, it makes little difference. I must part with Pietro, and the sooner I forget him the better. He does not know the meaning of true love. He loves me like a puppy dog which licks the hand of his mistress and jumps with joy when he sees her, but the moment she leaves the room, he forgets all about her and starts chasing his own tail."

Leonora quietly took her hand. "There will be other suitors."

Livia shook her head. "I have nothing to offer them. I am like a mottled pear left on a picked-over plate of fruit."

"You are too hard on yourself, my dear. You have much to offer. You are kind. You are witty. You are beautiful — slim and lithe like a young girl."

"Lithe? Thin, you mean. You know very well that men seek comfort in an ample bosom and like the sight of a round smiling face — like yours, my sweet Leonora. Men find your dimpled hands charming and your curved lips irresistible."

"My dear little flatterer! You make it sound as if I was a great beauty. But I know better, and before my happy union with Don Carlo, I was not sure at all that I could make a man happy. I trembled at the thought of my wedding night. But you are right in one point: men look for comfort in a woman. Let me tell you something in confidence — you must keep it to yourself, and I know you will. On our wedding night, after the roisterers left us alone at last, the prince took my hands in his and asked me to sing him a lullaby."

Livia could not help laughing. "A lullaby — that is a novel way of declaring love."

"Music is the pathway to Carlo's heart. As soon as he met me, he said, he knew he would find happiness with me. My voice made him glad. It was as comforting as a dulcimer. On our wedding night, as he led me to the bed, he spoke to me from a full heart. — Oh Livia, such eloquence, I no longer felt shy. We kissed, and I forgot everything." She caught her breath. "But I shouldn't talk like that to an unmarried woman."

Livia smiled. "I need not be a married woman to understand that love takes away all sober thought. Alas, I know it too well. I lost my reason when I fell in love with Pietro. Parting with him has one advantage though: I shall not regret leaving Ferrara."

But Love is a tyrant. And she did regret leaving Ferrara, never to see Pietro again. Gesualdo was so far away, and "never" such a cruel word. Why had she bid Pietro adieu in such final and immutable terms? Why hadn't she left the door open a chink through which he might return to her, and she to him?

CHAPTER 13

The dining room in the Palazzo dei Diamanti was aglow with the light of candles reflected in mirrors and silver dishes. As the guests sat down to dinner, Livia could see the anxiety in Leonora's eyes. She knew her mistress dreaded the evening, but the occasion could not be put off any longer. Almost three months had passed since her wedding, and courtesy demanded that Leonora invite her aunt, Donna Beatrice, before leaving for Ferrara. The old gossip was infamous for her plain speech, or rather, her rudeness. She prided herself on telling people "God's own truth, even if it hurts," but anyone who saw the glint of satisfaction in her eye when the words hit the mark, knew that it was not God but an evil genius that made her speak up. She took a malicious pleasure in being the bearer of bad news and seeing her victims suffer or pointing out their shortcomings and seeing them squirm. That is why Leonora had put off inviting Donna Beatrice, but here she was, her eyes glittering with malice as she marked every detail in the room and took in every word spoken.

Leonora had kept the number of dinner guests small and asked only those whom she could trust to be discreet. Apart from Donna Beatrice and her taciturn husband, she had invited di Grassi, the Prince's loyal mayordomo, her own dear Livia, and an elderly cousin of the Duke — safe, because she was too deaf to catch much of the conversation. Nevertheless, Leonora braced herself for an uncomfortable evening.

For a few short weeks, she had been allowed to live in newly-wed bliss. Gossip about the Prince had been suppressed for a time in deference to the Duke's diplomatic game, but once the marriage had taken place and the Este and Gesualdo families had been irrevocably linked, the rumours revived. And Donna Beatrice knew how to fan the flames. Lurid tales about the Prince's first marriage spread to every corner of the court. Giulia had already hinted to Livia that something was amiss, but now the whisperers had become brazen and said it out loud: The prince was mad! He was bewitched! He had killed a man, cut off his member and fed it to his dogs! Of course Livia knew better than to believe such nonsense and had done her best to keep the filthy gossip from her mistress, but tonight, with Donna Beatrice at the table, Leonora was in the direct line of fire. You could never tell what the old woman would bring out. In any case, Livia could not protect her mistress forever. The distressing rumours would reach her eventually.

Meanwhile, the guests had taken their seats and the servants were going around the table, pouring water into the silver bowls beside each setting. The guests politely dipped their hands for a moment into the rose-scented liquid and blotted their fingertips on the napkins, while the prince meticulously washed his hands, dried them, asked for fresh water, rinsed his hands again and was reached a fresh napkin to dry them a second time.

"Well, Prince," Donna Beatrice said, "It seems you are very particular about cleanliness. For a moment there I was afraid you'd rub the skin off your hands."

"It's a new fashion," her husband said. "When I was young, we never washed our hands at table."

Two sentences in a row! Livia thought. I don't think I've ever heard him speak at such length before. I suppose that will be his contribution for the evening. And maybe just as well.

"I shall lend you a book by the ancient physician Galen, newly translated from the Greek," the Prince said. "I found his advice on cleanliness most useful."

"What was that?" Donna Anna said, turning to Livia and pressing her silver ear trumpet against the side of her head. "I can't understand a word."

Livia explained about the ancient physician and set Anna off on a long lament about her poor health and all the aches and pains she was suffering.

"I'm more interested in Donna Leonora's health," Beatrice said. "No morning sickness as yet?"

Leonora coloured. "Let's not talk about sickness, Aunt, if you please," she said. "Why don't you tell us instead about your grandson, such a promising young man. I understand he has entered the service of the Duke of Florence."

For a while, Beatrice was sidetracked and proudly talked of her grandson, but then she saw the Prince covering his plate as he took a sip of wine. "Now what, in God's name, is the meaning of that?" she demanded to know, addressing herself to the table at large. "Why is he covering his plate?"

Di Grassi bent close to her and said in a low voice: "A Neapolitan custom."

When the main course was over and the dishes removed, the Prince asked for torches to be brought in and lit.

"Another Neapolitan custom?" Beatrice said loudly. Livia saw the servants exchange looks — was it Beatrice's rude question or the odd habit of their host that made them uncertain?

The Prince ignored the question and ordered the servants to bring in dessert.

"A Spanish custom, to be exact," di Grassi said to Donna Beatrice, answering on the Prince's behalf.

"An eccentric habit, if you ask me," she said.

"It would not be considered out of the ordinary in Naples, where the Spanish governor sets the example, Madam," di Grassi said.

But Beatrice wasn't shut up easily. She turned to Leonora. "I wouldn't tolerate those customs if I were you, my dear," she said. "Maria d'Avalos might have put up with them, but—"

Here the Prince interrupted her with a hoarse "No! No!"

All eyes were on him now. His face had turned a ghastly gray. He got up from his seat abruptly, his hands in fists and his body listing forward. The servants stepped up to the table in alarm, and Leonora too rose from her seat, a disturbed look in her eyes, but di Grassi had already taken the Prince's arm and steadied him.

"You are not well, sire," he said. "Let me assist you."

"I — I am not well, no," the Prince said with difficulty, in a rough voice.

"You must excuse us," di Grassi said, leading Don Carlo away. He gave Leonora a steady look. "With your permission, Madam, I will attend to the Prince."

Leonora sat down again. There was an embarrassed silence as the two men made their way out of the room. When the door had closed on them, Donna Beatrice turned to her husband.

"I am afraid we have tired the Prince," she said. "We should take our leave and take Donna Anna with us."

"I suppose so," he said drily and obediently got to his feet.

"I am sorry you must go," Leonora said in a stricken voice and signaled to the servants to escort the guests, while Livia explained to the deaf old lady what had been said.

Kissing her hostess goodbye, Donna Beatrice got in one last stab: "You'd better have di Grassi explain this business of the Spanish customs to the servants, Leonora, because they are spreading tales about the odd habits of your husband, you know. And another thing, about the Prince not 'feeling well'. It's more than his body that's ailing, my dear, at least that's what people are saying."

"What are they saying?" Leonora said faintly.

"That he is wrong in the head. I might as well tell you God's truth even if it hurts."

When they were finally rid of the blunt old woman and on their own, Leonora looked at her friend with languid eyes.

"Wrong in the head," she said, mechanically repeating Beatrice's ominous words. Her soft lips quivered, and her eyes brimmed with tears.

Livia took her hands into hers and said gently: "Pay no attention to that old dragon. You are the person closest to the Prince and understand your husband better than the gossips. Would you not be the first to know if there was anything awry?"

Leonora hesitated. "Yes, it's all a misunderstanding. Carlo is sensitive, and music absorbs him. They see him abstracted when he composes his motets and call it 'madness'. They do not understand what it means to be an artist."

"You are right, Leonora. They are too dull to understand the power of music or an artist's temperament." Livia had experienced the magic of the prince's compositions and the emotions they aroused in the listener. How much more keenly would they affect his own mind, the mind in which the music was born and taking shape. She was quite prepared to side with Leonora and make excuses for Don Carlo's eccentricities — and yet she was afraid that there was something of substance in the popular opinion. His erratic behaviour could not be explained by artistic impulse alone. Livia had seen the strange moods that seized the Prince sometimes, the quick change passing over his face like a summer storm gathering clouds and darkening the day. And what about his strange scene today, his hoarse cries of No! No! How could one explain that?

70

She was unsure how to go on with their conversation. Leonora was dabbing at her eyes. She was looking for comfort, not questions. Livia moved closer and gently took Leonora's hand in hers.

"You must admit that the Prince's mood goes from cheerful to bleak for the smallest of reasons or for no discernible reason at all," she started and stopped when Leonora cried out in anguish.

"Oh, Livia!" she sobbed, losing all composure and giving full rein to her tears. "It is true! My beloved Carlo is ailing, in body and in spirit. It is the death of his first wife that troubles him and blights his soul. If I could only get him to talk about it! She haunts him — that is all he will tell me. Her death is preying on his mind and making him ill."

"She haunts him? Does he mean-"

"Don't ask me what he means. I don't know. At first, I thought he was still grieving for Maria d'Avalos and feared that I would never replace her in his heart, but he assured me that I was his all now and that he felt our marriage was made in heaven. Then I thought it was the manner of her death that haunted him. They say she was killed by an assassin, you know. I meant to ask him about the circumstances, but I didn't know how to begin. Was she in great pain? I said to him. Did she suffer long? He only shook his head and put his finger to my lips as if to seal them. Do not mention her name to me again, he said. I could see he was in agony and asked no more questions."

"But the servants will keep talking," Livia said. "They observe the Prince's behavior and blather about it. They must be silenced somehow. Their gossip is disrespectful and damaging to the Prince's reputation."

"I suppose so," Leonora said in a strained voice. She was exhausted and wanted to put an end to the conversation. Livia acquiesced.

The subject was painful to her mistress, and she did not want to distress her friend further. But of course the servants kept on talking and the gossips kept on digging into the Prince's past and the circumstances of his first wife's death until they cracked open the secret and saw the naked truth. Then they spread it far and wide, in all its horrid colours.

CHAPTER 14

Two weeks after the distressing dinner, Livia was on her way to Leonora's apartment for their evening ritual, an hour's quiet reading at the close of the day. On the stairway leading up to the Princess' chamber, she met Donna Beatrice. Her brocade skirt rustled as she came to a halt on the landing and put out her jeweled hand to grip Livia's arm.

"Ah, Livia," she said, arresting her step. "You have come just in time to comfort your mistress. She is much disturbed by what she has heard."

More likely by what *you* have told her, Livia thought.

"It's about Maria d'Avalos — the Prince's first wife, you know. But of course you know. Everyone knows by now."

Livia's face tingled with a sense of foreboding. "I have heard only rumours," she said.

"Rumours? No, my dear — facts. God's own truth!"

"And what is the truth?"

"That the Prince murdered Maria d'Avalos. Well, perhaps I shouldn't call it murder. It was an honour killing."

"An honour killing," Livia echoed. No, she had heard nothing about that.

"I see you won't be of any help to your mistress. You look as stunned as Leonora did. I had to remind her that Duke Alfonso himself had acted in much the same manner to preserve the honour of his family. And if it was right for the Duke to kill Count

Ercole Contrari when he engaged in an illicit affair with a member of the Este family, it was right for Prince Carlo to kill his wife to preserve the honour of the Gesualdos. And as horrible as the truth may be, we must accept it." She stopped and gave Livia an impatient look. "Oh, for heaven's sake, pull yourself together, young lady, and don't make things worse for your mistress. As I said to Leonora, why be shocked? The laws of the land support honour killings. The family of Maria d'Avalos accepted it and did not seek to avenge her death. They bowed their heads in shame and consigned her disgraceful actions to oblivion. Quite rightly, in my opinion. Mind you, I would have thought they'd avenge the death of the innocent child."

"The death of the child?" Livia's voice was faint with horror. "I thought the boy was alive."

"The older boy, yes. But there was a baby, I am told, of uncertain parentage. Fathered perhaps by Maria's lover. They say the Prince killed the child, shaking his cradle until his little neck broke!"

Livia blanched. A chill seized her heart, but Donna Beatrice only pursed her lips. She gripped Livia's hand as if to transfer some of her own sangfroid to her.

"Well, those are the facts. Now wipe that ghastly look off your face, my dear, and try to cheer up your mistress."

She sailed past Livia, in a hurry, no doubt, to tell her friends how distressed Leonora was when she enlightened her about her husband's past, how naïve she was to be shocked by the cruelty of the world, and how foolish to be upset over what could not be changed.

Livia found the Princess' drawing room empty and the shutters of the windows closed tight. The cupids and garlands gracing the tapestries seemed to droop in the sparse light of a single candelabra on the console table. A quiet sob reached Livia's ears. When she parted the curtains separating the day room from the Princess' bed chamber, she saw Leonora lying curled up on her bed, tightly wrapped in the coverlet as in a cocoon, a hiding place for her grief.

She lifted her head when Livia parted the curtain, showing a face streaked with tears.

Livia sat down on the bed and pulled Leonora close. "Oh, my dear, don't let that old mischief-maker distress you."

"It wasn't Beatrice who distressed me," Leonora said, pressing a handkerchief to her swollen eyes. "She merely confirmed what I discovered on reading this." She handed Livia a small book that had been lying entangled in the folds of the coverlet, its pages crumpled and stained with tears.

It was an exquisite copy of Torquato Tasso's poems, with a red velvet cover and tiny metal clasps. He was Leonora's favourite poet. She regarded him as a genius. Surely it was not Tasso that had moved her to such paroxysms of grief.

"Someone left the book for me this afternoon," she said. "Someone who wished to remain anonymous — for good reasons, as I realize now, because it is the gift of a blackguard." Leonora wiped her eyes, trying to compose herself.

Livia opened the book to the first page and read the dedication of the anonymous donor. "To Princess Leonora. May the poet open her eyes to the truth."

"I began reading the verses, with great pleasure at first, until I came to the ode *On the Death of Two Most Noble Lovers* — you know the poem."

They had read it together many times. Livia knew the lines by heart. *Weep, O Graces, and bewail the cruel trophies of death. Weep, O Nymphs, for this horrible deed.*

"And it moved you to tears?"

"Tears of sympathy," Leonora said, "until I saw the words penned in the margin. That's when my sympathy turned to dread. But see for yourself."

Livia saw a wavering black line drawn from the title of the poem to the margin, where a childlike script, no doubt disguised, identified the "two most noble lovers" as "Maria d'Avalos and her paramour, the Duke of Gandia." Another line was drawn from the words "this horrible deed" to a second marginal note, which explained the horrible deed as "the bloody murder perpetrated by the cruel Prince Carlo Gesualdo".

She put the book down and stroked Leonora's arm. She felt powerless to comfort her mistress. Maria d'Avalos had betrayed her husband, and he had killed the lovers. Those were the facts, as Donna Beatrice had said. And yet she was unwilling to accept them. It was too horrible a thought.

"You mustn't believe anonymous accusations or the malicious tales of Donna Beatrice," she said at last, although she feared they were more than tales. "You must make further inquiries."

Leonora's tears were coming fast now. "That was my own reaction," she said. "I couldn't bear the thought of rumours being spread behind my husband's back. I thought it best to go to him directly. I told him of the accusations. — And he admitted that they were true."

Her face reflected the horror of his admission, and the two women embraced in silent misery.

"And did he give you any explanation?" Livia said. She was as badly shaken as her mistress.

"He said: How else was I to defend my name and the honour of my family when I found my wife in the arms of another man? In my own house, not fifty feet from my own bed! Any gentleman would have acted as I did."

Yes, Livia thought, that was the way of the world. Nothing mattered more to men than their honour in the eyes of their peers.

"What was I to do? he said. I owed it to my own dignity and to the honour of the House of Gesualdo to kill the lovers. I could not allow them to breathe the same air and walk under the same sun as I, or to be in my sight ever again. — That is the explanation Carlo gave me."

Leonora collapsed in Livia's arms and wept, but between sobs, she declared her resolve to stand by her husband. "It was an honour killing. I cannot blame him. Blame ought to be laid where it belongs," she said, trying to make her voice firm. "— the faithless heart of his wife."

Livia wordlessly stroked her shoulders until they stopped shaking and her face showed only a quiet sadness. "Then Aunt Beatrice told me another tale, more horrid than the first. That Don Carlo suspected her wife's lover had fathered the child to whom she had given birth a few months earlier."

"And he killed the innocent child?"

Leonora pressed her moist handkerchief to her eyes.

"I asked Don Carlo, and he denied the accusation outright. It was a shameful lie, he said. The child had been stillborn. And I believe him."

Thank God, Livia thought. At least he was not guilty of child murder. As for the rest, she could only sigh and repeat what Donna Beatrice had said already. The Prince had acted lawfully. A nobleman had the right to bear arms and to defend his honour with the sword. A man must guard his honour. And yet they were both crying, and Livia could think of no words to comfort Leonora.

"Perhaps I should not have questioned Carlo at all," Leonora said. "I should have simply believed that he did no wrong. He took offense at my questions, you know. He was angry that I interrogated him, as he called it. We parted on bad terms even though I promised never to mention the subject again. Oh, how will I spend the night, Livia? The apostle Paul says: Let not the sun go down on your anger. Then how can I sleep with Carlo wishing me Good Night so coldly, without the comfort of a kiss or the touch of his hand?"

"He will come to his senses and realize that you deserved an explanation, and not merely an explanation but compassion and understanding as well. The Prince's deed may be lawful, but it is shocking to a woman's sensibilities and troublesome to his own conscience as well, it seems—" Before Livia could say more, they heard a movement in the antechamber. Through the parted curtain, Livia saw the Prince enter the day room. Deep remorse and unhappiness was written on his face — no, more than that — a grey shade of despair.

Livia rose at once, curtsied to the Prince and left the apartment, praying that God would take pity on the couple and bring about their reconciliation. For a moment she lingered at the door and listened to their murmured conversation. Apologies, she hoped, and endearments.

Back in her own room, she thought about the appalling revelations the day had brought. Why had Pietro not told her of the murder when she inquired about the Prince on Leonora's behalf? Did he not know? But that was hardly credible. He had been in Gesualdo and attended the marriage negotiations. Surely these antecedents were mentioned or whispered about at any rate. Perhaps he did not think it was politic to let her know. He was well and truly on his way to becoming a diplomat! In spite of these sobering thoughts, her heart ached when she remembered that they would soon go their separate ways, she to Gesualdo and he to Rome — but why lament the mountains and plains separating them when they were even further apart in spirit, it seemed? Because love is a stubborn thing! she thought. That's why she still clung to him. Love did not go away when commanded to depart. She could not stop the string of memories — her last meeting with Pietro when they bid each other farewell, the earlier, happier tête à tête, when Leonora had sent her to question Pietro about Don Carlo and she was too giddy with Pietro's compliments to pursue her inquiry. Their meeting had been interrupted by Cesare, she recalled. Perhaps Pietro would have told her the sad tale of the honour killing if Cesare had not cut her inquiry short. Would it have made any difference? No, the marriage contract had been signed. Leonora was Cesare's pawn. She might have resisted if she had known all, but most likely to no avail. Cesare would have had no scruples forcing his sister to take the marriage vows, just as he had shown no scruples in his attempt to silence Livia.

And now — would the couple be reconciled?

When Livia went to her mistress in the morning, she was told to wait. A family council was in progress. She discerned the voices of Cesare and Donna Beatrice and feared the worst, but when the visitors departed and she was at last called into Leonora's presence, she looked refreshed by more than sleep. A spark of life had returned to her eyes which had been so dull the night before. Her full lips were curved into a gentle smile. They are reconciled, Livia thought, and Leonora confirmed it. The prince was full of remorse, she said. He agreed that he should have made a clean breast of his past earlier, but he was weak and could not overcome his own scruples. He apologized on his knees.

"He was ashamed of reproaching me because I had asked him questions. I had a right to know, he said. He begged me to forgive him. And he was especially sorry that he had disturbed me at this delicate time." She blushed rosy. "Yes, my dearest friend, I have happy news for you: I am with child."

Livia embraced her mistress and kissed her on both cheeks. "God bless you and the child," she said. "I am so glad to see you happy and at peace once more."

Even as she said it, she wondered: Was it peace or only a truce? Would Leonora's happiness last, and would she be able to love her husband as before? But she brushed away those dark thoughts to share in Leonora's joy.

"Of course it's too early to be sure," Leonora was saying. The telltale signs — nausea and the swelling of her breasts — were yet to come. She lowered her eyes as she considered the ever-present danger of a miscarriage. "It would have been better not to say anything to the Prince at this stage, but I did not want to wait. I was sure the news of my pregnancy would speed our reconciliation. Carlo could not remain resentful in the face of such tidings."

He had no right to be resentful in the first place, Livia thought. He had every reason to be grateful for Leonora's forgiveness. She was generous in her love for him. Or was it her sense of duty? Not long ago, Leonora had declared: *I could never love a cruel man.* The Prince had been cruel in the revenge he took on his faithless wife. He had shown no pity, sacrificing her on the altar of his honour. But Livia kept those thoughts to herself. For the time being, Leonora was happy. She had given proof of her ability to conceive. To a noble suitor a bride's fertility was as important as beauty and wealth, although it could not be written into the marriage contract. Leonora's eyes were full of pride and hope — pride in fulfilling the expectations of her family and hope of giving birth to a healthy son to perpetuate her husband's name. The Prince had a male heir already, a boy from his first, unhappy marriage, but an only child offered little protection against the wheels of fortune. Leonora hoped to present the Prince with another son and add another branch to his family tree. Livia did not have the heart to spoil Leonora's happiness with the question: After all you've come to know about your husband, can you still love him?

"You were right to tell the Prince about your pregnancy," she said. "And now that he knows, he will treat you with the consideration you need and deserve."

"The Prince was most solicitous when he heard the good news. He asked whether it was not too great a risk to travel to Gesualdo in my condition."

"That was my first thought as well," Livia said. "Should you not stay in Ferrara until the child is born?"

"The Prince cannot delay his departure. He has his duties to consider. He is a ruler and must rule. But I could not bear to be separated from Carlo for such a long time, not now when it is twice as important to nurse our love." She saw a shadow pass over Livia's face, faint lines forming around her mouth, and stopped mid-sentence. "My dear, dear friend, how thoughtless of me! To speak to you of avoiding the pangs of separation when you are obliged to put up with them and suffer. For I know you are suffering."

Livia lowered her eyes. "Yes," she said. "I can't forget Pietro — fool that I am."

"Loyalty is not foolish, Livia." Leonora folded her in her arms. "And knowing the power of love, you will understand me, and not urge me to stay behind in Ferrara, as Donna Beatrice did this morning, and even Cesare who does not care a fig about my health. It's all the same to him whether I live or die in childbirth. He worries only about his alliance with Carlo's family, which would end with my life."

"Of course you want to be with your husband," Livia said, "and in your place I would do the same. And think of Catarina Sforza's example! She rode into battle seven months pregnant to defend her city against the enemy. Luckily, you won't have to confront enemies. You will travel at ease, surrounded by people who wish you well and will make you comfortable."

Yet they both knew: there was reason to worry. Pregnancy brought a thousand dangers to a woman's life. How strenuous was the journey? they asked those who had come with the Prince from Gesualdo. But no one could advise them. They had taken the land route. This time, the Prince preferred to take the waterway: a barge along the Po to Venice, then a ship to sail down the Adriatic coast. He planned to turn inland at Barletta, which was only eighty miles from Gesualdo. Travelling on board of a ship was more comfortable than riding in a carriage, but the sea could be dangerous if the weather turned ugly. The inland journey was problematic as well. Would the summer come in with a vengeance and make them suffer from the heat? Would the child in Leonora's womb be safe if they spent days in a coach rattling over country roads? These were thorny questions, but Livia preferred to ponder them than think of Pietro and her own joyless future. Leonora's future could be painted in bright colours. A new and splendid life awaited her as the mistress of Gesualdo Castle and leading lady of a court renowned for its musical talents. And Leonora could dream of a healthy baby. Even the birth, so fraught with danger for a woman, was less menacing now that she had found a reliable midwife. Fina Capponi, who had delivered many of the children in the Este family had agreed to come along on the journey. When Leonora first asked Fina to accompany her, she begged off. She was almost forty, she said, too old to undertake so long a journey, too old to be uprooted from her native soil.

"My dear Fina," Leonora said. "You are as strong and healthy as a young woman. I have never heard you complain of ill health."

She promised the midwife a generous gift of money to make her old age comfortable.

"But what about my family?" Fina asked.

"You don't need anyone's permission, Fina. You are a widow. Your sons have a life of their own."

"Marco is still unmarried and living at home."

Leonora promised that the Prince would take Fina's youngest son into his service so that the midwife would not be deprived of his company on the journey, but no promise, however generous, could overcome Fina's reluctance. In the end, an appeal to her loyalty persuaded her to change her mind.

"You cannot leave me in the care of strangers," Leonora pleaded.

They all knew the horror stories. Witches masquerading a midwives got their hands on innocent babes and carried them off to the devil. Cruel midwives took pleasure in torturing young mothers by prolonging their labour, and ignorant helpers who pretended to knowledge bungled the delivery. Fina was experienced and knowledgeable. No woman in her care had ever died in childbirth. There were a number of stillborn children, but among those who saw the light of the world, none was allowed to slip away without baptism to save their little souls at least. Fina herself attributed her success to the grace of God and to a lucky birthstone she always carried with her.

The Prince supported Leonora's plea. It was not merely a matter of knowledge and experience, he said. Character counted as well, and Fina had a good name. She was a pious woman who had led a blameless life. One must weigh carefully whom to admit into the presence of a mother-to-be, he said. And so Fina agreed to undertake the journey to Gesualdo and be at Leonora's side when her time came.

They talked about the practical measures that needed to be taken. To begin with, Leonora must keep to a safe diet, avoid spicy foods that might hurt the unborn child, never drink red wine and certainly do without strawberries, her favourite fruit, because strawberries might cause red birthmarks. Under no circumstances could Leonora have hares on the menu because the very sight of them might cause the baby to be born with a harelip.

"And of course I will do without stomacher. I must not cramp him," Leonora said to Livia. They both smiled and repeated "him" in unison. It was every woman's fondest wish to present her husband with a son. Speaking of the unborn baby as a boy was a good as a prayer. One danger remained. Fina whispered about marital duties. Would the prince demand his rights?

"You know the old saying: When the ship is full, one must not admit passengers," she said.

"He won't insist," Leonora said, blushing. "He is too considerate a man to endanger my health and that of his child."

Considerate of his wife or of his lineage? Livia thought. Once again she bit back the question she wanted to ask Leonora: After all you have come to know, can you still love him?

CHAPTER 15

It was a bright day in June when the people of Ferrara prepared to bid farewell to the Prince and his bride. Family and friends were gathered in the large hall of the Palazzo dei Diamanti to say adieu to Leonora. The Duchess made a grand entrance with her ladies-in-waiting, sweeping into the room like an occupying force and besieging Leonora with eager questions and good advice.

Livia said her farewell to Giulia Morigi.

"And how is Giovanni di Grassi's battle going?" she asked. "Has he won your heart yet?"

"Oh, the Duchess is promoting his suit, you know, but my father is still making inquiries about his family. Like me, my father would have preferred someone from Ferrara. Don Giovanni's family is from Florence, but he looks like a Spaniard, all black and solemn. I suppose that's because he has lived under Spanish rule in Naples for so long." She sighed and her shoulders drooped a little. "There is nothing I can do if my father decides to sign the marriage contract. I only wish Don Giovanni smiled once in a while. That's what I told the Duchess, but she said I needed a grave husband to rein in my natural levity, and Don Giovanni was the right man for me."

"Then I might see you in Gesualdo before long," Livia said. The thought gave her pleasure because she discovered, a little to her surprise, that she had become fond of Giulia. Under all that talk, there was a good heart, and under all the giddiness, there was a good mind. Or at least an organized mind. Those lists Giulia kept on medical conditions proved it.

"The idea of seeing you again is the only thing that cheers me up," Giulia said, smiling wanly. Then her eyes wandered to the pastries and candied fruit that had been set out on silver platters, and she brightened.

"Come, let's have a taste of the quince tarts," she said. "I'm told they are heavenly."

Donna Beatrice was busy surveying the guests and keeping her ears cocked for news. She deftly maneuvered across the room and squeezed her broad rump into the circle around the Duchess.

"Leonora looks worried, don't you think?" the old gossip said to one of the ladies.

The Duchess heard her and took the wind out of her sails.

"Who wouldn't be worried," she said. "It's a long journey to Gesualdo."

"And in her interesting condition," Donna Beatrice said in a scandalized whisper. Everyone knew that Leonora was taking a risk, but the Duchess would not allow dark thoughts to intrude on the farewell gathering.

"She'll enjoy her stay in Venice at any rate," she said. Venice was the first stop on the couple's journey. The Prince wanted to consult with a printer there about publishing his newest musical compositions. The talk turned to the sights the city offered, the fashionable goods on display there and the elegant fashions.

But Donna Beatrice was not done with her insinuating talk. She wiggled close to Leonora and pinched her cheeks. "You look pale, my dear," she said. "It isn't only the journey that worries you, is it? I saw the Prince this morning, you know. Why was he looking so grim?" She heaved a dramatic sigh. "No, don't tell me. I suppose we women must put up with the moods of our husbands. It is not for us to question them."

"You are full of good advice today, Donna Beatrice," the Duchess said. "You will be quoting Barbaro's book *On Wifely Duties* next."

"There is no more edifying book for brides, madam," Beatrice replied. "And I *will* quote him. This is what he says about keeping the marital peace: *If your husband should scold you, bear his wrath silently.* I highly recommend the book to every young woman, especially the section on a wife's love." She gave the assembled ladies-in-waiting a stern look. "My mother made me learn it by heart."

"A hundred years ago," one of them stage-whispered to her companion.

She got away with this piece of impertinence because a servant entered at that moment with the Majordomo's message that the company was ready to depart. The Princess was requested to take her seat in the carriage that would convey her to the harbour. As the visitors surrounded Leonora for one last kiss and caress, Donna Beatrice sidled up to Livia.

"Donna Leonora is a model of virtue, I know, but tell me, how is she taking the Prince's ugly moods?"

"Like a loving wife," Livia said.

Donna Beatrice was not discouraged by her curt reply. "Ah, perhaps he cannot help his moods. You know what they say: he is bewitched, that is to say, a witch cast an evil spell over him."

This was too scurrilous to merit a reply. Livia only shook her head and hurried after her mistress. As they went out into the courtyard, they saw the Prince standing beside his horse, surrounded by a knot of people. Don Cesare was giving urgent directions to a servant.

"Oh, merciful God!" Leonora said, and faltered. At the same moment, Livia saw it too: The Prince was standing stiffly, one leg stuck out at an unnatural angle. The fingers of his hands were bent as if he was clawing an invisible object. When the two women drew nearer, they saw that his face was deathly pale and his eyes unseeing. The group of men parted to make way for Leonora. Don Cesare said: "I've sent for the doctor." Leonora waved him aside. She touched Don Carlo's cheek and softly called his name. At the sound of her voice, the Prince came out of his trance. He began to tremble uncontrollably. Then, all at once, his body slackened. He pitched forward and would have fallen to the ground if Giovanni di Grassi had not caught him in time. For a moment, he leaned heavily on the Majordomo, then he recovered his senses.

"Leonora, my dear," he said like one coming out of a dream.

"I am here," she said. "I am by your side."

He held on to her hand wordlessly.

"Would you like to consult a doctor?" she said.

He took in her words with difficulty. "No," he said at last, the strain still showing on his face. "A physician can do nothing for me."

Cesare bowed. "As you wish, Prince," he said, and sent one of the servants to call the doctor off. There was no pity in his eyes. He looked at Don Carlo with the contempt of a strong man for a weakling. "Then we are ready to depart, I take it. The Duke is awaiting us at the pier."

The Prince nodded. He seemed sluggish in body and mind, but after a little while he was able to mount his horse with the help of his page.

Cesare walked with his sister and Livia to the waiting carriage and handed them in.

"I suppose you will have to put up with those fits," he said to Leonora.

"Love bears all," she said.

"I'm glad you take it so meekly." His mouth curled into a sneer. "I just hope Don Carlo won't get any worse and make you a widow before you are a mother."

Leonora leaned back in the carriage seat and closed her eyes. "Enough, Cesare," she said. "Have you no mercy?"

"I leave those feelings to women," he said.

He gave them a sarcastic grin, raised his hand for a last salute, and turned to mount his horse.

As the carriage rolled out of the courtyard, Leonora said to Livia:

"Alas, this is not the first time the Prince has taken ill." Her voice was faint.

"And you never told me!"

"I could not bring myself to tell anyone."

Better so, Livia thought. It was wise to conceal the Prince's illness, whatever its nature, and protect him against schemers who might take advantage of his weakness. And against superstitious minds and mischief-makers. She remembered Donna Beatrice's insinuation that the Prince was possessed.

Leonora had shrunk back into the obscurity of the carriage and folded her hands over her stomach, as if she wanted to protect her unborn child from any further grief. They rode the rest of the way in silence.

CHAPTER 16

A stately ship awaited them in the harbour. It had been sent by the Doge to honour the couple and take them to Venice in comfort. The hull of the ship was richly decorated with carved gilt ornaments. The deck was equipped with a *felze*, a cabin to shelter the noble passengers from the elements. The two ladies took their seats on a sofa covered with a fringed throw of green velvet. Flower garlands had been strung along the top of the wall under a canopy of crimson silk, and a fragrant bouquet of jasmine and roses graced a low table set up in front of the cushioned seats. A delicate perfume filled the air. But there was one aspect that disturbed Leonora. The outside of the *felze* had been given a coat of shiny black lacquer.

Leonora sighed.

"I know the Doge meant honour us," she said, "and the ship attests to the elegant taste of the Venetians, but I wish the *felze* had not been painted black. There is something funereal about it. It is the second inauspicious sight to greet my child today — first his father's illness, and now the dismal aspect of black walls! What else is in store for him, I wonder."

The unborn child saw and heard through the eyes and ears of his mother. At the palace, Leonora had carefully arranged her rooms to cheer up the child and surround him with light and beauty, but she knew she would not be able to control every sight and every sound on the voyage. The colour black had the most sinister connotations, reflecting and doubling the appalling events of the morning.

"And I thought we would be safe by allowing the astrologer to pick the day of our departure." she said. "Now I'm no longer sure." Her voice was plaintive. "How will I avoid sudden frights, Livia? And how will the dampness of the riverbank and the marshes at Venice affect me and the little one?"

"Worry is more harmful than damp air, dearest Leonora. Keep up your spirits, and the child will rejoice with you. As for dampness, the winds will provide fresh air when we are on the water. And when we reach Venice, we must take the first opportunity to walk. They say that walking is by far the best exercise for a pregnant woman. And now, clear your mind of all melancholy thoughts and allow yourself to be distracted by the interesting sights around us."

She rose and looped back the curtain so they could watch the work of the bargemen, as they loaded the belongings of the princely couple and their entourage and the long train of carts, horsemen and mules carrying the rest of their baggage, as they moved off to take the overland route.

The Prince and his gentlemen were embarking now and taking their assigned places. Don Carlo nodded only curtly to them and moved at once to the back of the barge. He looked pale, but seemed to have recovered from his seizure.

"He keeps his distance from me," Leonora said, her face once again full of sorrow and care.

It was painful for Livia to see her looking at Don Carlo with longing eyes and to watch the Prince standing at the railing in a cloud of gloomy thoughts, oblivious to his gentlemen and indeed to everything around him.

"But you mustn't think that he is sullen or cold," Leonora said. "It is not moodiness that makes him keep his distance from me. It is fear."

"Fear of another crippling seizure, you mean?"

Leonora hesitated.

"He fears for his spirit more than his body. He is beset by demons, he says, and afraid they might harm me in turn. At first I thought he was speaking in the language of poets and using 'demon' as a metaphor. 'You mean temptations or afflictions of the soul?' I asked him. 'No,' he said, 'I am buffeted by Satan and his minions.' Oh, Livia, my heart nearly stopped. I asked no more. I yearned to put my arms around Carlo, to comfort him in his troubles, whatever they may be. I could see the need for love in his eyes, but he shrank from my embrace — to keep me safe from demons, he said."

Livia shuddered, remembering Donna Beatrice's dark hints about spells and witches and all the other stories she had heard about the Prince's first wife. Maria d'Avalos, they said, had used love potions to strengthen her hold on men, to make them subservient and drive them mad with desire for her. Was *she* the demon haunting the Prince?

"If you want to help the Prince, Leonora, you must draw him out. Let him name those evil spirits," she said.

"He is reluctant even to pronounce the words. He does not want the sound to strike the air. I must guard my language in the presence of the unborn child, he said. I must not subject you or the child to my moods and passions. They are infectious like diseases. Be your sweet and gentle self, he said to me."

"Indeed, there is nothing more harmful to an unborn child than melancholy and unpleasant thoughts."

"Of course, Don Carlo worries about that as much as I do. He wants to surround our child with everything that bodes well. He begged me to refrain from wearing necklaces, not even the one he gave me as a morning gift after the wedding, because our child could be born with the umbilical cord wound around his neck and suffocate. And when he saw me sitting with my ankles crossed, he asked me to change the position of my feet. He worried that crossing my ankles might deform the child. But most of all he worries about evil spirits hovering in the air."

"And he attributes the seizure we have witnessed to evil spirits?"

"Livia, please! No more talk about that ill-fated beginning of our journey!"

As the barge cast off and moved into the middle of the river, a farewell cheer went up from the people lining the banks, but there was no cheer in Leonora's eyes.

CHAPTER 17

Venice appeared to them like a great floating island. Di Grassi made it his business to show the ladies the sights as they entered the Grand Canal. He pointed out the magnificent old palace of Zorzi Corner, the brother of the Queen of Cyprus, and the great house built by the Most Serene Prince Francesco Foscari. He directed their attention to the fine glazed windows, splendid balconies and roof terraces, and the Campanile whose bells could be heard all over the city, signaling the beginning and end of the working day. Di Grassi was full of facts and figures, a dull guide — a dull man, if truth be told. Livia could quite understand why Giulia had not fallen in love with him, even though he was not bad looking — for his age, that is — and certainly a man who commanded respect. He had a good character and was reliable, but he had no charm and no words to engage the heart or mind. Today at any rate Livia did not mind him droning on. Even if his talk was not very entertaining, it served to keep Leonora's mind from other, more worrisome thoughts.

In Venice, the princely couple was lodged in the Doge's guest house. It was spacious and magnificently furnished. The main drawing room looked out on the Rialto Bridge, which had only recently been rebuilt at great expense — the Doge's gift to posterity. The guest quarters were elegant, the rooms hung with precious tapestries. In their honour, the bedrooms had been furnished with drapes and bedspreads in the colours of the House of Gesualdo. Everything was beautiful as well as comfortable. Leonora had every reason to be pleased, and yet her mood was subdued. Livia knew the cause. She was longing for the Prince's company, but he kept away all day, spending his time visiting the city's musical fraternities and listening to their choirs. He joined them finally at dinner.

The polished oak table, covered with a white damask cloth and bright with silverware, was designed for a party of twelve, but the Prince had no wish to entertain a large company and had invited only one guest, the music publisher Melchiorre Scotto.

The four diners were lost in the spacious room. The distance between them at table was like a signal, a manifestation of the Prince's aloofness and his desire to be left alone. He sat at the head of the table, while Leonora presided over the other end. Halfway between them, Livia and the publisher had only the width of the table between them, but could barely see each other. Their view was obstructed by a row of silver candelabras. The curved arms holding the candles wove a tangled pattern and formed a kind of screen between them. The conversation was halting. During the long silences, the smallest sounds became audible: the clink of the cutlery, the tapping of the servants' shoes on the marble floor, the stirring of the ladle against the terrine as they served the soup.

The Prince seemed immersed in a fog of private thoughts. He hardly spoke. His words floated across the table, rose to the high coffered ceiling, and hung over them like a cloud. He had brought with him a book of madrigals which he had composed during his stay in Ferrara and which he intended to publish. The manuscript was resting on a side table. In the intervals between the courses, the Prince cast longing glances at it, as if his appetite was for the music contained in those pages rather than for the food set before him. The lackluster conversation interspersed with long silences made the time creep. The meal seemed to go on for an eternity. Finally, when the dessert plates had been removed and the ordeal was coming to an end, the Prince said to Melchiorre:

"I shall visit your shop tomorrow afternoon and discuss the details of the publication. I am most particular about the paper, you know, and the quality of the ink."

"It will be an honour to receive you, my lord," Melchiorre said. "I have been told, however, that His Serene Highness the Doge has made arrangements to show you our beautiful city tomorrow. Should you find that your day is too full, I am at your disposal also in the evening."

"I will come in the afternoon as planned," the Prince said. "I have declined the Doge's invitation. There is no need to burden His Serene Highness with official functions. I am not on a state visit."

Leonora looked up, and said hesitantly: "I hope the Doge will not take it amiss-"

The printer did his best to smooth over the awkward situation. "Not at all, my lady. Lord Cicogna will not take it amiss. He is the most benevolent and obliging man, and merits the title of Serene Prince, which could not be said of his predecessor."

Livia had seen the Doge earlier at a reception in the audience chamber. His Serene Highness, wearing a cape of silver and gold embroidered damask and a matching cap, was an old man. He barely mustered the energy to rise from his ornamental seat to greet the visitors. Livia doubted that he had enough strength for any kind of emotion, good will or anger. He looked spent, a tired old man, bowed and white-haired, with a long thin beard, sunken temples and dim eyes. Don Carlo had made a polite little speech thanking the Doge for sending his barge to Ferrara, for his hospitality in Venice, and for his welcome presents of marzipan cakes, pots of ginger, syrup of violets, and other delicacies. The Doge replied in rotund phrases, taking labored breaths between each word and exhausting the patience of the Prince with his slow delivery.

"He is a saintly man," Leonora said to the printer.

"Ah, you have been told of the miracle?" Melchiorre smiled broadly, glad to move on to another subject. "The doge is a pious man, but I am not sure I believe the story of the sacred host miraculously rising up from the communion plate to seek his mouth."

"One should never discount the power of God," the Prince said severely, and Melchiorre wiped the smile from his lips.

"The Doge's reputation for saintliness is not in question, my lord," he said. "He treats everyone with benevolence and will readily accept a change of plans. No doubt he wished to honour you and take you to observe the glass blowers of Murano or our shipyard. Very few visitors are admitted to it, although many clamour for a sight of the halls where the ships are being assembled with the most advanced tools and methods."

"The shipyard. The shipyard. I'm tired of the very word," the Prince said. "Yes, the Doge proposed a visit, and I explained to him why I cannot go there. The clanging of hammers on metal would be injurious to my soul. As I need not tell you, my dear Melchiorre, the wrong kind of sound can create the wrong kind of mood in a man, whereas the right sound — or music, to give it its proper name—will calm our inner struggles and give us peace. It would be unwise to expose my ears to the chaotic noise of a shipyard. Nor would I want the Princess to be exposed to it if her interests ran to ship-building, which happily they do not. Donna Leonora will represent me tomorrow and go on an official tour of the city on my behalf, although it will be tailored to a lady's interests — the bazaars, I imagine — and will therefore exclude a visit to the shipyard."

"In that case I shall be glad to welcome you at any hour you name, my lord. I am sensible to the honour you do me in seeking out my shop here in Venice, when Ferrara does not lack music printers. I have no doubt that the Duke's own man, Vittorio Baldini, offered his services to you."

"In fact, the Duke did recommend Baldini to me, and I sampled his work, but I do not like the emblem he puts on the title page of his publications — Icarus flying toward the sun. The device horrifies me. I cannot understand why he would want to depict a man who challenged the powers above. We know the end of the story after all. Icarus was punished for his pride and met a fiery death."

The Prince rested his eyes on the flickering flames of the candelabra, which seemed to bring the story to life: the rays melting the wings of the bold aviator who tried to rival the sun. The prince's eyes followed the smoke curling from one of the candles, whose wick was drowning. His body went rigid, as if he had caught sight of something in mid-air, the soul of Icarus or the wrathful sun god. His face turned to marble. He seemed to have forgotten his guests.

Leonora half-rose from her seat. There was alarm in her eyes, a flash of fear. Was the Prince about to have another seizure?

"I am glad you find my emblem more attractive, my lord," the printer said. His words broke the spell.

The Prince gave Melchiorre a startled look. He coughed and wiped his mouth with a linen napkin. Leonora sank back into her seat.

"Your emblem," the Prince said. His voice was dusky. "Oh, yes, the three Graces and the motto *Virtus in omni re dominator* — Virtue conquers all. Yes, I like your device. It has an auspicious ring, and every aspect of a book is significant to me. The sight of a musical score on the printed page is as important as the sound of life music, for the score plays silently on our memory and can be as powerful as sound." The Prince looked around the table. His eyes rested on Leonora. "I am tiring you, my dear," he said.

"Not at all," she said. "It is pleasure to listen to you speaking of music."

"But I will not try your patience," the Prince said with finality and rose from the table. "We shall resume the subject tomorrow at your shop, Melchiorre."

CHAPTER 18

Leonora had allowed the Prince to think of her tour of the city as a lady's shopping expedition, but she had a different expedition in mind. In the morning she and Livia dutifully attended mass at San Marco and marveled at the gold and alabaster altar and even more so at elegance of the women in attendance: their jeweled hands, their strands of flawless pearls and intricate gold necklaces. But their main business came later in the day when their escort, the Doge's equerry who had been sworn to secrecy, took them to Tieffenbrucker's shop at the sign of the black eagle. Giovanni Tieffenbrucker was a renowned instrument maker, and Leonora wanted to buy a lute — a gift for the Prince's name day and an offering of love to cheer him.

Signor Tieffenbrucker himself waited on the ladies. With the natural verve of a salesman, he showed them two or three fine instruments, a little above the average, but nothing to arouse great interest. Then he brought out an exquisite lute, which he had kept back and showed them last to make them appreciate its quality. It was a masterpiece and bore the shop's trademark - an inlaid rose with a delicate pattern of interlocking rings set in the belly of the instrument.

"My favourite," he said. "All I have learned — the sum of thirty years' experience— has gone into building this archlute, which is quite novel and a great improvement over the angled lute. You will bear with me, ladies, if I brag a little about my craftsmanship. I cannot help it. I am in love with this instrument and would not sell it to just anyone. I show it to you only because you told me it was meant for the Prince. He is a connoisseur of music and of instruments, I know. I could not ask for a more appreciative client."

He went on in this way, praising the quality of the wood, its smooth finish, and the beauty of the design, although Leonora's smile should have told him that she needed no further convincing. He pointed to the top decorated with blossoms, butterflies, and birds and explained the pattern. "It recalls the most famous of the Tieffenbrucker instruments," he said, his voice soft with love and pride, "a viola presented to King Henry II of France by my grandfather, the founder of the firm."

"And the carved head?" Leonora said. She had never seen a lute quite like the one before her. The head of an animal sprung from some ancient myth surmounted the peg box. It seemed to watch the spectator with alert eyes and listen for music with erect ears.

"The dog of the goddess Rhea who guarded the infant Zeus," Giovanni said.

The ladies exclaimed with one voice. It was the perfect gift, and a wonderful omen! Could there be a more auspicious figure than the guardian of a divine infant?

"This will gladden the Prince's heart," Leonora said, but Tieffenbrucker raised up both of his hands.

"My lady," he said, "I cannot allow you to make a decision until you have listened to the sound produced by the instrument."

He beckoned to a slim young man, who had been waiting at the back of the room. He was of a dark complexion, with an unruly shock of jet black hair and a carefully trimmed beard.

"Benito Darrico will give you a demonstration," the master said.

The man came forward and bowed, but did not raise his eyes. His face was strangely closed as if he wanted to withdraw his thoughts and feelings from view. As if he was harbouring a deep secret he did not wish to give away to the onlooker, Livia thought.

Giovanni handed the lute to the man, and he reverently took it and began to play with consummate skill. It was then that his face opened up and mirrored the beauty of the music he made. Ah, Livia thought, I was wrong. What I took for secretiveness was merely a supreme effort to concentrate on the task.

Benito Darrico was an excellent lutist. His music delighted Leonora. The mellow sound issuing from the instrument confirmed her choice. She thanked the man and gave directions about delivering the instrument to their lodgings. The important thing was not to spoil the Prince's surprise, she said. The men who delivered the lute must tie up at the neighbouring dock and come around the side, by the gangway leading to the back of the house. They must bring the instrument to the servants' quarters, where it would be packed up with the rest of their luggage.

"The Prince will be with his majordomo in the evening to discuss the arrangements for our departure. That will be the best time to deliver the instrument," she said. "I only regret that Don Carlo did not hear your man play. I must mention him to my husband. Benito Darrico was his name, did you say?"

Giovanni hesitated. "The Prince knows Benito," he said. "He was the music master of Maria d'Avalos. He left Gesualdo when her household was dissolved."

Leonora's face darkened at the mention of the late Princess' name.

"You mean the Prince dismissed Benito?"

Giovanni had not failed to notice the clouded look that had come into Leonora's eyes and deftly changed tack. "Not him personally. The whole household was dissolved to erase that evil woman's memory," he said. "When Benito came to my shop and asked for employment, there was no need to show me a letter of recommendation. The knowledge and skill he displayed was recommendation enough. I did inquire into his character, of course, and heard nothing to make me hesitate or change my opinion of him."

"I wish you hadn't told me," Leonora said. "Or brought that man into my presence."

Afraid she would go back on the purchase, Giovanni made her an obsequious bow. "Accept my sincerest apologies for not anticipating your wishes, my lady," he said. "As for the rest, Your Ladyship's instructions will be observed to the smallest detail. I hope the happy emblems decorating the lute will brighten the Prince's name day and Rhea's dog will watch over his heirs."

The loose draping of Leonora's dress had not escaped his notice. He guessed her condition.

"Let us hope so," Leonora said and placed a protective hand on the little mound under the ample folds of her dress.

On the way home, she was quiet and kept her eyes on the dark waters curling under the gondoliere's strokes. Livia, too, looked thoughtfully at the eddies forming around the debris floating in the canal.

"I can't stop thinking about the lute player," Leonora said.

"Put him out of your mind, I beg you. Don't let his connection with unhappy events disturb you."

"But what a strange coincidence! That he should make his way from Gesualdo to Venice and be employed in the very shop I decided to visit —"

"Not entirely surprising, when you think of it. Tieffenbrucker is a renowned instrument maker. That is why you sought him out, and that is why Benito Darrico sought him out as well. There are few craftsmen to satisfy Tieffenbrucker's standards, I imagine, so few in fact that he was willing to take on a man without a letter of reference, on the strength of his skill alone. And so I would not make too much of the coincidence."

"But perhaps it wasn't coincidence, Livia. Perhaps it was fate."

CHAPTER 19

Leonora was preparing for bed. The chamber maid had brought in a basin with hot water and towels scented with lavender. Livia was looking through a book of poems for a bedside reading to cheer up her mistress, while the maid helped the Princess undress. She unpinned the chignon at the back of Leonora's neck, took out the shell combs, and brushed her long hair until it shone. She slipped the lace-trimmed nightgown over Leonora's head and shoulders and took away her skirt to be brushed and cleaned.

Leonora stopped the girl at the door.

"Ina," she said. "I made a purchase at the shop of an instrument maker this afternoon. Has it been delivered?"

Ina curtsied. "Yes, my lady. And the Majordomo said to put it away immediately and keep it a secret from the Prince."

"I have no secrets from my husband, Ina. It is a surprise."

Ina bugged her eyes, looking first at the Princess and then at Livia. "Oh," she said. "A surprise. But the Majordomo said to keep it secret."

"Then you must do as the Majordomo says," Livia said and bundled her out the door. She turned back to Leonora and laughed. "You have confused the poor girl. I hope she won't be going around telling everyone that it's not a secret after all."

"It's a good thing we are leaving tomorrow. I wish I hadn't asked Ina about the lute. I doubt that giddy girl can keep anything to herself. — Oh, Livia, this day has been altogether too much for me and my little one. Come, sit with me, and read until I am at peace again."

It did not take long for Livia's voice and the poet's words to soothe the Princess. Her fingers which had been pressing Livia's hand slackened, and her breathing became even. Livia rose quietly, took the candle, and tiptoed out of the room.

Walking downstairs, she thought of inquiring once more about the delivery of the archlute, to make sure that the precious instrument had been stowed away safely. As she crossed the lower corridor to the servants' quarters, she became aware first of a scraping sound, then of a movement just beyond the narrow circle of light cast by her candle. She stopped and raised the candle to illumine the stairs and caught sight of an old woman, crouching low as if she had been arrested in the movement of creeping up the steps. The woman raised her bronzed peasant face, and for a brief moment Livia looked into her amber cat's eyes. The next moment the woman pounced with a force and agility unexpected from an old crone. The candle holder in Livia's hand cluttered on the floor, the candle sizzled and went out. Bony hands gripped her throat, and she could utter only a low cry before the fingers closed around her neck and shut off her breath. She struggled with her assailant in the lightless corridor, flailing her arms, but the old woman seemed to have demonic strength. Livia felt a burning hollow open up in her chest. The last thing she remembered was an acrid smell entering her nostrils, of sweat and burned leaves. When she opened her eyes again, she looked into the light of a candle burning brightly and the anxious face of the cook kneeling by her side.

"Are you alright, my dear?" she said, putting an arm around Livia's shoulder. "We heard a noise, Paolo and me, and went to see what was going on."

A narrow door at the end of the corridor stood wide open, the door panel slammed back against the wall. Through the dark opening, Livia could see the iron railing of a gangway and the spangled shimmer of the canal below, reflecting the moon.

At that moment Paolo the porter appeared in the open door with a torch. He had been looking for the intruder. "She's gone," he said. "Vanished like a ghost." He shut the door behind him. "Are you hurt, Donna Livia? Did she take anything from you?"

Livia sat up slowly. She rubbed her neck. The room was spinning, but her first thought was for Leonora. Had anyone told her of the intruder? She must not be alarmed or disturbed!

"I'm alright," she said quickly. "Just shaken." It seemed her legs had seized up and she had to unlock them one after the other. She heaved herself upright and smoothed her skirt. The smell of burned leaves the intruder had given off, seemed to cling to her hands and to the fabric of her dress. "Do you know the woman who attacked me?" she asked.

"She's just riff-raff," the porter said. "People of her kind go around at night, trying doors and windows to see if any have been left unlocked, so that they can steal valuables."

"Someone will have to answer for this piece of negligence — leaving the door unlocked," the cook said. "I warrant it happened when they made that delivery, all hush-hush." She pursed her lips. "I don't like it if things go on behind the master's back, and I didn't like the looks of the men who made the delivery, shady characters up to no good, if you ask me."

The porter nodded his agreement. "There's too many of them around, beggars, thieves and cut-throats, and too many bridges from which to toss corpses." He slid the bolt across the door and rested his hand on it as if to make sure it stayed in place. "Thank the Lord, we were in time to chase them off."

The room had stopped spinning, and Livia's brain stirred into action. "Thank God indeed, but I beg you, do not allow news of this incident to reach the ears of the Prince. I would not want to disturb him or upset my mistress, who is in a delicate condition."

"I don't see how I can *not* mention it," the Porter said. "It is the duty-"

"It is the duty of Signor Despini to see that the house is safe," Livia said. "He is the Doge's man of business. By all means report the incident to *him*, but I do not see why you have to trouble the Doge's guests, especially when we are set to depart in the morning. There will be enough excitement, what with packing up and boarding the ship."

"Donna Livia has a point, you know," the cook said. "There is no need to go about spreading bad news. Signor Despini will not thank us for blabbing, Paolo. It will be better to be discreet and keep what happened to ourselves."

"I don't know about that," Paolo said, unwilling to take advice from two women. "I will speak to Signor Despini tomorrow and take my lead from him."

CHAPTER 20

Venice was slowly fading from view. On board of the ship carrying the travelers away and sailing down the Adriatic coast, the Prince kept his distance from Leonora as before and remained in the forward part of the ship. But he seemed in better spirits and had promised to join his wife for dinner in the "great cabin" as the master of the ship called their quarters at the stern of the ship. It was a stately room, handsomely and comfortably furnished and equipped with moveable panels to separate the sleeping quarters in back from the front room, which looked out on the deck through a row of windows.

Fatigued from the commotion that attended the embarking, Leonora retired to the elegant little pavilion erected for them midship. It was decked in bright colours inside and out, unlike the black-walled *felze* on the barge that had carried them to Venice. It provided the ladies with shade and protected them from wind, but also let them enjoy the fresh air and the ever-changing vistas along the coast.

Livia herself was too unsettled to rest or sit still after the trying events of the previous evening. She stood at the railing watching the harbour recede into the haze of the morning. The gaffs, mizzens and bowsprits diminished in size until they looked like toys and became a blur on the horizon. Soon Venice was no more than a mirage. The ship left behind the great swampy reaches that formed the river delta and reached the open sea. Brisk winds kept the sails taut and sped them along.

Livia grasped the edges of her hood to keep it from ballooning out as she faced into the wind. If only the breeze could blow away the memories of yesterday's fright. This morning, looking into the mirror, she had seen the bruise that had formed on her neck overnight, a shadowy reminder of her struggle with the old woman — yet if it had not been for the faint purple marks on her neck, now carefully covered with a scarf, she would have dismissed it as a warped vision, a bad dream. The attack had been so sudden that it barely entered her mind before she lost consciousness and the woman's face faded to black. Livia brushed her fingers over the sore spot on her neck and winced. Another attack on her life, and this time she could hardly blame Cesare for it. Even if his power reached as far as Venice, he no longer had a motive for wanting her out of the way. Or did he? It was good at any rate to get away from last night's terrifying experience in time and in space. She took a deep breath of the air salted by the Adriatic Sea and looked up into the sunlit sky with eyes half-closed.

"Donna Livia," a voice said close to her. She opened her eyes. "I beg your pardon," the Majordomo said. "I am imposing on you, but may I have your ear for a moment-" He looked around cautiously.

"What can I do for you?" Livia said politely.

"I was told of the unfortunate incident last night. I hope you have recovered from the fright."

"Who told you? I asked the porter specifically not to report the incident. I did not want to alarm Donna Leonora or disturb the Prince."

"My sentiments exactly. I am very grateful for your discretion, Donna Livia, but the man felt obliged to report the incident to his superior, and he in turn came to me. I made sure it went no further. To be on the safe side, however, I think the matter should be investigated. There are persons in Venice who are ill-disposed toward the Prince, who bear a grudge and may wish to harm him. I have reason to think that the attack was not aimed at you. The intruder was trying to enter the Prince's quarters. You just happened to be in the wrong place at the wrong time."

"And why would anyone in Venice bear the Prince a grudge, if I may ask?"

The Majordomo hesitated, but he could not expect Livia to answer his questions if he refused to answer hers. "To avenge their dismissal," he said. "After the death of Maria d'Avalos, the Prince dissolved her household, and although he did so on generous terms, it caused resentment and in some cases hardship." He pressed his lips together, determined to say no more.

"Are you referring to Benito Darrico?"

She had caught him out. He raised his eyebrows. "You know of Benito?"

"The Princess and I were introduced to him at the shop of Tieffenbrucker."

"An unfortunate encounter! Yes, he was one of the men dismissed by the Prince — against my advice, for he was an excellent musician and hard to replace. But he wasn't the intruder?"

"No, it was a woman who attacked me."

"That is what I was told — can you describe her?"

"I saw her only for a moment. She was an old woman with a dark complexion and amber eyes. She was surprisingly strong for her age, too strong for me to fight off. I can't tell you more, except that there was a strange odour about her, as of medicinal herbs."

"Benito's mother, I suspect. She was Maria d'Avalos' maid and mistress of her wardrobe. I was not sorry to see *her* go. An evil woman. She was reputed to be a poisoner, or worse. Some called her a witch. I have engaged a man to look into-" The Majordomo broke off when he saw two gentlemen in the Prince's retinue coming toward them. "That is all I wanted to know," he said hurriedly. "You have confirmed my suspicions, Donna Livia, and I take it we agree that this must remain between us."

He left her and joined the two gentlemen.

Livia breathed deeply to rid herself of the tension she felt in her shoulders and arms, then turned away from the railing to join her mistress. She entered the pavilion quietly, expecting Leonora to be at rest. But she was awake and seemingly pleased with her surroundings.

"There you are, Livia," she said. "How do you like our pleasure tent?"

The cabin was hung with crimson cloth and furnished with an oriental carpet. Comfortable settees surrounded a low brass table. Livia tied back the curtains to allow them to watch the scenery. The sea was calm, the swell hardly great enough to break into billows. The ship was keeping close to the shore, taking them past villages and terraced fields. Houses dotted the hills, and footpaths crisscrossed like lines drawn on an immense canvas.

The vista had put Leonora in a cheerful mood, or perhaps she was still animated by the smiling countenance of the Prince when the captain took him around the ship and stopped to inquire if the ladies were comfortable. The vital spark had returned to the Prince's eyes.

"This morning he seemed unsettled, but now he feels at peace with himself again," Leonora said.

I wish I could be at peace with myself, Livia thought, but she pushed away thoughts of the mysterious intruder and of the other matter which dulled her spirits — lost love. Only time could cauterize that wound. She took a deep breath and brought an air of cheerfulness to her voice, falling in with Leonora's good mood. The day passed tolerably well. They read a little, took a walk on deck, and talked of Leonora's favourite subject, the child. Boy or girl? That was the big question.

"If it's a girl, I want her to be like you, Livia. Beautiful, lively, clever."

"And a fool for love?"

"That, too. A fool for love, like you and me. But look at my right cheek, Livia. Do you see a spot there, right below the eye, because you know what they say, if your face is marked, the child will be a girl."

"I see no more than a shadow."

"Only a shadow? Go and ask Fina to join us. She knows about these things."

Livia went to fetch the midwife. She came, a short, corpulent woman, walking heavily on large flat feet. She had a gentle face, no chin, and large wet eyes like a faithful old dog. Her forehead was lined, but those lines were not caused by frowns. They were a palimpsest of hearty laughter and complemented by the sparkle of good humour in her eyes.

Fina studied Leonora's cheek.

"Hmm," she said, but would not commit herself. "I tell you what you can do, my lady, to make it more likely that the baby will be a boy. Get out of bed every morning on the right foot."

"Oh, I always get out on my right foot," Leonora said.

Fina was devoted to her mistress. Every evening she brought out her oils and liniments and applied them diligently to Leonora's bosom and her belly to keep the skin smooth and elastic.

"What do you think, Fina? Is my belly pointed?"

"Not at all, madam," the midwife said. They both knew: A pointed womb meant a girl.

"Then it will be a boy," Leonora said eagerly.

"Well, no one can tell for sure, but I see your right leg is slightly swollen. And that's usually a sign that the baby will be a boy."

Leonora fidgeted.

"I've been told the surest way to tell the sex of the child is to take two little garments, a boy's and a girl's, and float them on the water to see which sinks faster," Livia said. "The one that prevails determines the sex of the child, they say."

"Then we must make trial tomorrow morning," Fina said placidly.

But the thought made Leonora tremble. "I'm not sure I have the courage to know," she said to Livia after the midwife had gone and they stood at the railing, admiring the sun setting in a golden blaze over the water. "What if I am disappointed?" They watched the sea silently until the sky emptied of colour and they put in at the harbour of Ancona for the night. Another day passed quietly under a benevolent sky, and they were received with great hospitality by the Lord of Pescara.

In the morning, a fine mist veiled the sun. The sky looked mysterious, inviting prophesy. They decided to try the omens. They had no baby clothes on hand, but on Fina's suggestion they floated a red and a blue piece of cloth instead — red for a girl's warm heart, blue for a boy's cool courage. Thank God the blue floated merrily, while the red was swamped by a wave almost immediately. And was it not ever so? Livia thought. The warm heart sinks. Cold blood prevails. Beyond that, she did not put much stock into those "signs", and even Leonora who was more alive to tradition, wondered: Were those bits of cloth reliable omens? Fina's advice was to repeat the test in the afternoon, just in case, and she promised to look for something that held a more prophetic promise than ragged squares of red and blue. But after lunch, a stiff wind blew up and streaked the sky with fast-moving clouds. They rose above the foothills, descended upon the shore, and thickened to a menacing purple. Thunder was crackling in the distance, the air grew heavy, and darkness spread over the leaden sea. Soon rain came down in sheets, the ship rocked among great rolling billows. The crew reefed the sails, and the Prince's equerry hurried the ladies to their quarters in the stern of the ship. They reached shelter just as lightning ripped through the clouds above them. Leonora's chest rose and sank with rapid, nervous breaths. Livia made her lie down on the bed and took her hand.

"Be calm for the baby's sake, my dear," she said, trying to put conviction into her voice. "The storm will soon blow over." She squeezed Leonora's hand and murmured encouragements.

The ship bucked and rolled. Leonora's face grew more pallid. The thudding of the wind against the spars and the juddering of the floor sickened her. In a spasm of retching, she called for a basin. Livia cradled her head as she bent over the bowl, brought up bile and sank back again, tears running down her cheek.

Fina fetched her medicine box from below deck, where it had been stored with the chests containing Leonora's dresses and finery. She set it on the floor beside the bed and opened it up.

"We'll have you right in a minute, madam," she said. Livia blanched when she saw the lancet and the calibers among the bowls and pewter jars in Fina's miracle box. She hoped they would never be needed. Meanwhile, Fina had found what she was rummaging for. "Dried ginger," she said. "Chew it slowly, madam. It works without fail."

As always, the midwife was right. The ginger root steadied Leonora's stomach. It also helped that the rain was easing off and the rolling thunder was more distant. The storm passed as quickly as it had blown up. Fina stowed away her box, and within an hour the waves grew calmer and resumed their cradling motion.

Livia went out on deck to see how their pavilion had fared. The servants were already at work, straightening the screens that had been kicked awry by the sudden gusts. They removed the sodden carpet, replaced the damp cushions, and brought out a different settee and chairs. The clouds were breaking apart, and the first thin rays of the sun cast an interplay of light and shadow over the shore and the foothills. Leonora returned to the middle deck on Fina's arm and took her seat in the shelter again. She was still pale and shivery, but glad to escape the oppressive closeness of the cabin and breathe the fresh sea air. Livia plumped up the cushions on the sofa and put a soft woolen blanket over Leonora's shoulders. "There," she said. "Close your eyes and think of pleasant things."

Fina meanwhile had gone back below to find more suitable tokens to predict the sex of the baby and repeat the test, as she had promised Leonora, but a moment later she was back, looking rattled. She stopped at the entrance of the pavilion and furtively signaled to Livia to join her.

As soon as she came within reach, Fina grasped her arm and pulled her close. "Come below," she whispered. "Someone has been into my things." Livia cast a look back at her mistress now resting peacefully and followed the midwife. The women descended the narrow stairs to the storeroom which also served as Fina's sleeping quarters. There was her precious medicine chest, overturned on the floor, jars rolling about, vials broken, and implements strewn across the room. Livia's mind immediately flashed back to Venice and old woman who had ambushed her on the stairs.

"Who could have -" she started, but Fina put a finger to her mouth, and now Livia heard it too: a rustling in the far corner and a flitting shadow. The two women stood frozen with fear, staring into the murky darkness beyond the circle of light cast by a single lantern swinging from the rafters. But the room had gone quiet. There was no sound now other than the muted tread of boots on the planks above them and the creaking and wrenching of the ship.

"Whoever did this is gone," Livia said at last, but she took down the lantern and searched the corners of the cabin, lighting up each crevice. The culprit must have been lurking there, behind the chests and boxes piled against the wall and must have taken his chance as soon as Fina had gone up on deck.

The two women gathered the jars and swept up the broken pieces of glass. "Careful!" Fina said, as she wiped the spill with a towel. "Some of those elixirs are caustic in the undiluted state, and I don't know what a mixture of them will do. All I know is that I'll have a hard time replacing them. — Better leave the clean-up to me and ask one of the servants to heat a kettle of salt water for us to cleanse our hands thoroughly. As for the towel, I'll throw it overboard — the sea will take care of the noxious stuff."

"And the rest of your things — is anything missing?" Livia asked.

"Oh, my poor bundle can be of no interest to a thief," Fina said. "And everything else looks untouched."

Livia did another round with the lantern to check the locks on Donna Leonora's chests. They were intact and undisturbed.

When the two women got back to the pavilion, Leonora was sitting up and wanted to know where they had been. They told her of the intruder reluctantly, and sent for Di Grassi to ask for his advice. He looked grave on hearing of the incident. No doubt, he too thought of the intruder in Venice and wondered whether there was a connection.

"I shall speak to the captain," he said, "and question the sailors one by one. In the meantime, the cabins below must be searched and secured and guards be posted at your quarters, madam, to ensure your safety. — I shall have to inform the Prince as well."

"I beg you, do not disturb Don Carlo," Leonora said at once.

"Believe me, I am most reluctant to disturb his peace, madam," the Majordomo said, "but this is too serious matter to leave him in ignorance. In the meantime we must keep our eyes open —"

But before he could finish what he had to say, a cry went up from a sailor at work with the cordage and all eyes turned to where he pointed. High up in the rigging, a brown creature was jumping nimbly from rope to rope, a bare-chested little imp in emerald green pants, his neck adorned with a gleaming necklace. He was cackling with glee as he nimbly swung from the halyards. On the command of the captain, two sailors went after the creature but before they could reach him, he flung himself into the sea and made for the shore, paddling vigorously.

Everyone rushed to the railing to get a better view and backed off again in alarm as the ship began to list under the lop-sided ballast and the sailors shouted a warning. The three women huddled in their shelter and begged di Grassi to stay with them. There was no more need to inform the Prince. They saw him standing on the bridge with the Captain, who was bowing and speaking volubly.

They could still see the head of the little creature, bobbing above the waves, halfway to the shore. The water had slicked back his hair, exposing the wrinkled brown face of an old man.

"Don't look!" Fina exclaimed, obliging Leonora to turn her back to the sight. She was certain that the thing was a demon from hell, although to Livia it had looked more like a wizened dwarf. A knot of people surrounded a mate who had trained his spy glass on the swimmer. Now they raised a confused shout. Livia thought she could make out one word, repeated over and over: A monkey!

"Could it be?" she asked di Grassi.

"Whatever it may be, Madam," Fina said, "it's an ill-omened sight. Don't look at his ugly face. It might rub off — but I won't say more."

"It is a monkey, I can see it now," di Grassi said. "It's the newest fashion. I saw a pet monkey at the court of Count Rovere not long ago. It was the Count's pleasure to have the animal dressed up in a velvet suit and trick ignorant people into thinking it was a child or a misshapen dwarf. A foolish craze, if you ask me."

"I have heard of it too," Leonora said. "A foolish thing indeed. I am told that monkeys are the most-ill tempered pets and prone to bite. But how did it get on board?"

In the meantime, a boat had been lowered down the side of the ship, and two sailors rowed out to the creature struggling in the water. They threw a net over the monkey, hauled him in with a victorious shout, and rowed on, taking their captive to shore.

The Captain explained the mystery. Last night the Prince and his entourage had been the guests of Francesco of Pescara and spent the night at his castle. The monkey belonged to their host. Don Francesco had been given the animal by a merchant. At first he found the monkey's tricks entertaining, but it did not take long for him to become heartily sick of his mischievous pet. Accordingly, he asked the captain to take the animal to Barletta and sell him at the market or display him for money or do whatever he pleased with the creature as long as he never saw it again. The Captain had agreed reluctantly, or so he said. He was not keen on taking responsibility for the Count's unruly pet, but he was afraid of giving offense to the noble lord. In any case, he thought, it was only a matter of putting up with the beast for twenty-four hours. Within a day they would reach the harbor of Barletta, where he could rid himself of the unwanted cargo.

"Of course, he should have obtained permission from the Prince to take the animal on board," di Grassi said, retelling the story to the ladies. "And if you ask me, he wasn't nearly as reluctant to take the monkey on board as he wants us to believe. He expected to sell the animal for a tidy sum to the next fool who came along and he was afraid the Prince would refuse him permission to take the monkey on board and spoil his chance of making a profit."

The Captain had given orders to lock the monkey in a cage, he told them, and to chain a wooden clog to his leg for extra security, but the animal resisted so valiantly and bared his pointed teeth at the sailor who had been assigned the task, that the man gave up and merely secured the door of the cage with a lock and chain. The chain must have come undone in the storm or was undone by the dexterous fingers of the animal. At any rate, the monkey escaped with the unhappy result of getting hold of Fina's medicine box.

And that was the worst part of their sea journey. The remainder of the day passed peacefully and they reached the harbour of Barletta without further incident. Now that the more perilous part of the journey was over, Livia noticed with surprise that the rapid succession of events and new vistas had left her no time to reflect. The onslaught of the new had crowded out the old. It was as if she was coming home to herself after a long absence and had time at last to take stock and inspect the furnishings of her soul. Alas, everything was as before. The pain of lost love was still there, and the memory of Pietro had lost none of its sting. She tried to expel it with a deep breath, but a lump remained stuck in her throat, too hard to swallow.

CHAPTER 21

The sky was cloudless, when they began their overland journey the next morning. The locals predicted that the storm and downpour which had made their final day at sea so uncomfortable was bound to be the last for a while. The hot, dry season was about to begin.

The rainstorm had left the air heavy and humid, and when they reached the outskirts of Barletta, the horses and mules had to plod through mud and puddles. The road wound through a low-lying plain dotted with vineyards and olive trees. The Prince and his men rode ahead. A troop of hired soldiers made up the rearguard. Livia had joined her mistress in a coach fitted with a velvet bench and satin curtains. But the luxurious inside and the sturdy construction did not protect them against being jolted, as the coach rumbled along the deeply rutted road. Fina had wrapped wide linen bandages around Leonora's thighs and waist to cradle her belly and protect it against the bumping motion of the carriage. The bandage provided a measure of relief, but Leonora was now also suffering from morning sickness, the bane of all women in the early stages of pregnancy.

As the morning passed and the waves of nausea eased, Leonora cheered up again and passed her time watching the stream of peasants pulling handcarts along the road or leading donkeys to the market, loaded with baskets of greens. Her pleasure in the rustic tableau was cut short, however, when they encountered a funeral procession. Livia immediately put her hand over Leonora's eyes to shut out the baneful sight, the widow beating her breast, the coffin swaying on the shoulders of the men, the keening mourners — Leonora could close her eyes to the sight, but could she shut it out of her mind? What if the child was affected by the mental image and was born as yellow as death or as pale as a corpse? Fina, who was riding a sturdy mule, stopped at the sight of the cortege and slid out of the saddle.

"Confound those people!" she cried, as she walked back to their coach. "Why are they carrying their dead along the public road in broad daylight? Why don't they have the decency to use the byways?" She pulled open the door of the coach. "Quick, my lady," she said to Leonora, "cross yourself and say a prayer. And thank God for the talisman I have brought along." She patted the leather purse hanging from her belt, reached into it and brought out a greyish-green stone banded with silver. "Brought back from the Holy Land by a crusader," she said. "My grandmother left it to my mother, and she left it to me. And if God had given me a daughter instead of three sons, I would have handed it on to her."

"Let me see your treasure," Leonora said and eagerly passed her fingers over the miraculous stone.

"We must tuck it into the bandages around your belly," Fina said. "It will certainly undo any damage that has been done and will serve as a fortress against future evil. And when your day comes, my lady, you can hold the stone in your hands and hang on to it with all your strength, and it will shorten your labour and speed the delivery."

She clambered into the carriage and busied herself rearranging Leonora's bandages to hold the stone securely against her pregnant belly. "It's a great treasure and irreplaceable, my lady. I don't like to let it go and usually apply it only at the moment of delivery, but the road is full of danger and maybe it's time to let the stone work its magic. Only promise me to guard it well, madam."

Leonora assured the midwife she would take good care of the stone. For good measure, she asked Livia to lower the curtains on the windows of the coach to guard against another ill-omened sight.

As the day wore on, the air thickened. The sun dried up every bit of moisture and left the interior of the coach stifling hot. Peeking out between the folds of the curtains, Livia saw that there were fewer people on the road now. Most had sought shelter from the blazing sun. The ones who drudged on looked limp and hollow-eyed in the dull airless heat, the brims of their hats a weight that bowed their heads. Livia felt the soles of her shoes sticking to her feet. She dabbed at the sweat pearling on her neck and collecting in the hollow of her collarbones.

In the afternoon when the heat became unbearable, the Prince gave orders to stop at a copse of tall trees and rest for a few hours in their shadow. They would continue their journey in the evening and take advantage of the cooler temperatures at night. The horses and mules were fed and given a rest as well. When the sun sank to the horizon, the carters harnessed the animals again, the riders remounted their horses, and the caravan moved on along the dusty road. The manor house where they were to spend the night was still miles away.

Night fell, but the earth held the heat like a giant clay oven. Leonora had fallen asleep, leaning against the side of the carriage, a pillow cushioning her head against the knocks of the road. Livia was dozing in the other corner. A warm breeze blew through the open window and fanned her face, but it was not enough to provide relief, and her forehead was bathed in sweat. She was slipping into dreams when she was startled by a woman's high-pitched scream. The carriage came to a sudden stop. Leonora, too, was jolted awake. She sat up stiffly and groped for Livia's hand in the dark.

"What was that?"

The road was passing through a stand of pines which obscured the stars and the moon above. Livia reached for the latch of the carriage door. "I'll go and see."

"No, stay," Leonora said in an uneasy whisper. At the same moment they heard men shouting and the sound of horses galloping away.

The driver of their carriage jumped down from his seat and lit a torch illuminating the thicket by the side of the road. In the flaring light, they saw half a dozen soldiers charging through the pines in pursuit of two riders. They were flailing the rumps of their horses, urging them on.

Livia leaned out of the carriage window and called Fina's name, but there was no answer. The midwife and her mule had disappeared from sight. Marco, Fina's son, who usually kept her company, was gone as well. The caravan was in disarray. The carts had come to a stop.

Leonora's voice trembled when she asked their driver what was going on.

"An ambush, my lady," he said. "But there is no reason to concern yourself. The men will take care of everything."

"But where is Fina? She was riding just ahead of our carriage."

"I saw her son go after the robbers, my lady," the man said. His voice was hesitant as if he did not want to be the bearer of bad news.

"And Fina?" Leonora persisted.

"Let me make inquiries, my lady," he said. "Those men over there may have seen more than I." He pointed to a group of guards standing at the edge of the road. Two of them were carrying arquebuses.

"Why didn't they shoot the robbers?" Livia asked.

"Because they were afraid of hitting the wrong mark. Those things are as accurate as a lightning bolt, if you ask me, madam."

He walked off and was still talking to the men shouldering the arquebuses when they saw the soldiers coming back through the pines. They were riding at a slow trot now. As they came nearer, Livia could see the froth on the necks of the horses and smelled the pungent scent of horse sweat. Then she caught sight of Fina in the arms of her son. She groaned as he lifted her over the ditch and set her down on the road. Her hair was in a tangle. Tears were running down her cheeks mingled with streaks of blood. Her dress was torn and smeared with dirt.

Livia climbed down from the carriage and ran to her.

"Fina!" she cried, catching her up in her arms. "You are hurt, my dear! You are in pain!"

But it was the shock more than the pain that made Fina cry. The blood on her face was from the nicks and scratches scored by stones when she was dragged along the forest floor.

"Trying to hang on to her bag," Marco said. "How can you be so foolish, mother? You could have lost your life over a few coins."

The midwife shook her head. "More than coins," she said, wiping the blood and tears from her cheeks and wincing as she brushed the pine needles off her skirt. "There was a picture of Saint Agnes in my bag, blessed with the waters of the River Jordan. She has protected many a woman in childbirth."

"But not against robbers," Marco said.

"That's where you are wrong," she said and drew a deep breath to calm her pounding heart. "She protected me when I gave birth to you, and your strong arms defended me against the robbers in the time of need."

"Then let us give thanks to St. Agnes and to Marco," Livia said.

"And to your good luck, mother," he said. "If the strings on your purse hadn't broken when they did, your arm would have been pulled from its socket."

Livia hugged Fina and led her to the carriage. "Come, we must let Leonora know that you are safe."

The commander of the guard was already answering the questions of the Princess and explaining that his men had gone after a pair of robbers.

"A pair of robbers and a wolf," Fina said.

"A dog, mother," Marco corrected her.

"Call it what you want. It was a monster. He jumped my mule and tore its flank open before my very eyes. And the mule let out a shriek! Mother of God, what a shriek! It pierced my heart. It was like a human crying in agony, and here I was on the ground, dragging along and powerless to help the poor animal."

The guards confirmed Fina's story. A mastiff had been with the robbers and attacked the mule. They had chased the hound off with torches, but could not save the mule. They caught one of the robbers, pulled him off his horse and slashed his throat. The other, a long-haired youth, got away, protected by the snarling dog.

"I had only a glimpse of his face," one of the guards said. "Smooth as a child's. If I did not know better, I'd say it was a woman. But no woman could have unseated Eduardo with the ease that fellow did. I could hardly believe my eyes. A bull of a man like Eduardo knocked down by a beardless youth!"

"I don't know how it happened," the guard named Eduardo said, shamed by his defeat. "I saw an arm swinging at me, then something whacked me across the face, and everything went dark."

"He fell off his horse like a man shot by an arrow," someone else said. "And the horse stumbled too, struck in the head, it looked like. It was an odd thing."

"Call it odd," Eduardo said. "I call it unnatural."

"Next thing you'll tell us that the devil whacked you across the head."

"It was some kind of black magic. My mind was clear gone."

"So is my bag, which is worth a great deal more than your mind," Fina said. "But if you ask me, those scoundrels were after the carriage, and it was only when I screamed and Marco gave a great shout to alert the guards —"

"Mother, you talk too much," her son said. "And here is his Lordship." He took off his cap and bowed as he saw the Prince riding up with Di Grassi at his side.

119

Don Carlo stopped by the carriage.

"My dear," he said to Leonora. "I am happy to see you safe, and the attack fended off."

Leonora saw that his horse stood with its head hanging low and its flanks moving rapidly in and out. "You did not go after them yourself?" she asked anxiously. "You would not endanger your person chasing a pair of robbers!"

"Would you have me act like a coward, my dear? I owe it to my honour as a gentleman to protect your life. It would have been the act of a craven fellow to stay behind and watch others give chase. Besides, it was entirely possible that there were more than those two robbers, that a whole pack of them were lying in wait for us. But we searched the woods on either side of the road and saw no one. Perhaps we scared them off."

Leonore saw the exhaustion in the Prince's face as he spoke. His hand holding the reins trembled.

"I trust my lady was never in danger, sire," the man in charge of the guards said. "It is one thing to set upon a helpless old woman riding a mule and another to attack a carriage with an armed driver and half a dozen guards in the rear."

"And what would a robber gain from attacking an old woman, I'd like to know?" Di Grassi said. "It's quite unlikely that she was his mark."

"I suspect the attack on her was a clever tactic, a diversion to draw you off," the Prince said. "They were just decoys. The main party of robbers would have attacked the carriage next. And you, like the fools and asses you are, left it unprotected and rode off without giving a thought to the safety of your mistress."

The commander of the guards had no answer to that reprimand. He offered an abject apology. The Prince turned away from him impatiently and gave orders to move on. He wanted to leave that treacherous spot behind and gain the open road. "We shall talk about your conduct in the morning," he said. His voice was implacable.

They men bowed to the Prince, but behind his back Livia heard them grumble. This wouldn't have happened, they said, if the Prince had listened to the advice of the guards. It was too dangerous to travel this road during the night. Better suffer the heat of the day than risk the attack of robbers.

In the meantime, Leonora had invited Fina to share their carriage.

"You must come with us," she said, and Fina gratefully climbed in and squeezed into the corner beside Livia.

120

"Oh, my poor bones," she said, rubbing her arms and legs. The knuckles of her right hand were swollen. It was only now that she began to feel the pain of being yanked from the mule and tumbled to the ground. She was sore in body and soul. The two women did their best to soothe Fina after her ordeal and restore her peace of mind after the fright she suffered and the shock of seeing her mule attacked and killed by a vicious dog.

The men returned to their places. They heard the driver of their coach get back into his seat and spur on the horses. The caravan made its way to the nearest inn. It was a poor refuge for the noble company, but they made do. Fina was looked after, Leonora, exhausted, fell asleep at once, but Livia kept tossing on her bed. She slept fitfully and dreamed of slashing knives and frothing horses. Waking with a start, she was relieved to find that it had been only a dream, but as soon as she went back to sleep, she drifted into another nightmare. This time she was sinking into murky waters, grasping for Pietro's hand and unable to hold on to him. She woke up groaning and was glad to see that it was dawn and time to rise.

Fina joined the two ladies at breakfast. Her face was bruised and her right hand bandaged.

"Perhaps that big oaf, Eduardo, was right after all, and the devil was in it," she said. "Marco tells me that the guards searched the wood in case the robbers had accomplices, but they found nothing except my bag torn to shreds and a piece of cloth near where Eduardo had taken a fall. The man who picked it up thought there was a strange odour about it, and when he put it to his nose and sniffed at it, they told me, his sight grew dim and he fell to the ground. The piece of cloth dropped from his hand, and no one was willing to touch it afterwards. There was something uncanny about it, they all said. And the servant girl at the inn told me that the pinewood is cursed. A coven of witches meets there every solstice. So that long-haired youth they told us about may have been the devil after all, and that mastiff a hell hound."

Leonora put her hands over her ears. "Spare me, Fina. No more talk about hell hounds and devils."

"I beg your pardon, my lady," Fina said. "You are quite right. I shouldn't have named the Evil One."

After breakfast they set out, comforted by the daylight and the thought that they were now close to Gesualdo and approaching the end of their journey. In the afternoon, they crossed into the territory of Venosa, which was one of the Prince's fiefs. A guard of honour met them at the border to escort the Prince and his bride on the last leg of their journey. The welcoming party had brought along a luxurious sedan chair covered with brocade and fringed in gold and presented it to Leonora with their best wishes. They hoped that the bearers, whose livery matched the brocade of the chair, would provide the Princess with a gentler and more comfortable ride over the rough road than the carriage.

The company moved on, eager now for a first glimpse of Gesualdo, their final destination. But fate did not let them escape without a last reminder of its power and caprice. The axle of a cart broke, weakened perhaps by the wretched roads they had traversed. It was the vehicle carrying the Prince's music instruments. He stopped in alarm and turned back to inspect the damage. The cart had collapsed and was listing to one side. Two boxes had slid off. One was lying in the road open-jawed, spilling a collection of flutes. The Prince watched the men drag it out of the way. His brow furrowed as he pointed to the second box, which was still intact except for a dented corner.

"I do not recognize that one," he said and asked to have it opened.

The carter hesitated. He hemmed and hawed.

The Prince turned to his equerry. "What is that idiot mumbling about?" he said, tapping the side of his boot with his riding crop. "What is he waiting for?"

The equerry knew the reason for the man's hesitation. "Do not fault him, sire. The Princess gave strict orders to keep the box out of your way. It contains a gift my lady meant to present to you on your name day."

In the meantime the man had reluctantly pried open the lid, and the Prince exclaimed with alacrity: "An archlute!"

He jumped down from his horse, took the instrument from its padded container and cradled it in his arms as tenderly as a newborn babe. He inspected it carefully, turning it this way and that, and set it down with a look of admiration on his face. "A masterpiece," he said. "I recognize the work and emblem of Tieffenbrucker."

Walking back to where Leonora was anxiously waiting in her sedan chair, he saluted her with a deep bow. Leaning close, he said in a low voice: "My dear, you chose the perfect present. Only one gift could make me happier — a son, and that is in God's giving."

He took no less pleasure in the lute for being presented to him so unexpectedly, he said, and he did not mind celebrating his name day early. Indeed he could not wait to give her a private concert when they arrived in Gesualdo. He bent down and kissed

Leonora's hand gallantly. The reluctance he had shown during the journey to come close to her was gone in his joy over her gift. Music had worked its benevolent magic on him.

An hour later, the princely pair entered the town of Gesualdo. Leonora was riding the short distance from the city gate to the castle mounted on an elegant palfrey whose satin coat and smooth ambling gait raised admiring glances. The blue-figured silk of the gown she wore enhanced the soft grey of her eyes, and a happy smile graced her face. The Prince too looked contented and acknowledged the cheering crowd that lined the street with a benevolent wave of his hand.

From their perch in the carriage, Livia and Fina listened to the cheers of the crowd, hailing the couple with cries of "Long live the Prince and Princess!"

"They look like friendly people at any rate, and pleased with their ruler," Fina said. "He is such a stern man, though, and I was afraid he'd get a cold reception after what he did to his first wife and now that he is bringing home a foreign bride. But I suppose they have forgiven him."

How naïve Fina is in spite of her age, Livia thought, and how innocent of the ways of the world! Of course the people will welcome a Prince, whose servants distribute coins among them. Besides, they do no more than their duty and would be punished if they didn't. No, the cheers of the people meant little, Livia knew, but she kept her thoughts to herself. Better to be innocent and enjoy life than understand the world and be forever wary and suspicious.

The festive procession wound its way between houses decorated in the couple's honour with scarlet cloths and flower garlands. The bright day added its lustre to the welcome. Sunlight glanced off the shop signs, the helmets of the guards, and the gilt edges of the ensigns. The couple halted at the church of Santa Maria delle Grazie and were presented with gifts of handicraft — embroidered caps and cushions, terracotta birds, and delicately scented handkerchiefs. The parish priest said a prayer for the happiness of the princely couple, and the choir intoned a joyful psalm, *The Earth is full of the Goodness of the Lord*. From the church, they rode on to the castle, an imposing fortress overlooking the Fredane river and a fertile plain with meadows and fields stretching to the horizon.

The coach and the procession of riders passed under two stone arches and entered the inner courtyard of the castle. The Prince dismounted and led Leonora through a bough of flower garlands into the hall. There they were greeted by the members of the court. The ladies curtseyed and the gentlemen bent their knees in obeisance to the new mistress of the castle. The staircase was lined with pages dressed in vermillion liveries, gleaming white stockings, and shoes with silver buckles. At the foot of the staircase, a crowd of servants, cooks and kitchen helpers, valets and ladies' maids were waiting for a glimpse of their new mistress, but keeping a respectful distance. Dressed in their Sunday best, they nodded and smiled and bowed deeply as the princely couple walked by.

"They do make you feel welcome," Fina said and smiled broadly at the women of the household, whom she would join shortly. But Livia could not help feeling a chill as she looked up at the solid walls of the castle. They seemed prison-like to her. She silently reproached herself. Why harbour sinister thoughts in the midst of joy? Gesualdo was Leonora's home now, and it had a majestic beauty even if it could not match the splendour and opulence of Ferrara, even if there was something forbidding about the unadorned stone façade, the parapets and watch towers of the castle.

The housekeeper took Fina under her wing, while Livia followed the couple upstairs. They entered a high narrow corridor with a vaulted ceiling that breathed the spirit of a bygone age. But when they came to the private apartments, Livia had to admit that they rivalled in elegance anything Ferrara had to offer. There were marquetry tables and dainty chairs, cabinets displaying fine china, and wall hangings depicting peacocks and unicorns frolicking in a garden. The rooms had been refurbished in Leonora's honour, a welcome-present from the Prince to his wife and a token of his love. The smile on Leonora's lips and the gratitude in her eyes showed how highly she valued his present.

Leaving Leonora in the hands of her maids, Livia went to inspect her own rooms. They were well and comfortably furnished, befitting her new post. She was Leonora's principal lady-in-waiting now and in charge of the attendants and servants the Prince had put at his wife's disposal. She washed off the dust of the road, changed into a fresh chemise, new stockings, and a clean skirt, which had been laid out carefully by a young servant girl. Livia rewarded her with a friendly smile but the girl looked at her with a respect that bordered on fear. Livia had sensed an aura of fear, in spite of the cheers that welcomed them, but perhaps it was all in her imagination. Should she trust vague feelings in the absence of any concrete signs? There was another thought that bothered her as well. She had seen no family members among the crowd welcoming them. She knew that the Prince had no brothers and sisters, but why were there no cousins, no aunts and uncles among his retinue? And where was the Prince's son? His absence had been conspicuous. Livia wondered why he was not among the ladies and gentlemen in the reception line. What did this absence mean? Was the Prince ashamed of his child? Was he apprehensive about Leonora's feelings for her step-son? She had no reasonable answer to these questions.

Putting her maid at ease with a few gentle words, Livia left her to finish the work of unpacking and set out to explore the castle, her new home. She wandered through the great hall, the reception rooms, and the library, a peaceful refuge two stories high with a timbered ceiling. She looked into the Prince's music room, a chamber with a decorative motif of vines, where two servants were setting up chairs for an evening concert. They bowed politely to Livia and, on her request, showed her the storeroom where the instruments were kept — lutes, woodwinds, trombones, and a clavichord. From the music room she sauntered into a gallery adorned with portraits of Don Carlo's ancestors. At the far end was a glassed-in loggia connecting the quarters of the prince to another which housed the members of his court. The windows of the loggia looked down on a private courtyard, a tidy square of green edged with yews and dissected by gravel paths in a star-shaped pattern. The four corners of the lawn were marked by topiaries cut in the shape of lions and unicorns. A fountain with a stone nymph pouring water from an ewer stood at the centre of the courtyard. It was there that Livia saw a boy playing with a kitten.

Could this be the Prince's son? Livia went downstairs and entered the garden. The boy looked up, quickly gathered the yarn he had dangled to make his kitten jump and dance, and ducked into a doorway on the far side.

The kitten ran after him disappointed, then spying a new playmate, turned and sprang toward Livia. She bent down, stroked its silky fur and, when it rolled on its back, tickled its rosy belly. As she turned to go back into the house, the kitten followed her, capering along.

"Don't take him away!" a pleading voice called out.

The boy had observed her and was running after her now.

Livia stopped. "Don't worry, I won't take him away," she said. "Is he yours? What is his name?"

The boy picked up his kitten and gingerly held him against his chest. "His name is Rufus. Cook gave him to me on my birthday a week ago."

"Congratulations and many returns. How old are you?"

"Nine," he said. He was a pretty boy with a round face like a putto and large soulful eyes.

"And what is your name?" she said.

"Emmanuele da Venosa."

He was the Prince's son!

"Have you come from Ferrara?" the boy asked.

"I came with your father and step-mother, but I don't recall seeing you among the people who greeted us on our arrival."

The boy offered no explanation for his absence. Instead he asked:

"Is my step-mother beautiful?"

"Donna Leonora is beautiful as well as good, and that is more important, don't you think?"

"That is what my tutor says." He looked past Livia at a slim young man coming toward them on the gravel path. He cut an almost comical figure as he hurried along with mincing steps, keeping his upper body rigid in an effort to preserve his dignity.

"Emmanuele!" he called. "Recess is over. Please to go back into the schoolroom."

He took off his cap and bowed to Livia. "Antonio Paulella at your service, madam." He ran his hand over his thin hair as if to check that it was unruffled before replacing his cap. His angular face was a mask of correctness, his posture as stiff as a wooden puppet's. "And with whom do I have the honour—" he asked.

"Livia Prevera," she said. "Lady-in-waiting to the princess."

"There is an ancient writer whose name sounds like yours," the boy said. "Titus Livius. He wrote the history of Rome from its beginnings. Have you heard of him?"

"I have indeed," Livia said, smiling.

The tutor gave the boy an approving look. "And can you explain the a-ending in the lady's name?"

"Livia is the feminine form of Livius," the boy said promptly.

"Correct," the tutor said, and his lips curved a little. "But now you must leave your pet with the cook and join me in the school room without delay, *stante pede*, as the Latins say. Remember the phrase, Emmanuele, and repeat after me. *Stante pede*."

"*Stante pede*, without delay," the boy said, bowed to Livia and rushed off with his kitten.

126

"The backstairs, Emmanuele!" the tutor called after the boy. "Please to use the backstairs."

He turned to Livia. "I hear the Prince's caravan was attacked on the road."

"By two robbers. But with God's help, we escaped the ambush."

"Robbers? Evil spirits, I was told."

"That is idle talk. They were highway men. The guards killed one of them and chased off the other."

The tutor looked doubtful, but Livia did not give him a chance to ask another question. She was unwilling to encourage fantastic tales or dwell on the frightening incident longer than necessary.

"We were certainly glad to reach our destination and to receive such a warm welcome," she said. "But I did not see Emmanuele at the reception. I imagine he will be presented to his step-mother at dinner tonight."

The boy had been evasive when she asked him why he had not come to meet them on their arrival. Don Antonio added to the mystery when he said:

"That will not be possible, I'm afraid. Emmanuele does not take his meals with his father. I am instructed to keep him out of the Prince's eye."

"How can anyone resist looking into his angelic face?" she said, surprised to hear of Don Carlo's command. Was this another of his eccentricities?

"Emmanuele is a handsome boy, but he has the misfortune of resembling his late mother, an evil woman in league with the devil," the tutor said. "God has denied her soul eternal rest and condemned her to walk the earth as a ghost."

Dismay flooded Livia's eyes. "A ghost!"

"I have not seen her myself," the tutor added, "but people say that she haunts the castle and has appeared on the parapet as if she wanted to cast herself into the river below or take wing like a witch."

"And who are the people who claim to have seen her ghost?"

The tutor's voice sank to a cautionary whisper. His mouth was a dark smudge in his pale face. "The Prince himself has told us so. And he does not like to be contradicted."

He clamped his lips shut, as if he was afraid to say more, afraid even of letting too much air escape from his prim mouth.

CHAPTER 22

Pietro left Ferrara on a rainy morning in September. Ragged gusts of wind buffeted horse and rider as they crossed the Po river and set out on the road traversing the level country south of the city. Bad luck! he thought, but worse for the poor sods making their way on foot. A rivulet of water was snaking down the middle, the runoff from the relentless rain. The road was banked up on both sides, so that those hapless travelers had no way to escape the mire. Some of the country folk wore clogs half a foot high and staggered along as if on stilts. The others trudged along, their clothes splattered and their boots caked with mud.

Pietro was traveling in the well-guarded wagon train of Luca Panetti, a silk merchant. It was the safest way to cover the distance to Rome, but also the least convenient for a young man who wanted to see the sights. Time was of the essence for the merchant. The caravan moved on steadily, sun or rain, and halted only when the animals needed rest. They continued on their way until sundown, expecting to cover thirty or even forty miles on a good day. They took the shortest rather than the most picturesque route. As a rule, the company did not stop in large cities, but stayed at village inns, which offered cheaper accommodation.

Pietro thought of his journey last spring, when he was one of the company escorting Prince Carlo to Ferrara. How little he had appreciated the comforts provided for him then! The clean bed, the services of a polite groom, solid meals served with decent local wine. Now he was obliged to pass the nights, sharing his room with a snoring fellow and was told to count himself lucky that he didn't have to share a bed. They slept on thin straw pallets, and more often than not had to put up with a peasant meal for supper: soup made of scraped parsley and ginger root, a piece of boiled meat that was tough and tasteless, and coarse bread. To wash down the meal they were served young wine that was apt to give a man the colic. In fact Pietro suspected it was the same acidic wine the stable boys used to wash the grime off the horses. And the lard they rubbed into the places where the leather harness had chafed the animals was perhaps the very same that was slathered on his bread. But even if the fare had been better and the wine more potent, the merchant saw to it that the evenings did not become too lively. He did not want the men to get drunk and boisterous, and have to deal with complaints that they bothered the serving girls or had broken crockery in a drunken stumble. He made sure everyone retired early and rose as soon as dawn broke.

To pass the time on the road, Pietro watched the changing landscape and the panoply of fellow travelers — peasants, merchants, soldiers, bands of itinerant jugglers, and couriers galloping south with urgent letters. He often rode in the company of the merchant's son, Matteo, who had made the trek back and forth to Rome several times and could explain the baffling sights along the road.

Who were the men sidling up to the merchant every time they approached a town? "What are they up to?" Pietro asked.

"They are hawkers," Matteo said. "The landlords send them out to lure travellers to their inn. They promise you heaven if you stay with them, but after you've settled in, you find that they starve your horse, or let you freeze, or provide you with two stumps of candles to light your room, and expect you to sleep on linen that hasn't been washed in a month."

"That was certainly the case last night. My sheets reeked of sweat or worse. And the walls were as thin as paper. I could hear my neighbour cough and fart," Pietro said.

"You did better than I. My neighbour was drunk and puked all night." Nothing about inns surprised Matteo, not enough at any rate to slacken his square jaw or lift his thick brows. "That place last night was rotten, I agree, but on the whole the landlords try to oblige my father because they value his custom," he said. "He makes the journey two or three times a year, and they don't want him to give their inn a bad name and scare off other customers.

That's why we are spared the worst of the lumpy mattresses and stinking blankets."

Pietro's thighs and shoulders were sore and stiff from riding all day. Matteo was used to life on the road. He didn't mind the long hours in the saddle and had a store of amusing anecdotes and dirty jokes, but his interests were narrow and focused on his father's business, which he expected to take over in a few years. He lamented the decline of currency and talked about the fluctuating price of silk. He was willing to broaden the conversation to include the subject of diseases and speculate about cures for syphilis and dysentery or the best treatment for a sick horse, but he showed no curiosity in books or in the architecture of cities or even the wonders of nature. Pietro would have liked to make a detour to Pietramala and see the emanations of coal gas said to explode into soaring flames or the lake whose waters could be set on fire. Matteo shrugged his shoulders.

"Why would you want to go out of your way?" he said. "If you like to see that kind of trick, any troupe of jesters will oblige and breathe fire on you or jump through burning hoops and all that stuff, without you having to ride over wretched roads and ruin your horse."

In a way Pietro envied his companion. He led a life of simple purpose. His goal was well within his grasp, while Pietro did not know where to stake his claim. His heart was divided between love and ambition. He was feeling at loose ends. The novelty of the road and the ever-changing landscape, which had exhilarated him at first, oppressed him now. He missed the congenial company of his friends in Ferrara. He longed for Livia, for a touch of her soft cheek, the feeling of her fingers against his palm, her voice, the smile playing on her face. He told his wayward soul to keep still and submit to reason, but Livia remained lodged in his heart. He could not suppress his yearning for love, for the kind of romance described in *Floridoro,* the book he had failed to return to her. He read in it every day as in a prayer book. At night before extinguishing his candle or in the morning before setting out, he opened the book at random and read a few verses, a blessing for the road. The lines he had read that morning echoed in his head:

He armed himself and took his leave from her
whose lovely face he had engraved upon his heart,
her fair visage, so noble and serene-

The words seemed to describe his own leave-taking from Livia, and it took a long time for the image to fade, a long time to chase the verses from his mind and replace them with more prosaic thoughts. He was no knight, and his future wife no princess. If he came to some arrangement with Amosto in Rome and married his daughter, it was just that — an arrangement to further his career. Romance did not enter into it. If everything went well, he might become fond of his wife, or at least get along with her. It was time to curtail his fantasies of love and put away *Polidoro*, but he could not bring himself to abandon all thought of Livia. Life without romance was too dreary.

The company had now reached the Apennine Mountains. They were riding through silent woodlands and along rocky ledges. In the afternoon they reached the summit and began the descent to the Tuscan plain. Passing between terraces of vines and olive trees, they saw before them the walls and towers of Florence, gilded by the setting sun. Pietro had already missed out on the wonders of Bologna, its porticoes and palaces because the merchant's itinerary left no time for sightseeing. He fared no better in Florence. He had to be content with fleeting glances of the Duomo, the solid walls of the Bargello, the old palace and the new Uffizi. Nor did Pietro see much of the town of Siena except its beautiful market place, but he comforted himself with the thought that Rome at least would be his to explore. No doubt he would have plenty of leisure there, since it was the habit of those in power to keep the unimportant waiting.

Two days later, they entered the Papal State. The road narrowed to a track as the company traversed a stony valley in the shadow of barren and forbidding mountains. They had been warned about roving bands of brigands and kept a sharp look-out on the way to Montefiascone. As they reached the little town, which hugged the summit of the mountain, the view opened up and offered them an astonishing sight. On the plain below, two armies confronted each other, arraigned in battle formation — blocking the route to Rome. They could see the pennants waving in the morning breeze, a train of pack wagons lined up in the rear, camp followers huddling behind the lines — whores and peddlers, most likely.

The merchant's caravan came to a stop. Every man gaped at the troops below assembled as if on a stage and about to perform a play for the benefit of the people in the caravan. They watched teams of oxen pulling gun carriages to the fore and heard the beat of drums start up. Trumpets blared, as the armies on both sides advanced. Orders were shouted, and the next moment, the combatants broke into a run, their swords drawn. The front lines came together in a clash of metal and unleashed pandemonium.

The soldiers engaged in strenuous combat, charged and fell back in a boiling and eddying movement. A cloud of dust rose up, veiling the scene from the onlookers, but the battle noise was all around them, echoing from the hills — the neighing and bellowing of beasts, the wild yells of men, the clanging of armour, the crack of shots and roar of cannons.

Matteo, who had gone off to reconnoiter, returned and told the company what he had heard from the locals.

"They are troops hired by the pope to fight Marco Sciarra and his army of bandits."

Pietro had never heard of Sciarra.

"A robber baron from the Abruzzi mountains," Matteo explained. "He wants to be King here. Or perhaps I should say 'pope' since we are in papal territory now. They told me Sciarra catches monks and makes them kneel down and lick his boots. And now he has started to collect taxes around here. The people of Piceno refused to pay tribute to Sciarra, so his men raided the town. They slaughtered whoever got in their way, raped the women, drove away the cattle, and burned down the houses. What happened in Piceno was enough to cow the other towns. They didn't want to suffer the same fate and submitted to Sciarra's rule. The Pope was forced to take action then, or lose his territory to the brigand."

Matteo had brought back with him a local guide, who was prepared, at a price, to lead the merchant's caravan along a path skirting the battle ground. The change of route was bad news for the company. It was longer and had narrow turns that were difficult to negotiate for the cart drivers. The mules plodded along at the same steady pace, but the horses were much slower on the stony path than on the road cutting through the plain.

The caravan made its way to the accompaniment of a dull roar, the muted noise of battle, pierced occasionally by cries and the booming of cannons. Two hours on, after a steep descent, slippery and treacherous, they reached flat terrain.

"In the clear at last!" Matteo said and kissed a little bag hanging around his neck. "Fennel and fox' teeth," he said. "There is no better protection against misfortune."

"You don't trust in God's protection?"

"Of course, I trust in God. What do you take me for, Pietro? A heathen? But it does no harm to have double protection." He padded the cotton bag and tucked it back inside his shirt. "And by the way, I couldn't help noticing that little book you carry around with you. Haven't I seen you pressing your lips to it in prayer? So let's just say: you have your talisman, and I have mine."

Pietro grinned sheepishly. Matteo was right. He guarded Livia's book as superstitiously as a pagan idol. Of course it was asinine, and he had reasoned with himself about his attachment to a useless token, but to no avail. His foolish love for Livia prevailed.

The company was now past the battle lines and out of the fray, or so they thought until they heard the thunder of hooves and clattering of armour coming up behind them. Looking back, Pietro saw a dust cloud heralding a troop of riders.

"Mother of God, protect us!" Matteo said, as the company hurriedly moved to the side of the road. They had hardly taken up defensive position, scrambling for shelter behind the carts, when the ground shook and a horde of fleeing bandits rushed by them like a swarm of locusts. A single rider was lagging behind, whipping his horse and straining to catch up with the others. He was leading a second horse by a rope, a beautiful chestnut, no doubt captured in battle. His own horse was burdened with a double load— the rider himself and a figure wrapped in a coat and slung across the horse's back. As the bandit passed Pietro, flashing a bearded wolf's face, he saw that the second man was trussed up with cords. A hostage!

Without taking thought, Pietro urged his horse into the road, dug in his spurs, and gave chase. The bandit cocked an eye over his shoulder. Half turning, he raised an arquebus and delivered a shot, but his awkward position and the uneven ground made it difficult to aim. The bullet missed its mark. At the crack of the shot the chestnut horse led by the bandit shied, arched its neck and pulled away. For a moment it looked as if it would knock the rider off balance, but he jettisoned his human cargo and managed to regain control over his mount. Pulling hard on the rope and making the booty horse fall in line, the bandit sped off. He rounded a bend in the road, and was gone from sight.

The animal was worth more to him than the hostage. Naturally — Pietro thought. He prefers the price a fine horse will fetch in the market over the uncertain chance of collecting ransom on the hostage.

The trussed-up body of the captive had hit the road with a thump and rolled into the ditch. Pietro reined in his horse and jumped down to untie the robber's victim and see how badly he was hurt in the fall. Too late he understood the bandit's maneuver. The man had only waited for Pietro to dismount before wheeling around and coming back at a gallop, charging him head-on, sabre in hand and ready to cut him down. Death flashed before Pietro's eyes. He could see the blade come whistling down on him, but at that very moment a shot rang out. The bandit's horse reared up, blood running from its nostrils. It stumbled, collapsed on the ground, and lay there, kicking and thrashing in mortal agony, pinning the rider under it.

It was Matteo who had discharged his arquebus and saved Pietro. Two muleteers came running up as well when they saw the bandit's horse flounder, and together dragged the man out from under the horse. His legs were mangled and stuck out at unnatural angles. His mouth gaped open as if he wanted to scream, but no sound emerged except a rasping breath. He was dying. His eyes rolled up in his head. His body gave a last twitch and lay still. The muleteers cursed violently because death had deprived them of a chance to punish the man. They would have liked to string him up on a tree, and were clamouring to be allowed to quarter his corpse at any rate and leave it by the side of the road as a warning to other highwaymen.

By this time Matteo's father had caught up to the scene and called them off impatiently. "Enough time wasted on this skirmish," he said, and the muleteers had to content themselves with robbing the robber of his arquebus and sabre.

The merchant meanwhile remonstrated with Matteo, who had jumped off his horse and joined Pietro, bending over the wounded captive.

"Idiots!" the merchant shouted, including Pietro in his tirade. "Hotheads! Endangering the whole caravan so you can play heroes. And what if the bandits come back to check on their comrade-in-arms and attack us? Wait until they give you a taste of their cutlasses, and we'll see if you still like being heroes." He carried on, spit gathering in the corners of his mouth.

Pietro turned to offer an apology to the angry man.

"I'm sorry if I acted rashly, Signor Panetti, but I could not bear seeing a man carried off like a piece of mutton. In any case, no one has come to harm, except the scoundrel himself."

"Don't count your blessings yet. The rest of them might come back and avenge his death."

Matteo was unperturbed by his father's wrath. "They aren't coming back," he said. He was sure that the troop of robbers had abandoned their comrade. "They are more interested in making their getaway after losing the battle."

The other men agreed with his speculation. They clapped Matteo on the shoulder, shook Pietro by the hand, and applauded the bravery of the two young men. Only Panetti kept grumbling. "We haven't seen the end of the affair. The bandits will go to earth for a while, hole up in their dens in the Abruzzi and regroup as soon as the pope has dismissed his soldiers. He can't keep paying their wages for ever. Then the Sciarra clan will come back with a vengeance."

The merchant made his sinister predictions, thinking of the return journey which would take his company through the same territory. Meanwhile Pietro had turned back to the bandit's hostage, cut the leather cords binding his arms and legs and removed the gag from his mouth. The victim turned out to be a young gentleman, his face wind-burned, although pain had drained it of all colour. He gave his name as Orazio Farnese — a family name that got instant recognition from the onlookers and smoothed even the brow of the merchant. The Farneses, as everyone knew, controlled large estates in the area and wielded a great deal of power both in the countryside and at the papal court. There might be a reward for the rescuers!

A barber-surgeon in the merchant's train was fetched and knelt down beside the injured man, whose hair was matted with blood.

"My arm," he groaned. "My shoulder." His face was distorted with pain. His sleeve was ripped and clots of blood surrounded the holes in his leather jerkin where his skin had been punctured and cut by a knife, it seemed. The barber pulled off the young man's shirt and padded vest. A soldier's body, Pietro thought, seeing his powerful shoulders and sinewy arms, which were at odds with the delicate features of his face and the fine white linen shirt he wore, a garment more suited to a dandy than a fighter.

The barber passed his hands over the man's limbs, felt along the bones and declared that nothing was broken, but the shoulder had been dislocated. "The sooner I can reset it the better," he said. "Before it gets infected."

Orazio Farnese nodded and said. "Do what you have to do."

The barber gripped his arm and pulled sharply. The stricken man turned ashen and gave a scream that cramped Pietro stomach, but the barber declared the procedure a success.

"It's popped back in," he said. He angled the young man's arm and bound it to his chest with a linen bandage. "Keep it tight for a few days," he said, "and don't wrestle with anybody — no matter how willing she is to take a fall."

The onlookers laughed and gave their own estimate of the time it would take the young man to recover. Nothing to it, one said, he'll be as right as rain in a day or two. Others were more cautious. As long as he doesn't develop a fever. Those wounds on his chest should be washed out with wine as soon as possible.

Orazio smiled wanly and tried to get to his feet, but sank back, overcome by the pain and loss of blood. On the merchant's direction, two men lifted him up and laid him into a rack wagon padded with bales of hay. One of the muleteers, meanwhile, had recovered the booty horse. The men gathered around to admire the fine animal, every one of them a connoisseur. They praised his gait and the curve of his arched neck, and fingered the saddle stamped with heraldic colours until Panetti came and put an end to their talk.

"We've wasted enough time," he told them gruffly. "I'm not paying you for standing around and gabbing about horses."

The caravan moved on and reached the next village by nightfall. The patient was received with the greatest deference at the local inn. The landlord, the ostler, and the stable boy vied to be of service to him and anticipate his every wish.

The landlord himself offered to ride to the Farnese estate and deliver the news of Orazio's rescue to his father, Lord Ranuccio, but the young man waved him off.

"No, no," he said. "There is no need to alarm him or my mother. She will collapse in tears and hang around my neck, crying. You know how women are." Even so he did not escape female attention. He was young and handsome after all, tall and lanky, with a pleasing face marked by high cheekbones and frank intelligent eyes. And even if he had been ugly, his family name gave him a right to be pampered. He was taken to the best room upstairs and fussed over by the women of the house.

"Come along," he said to Pietro. "I am being besieged and need reinforcement." He made a show of leaning heavily on Pietro's arm as if he needed support, although he was laughing. The colour had returned to his face. He bore his injuries bravely.

Upstairs, he shooed away the maids. "Like a peck of hens," he said. "Leave me the plate of meat, girls, and the carafe of wine, and I will look after myself."

"I see you have recovered," Pietro said. "Or are putting on a brave face."

"That shoulder will keep me out of action for a while, I can tell," Orazio said, no longer smiling. "But the worst is yet to come:

facing my father, who called me a fool for joining the battle and will say I proved him right."

"He will be glad to see you alive."

"Let's drink to that," Orazio said and poured two glasses of wine for them. "I haven't thanked you properly for rescuing me."

"It wasn't just me," Pietro said. "Matteo Panetti, the merchant's son, shot the bandit's horse. If he hadn't been ready with his arquebus, the affair might have turned ugly, for me at any rate, because the bandit was about to split my head with his sabre. But tell me, how did he take you captive?"

"With the greatest ease," Orazio said. "Because I am a fool, as my father says, mistaking a battle for a tournament and finding out the hard way that gentlemen's rules don't apply."

"Not if you are fighting bandits, at any rate."

"I've learned my lesson. Don't ride a fine horse into battle against men who have no honour and who think only of loot, not of glory. I had hardly joined the battle when I found myself between two bandits, jostling Bucephalos — that's my horse."

Pietro laughed. "Bucephalos! You named him after the favourite horse of Alexander the Great?"

Orazio nodded. "My hero."

"We share an idol then. But while I merely admire Alexander's heroic spirit, you have manifested it already. You are living the life of a soldier."

"And will die like Alexander, my father says, before I am thirty-three."

"But continue with your story. Two bandits surrounded you, and then?"

"One of them slid a noose around my neck and pulled me down into the dust. The other jumped from his horse to mine like a circus acrobat, and galloped off to the sidelines. His partner meanwhile tightened the noose until the world turned black before my eyes. When I regained my wits, I found myself tied up like a bundle of rags, and the fight raging on without me. When it looked like Sciarra's men were losing the battle, my kidnappers decamped. I tried to put up a fight, but they threatened me and nicked me with their knives to teach me a lesson. You know the rest of the story. I am glad at any rate that the papal troops won the day, or so it seems, since the bandits were in full flight."

They heard the wheels of a carriage rolling into the courtyard.

"What's going on now?" Orazio said.

Pietro stepped up to the window and saw that a carriage had come to a halt in front of the inn. It bore the Farnese arms. A gentleman alighted and spoke to the ostler in a commanding voice used to giving orders.

"My father!" Orazio said. "I recognize his voice. The landlord has ignored my wishes and informed him, hoping to curry favour of course."

As it turned out, it was Matteo who had volunteered to take the news to Ranuccio Farnese. He told the tale of Orazio's rescue and was rewarded with a purse of silver pieces. No doubt that was his purpose in the first place.

Farnese had come in the carriage to take his son home. He was shown into Orazio's room and introduced to Pietro.

"From Ferrara?" Lord Ranuccio said after thanking Pietro for his part in Orazio's rescue. "You must tell me about the famous horse races the Duke holds on St. George Day. I have organized something of the kind on my estate to celebrate our patron, St. Raynaldo. — Nothing as grand as the festivities in Ferrara, you understand. I don't have bolts of gold brocade to give away, like the Duke."

"The first prize in our race is a game cock," Orazio said. "Yet the competition is fierce. You might want to enter the lists."

"Indeed," Lord Ranuccio said. "Do come back with us and enjoy our hospitality for a few days or as long as you please."

"I am honoured by your invitation, sir," Pietro said, "but Luca Panetti will hardly wait for me. He is in a great hurry to make up for the time we lost skirting the battle field. We hope to reach Rome in two days' time."

"That should not keep you from joining us. Let the merchant go on. We will find another escort for you and see that you reach Rome safely."

"Yes," Orazio said eagerly. "Stay on, and we'll ride to Rome together. I have business there next month."

"The kind of business young men have," his father said irritably. "And what about your injuries, Orazio?"

"They will be healed by then." He turned to Pietro. "Well, what do you say?"

Pietro would have liked to accept the invitation, but he could not delay his business, he explained. He was on a mission for the Duke.

He saw a glimmer of interest in Ranuccio Farnese's eye. "You are going to the papal court?" he asked softly, making it sound like a disinterested question, but the light in Farnese's eye warned Pietro. He remembered Cesare's caution: A courtier keeps his mouth shut.

139

"On a family matter," he said. "I am no diplomat, sir. I am the duke's archivist."

"You are a rare bird then," Farnese said. "A man of learning with the bravado of a soldier, for I understand it took some courage to tackle the bandit, as you did to rescue Orazio. But if your duties will not allow you to come with us at this time, perhaps you will stop on your way back to Ferrara and take advantage of our hospitality then."

"And if you are still in Rome next month, I shall look you up," Orazio said. "In any case, let me have an address where I can reach you."

Pietro was about to give him Amosto's name, but thought better of it. Perhaps the two families were not on the same side of the eternal diplomatic battles being waged at the papal court. "I am not sure where I will be in a month's time," he said and gave Orazio the address of the banker with whom he was to deal. "Cigi will know where to find me."

He accompanied father and son downstairs and took his leave of them in the courtyard, not without receiving from Orazio's hand a gift to remind Pietro of their common danger: his saddle, a splendid piece stamped along the edges with the emblem of the Farnese: a golden unicorn.

Pietro protested that he could not accept such a costly gift, but Orazio would not be denied, and the two young men parted with mutual assurances of friendship.

When the company set out the next morning, Matteo was the first to admire Pietro's new saddle.

"Worth more than the purse of money Farnese gave me," he said. "But I know my place."

He did not complete the thought: Pietro was a gentleman. He was a merchant's son. Orazio Farnese was as far above him as the clouds in the sky. The world was neatly divided by rank and money. That's how it was. No use fighting it. Matteo accepted the world order with equanimity. He had no ambitions beyond carrying on his father's business.

"I hear you got an invitation to visit the Farnese estate," he said to Pietro.

"And watch the horse race to celebrate St. Raymond's Day — yes, but I declined. My time is not my own. The Duke is my paymaster."

"If I were you, I'd have accepted the invitation, and the Duke's business be damned," Matteo said. "You sit your horse well, you know. You could have entered the race."

"Never! You need years of training for a race like that. I would have cut a ridiculous figure. But I wish I could have enjoyed Orazio's company a little longer. I like him a great deal."

"You like him? A great deal?" Matteo's mouth curled into a lascivious grin. "I hope you aren't one of those—." He waved a limp wrist at Pietro.

"What are you talking about?"

Matteo winked. "Those men who like each other a great deal. There is a lot of them in Rome. You know what someone told me? A few years ago, two Spaniards actually got married. Two men. In a church ceremony."

"What!" Pietro said. "You are making that up."

"You don't believe me? Ask anyone in Rome. They'll tell you it's true. It was a big scandal. The lot of them was burned at the stake — the two perverts together with the priest who married them."

"I don't believe a word of it."

"You'll believe it once you have spent a week in Rome. But let me tell you about the women—"

All day, on this last leg of their journey, Matteo had a single topic: the whores of Rome. He crackled with restless energy. His whole mind was bent on carnal pleasure.

"Aren't you afraid of catching a disease from them?" Pietro said.

"You have to be careful, naturally, and shop around. There's a difference between a streetwalker conducting her business under a bridge and a cardinal's whore, and there are many in between. The best — the honest courtesans as they call themselves — are too expensive for you and me, but looking doesn't cost anything. Walk around in the Ortaccio — that's where the whores ply their trade — and you'll get an eyeful free of charge. Tits pushed up almost to their collarbones, painted nipples and what not. If it's a cold night, they may keep the goods under wraps, but they'll open their capes and show you their tits if you ask for it. And there are hundreds to choose from." Matteo smiled happily, thinking of the pleasures in store for him.

"And you don't worry about committing a deadly sin?"

"There is nothing to worry about. I go to confession afterwards and get my absolution from the priest. Besides, if that's what bothers you, there are pious girls even among whores. I've seen it myself. One girl I hired removed a chain with the image of St. Mary before doing it with me, and another stopped humping at the sound of the Ave Maria bells and got out her rosary."

141

"I don't call that pious," Pietro said.

"What do you call it then?"

"Superstitious."

"Come on, let's not quarrel over words. Those girls are okay. I mean, they aren't beasts with horns."

For a while they rode on in silence, then Matteo started up again.

"We'll arrive in the city at the right season at any rate. Last year the governor of Rome had a wall built around the Ortaccio and installed a gate. It stays closed during Lent. When it opens up again after Easter, people go wild. It's like any other business, you know. A matter of supply and demand. There is a pent-up demand after Lent, and the prices are high."

"And now the demand has fallen off?"

"And the prices have come down. So I advise you to take advantage of the market."

Matteo's talk about loose women was having its effect on Pietro. "You are making me curious," he said.

"Aha! So you aren't dead to the world after all."

"I might go and take in the sights."

"Just stay away from the dreary hovels and tenements near the Tomb of Augustus. You'll get lost in the warren and get your throat cut. Keep to the upscale establishments further away from the river. You'll find women preening at the windows, showing their wares from behind lattices. Their dresses are cut practically to the navel. I took the plunge once and asked for admission, but let me tell you the woman looked better in the window — it was some trick of light. Up close she was quite ugly, with a scar on her cheek, and a gut like an old hag. Well, maybe it was just bad luck and I picked the wrong one."

"I'm surprised the Church allows such goings-on."

"Oh, the Governor tried to get rid of the whores. The Pope outlawed prostitution and ordered the women to leave the city, but there was an outcry from the merchants and tradesmen. The whores are an economic force, you see. Their customers spend money on food and drink and lodging and on gifts for the girls. So in the end it was decided to restrict the evil to one area of the city. Venice did the same with the Jews. They are a cursed tribe, but people can't do without money lenders. Or whores. So let the authorities confine the dirty business to one district, and everyone is happy."

Pietro had no answer to Matteo's reasoning, but he thought that Christian charity was in short supply, and the city which was regarded as the centre of Christendom, was no better than Sodom and Gomorra.

The next day, the caravan reached Rome. The domes and towers of the famous city began to rise before their eyes. The company picked up the pace with shouts of excitement.

"I'll give you one last tip," Matteo said, "but this is between you and me. There is one place — it's called The Barn — where the women are fantastic. You won't find anything like it anywhere else. I'm going there tomorrow night, and if you want, I'll take you along."

"No, thanks," Pietro said. "I'll be settling in with my host."

"You don't know what you're missing."

But now they had arrived at the Porta del Popolo, the northern gate of the city, and the talk dried up. They joined the line of carts and riders, peasants, beggars, and pilgrims wanting to enter the city. As they approached the gate, the line slowed. The gatekeepers had pulled one man aside and rifled through his saddle bags.

"What's going on?" Pietro asked.

"They are searching people's luggage," Matteo said.

"What for?"

"Stolen goods. Illegal stuff. Any books that don't bear the stamp of the papal censor. Dirty pictures. Lutheran tracts."

The guards had taken a book from the man's bags and were roughing him up, searching his body. He argued with them, mixing German and Italian in a desperate bid to clear himself.

"Shut up," one of the gatekeepers said. "You can tell your lies to the inquisitor. That's one of Luther's books."

"No, I swear, it isn't by Luther," the man repeated over and over.

"Why else would the title page be missing?" the guard said with irrefutable logic. He hawked a gob of spit into the dirt. "That's what I think of German heretics like you. I spit on them. They are a worse plague than the rats."

The man was marched off to the jeers of those waiting to pass through the gate.

The line began to move more briskly.

"Who'd run the risk of carrying Luther's writings?" Pietro said, looking back at the German, now clapped into irons. "He must be insane."

Luther's books were on the Index of Forbidden Books and anyone found in their possession was liable to be burned at the stake. And yet they circulated throughout Italy, he had heard, smuggled and carried from one city to the next.

"Don't ask me why those madmen want to risk their life for a book," Matteo said. "I don't read Latin or German and have no interest in theology. But the guards are also looking for books on alchemy and black magic. They are outlawed as well. Still people try to smuggle them in. Witches and alchemists have their secret hangers-on, just like Luther. That little book of yours, the one you keep hugging to your chest — that's not black magic, is it?"

Pietro smiled. "It has a certain magic for me, but it contains only innocent verse, a tale of chivalry."

The merchant's party had reached the front of the line. Matteo knew the customs men and hailed them. Soon they were trading jokes. "Show them your book," he said to Pietro and grinned. "My friend here is reading up on chivalry. He's into jousting."

The guard gave Pietro a friendly cuff on the shoulder. "Jousting in the Ortaccio games, hey? Well, good luck."

"He doesn't need luck," another said, "He needs money."

There was more ribbing until finally Pietro was allowed to pass and followed the merchant's company to a nearby inn. There he asked for directions to the house of Leonardo Cigi, the banker who held his funds.

"If you change your mind about The Barn," Matteo said as Pietro took his leave from the company, "meet me here tomorrow at nightfall."

CHAPTER 23

A glorious scene greeted Pietro as he made his way to the banker's house: a vision of domes, churches, and a long perspective of streets aglow in the ruddy gold of the evening sun. Following the directions he had been given, Pietro came to a maze of streets so narrow that the balconies and loggias of the houses almost touched in the middle. It was like riding under a canopy blocking out the sun. Pietro made his way slowly through a crowd of hawkers, porters, tradesmen and peasant women selling eggs, nuts, and vegetables out of their aprons. Gradually, the vista changed. The streets became wider, the houses larger. Mansions lined the road. They were old and rundown but still preserved an air of grandeur. At last, Pietro reached the bridge over the Tiber leading to the fortress of Castel Sant'Angelo, and entered the enclave of the Pope.

The banker's house was near the Vatican. It was a stately building, three stories high, with a façade of smooth masonry and a tall arched entrance that spoke of the owner's wealth. Cigi himself welcomed Pietro, but the young man understood very well that the banker was honouring the House of Este rather than him, the Duke's lowly emissary.

Cigi showed Pietro into his study. Lodgings had been arranged for him nearby, he said.

"But first let us drink to your health, and then you must tell me about your journey."

"I wouldn't want to presume on your time, Messer Cigi," Pietro said.

"My time is at your disposal," the banker said. "Indeed, you might say it is my business to be inquisitive on behalf of my clients. The safety and the condition of the roads are of concern to everyone who has money invested in commercial enterprises."

He listened with interest to Pietro's account of the rout of the bandits by the papal troops.

"That's good news, but I am afraid Sciarra's defeat will bring only temporary relief. His men will regroup and attack again. His Holiness the Pope would have to keep a standing army in the area, and that is an expensive proposition."

"Why don't the towns band together and set up a militia?"

"I suppose they have done the sums and found it cheaper and more convenient to pay protection money to Sciarra."

A lesson in politics! Pietro thought.

"But you were fortunate," the banker continued. "Your adventure ended well, for yourself and for young Orazio. And it is always good to oblige a Farnese. Orazio's father may be bankrupt, but other branches of the family remain powerful, especially at the papal court."

Pietro raised his eyebrows in surprise. "Ranuccio Farnese did not make a bankrupt impression on me," he said, thinking of the handsome reward he had paid to Matteo. "And his son was riding a fine horse. It would have fetched a great deal of money if the robber had gotten away with it."

The banker nodded. "The old man will live and die in style, but his son will inherit nothing but debts. No wonder he joined the papal troops. He might as well hone his fighting skills. He may have to earn his living as a mercenary, unless one of his relatives here in Rome obtains a sinecure for him. And speaking of financial matters, you have come to draw a sum of money from me, have you not?"

That was the main purpose of Pietro's visit, and he presented the draft he had been given to cover his expenses.

"If I may give you the benefit of my advice, young man," the banker said. "Don't keep too much ready cash on hand. Rome is full of thieves and robbers. Your lodgings are most respectable, but even so your landlord cannot protect you against their tricks. There is no strong box that can't be rifled. Mainly, do not make the mistake of walking around at night on your own. The robbers are getting bolder every day. They fear nothing and cut your throat for the clothes on your back. They even assaulted the papal nuncio of Naples."

"What, not even a representative of the holy church is safe!"

"Well, as to being holy — I don't know what business the nuncio had in the disreputable quarters where he was attacked. But no one is safe."

Pietro thanked Cigi for his warning.

"One more thing," the banker said. "A servant came yesterday from Tommaso Amosto to inquire whether you had arrived. He left this note for you."

Pietro unfolded the sheet. "An invitation to dine with him," he said. "Perhaps you could give me directions to his house."

"Your business is with Amosto?"

Pietro was unsure how much to tell the banker. He decided to keep it vague.

"You could call it business," he said. "Family business."

The banker gave him a knowing smile. "Involving Amosto's daughter?"

There was no need for secrecy, then. Cigi must have been told of the proposed arrangement.

"The Duke has been gracious enough to take an interest in my affairs and has recommended me to Tommaso Amosto," Pietro said. "Amosto is a friend of my father's, but I have no personal acquaintance with him or his daughter. Do you know her by any chance?"

"I have met Donna Isolda once or twice in the company of her mother. She is a handsome young woman with a pleasing figure — if that answers your question."

"I am curious about her appearance of course, but my real question is: why would her father favour my proposal? If Donna Isolda is as handsome as you say, she must have many suitors."

"Ah, that is a question I cannot answer," the banker said, and yet his eyes told Pietro that he could tell him more if he wanted to. There was a pregnant pause, but it was clear that Cigi was not going to furnish him with more information. Pietro changed the subject.

"My business proper is with Cardinal Gesualdo," he said.

"So I was told when I received instructions from Don Cesare to assist you during your stay in our city. But I'm afraid you'll have to cool your heels. The Cardinal is out of town, staying at his villa in Civitavecchia. A fashionable rural setting, you know, especially for hunting expeditions in the marshes."

"I will wait for his return."

"You may have to wait a good while. But let's go and get your money," Cigi said and showed Pietro into his *contado*, where a clerk received Pietro's draft and counted out what he needed. Soon he was on his way to his lodgings, following a porter through the streets. In one short hour with the merchant, Pietro had learned two important lessons: thieves were everywhere, and there was something about Amosto's daughter that Cigi was unwilling to tell him. One more lesson was in store for him: the grandeur of the Pope. Just as he left Cigi's house, outrunners called for everyone to stand clear, and people pressed themselves against the walls of the buildings to make way.

"What's going on?" he asked the porter, as they hurriedly moved into an alley.

"The Pope is coming through," the man said. At the same moment they saw the horse guard riding by in formation, bearing the papal ensign. They were followed by the pontiff himself riding a white horse decked in red velvet to match his outfit, the red hat and the cowl covering his white surplice. He was followed in turn by a troop of men, fully armoured and bearing lances. A hackney, a mule and a sedan chair formed the conclusion of the parade, in case the pope desired an alternative mode of transportation.

The Pope and his retinue passed and were gone in a minute. Pietro looked around as the wave of people closed up again, and the porter carrying his baggage led on. Everything in this dazzling city seemed as unreal as a mirage. It will become more solid, Pietro thought, once I put my thoughts into words and enter them in my notebook. He had begun to keep a log after he was entrusted with writing the history of Ferrara. At first he thought of it as a writer's tool and jotted down what was relevant to the history of the city or might help him in his career as a courtier, but soon he began to jot down his personal observations as well, and now he wondered: Was he experiencing the world, or was he merely recording it? Something had changed inside him since he had started on his log. It was as if a channel in his mind had been blocked and the flow of his blood staunched. He was living life at a remove, always thinking of it as a narrative in which he appeared as "he" rather than as "I". Whatever he saw and heard, entered his head and turned into words and sentences to be put into a chapter of the Este chronicle or into a letter to Cesare to impress his patron. He tried to remember how it was when sights and sounds entered his mind unmediated and turned into experiences, into something laid up in his brain or in his heart and taking root in his memory. When was the last time he had been truly himself and allowed life

148

to enter his bloodstream? The night when he said farewell to Livia perhaps. That scene was sharply etched in his mind with all the attendant feelings — shame, heartache and remorse. What followed, the whole of his journey, was only fodder for reports. Once he had put the words on paper, his mind was left blank. There was no residual feeling. No, that wasn't entirely true either. Rescuing Orazio Farnese had been a spontaneous action without any thought for the consequences. The moment of danger was present in his mind and could still set his heart racing. His talk with Orazio at the inn had stayed with him as well, with all its animation — two young men speaking their minds freely. Yes, those had been genuine experiences, genuine feelings that could be revived perhaps if Orazio came to Rome next month and looked him up. He could be himself then, not the emissary of Cesare trying to play the courtier, or the inexperienced traveler trying to keep face, or the suitor of Amosto's daughter trying to strike a bargain. He would be Pietro Paci, who wanted to live life to the fullest. But could a courtier ever be his own man? Pietro feared he had made a wrong turn somewhere along the way and was lost in a world of artificial arrangements.

Wrapped in melancholy thoughts he arrived at the guesthouse. But after washing off the grime of the journey and settling into his comfortably furnished rooms, his courtly ambitions revived. He sat down to write a letter to Cesare d'Este. He had nothing of importance to report as yet, but he felt obliged to notify his patron of his arrival in Rome. Accordingly, he composed an eloquent travelogue and was very pleased with the cultivated tone he had given to his missive.

The next morning, he made his way to Cardinal Gesualdo's palace. He knew that the prelate was out of town but he left a note, asking permission to present himself on his return. The gatekeeper looked Pietro up and down, resting his eyes for a moment on the saddle with the Farnese emblem, and accepted the note — hesitantly, or so it seemed to Pietro.

"When is his Eminence expected to return?" he asked.

The man only shrugged. "Can't tell you, sir."

"In a week? In a month?"

The man observed him through half-closed eyes.

"I really don't know, sir."

Boorish fellow, Pietro thought as he remounted his horse and rode away. The man's clipped answers angered him. He knew he had been slighted. I didn't act with enough authority, he thought. Does the fellow think I am a yokel? He looked down on his jerkin and plucked at the coat he had slung over his shoulders. Perhaps they weren't fashionable enough for Rome. He would dress more carefully in the evening when he presented himself at Amosto's house.

With no other business on his hands and hours to pass before he was expected for dinner, he spent the remainder of the day sightseeing. The pomp and splendor of the Church was on display everywhere. Rome was the city of the Popes. For centuries it had been the city of the Caesars, but the glory of their empire was no longer in evidence. The Rome through which Pietro wandered was a giant cemetery of ancient ruins buried in the ground. Here and there, coins and pottery fragments were unearthed, brought up by carriage wheels rumbling over the old roads. Columns poked through the rubble, some upright, some toppled, and the shape of walls and buildings could be seen like broken hills, overgrown with brush. A few vestiges of Rome's grandeur survived in the Baths of Caracalla and the Colosseum, but most of the sites had long ago been quarried by builders for their own use. The ruins had been plundered for its statuary and its friezes. The ancient marble gods had been carted away and were now on display in the courtyards and villas of noble families. The Forum Romanum, the hub of the ancient city, was gone except for a few bronze statues kept in memory of an era long past — the twins Romulus and Remus suckled by a wolf, the Thorn Picker, and Emperor Marcus Aurelius on a noble steed. Again Pietro had that feeling of distance, of being removed from the present, as if he was merely eaves-dropping on a life in which he had no part. Even as he looked at the sights, he was already putting them in order and shaping them into a story, another letter to Cesare, although he doubted that his patron had any use for ancient lore. He argued with himself: Why could he take no interest in anything without thinking of putting it on paper? If he could talk to someone — to Livia— would the sights take on a different hue, would they come to life? He longed for Livia, for their familiar talk, when every word spoken was caught by a sympathetic ear and resonated in a sympathetic breast. Would Amosto's daughter be able to fill that role? No, Livia was irreplaceable! He feared he was condemned to loneliness.

Pietro was jolted from his thoughts by a tug at his jerkin and was just in time to wheel around and arrest a thief's hand poised to cut his purse. A warning cry went up. Someone moved alongside and helped him hold down the man, a thin fellow dressed in rags, with the beseeching eyes of a hungry beggar. Pietro almost felt

150

sorry for him. He loosened his grip and felt a sharp sting as from a lash. The thief had concealed a knife in his fist. He had turned on Pietro with lightning speed, knicked his hand with the blade, twisted free and disappeared in the crowd.

Blood trickled from a cut across Pietro's knuckles. So much for feeling sorry for a beggar, he thought. The rogue had the skills of an actor on the stage and knew how to arrange his features to make you feel pity for him and catch you unawares.

The man who had helped Pietro hold the man now rushed after the thief, but he was too late. The man had slipped away.

Pietro wound his handkerchief around his hand to stop the wound from bleeding.

"Did he get your purse?" someone asked him.

Pietro reached for his belt. His purse was intact.

"Lucky you," the man said. The crowd that had gathered around cheered and thinned out, seeing that the excitement was over.

It was only when Pietro arrived at his lodgings that he realized what was missing. He had lost something more valuable than money: his keepsake, Livia's booklet. It must have slipped out of his jerkin when he grappled with the thief. It wasn't credible that the man would make a play for the book in preference to his purse. Pietro went over the scene in his head, the light tug he had felt, the thief's arm in his grasp, someone else brushing up against him, helping him to hold the man down. Or, it occurred to him, sidetracking him and helping the man to free himself? Was it just luck that he remained in possession of his purse and suffered only a slight wound, or was it design? If the second man, the would-be helper, was in fact an accomplice of the first — no, the idea was too absurd, Pietro thought. There was a simpler explanation for what happened. He dropped the book in the commotion, and although the loss made his heart sore, it merely underlined the truth: Livia *was* lost to him. He might as well face it and resist hanging on to her memory. He thought ruefully of the love poem he had composed for her. He had written it out on a sheet of paper and folded it into the booklet, thinking that one day he would send it to Livia. He had read and reread his composition so often and tinkered with the words so long that he knew them by heart:

Where is thy magic now, Livia,
Where the bewitching smile
That cast a spell o'er me?
You frowned when last I saw you.

151

Have mercy on me, Livia.
Your frown is lethal to my soul,
Casting me down
Into the depth of Hades...

Just as well he never sent his effusions to Livia. He had been carried away by the verses of *Polidoro* and inspired by them to try his own hand at rhyming, but poetry was not his strong suit. Those awkward lines would not have pleased her. And in any case, what was the use of writing to Livia? he thought. We have said our farewells, and she has long forgotten me.

CHAPTER 24

In the evening he made his way to Amosto's house. What Cigi had said of Isolda relieved him of the fear that she was ugly or disfigured, but what the banker had left unsaid under the plea of ignorance deepened the mystery. Why was there no swarm of suitors vying for her hand if her father was rich and she was beautiful? Pietro was determined to discover the reason.

At the house of Amosto, he was welcomed by the master and introduced to the family who had gathered to greet their guest. Isolda, he saw at a glance, was indeed shapely and moving with grace. Her complexion was smooth, her hair arranged prettily in soft waves, her mouth curved in a pleasing smile, but her eyes — her eyes were still and impenetrable. Pietro could not help comparing her frozen look with Livia's natural radiance and vivacious eyes, but he banished her image and pushed it to the back of his mind, where it belonged, among the memories of an irretrievable past.

Dinner was served.

"You must tell us about your journey," the host said.

He obliged and tried to give some charm to his tale of bandits and bravado. Isolda watched him attentively, but it was as if her attention was meant not for him but only for his words, so that she might smile convincingly or nod in the appropriate places. Her body remained as still as a sleeper's, and when she batted her eyes, that too seemed the movement of a dreamer. She was like a cunningly manufactured image of a bride. She ate daintily, barely moving her mouth to chew, swallowing without tasting the food, it seemed, as is the food on her plate was made of paste. There was no life in her and no sweetness. Again he thought of Livia, the little gestures that were peculiar to her and her alone, the way she tapped her toes when she was uncertain, or fluttered her hands when she was excited, or smiled with the tip of her tongue protruding between her lips, ah, her lips —

"Now that young man you rescued," Amosto was saying. "What did you say his name was?"

Pietro straighten up and recalled his straying thoughts.

"Orazio Farnese," he said.

"Never heard of him. Must belong to a minor branch of the family. Did you have a chance to visit his estate?"

"He invited me, but the merchant with whom I traveled would suffer no delay, and I did not think it wise to abandon the safety of his caravan."

"In your place, I would have let the merchant go on without me. It's always worthwhile to see where and how a Farnese lives. That would tell you whether they have money or are just land agents for the more prosperous branch of the family."

"They have no money, I am told, but Orazio's father was liberal. He gave a generous reward to the merchant's son, who aided in the rescue."

"I would expect no less. A man's life is worth a great deal, or should be to his father at any rate, whatever others may think. And others may not think too highly of a young man who hires himself out as a soldier. I for one would not allow a son of mine to become a mercenary and fight a horde of robbers. There is no honour in such an enterprise."

"I suppose not, but it was necessary to fight them, or Sciarra would have made himself lord of the papal territory."

"Well—" Amosto said, looking annoyed. He was not used to having his opinions challenged. "I meant to say I am no admirer of the Farneses. It is all very well that you rescued that Orazio fellow. It shows your mettle no doubt and is to your credit, but remember, the Farneses aren't exactly promoters of the House of Ferrara. Need I say more? I was talking to a friend of mine at the papal court the other day — I won't mention his name, but he belongs to the innermost circle and knows what's going on. The Farnese gang is up to no good, he said to me. And as I myself said to the Holy Father — ah, I see you are surprised to hear that I have the Pope's ear occasionally — as I said to His Holiness—" He hesitated and did not complete the sentence. "But that's no topic for a dinner conversation and will hardly interest the ladies."

Amosto went on in this disjointed fashion, dropping names and leaving sentences unfinished. Pietro wished his host would speak clearly and explain himself, but Amosto stuck to hints and muffled his meaning, almost as if he didn't want Pietro to get a clear picture and didn't quite trust his good will. It was, Pietro thought, another lesson in courtly diplomacy.

"But to come back to the business of travelling, I could tell you some stories, young man," Amosto said, and he did, at great length. Pietro could tell from the bored expression on his wife's face that she had heard those stories before. Isolda's face remained unchanged. She might have been a wax image. She looked at her father with placid eyes, sat back languorously, and had nothing to contribute to the conversation. It occurred to Pietro that this might be the reason she had not been wooed. She was dull. But a good dowry easily outbalanced a lethargic temperament. Pietro speculated that there was another, more serious flaw he had not yet discovered.

In the meantime Amosto carried on, relating his own adventures as a young man when he had travelled in his master's train to France.

"A dangerous journey, and endless, it seemed. Long hours in the saddle, let me tell you, but I never complained. Not I. I thanked God for the leisure riding afforded me after the frantic packing up in preparation for the journey. Although perhaps I shouldn't call it leisure. It was my responsibility to look after the lodging and food supplies on the journey, and that was a daily problem I had to wrestle with. You didn't have to worry about any of that. Someone else took care of those details for you, I take it."

"Indeed I had that advantage. The merchant made all the arrangements."

Amosto nodded. There was a pause as if he was waiting for a more fulsome acknowledgment of his labours, but Pietro was not about to truckle to his host. In truth, he was tired of the old man's superior manner. Isolda had lowered her eyes and was picking at the table cloth. Amosto's wife came to the rescue and revived the conversation.

"I understand you are in the Duke's service," she said to Pietro. "You must tell us about your work."

"I am in charge of the archive and am writing a history of the House of Este."

"Then you must have impressed the Duke with your literary talents."

"I hope I will have an opportunity to prove my worth to the Duke. It was my patron, Cesare d'Este, who recommended me to him."

"My master would never have relied on the judgment of others," Amosto said with some asperity. "When he chose the members of his household, he put them to the test himself. We were all handpicked. Indeed you might say we became the master's associates, his eyes and ears. Of course we were well paid for our loyalty." He gave Pietro a calculating look. "I hope the Duke is as generous with you as my master was with me."

"I am afraid my stipend is modest," Pietro said.

There was another pause, almost as if Tommaso wished to be informed of the exact sum paid to Pietro. He felt Isolda's glances touching him as well, a gleam of interest coming alive in her eyes. When Pietro said nothing, Amosto continued.

"Of course, an archivist's position does not compare with that of a majordomo, which has considerable reach. I was in charge of purchasing, maintaining and repairing the household goods — clothing, armour, weapons, furnishing, tapestries, paintings, bed hangings, and what not. And of course I had a large staff reporting to me: buyers, bookkeepers..."

The list of Amosto's duties and accomplishments was endless. He wants to trump me at every turn, Pietro thought. Whatever I have done, he has done better. Whatever my experience, his is larger. Here was another skill to be learned if he wished to prosper as a courtier: the art of one-upmanship, the skill to put himself forward, to outdo the other man, to come in first.

Dessert was served and Amosto embarked on another tale of glory. Isolda sighed softly, a message that even the boring can be bored. Recognizing the sign perhaps, Amosto capped his talk and expedited the meal.

Pietro escaped, but had to promise to come back in the morning to "speak of business" as Amosto put it, without pinpointing the nature of their business, marital or diplomatic, affairs at any rate that would be conducted without the women.

CHAPTER 25

Riding home full of misgivings, Pietro decided to meet up with Matteo after all. He needed someone or something to take his mind in a different direction. He was dissatisfied and frustrated because he had failed to read Amosto's hieroglyphic mind or make any headway deciphering Isolda's character. Perhaps he had drunk too much of the full-bodied Falernian served at dinner while he suffered Amosto's interminable stories. The wine had addled his brains. He stopped at a fountain and splashed cold water on his face. To hell with propriety and decorum, he thought, as he wiped his face with a handkerchief. He needed diversion after that strenuous evening, a walk on the wild side to loosen the knot in his stomach.

At the inn, Matteo greeted him with a shout and eyebrows raised in exaggerated surprise.

"Pietro! — I'll be darned. I guess I misjudged you. I took you for one of those mealy-mouthed fellows who warn others about the sins of the flesh because they can't get it up themselves. But maybe there's more than lamb's wool in your codpiece." He looked Pietro up and down as if to check his manliness. "So you've decided to come along for a bit of fun?"

"I'll come along," Pietro said, but his tongue moved sluggishly. It wasn't only the effect of the wine he had drunk. He wasn't sure he was doing the right thing, but he could think of no other way to silence the memory of the futile dinner conversation and relieve the frustration that was roiling his guts.

"You are too well dressed for the occasion, my friend," Matteo said. "Come in. I'll get you something a little less fashionable, something that can take the wear and tear of an evening with the girls."

He supplied Pietro with a soiled linen shirt and a greasy leather jerkin smelling of sweat and horses. "There you are, that's better," he said, all business now, like the director of a play that needed careful staging.

"How much money did you bring with you?" he asked and laughed when Pietro opened his purse, "That's enough for three whores! You won't be able to hold on to your coin, no matter how careful you are. Those girls are expert thieves. Tell you what — you might as well spend up front what you've got there. We'll strike a bargain with them. We'll have three whores to service us and triple our fun."

"One is good enough for me," Pietro said, but it came out an inarticulate mumble.

"It looks like you've fortified yourself for the task," Matteo said, nudging him with his elbow. "Had a little too much wine? I hope you can still get it up."

"No worry," Pietro said with a conviction he did not feel. "But three — isn't that a bit rich, not to say degenerate?"

"What, degenerate? De-generate? No, my friend, that's the way of the world, and the sooner you wise up to it the better. You've got business with the papal court, isn't that what you told me? Well, you'd better learn their tricks. Those churchmen know all about degenerate. You have a long way to catch up. First they scare you shitless with their hell and brimstone sermons, then they make you confess, and finally they make you pay in coin for absolving you from your sins. What a racket they have going! Are they degenerate because they listen to what men do in the privacy of their bedrooms and how they like to take their women, back or front? No, they make clever use of their knowledge!"

Pietro could think of no reply.

Matteo was irrepressible. "Here is a song to get you into the mood," he said as he saddled his horse in the courtyard of the inn.

"*Io 'l voglio in cul, tu mi perdonerai / O donna, io non vo far questo peccato...*" He belted out the lewd sonnet to a chorus of laughter. Two of the men in the yard joined in and mimicked the action described in the song, one sticking out his bum and squealing in a woman's voice high with delight, the other humping

158

his back vigorously. The pantomime had its effect on Pietro even in his sodden state. He was not quite as innocent as Matteo wanted to make him out. Like every lad, he had studied the dirty pictures of copulating pairs, squares of paper grimy from frequent handling and crumpled from being hastily concealed in pockets. He had been eager to look at the images of forbidden embraces even as he was ashamed of the lascivious thoughts rising up in his mind and convulsing his body. Of course it was wrong to contemplate or even fleetingly think of acts that were against nature, as he had been told by the parish priest. That kind of copulation was forbidden even to married couples. Marriage was for procreation — that was the message dinned into his ear, and intercourse "in the wrong orifice", or intercourse "in the wrong manner" that did not produce offspring was against God's will.

Alas, listening to the stern words of his parish priest had brought on thoughts more impure even than the smutty pictures which had drawn a confession from him in the first place. The prohibitions listed by the priest only made him ponder: What can it be like to lie with a woman "laterally"? And would it be pleasurable "to sit or stand during intercourse"? Or "to copulate like animals." Instead of feeling revulsion at these illicit positions, Pietro became fascinated with them, although he never had an occasion to try them out. He did not like to admit it to Matteo or even to himself: his excitement was rising as he listened to the song and watched the men in the courtyard acting out their dirty fantasies.

Matteo saw Pietro's hot face and laughed.

"I see you are ready to sweat it out with the girls," he said, as he swung into the saddle and led Pietro along the narrow streets to his favourite brothel by the city gates. From the outside, it looked like a dairy farm, with a dirt-packed court and straw-thatched outbuildings, but the stalls were furnished with pallets and the creatures there weren't livestock. They were human, women of every description, thin, fat, mature, girlish — and not only women. There were young men also for those with a taste for something different. Here was humanity in every form, yet the bleating and bellowing and groaning coming from the stalls was much like the noise heard in a barnyard.

Pietro had never seen such abandon before, such writhing of bodies sleek with sweat, such boiling and bubbling of lust, the very cauldron of Hell, it seemed to him. The effect of the wine he had drunk was wearing off. He was filled with desire and disgust in equal measure. The slovenly young woman with whom he was

159

paired was willing enough to shift in any way he desired, to lie still or climb on top of him or offer her lush fruit to his mouth, but Pietro faltered before her generous offer. The ripe scent emanating from her well-used body, the mingling of her sweat with other men's juices revolted him. In spite of her enthusiastic groping and handling, he remained limp.

Matteo, rolling off his girl after a joyous discharge of pleasure, proposed a swap.

"Hey, Pietro! Try this one," he shouted. "She's good. I'll take care of number three."

Pietro's next lover was a fat little woman with a face like a pug, less popular than the prettier hussies, and therefore cleaner. The mountainous folds of her body, the round curves and soft flesh might have pleased Pietro, but the one and only lamp illuminating the barn was right above them and shed too much light to conceal the girl's coarse face. Pietro closed his eyes, shutting out the sight of the wretched woman and trying desperately to substitute for it some heavenly figure. He resorted to voluptuous imaginings, replacing the woman's ugly face with more elegant features, a clearer brow, but it was Livia's image that occurred to him. Her features, her luminous eyes, her full lips, came to him unbidden, and he froze with shame.

He shoved the whore away and got up. Pushing through the boisterous crowd, he stumbled out into the cool night. In the shadow of a tall oak, he stopped and groaned with deep self-loathing and shame for the weakness of his character and the insistent demands of his body. He wanted nothing more than leave this wretched place but he was unsure of the way back and wary of crossing the town at night, on his own. Remembering Cigi's warning about thieves and cut-throats, he decided to wait for Matteo and settled down on a grassy knoll. Left alone with his thoughts, he could not fend off the pangs of conscience, his betrayal of Livia's love. He reproached himself for dragging her, even in his mind, to this place of execration. He felt diminished by his animal lust and made an impetuous promise to himself: He was done with women once and for all. He would mortify his flesh with prayer and fasting. Then he lay back and sighed. He knew he was too weak to live up to such a vow, but the resolution soothed his qualms. He shut his eyes and was asleep in an instant.

It was dawn when Matteo shook him awake.

"There you are!" he said. "Why did you run off? You should have gotten your money's worth. I know I did."

CHAPTER 26

Remorse clung to Pietro for days, like a stench that water could not wash off. He had a nagging sensation of worthlessness, from which — he feared — no penance could release him. Yet he went to church and sought the solace of confession.

He dipped his fingers into the font of holy water and slunk guiltily past women lighting votive candles and murmuring prayers, rosary beads gliding through their fingers. He genuflected before the altar, and walked past the stations of the cross with his head bent low. The sun slanted through the windows and cast coloured squares on the marble floor as he knelt down in the confessional. The panel in the screened window shuttled back. He mumbled the conventional preamble and related his sinful doings to the priestly shadow hidden by the screen. His voice came out as a rough whisper. "I have sinned against the sixth commandment. I have visited a brothel, Father." The words stuck in his throat. He waited, expecting a sharp reproach, and could hardly believe his ears when the priest sent him away with a benign admonition and a penance of three Hail Marys.

Three Hail Marys!

"Is that all?" he asked, astonished.

"If I had a farthing for every Hail Mary I impose on a young man for lechery," the confessor said mildly, "I could build a cathedral to rival St. Peter's and finance a campaign against the

Infidel with the rest." He laughed, pleased with his own witticism. "Go in peace, young man," he said and slid the panel back in place.

For a moment Pietro knelt in the dark. Then he rose to make room for the next sinner. Three Hail Marys might reconcile him with God, he thought, but nothing could undo the memory of the filthy brothel and his disloyalty to Livia. Why did he go to that godforsaken place or, for that matter, what was he doing in this godforsaken city? Was a career at court worth all the anguish he was suffering?

For days he was sullen and irritable, indifferent to the solicitous questions of his landlady, the bantering of his fellow boarders at the lodge, and the conversations at the dinner parties he was obliged to attend. That was the worst part of his unwilling courtship. Amosto insisted on introducing him as Isolda's suitor to every one of his numerous uncles and cousins and second cousins, as if he wanted to tie him down with social obligations and leave him no escape, no honourable way to change his mind. God is punishing me for my ambition and my disloyalty to Livia, he thought.

Then a miracle happened that suggested a heavenly amnesty. Livia's book was returned to Pietro. A man had found it lying in the street and delivered it to the banker's house. No doubt, he hoped for a reward when he took it to the address written on a sheet of paper inside the book. Pietro had put Cigi's address on the back of his poem for Livia, in case he'd gather enough courage to send it off, and she cared enough to send him a reply. And there it was still safely tucked into the pages of *Floridoro*. A sign from heaven that all was forgiven! Pietro rewarded the bearer with a generous tip.

The recovery of Livia's book raised Pietro's spirits, but now that it was lodged once more inside his jerkin and pressing against his heart, the work of courting Isolda was harder than ever. To go on with it, he had to erect barriers in his mind. In one compartment, he kept romantic love, which he allowed to range freely only in the drowsy minutes of falling asleep at night and waking up in the morning. In another corner, he had corralled his diplomatic career, to be pursued with tenacity and a mind alert to every opportunity. Packed on top, like extra baggage, was the task of courting Isolda, which was turning more onerous every day.

He looked at his obligatory visits to Amosto's house as a penance to atone for his sins. He skipped a few days, declined a few invitations, but he could not always pretend to be engaged in business. In fact, time was hanging heavily on his hands. There was nothing to divert his thoughts from his dreary obligations. The Cardinal was still out of town. To pass the days, Pietro had taken to walking the streets in his neighbourhood, restless and with unseeing eyes. Sometimes he borrowed a book from Amosto's well-stocked library and buried his head in the pages of an ancient historian like Tacitus or studied the court speeches of Roman orators.

Isolda's mother was an indulgent chaperone when he called on her daughter. She was willing to close her eyes and take a gentle nap to allow for the intimate moments so coveted by lovers. But Pietro's heart remained unmoved in Isolda's presence. His lips chilled at the thought of planting a kiss on her hand or her cheek which looked as hard as marble. Isolda, too, kept her distance, lowering her eyes and withholding her thoughts from him, allowing only the most trivial words to pass her lips. There was no love lost between them. Of course, an arranged marriage wasn't about love. It was more like buying property, but when Pietro inspected what was on offer, he discerned neither virtues nor faults. Isolda was like a property without landmarks, flat and uninspiring.

One afternoon when he was admitted to Amosto's house, he was surprised to find Isolda lingering in the hallway. Was she waiting for him? Hardly! Not after their lackluster conversation the previous day.

He greeted her courteously. In response, she screwed up her eyes in a peculiar, pleading fashion. She had him puzzled. Was it a look of melancholy? Of indigestion?

They carried on a halting conversation.

"I hope you had a pleasant morning," he said.

"Ah, yes," she said. "I had my singing lessons."

"You enjoy singing?"

"I do."

It seemed they had exhausted that particular subject, but she started up again.

"I was going to talk to you about that," she said with something like animation. It was the first time Pietro had seen life in her eyes.

"My music teacher—" she said and looked him fully in the face. Another first. Usually he got only sideway glances. And there was that imploring look again. What could it mean?

"Yes?" he said. "Your music teacher — is he to your liking?"

She blushed. Perhaps he shouldn't have put it that way. He rephrased his question.

"Is he a competent teacher?"

"I wanted to say—" She stopped, seeing her father come out of his study.

"And what are you two talking about?" he said cordially, taking Isolda's arm.

She opened and shut her mouth rapidly like a fish out of water.

"I asked Don Pietro if he likes music," she said. Her face had gone blank and her voice returned to its usual flat tone. Pietro did not know what to make of it.

The weeks passed. Pietro went through the motions of courtship reluctantly and felt the rope tighten around his neck. He felt he knew Isolda no better than on the first day, but having come this far and knowing the whole clan by now, he could no longer break off relations without giving offense. He could not put the evil day off much longer. Amosto expected him to make a formal declaration soon and begin the marriage negotiations in earnest.

Since Pietro was hanging back, Amosto was obliged to broach the subject himself one afternoon. He had offered to show Pietro the Vatican gardens. They left their horses at the guard house and were ambling along the gravel paths.

"Not everyone has permission to come here," Amosto said with his usual bluster meant to show his superiority over the young man. "It is a special privilege granted me by the Holy Father. You can never tell whom you might run into here — a foreign dignitary, an ambassador, a cardinal. Maybe even the Holy Father himself."

At this time of the day, however, the city was caught up in a gentle afternoon slumber, and the garden was deserted. Clearly Amosto had chosen the hour because he wanted privacy.

They had not walked far before he started in on the business at hand.

"You have been a frequent visitor to our house, Pietro, and a most welcome guest, I hasten to say, especially to Isolda. Clearly you have captured her heart."

Pietro kept his mind firmly on his career, and yet he felt he was doing violence to his heart when he brought out a few well-rehearsed words of praise for Isolda. She was graced with beauty, he said, and would bring honour to any man fortunate enough to win her heart.

Amosto took him up at once.

"I am pleased to hear you say so," he said. "You are the son of an old friend after all, and if you admire Isolda, and Isolda is fond of you in turn, I will not stand in your way — unlike some fathers." He paused for emphasis. "There are men, I know, who will consider only the standing of a suitor, his position in society and his wealth. I won't deny that financial considerations enter into the question and are of concern to me as well, but I feel that the friendship between our families should count for something —"

"As should the Duke's recommendation," Pietro said. The negotiations had begun, and he was paring Amosto's moves skillfully. Just as well he was not in love with Isolda. It made bargaining easier.

"Duke Alfonso's word counts with me. That goes without saying," Amosto said. "He let me know that he favours the idea of our two families joining hands. As I said, your father and I are old friends and remain so even if our careers diverged early on and he has not always been fortunate in his pursuits. Mind you, he could have been as successful as I, if he had not been so unbending in his preferences."

The thrust of Amosto's words was clear. He was hinting at the elder Paci's lack of business acumen and his unprofitable marriage. Pietro's mother had added little to her husband's assets, whereas Isolda would bring Pietro a substantial dowry. "Of course a love match rarely benefits anyone," Amosto said. He was setting himself up as the dominant party in the negotiations. He brought the money to the table and he meant to dictate the conditions.

"You are a young man with a future — I'll give you that," he said amiably. "You have one foot on the career ladder already and are looking at marriage as a means of enlarging your prospects. And that's all very proper. I respect a young man who knows what's what and who can subject his passions to reason. I will not be ungenerous to my daughter, and since I have no sons, she will inherit — not everything because much is indentured to my wife and will go to her family — but a respectable sum at any rate."

"Perhaps we should draw up a preliminary contract," Pietro said, "and I will consult with my father."

This response was a little too cool for Amosto's liking. He wanted the match to be regarded as a great honour to the Pacis and had expected eager gratitude rather than businesslike reserve.

"Consult away," he said, switching his tone from amiable to stern, "but I will not haggle with your father."

"I don't mean to suggest we should haggle, as you call it," Pietro said, undisturbed by the Amosto's peremptory tone. He knew it was the old man's strategy to keep him in place. "I only meant to say that I do not wish to make a hasty decision. I am sure you will agree with me in that point. It is better to consult all round, and make sure not only that the sums add up but also that your daughter and I are compatible, that our characters and aspirations match. You say I have won your daughter's heart, but I myself am far from convinced that I have gained her favour."

Amosto had expected smoother sailing. His brows contracted when he answered: "Very well, we won't talk of love then. Isolda certainly knows her duty. She has been brought up to respect the wishes of her parents. She will give her favour to the man I favour, although I am no brute and will not force her into a marriage that is hateful to her. So far she has given me no reason to think that this is the case. Of course, if you wish to delay the decision and consult with your family, that is your privilege. I, in turn, may have second thoughts about the matter."

Pietro bowed. "I quite understand," he said, keeping his voice level and his thoughts to himself.

"Much will depend on how your mission here goes," Amosto said, giving him a shrewd look. "Cardinal Gesualdo has returned to Rome, they tell me. Have you been to see him yet?"

The prelate had not replied to Pietro's request for an audience, or perhaps never received it. This was the first Pietro had heard of his return.

"I expect to see him within a few days," he said, hoping Amosto would take his vague answer for the discretion of a courtier. "The Duke's mission is uppermost in my mind of course."

Amosto nodded. "I wish you success and, may I add, a promotion and an appropriate reward for your labours."

"My own hopes exactly."

They returned to the gate, mounted their horses and rode back, making desultory talk. As they turned into the street where Amosto lived, they saw a young man hurry along, then slow down as he approached Amosto's house. The front door opened like magic, guided from inside by an unseen hand. Pietro had a glimpse of Isolda in the darkness of the hallway. Then the door closed on the man.

Before he could comment, Amosto said: "Ah, Isolda's singing master."

Pietro thought he detected impatience and barely concealed anger in his voice. What was going on? Instantly he remembered the day when he had found Isolda lingering in the hall, her beseeching eyes when she mentioned the music master, her halting words *I meant to talk to you about that.* Had she been waiting for that man? Was there something between them?

166

"I don't know your opinion of young women taking singing lessons," Amosto said, "but my wife thinks it would be better to have Isolda learn to play the clavicembalo. What are your thoughts on the matter?"

"I have no strong opinion about singing lessons," Pietro said and eyed Amosto curiously. The man's discomfort was noticeable now in spite of his effort to mask his agitation and speak in an offhand manner. Something was amiss. Was the music teacher the answer to the question why there were no other suitors for Isolda's hand? Was she in love with him and had been on the point of making a confession to Pietro when they had that awkward encounter?

"By the way," Amosto said. "I am thinking of taking my family to Bulicame. The doctor has urged me to visit the thermal baths there and promised me wonders for my aching bones. My wife, too, is eager to go, as the springs are supposed to relieve the headaches that have been plaguing her lately."

"I will miss your company," Pietro said.

Amosto gave him a doleful look. Pietro had pointedly omitted any reference to missing Isolda, but his prospective father-in-law was not about to let him off so easily. "I know it will be hard on you not to see *Isolda* for a time," he said, stressing her name, "but it can't be helped. Health is a fickle thing."

"I quite understand," Pietro said, "and wish you a pleasant journey."

His heart grew light at the thought that he would be released from his duty visits for a time or perhaps forever, if there was something untoward going on. He lost no time visit Cigi's house and relate the conversation he had with Amosto to the banker.

"I wonder about Isolda's music teacher," he said.

This time Cigi did not hold back. He laughed softly.

"So you have seen the man?" he said. "Perhaps he has taught her too much already."

It did not take long to get the rest of the story out of him. Rumour had it that the music master had seduced Isolda or at any rate exchanged compromising letters with her. In other words, Amosto had tried to pawn off damaged goods on Pietro.

"Why doesn't Amosto dismiss the man?" Pietro said.

"What good would that do? It would only lend substance to the rumours and innuendos. No, it was a clever move on his part to pretend that nothing had happened. He will keep the man on for a while and carefully watch his every move, then send him away on some pretext or other."

"Or take Isolda away."

"No doubt that's the best thing he could do in the circumstances," Cigi said. "And when he comes back — if you are still interested in the daughter, that is — you should demand a large dowry to compensate for the rumours. It may turn out to be a lucrative settlement for you. I doubt the rumours will follow the young lady to Ferrara. You will be in the clear there. All in all, it's a prestigious match. Amosto's name is worth something, you know."

Pietro thanked the banker for his advice, but as he left, he put his hand to his chest, feeling the edges of Livia's book against the fabric of his jerkin. Her name counted for more with him than Amosto's.

The following day he received a note from Amosto. He had made arrangements for the family to depart for Bulicame in the morning and intended to stay there for a fortnight. Nothing more was said of drawing up a marriage contract.

CHAPTER 27

It was the end of October, and the nights had turned chilly. The rain was coming down steadily, lashing the cobblestones and enveloping the street in a curtain of mist. It was not a good day to go out, but Pietro was newly determined to pursue his business, or rather the Duke's business, and to call at the Cardinal's palace now that he knew the prelate had returned to Rome. The message he had left for him had never been answered, although he had inquired repeatedly, but he intended to try again.

He was pulling on his boots when the landlady knocked on his door and announced a visitor.

Pietro's eyes lit up with pleasure when he saw that it was Orazio Farnese.

"I was wondering what happened to your promised visit," he said, waving him in.

"My father found reasons to delay my journey. He doesn't like to see me go to Rome and waste my time and his money, as he puts it. — And how is your Roman mission going?"

"Not very well."

"Have you really come as the Duke's emissary or did you make that up on the spot?"

"Does it seem so unbelievable that I should be entrusted with a diplomatic task?"

"Depends on what the task is."

"To present a brief to the Pope."

"No reflection on your ability, Pietro, but if the Duke wanted to present a brief to the Pope, he could have channeled it through Cesare's brother Alessandro. Surely, that would have been more efficient. They say he is in line for a cardinal's hat. Why would the Duke not ask him to present that brief whatever it is and push his own case while he's at it? — How would you even go about obtaining an audience with the Pope?"

"Cardinal Gesualdo was to arrange it for me. The Duke gave me a letter of introduction to him."

"Ah. Cardinal Gesualdo. Then I take it the object is for you to spy on the old man and report back. Is that it?"

The two young men looked at each other, Orazio inquiring, Pietro caught out by the question and on the defensive. Yes, it was part of his mission to report on Gesualdo. Orazio had guessed rightly, and Pietro's stunned silence served only to confirm it. Orazio followed up his question with another.

"I suppose the Duke wants to know what the old man is doing to promote the cause of Ferrara at the papal court. Am I right?"

There was no use denying what Orazio knew already. Pietro gave him a probing look.

"How much do you know about the Duke's cause?"

"How much do I know? Everyone knows that Cesare d'Este wants to be the next Duke of Ferrara and has traded his sister for Gesualdo's good services. But will he be able to deliver the goods? And are you the man to find out?"

Pietro had asked himself the same question. Why send an unimportant man like him to Rome? He ventured an explanation.

"If the Duke wants to keep things confidential, sending Alessandro d'Este might be too conspicuous a move. I'm unimportant and may pass unsuspected."

"I doubt it," Orazio said. "My father at any rate suspected your business at once. And — have you seen Gesualdo?"

"Not yet."

"Not yet! What are you waiting for?"

Pietro hesitated. He liked to think of Orazio as a friend. Looking into his open face, he decided to trust him and disregard Cesare's warning about keeping his mouth shut. "The Cardinal was out of town. I left a note with the gatekeeper, but I am not sure it was delivered. The man did not show me much respect. Perhaps if I had dressed more elegantly or ridden a better horse-"

"Or tipped him more generously. How much did you slip him?"

170

When Pietro named the sum, Orazio threw up his hands in mock despair.

"Well, that explains it. You should have given him twice as much. He has to share the money with the Cardinal's valet, who is the essential link in passing on messages. I bet your message ended up in the gutter."

Pietro could not hide his embarrassment. "I should have known better," he said.

"I always try to keep on the good side of a man's servants," Orazio said. "They are familiar with their master's habits. They are aware of what's going on in his house. You never know what you might learn from them and what bits of information might turn out to be of advantage to you."

"I'll send another note."

"Why don't you take the bull by the horns? Present yourself at the Cardinal's door and ask to be announced. What have you got to lose? He may turn you away, or he may have nothing better to do and see you out of curiosity."

"When do you think is the best time to present myself?"

"No better time than now." Orazio pointed out the window. "Look at the dreary weather. The great man is probably sitting at home, twiddling his thumbs. Let's go. I'll join you. I'd like to meet the old roué and see whether the stories circulating about him are true."

"What stories?"

"I'll tell you after we've seen him. You are booted and spurred, I see. Ready to go?"

The Cardinal's palace was in the Via del Corso. As they came up to the guard house, Orazio took the lead. He rode by the gatekeeper without deigning to give him a glance and stopped only in the courtyard. There he dismounted and with a nod gave Pietro to understand that a tip was wanted by the lad who stepped up to take their horses away. The two young men mounted the stone steps to the grand entrance, an oaken door flanked by marble pillars. The valet who received them in the hall inquired after their business. Orazio explained their purpose, passing a coin into the man's hand so discreetly that it seemed a sleight of hand.

There is a man worth watching, Pietro thought, observing Orazio's effortless superiority — the self-possession and sense of entitlement that comes with pedigree, with being a Farnese, he thought.

"Announce us to His Eminence," Orazio said. "Pietro Paci from the court of Ferrara and Orazio Farnese of Orvieto at his service."

He dispatched the valet with this message, treating him as if he was of no more importance than a tray bearing a note.

"So far so good," he said when the man had left, "but we may be stuck here."

They looked around the elegantly furnished waiting room, decorated with Spanish leather hangings and exquisite paintings.

"And what do we do if we are rebuffed?"

"Not to worry. Now that the valet's nose has caught the scent of money, we may rely on him to present our request again at a more opportune time."

They did not have to put Orazio's theory to the test. The valet returned with a summons to present themselves to the Cardinal.

They entered the audience room through a door hung with red velvet. The walls were covered with finely woven tapestries depicting a hunt. Gesualdo awaited them. He was sitting on a throne-like chair, which had been placed on a dais against the backdrop of rich drapery. The two men advanced, their steps ringing on the inlaid marble floor. Gesualdo rose and held out his hand to be kissed — a beautiful white hand adorned with rings of ruby and turquoise set in gold. The scent of citrus and jasmine oils filled Pietro's nose as he bent over the prelate's hand.

The Cardinal was an old man, but he carried his years well. His dark eyes retained a sparkle of youth, and a well-trimmed beard camouflaged his sagging chin.

"I expected your visit," he said to Pietro. A faint smile was playing on his lips as if he was secretly amused at seeing him in the audience room. He turned to Orazio next. "And I am pleased to make your acquaintance." He contemplated the young man's face and figure. "They say that the Farnese men are without exception handsome, and I see you prove them right."

Orazio bowed in acknowledgement of the compliment.

"What can I do for you, gentlemen?" the Cardinal said, all shallow smiles.

Pietro explained that he had come in the hope that His Eminence would arrange an audience for him with the Pope. It was his intention to present a brief to His Holiness.

The Cardinal regarded him steadily. "Ah, yes," he said. "The brief. The Duke mentioned it in a letter to me."

Under the Cardinal's probing look, Pietro felt beads of sweat forming on his brow. Coals were glowing in a brazier to take the chill and damp out of the air, but it was not only the closeness of the room that made him uncomfortably hot. It was the sense of inferiority which had overcome him, facing the Cardinal in his full regalia. He wore a red skullcap, a cassock trimmed with scarlet, and a matching cape open at the neck and showing the top of a linen shirt. A wide purple sash gathered the folds of his floor-length soutane.

Pietro shrunk under the Cardinal's eye. He was unsure whether he had used the right phrases and worried that he had been too direct in his approach.

"As for arranging an audience with His Holiness," the Cardinal said, keeping his watchful eyes trained on Pietro. "I don't know how long that will take. It can't be done on the spur of a moment. His Holiness is not in the best of health, you know, but we shall see —"

Pietro thought he heard a note of weariness in his voice. The interview was going badly. He gave the great man a resigned bow.

"We are presuming on Your Eminence's time," Orazio put in.

"Not at all," the Cardinal said. His voice recovered its cordial tone. He stroked the large cross dangling from a chain of gold, which adorned the front of his cassock like a crest. "I hope you will not deprive me of your company after so brief an acquaintance and will honour me with your presence at table. I am in the habit of foregoing breakfast and eating my midday meal at an early hour, an unfashionably early hour, I'm afraid. In fact, the table is being set as we speak."

Orazio thanked him for his gracious invitation.

"Nothing would give us more pleasure than joining Your Eminence," he said, and Pietro echoed his words.

The Cardinal gave directions to his valet to show the visitors to his private dining room. "I shall meet you there shortly," he said, and put out his hand once more as if he wanted to bless them before retreating from the room.

Orazio cast a triumphant look at Pietro as the servant conducted them upstairs and ushered them into the Cardinal's dining room. It was furnished with the same sumptuous taste as the rooms they had seen earlier. The chairs were covered with purple brocade and fringed in gold. The table was laid with three cloths, one on top of the other, to cushion the fine china and crystal settings.

In due course, the Cardinal entered, followed by a slim youth of delicate features whose long hair was bleached to the colour of wheat. He wore tight breeches and hose that showed his calves to advantage. The short, belted tunic of yellow velvet matched the velvet uppers of his shoes. He looked no older than sixteen, but was introduced by the Cardinal as his secretary, Ricardo Ascone.

They took their seats, the Cardinal at the head of the table, Ricardo next to him. The youth took off his tunic and slung it negligently over the back of his chair, revealing a doublet of leonine orange with studded silk knots, and a satin shirt with embroidered frills at the neck and wrists. His eyes rested, first on Orazio, then on Pietro. At last he wiggled his shoulders and sighed with resignation as if attendance at the meal was a great sacrifice on his part.

After the Cardinal had said grace, a servant brought in basins to wash their hands. The servers placed a plate before each diner and beside it a starched napkin, silver cutlery and bread. Next, they set out carafes of wine edged with silver together with small pitchers of water for mixing, as was the general custom. A carver went to work on a roast fowl waiting on the sideboard, and the servants handed out portions stuffed with almonds, arranging them deftly on the plates.

Pietro, who had been primed by observing the customs in Amosto's house, knew that in these hallowed halls no one ever touched food with their hands or shared their portion, as was done in the hinterland of his parents' home. Here the meal seemed to be a sacred rite with each course presented reverently and with close attention to form and elegance.

The Cardinal asked about Pietro's journey, and he told his story in amusing anecdotes while Orazio took up the tale of the battle with Sciarra. The Cardinal listened with interest.

"Sciarra!" he said, "God's scourge, or to give him the name he has chosen for himself, the scourge of usurers! He pretends to be a friend of the poor, and for all I know he may be the gallant gentleman of lore who leaves his victims half their money, but his followers are barbarians, or rather animals. They make no difference between high and low when it comes to cutting throats. You were lucky to escape with your life, my friend, although I hear the robbers were routed in that particular engagement."

A lively discussion followed about the brutal methods of the robber baron and the best way of ridding the country of this pest. The secretary never opened his mouth except once, to yawn broadly. The Cardinal gave him an indulgent smile.

"My dear Ricardo," he said, "I know I have kept you up very late last night, and you've worn your fingers to the bone working

174

for me, so I am not surprised to see you fatigued. Perhaps you would like to withdraw?"

The youth promptly rose. "If you don't mind, Your Eminence, I'll retire. Gentlemen—" He nodded curtly to the company, scraped back his chair, and left, not without smoothing down his hair and checking his profile in the mirror on the way out.

A smile lingered on the Cardinal's face as he looked after the receding figure.

"Ah, youth!" he said. "I have pledged myself to Ricardo's father and promised on his deathbed to make something of his whelp, although at times it looks as if I may not be able to fulfil my promise. Poor Ricardo. He can't be tamed."

"Lion tamers use the whip to good effect," Orazio said, looking straight at the Cardinal.

Pietro held his breath, but the prelate did not seem to take offence.

"Some men are inclined to use force," he said without raising his voice or betraying any annoyance. "You are a soldier, my friend, and inured to cruelty perhaps. I am too soft-hearted to resort to harsh means. I believe in returning wild things to their natural habitat and allowing them to follow their inclinations. As much as it pains me, I may have to let Ricardo go. — But to return to our subject, which is not entirely unrelated, for Sciarra too is a wild man."

"And has returned to his natural milieu — the battleground," Orazio said.

"So I have heard. It appears he got away and is now in negotiation with the Venetians, who are looking for a man to do battle for them against the pirates in the Adriatic Sea."

Pietro was amazed. "The Venetians would hire a notorious criminal like Sciarra?"

"Who can offer better qualifications for the job?"

"And so he is to be rewarded for his crimes with a lucrative contract?"

"I am afraid so."

"At least His Holiness the Pope can take satisfaction from the fact that he rid himself of that lawless band."

"I am not so sure of that. My informants tell me that Sciarra has left his brother behind as a deputy, who will rally his old companions and continue the extortions."

"And Venice does not fear the wrath of Rome when they favour a man who has done His Holiness great injury?" Pietro asked, hoping to impress the Cardinal with his concern for the pope's interests.

"Venice has sided with the enemy before, unlike loyal Ferrara — as you demonstrate in your brief, or so I am told," Gesualdo said, smiling his sphinx' smile.

The dinner passed pleasantly in this fashion, but Pietro felt that he had gotten no hold on the Cardinal. His talk was like the plashing of a fountain that leaves no permanent impression in the pool below. The drops hit the water and cause a ripple, which flattens out again. The Cardinal's conversation was like that. He referred to the murderous deeds of Sciarra, to the misbehavior of his little secretary, and to Pietro's brief all in the same light tone of amusement, as if he had no hope of changing anything and indeed, no preference for one thing over another.

Pietro felt there was a great deal going on behind the scenes of the Cardinal's words. He made every phrase do double duty, in its straight sense and in a second, more elusive meaning. A courtier's business was slippery, he thought and asked himself, not for the first time, whether he was sly enough for that profession. In the end, however, it appeared that he had achieved something to the purpose. When the Cardinal bid them farewell, he asked Pietro to return in a week's time, when he hoped to have news for him concerning an audience with the pope.

CHAPTER 28

It had stopped raining when the two friends left the Cardinal's palace, but the sky was the colour of lead and threatened another downpour.

"Well, now you can tell me what they say about the Cardinal and whether you think it is true," Pietro said as they turned from the Via del Corso into a quiet street too narrow for wagons and carts.

Orazio gave him an amused look. "Surely you can judge for yourself. You've seen that jackanapes of a 'secretary', as he calls his *fanciullo*. Did you see how he opened his jerkin to display his codpiece? That's all the proof I needed to make up my mind about the rumours. The Cardinal has a taste for young men."

"Then you don't believe the story he told us about his pledge to Ricardo's late father. Is it only camouflage?"

"A transparent lie, but at least he keeps up appearances, which is more than can be said for some men I know who kiss and fondle their catamites in public."

"Then the outrageous tale I have heard about two men getting married in church is true?"

"The two Spaniards you mean? It's true but it happened some years ago."

"And so you would not be shocked, as I was the other day, when I heard a man say that his tastes vary with the seasons. The whores stink in the heat of summer, he said. By August he found them unbearable and was obliged to resort to boys prettified and dressed up in a girl's finery. They are the next best thing to women, he told me without a blush."

Orazio shrugged. "Indeed it has become fashionable in certain circles to keep company with young men, and the theme of boyish lovers is all the rage in the decorative arts. I should get you an invitation to my uncle's palace. The ceiling in his great hall has been decorated by Annibale Carracci and depicts the rape of Ganymede. The scene has been much admired by his guests."

They rode on in silence. Pietro thought of the question Orazio had raised earlier about his mission: why was Pietro sent to Rome when there were men here more experienced and more capable of accomplishing the task. The truth dawned on him. It was not because he was too unimportant to attract attention. It was on the off chance that he might attract the attention of the Cardinal, catch the old man's fancy and gain some influence over him or at least pry valuable information out of him. Was this Cesare's revenge for getting in his way and rescuing Livia? Or merely his idea of a cruel joke?

He turned to Orazio. "I wonder," he said. "Did the Duke send me as bait for the old lecher?"

Orazio gave him a telling look. "The idea crossed my mind, too. They sent you to spy on the Cardinal, but he is an old fox and won't tell you anything unless he loses his head. Some men become slaves to their lovers, but he is too smart for that, and too calculating, if you ask me."

"And I don't think I've caught his eye," Pietro said.

Orazio laughed. "No," he said. "Your skin is too rough and your shoulders too broad. No, you won't do as a lover boy."

"Then why did he invite me back?"

"You will find out, no doubt. He may be putting on a show of power or good will, but he can't be of service to the House of Este and won't be able to pull the wool over their eyes much longer. The days when he was a voice of authority at the papal court are over. He was a man of influence under Pope Innocent when he was Dean of the College of Cardinals, but he is not in favour with the present pope. That's why he was named Archbishop of Naples earlier this year — to get him out of the way. So far he has managed to hold on to his Roman quarters, but your master, the Duke, will have to start over again with his campaign to have the law of succession changed. The thing is to find out who will be appointed cardinal next. The pope has a dozen names on his list, including Alessandro d'Este. His promotion would of course be a boon to

Ferrara's cause, but being on the list does not mean much. It's like being shown the last will of a man who is still alive and may alter it any time and in any way he wants."

They reached Pietro's lodging and came to a halt. It had begun to drizzle again, and the moisture covered the mane of their horses like beaded silver.

"Don't go away yet," Pietro said. "We have talked a great deal about my affairs, and it's good to listen to someone who is in the know and not afraid to speak his mind. Everyone else has been talking to me in riddles, giving me a hint here and a pointer there, but always stopping short of the whole story. Listening to you has been an eye-opener. But now let's talk about your affairs. Tell me what you're up to."

The maid took away their coats to be brushed and dried by the fire, and when they were comfortably settled in Pietro's room, Orazio said:

"My affairs can be summed up in a few words: I intend to go to Naples and offer my services to Count Olivares."

"I thought all the gentlemen in the Viceroy's court are Spaniards."

"I have no ambition to join his court. I intend to enlist in his army."

"So you haven't lost your taste for fighting, and the battle with Sciarra has not discouraged you from a military career?"

"What other career is open to second sons? My brother will inherit our estate, such as it is — for I will not conceal from you what is well-known already. We are burdened with debt, yet my father is unwilling to change his ways and will go on in the grand style to which he has become accustomed."

"Second sons usually pursue a career in the church, and there are illustrious examples in your family."

"No, a career in the church does not suit me. Nature has made me a soldier. I rode into the battle against Sciarra with a sense of destiny, with a sense of fulfilling my mission in life. I will always be a soldier, and there will always be wars. The thing is to find a worthy opponent. Princes change sides, alliances are made and broken again. In other words, the paymaster may change, the cause may change, but the name you make for yourself by showing skill and courage in battle will stay with you."

"And Naples offers you a worthy opponent?"

"That is my hope. I much regret that I was too young to fight by the side of my uncle, Alessandro Farnese, when he was regent of the Netherlands and put down the Dutch revolt. Now *there* was a good paymaster and a cause worth fighting for. Those men fought for their beliefs!"

"And Naples? The Habsburgs are keeping a tight leash on the territory, I know, and the place is rife with unrest. But is the Neapolitan mob an enemy to your taste?"

"You are thinking of what happened ten years ago, when the mob lynched Vincenzo Starache. The situation is different now. I grant you the people who killed Starache acted no better than wolves when they castrated his dead body, dragged it naked through the streets and dumped it on the steps of the Viceregal palace. Of course, Starache was an animal himself, the lowest of the low, a grain speculator. So, to answer your question: No, there was no honour in fighting Sciarra's band of robbers and there would be no honour in fighting an unruly mob, but the revolution threatening Naples now is different. It is led by a philosopher, Tommaso Campanella, and his followers will be fighting for a principle, for freedom and equality. It may be a crazy idea that every citizen should have the same rights and that there should be no distinction between commoners and noblemen, but it is at any rate an idea that is driving them rather than the desire to fill their stomachs or their purses. The fear that Campanella will stir up the people has prompted the Viceroy to take precautions and hire soldiers."

"All very well, Orazio, but I wouldn't risk my life in any war, however respectable the cause. I am a man of peace. Diplomacy is where I mean to make my mark." Pietro stopped when he saw the look on Orazio's face. He was curling his lip in disgust.

"What!" Pietro said. "Is a career at court so unpalatable to you?"

Orazio lowered his eyes and shrugged. He stretched his long legs and leaned back as if to say: Your aspirations are none of my business.

"Do you think so little of a career at court?" Pietro insisted. He wanted an explanation for the disdain he had seen in Orazio's eyes.

"Perhaps you can turn that career into something worthwhile," Orazio said, "but most courtiers are nothing but lickspittles and yes-men. It's in the nature of the job. Diplomacy is a pretty word, but what does it mean? Lies and intrigues. Glib talk and playing games with people's minds. That is the essence of diplomacy, and a courtier is nothing but a privileged lackey."

"You could argue about soldiering in the same way," Pietro said. "You speak of courage and honour, but war isn't a game of chivalry. You are making a romance of it. If you take a closer look, soldiering comes down to killing your fellow man. Diplomacy seems benign by comparison. And as you said yourself, a man who does not inherit wealth has few choices. Enter the church. Enter the military. Become a courtier —" He paused and laughed ruefully. "Or marry a rich woman."

Orazio joined in the laughter. "And — will you become a courtier or marry a rich woman?"

"I was about to take the second route, but it didn't come off. The Duke of Ferrara recommended me to a man who made his fortune at the papal court. He was prepared to accept me as his son-in-law, but there was a reason for his willingness to consider a penniless suitor. The reputation of his daughter is compromised, as I discovered."

"You should have bargained for a larger dowry."

"I could not love the lady."

"We have debunked the lives of soldiers and courtiers. Why not take a cold look at marriage as well? You talk of love, but that is a romantic conceit. Marriage is a business proposal."

"If you can say that, Orazio, you have never been in love."

"And you have?"

"I am in love, and have decided that the lady of my heart is worth more to me than money, and more than a career at court, but I fear I have spoiled my chances with her."

It was not until Pietro said it out loud that the half-formed thoughts in his head came together. It had been a mistake to put his career above his feelings. His love for Livia was irrepressible. He could never be happy without her. Was it too late to reverse the course?

"You *fear* you have spoiled your chances, but you aren't sure? Then why not ask the lady and find out?" Orazio said.

Pietro looked at him like a man awakened by a trumpet blast.

"You are right," he said. "I will ask her."

The love poem he had written for Livia was still between the pages of the book. He would send it to her this very day and ask her pardon for being a fool and letting her depart for Gesualdo without a commitment.

Orazio caught his distracted look. "I see you have grave matters on your mind," he said smiling. "I will take my leave, then. Good luck in the battle for your lady's heart."

"And good luck to you in Naples."

The friends parted with a warm embrace and the assurance that they would keep in touch. An hour later, Pietro was on his way to the banker, who received and dispatched messages every day and had conveyed his letters to Ferrara on other occasions. Pietro had written two letters, one to Livia in Gesualdo, asking her to forgive his foolishness and become his wife, and another to Cesare d'Este in Ferrara, describing his meeting with the Cardinal and adding the insights he had gained from Orazio. The Cardinal was no longer at the peak of his power, he wrote. However, Pietro expected to obtain an audience with the pope the following week and hoped to present his essay to His Holiness at long last and to good effect.

Cigi looked at the two letters Pietro handed him.

"A letter to a lady at the court of the Prince of Venosa?" he said. "Has Don Cesare broadened the range of your mission?"

Pietro was not fast enough to wipe a certain hue of embarrassment from his face, but he quickly recovered and met the banker's inquiring eye with a steady reply: "Broadened? No. The actions of the Gesualdos — uncle and nephew—have always been at the centre of his interest."

Cigi gave him a long look from under his brows, but asked no further questions. Pietro could tell that he had not convinced the banker of the official nature of his letter and regretted that he had not made an effort to find a messenger of his own. But where would a stranger in Rome find a reliable messenger to a place that was not on the main road to Naples, but required a side trip?

CHAPTER 29

A week later Pietro presented himself at Cardinal Gesualdo's palace, as requested. His business there no longer seemed as urgent as it had been when he was eager to climb the diplomatic ladder. His career was in Livia's hands now. The letter had been dispatched, and he was waiting for her reply, waiting for a sign to direct his future. Would she take him back or dismiss him? How the balance of his life had shifted! He was a disinterested observer of Roman affairs now. The importance he had attached to his essay, his eagerness to hand it to the Pope — an action to which he had attributed symbolic significance as the inauguration of his diplomatic career — all those hopes and expectations struck him as faintly ridiculous now. If a man of the Cardinal's stature did not have the ear of the Pope and, according to Orazio, was in no position to help the cause of Ferrara, what difference could his own paltry rhetorical composition make? Politics moved in an atmosphere more rarified than common mortals breathed, he thought. He was more convinced than ever that Cesare had not sent him to Rome as a favour, to help him along in his career. Cesare was a man who took pleasure in the troubles of others. He had sent him to Rome out of spite, to humiliate and ridicule him, to set him up as a prey to the lecherous Cardinal and a dupe to Amosto, whose daughter would marry him only to make a cuckold of him. Yet when the Cardinal sent him a note that an audience had been arranged, Pietro decided to take advantage of the opportunity to speak to the Pope. He had composed a brief. He might as well deliver it to His Holiness. And he was curious to see the august head of Christendom with his own eyes. The chance would not come his way again.

He presented himself at the Cardinal's palace at the appointed time and was conducted to His Eminence's study. He found the prelate at his desk, writing.

He put down the pen and gave Pietro a welcoming smile.

"You see me reduced to writing my own letters," he said. "I had to dismiss Ricardo. Poor child. Nature has been a stepmother to him, making him neither patient nor submissive, qualities essential to a man in his station of life. He will pay dearly for his shortcomings."

"I am sorry to hear it," Pietro said, unsure what to make of this piece of information.

The Cardinal rose from his desk. "Perhaps you could help me out," he said. "My fingers are going numb from holding the pen. Be good enough to complete this draft for me. It is addressed to your patron, Don Cesare, and you might as well be apprised of what I have to say to him."

Pietro bowed and sat down on the chair vacated by the Cardinal. The sheet before him was empty except for the words "Honoured sir!"

The Cardinal walked up and down the room as if to gather his thoughts and began his dictation:

"To answer your inquiry about Pietro Paci: I find him a most pleasant young man with a ready tongue and an open face, too open perhaps, but experience will temper that fault. I have arranged for an audience with His Holiness the Pope and hope the essay prepared by your emissary will have the desired effect. You inquire about my affairs at the papal court, and I can only answer you with sighs. I thought I had seen the worst at the conclave in which we elected that cunning snake, Sixtus. He made us believe that he was as dumb as an ox and as easily led. He pretended to be riddled with disease and suffering from the infirmities of old age, and acted like a man with one foot in the grave. That's why we voted for him, why we made him pope, I won't deny it. We thought we had a man after our taste, a man we could easily control. But as soon as he had the requisite number of votes, he jumped up like the proverbial cripple in the Bible, threw away the staff he had used as a crutch, and straightened up —"

The Cardinal waited for Pietro to catch up. What a strange letter, Pietro thought, and what an astounding piece of information, but he was hard pressed to keep up with the speed of the prelate's dictation and had no time to dwell much on the content.

"I could see that Sixtus was going to make fools and asses of us, once he was pope. The next day he invited us to a banquet, at which he ate heartily. I gave him a sarcastic smile and said: 'Yesterday you weren't feeling so well.' And the Pope answered me smartly: 'Yesterday I wasn't pope.' So we were stuck with him until, thank God, he succumbed to malaria. Then came a whole series of short-lived popes, and now we are saddled with Clement who has shown no inclination to favour Ferrara —"

The Cardinal stopped pacing the room. His valet had appeared at the door to announce that His Eminence's horse was saddled and waiting in the courtyard.

"Then we shall finish the letter another time," the Cardinal said to Pietro. "It would not do to keep His Holiness waiting."

Pietro sprinkled sand over the lines he had written.

The Cardinal came around the desk and peered at the sheet.

"You write a neat hand," he said. "Perhaps you would like to take Ricardo's place in my household. You strike me as an eminently qualified scribe." He placed his hand on Pietro's shoulder and rubbed it. Pietro turned cold.

"I am grateful for your Eminence's offer and touched by your trust in me, but I regret I cannot remain in Rome much longer. Family affairs oblige me to return to Ferrara."

"Ah, of course," the Cardinal said mildly. "Don Cesare intimated as much in his last letter to me."

What, exactly, had Cesare intimated? Pietro wondered.

"And what would you like me to do with the unfinished letter?" he asked the Cardinal. "Shall I leave it on your desk?"

"Tear it up, my boy. Tear it up. It is much too candid, come to think of it, and candor is a fault to be avoided at all costs. Let this be a lesson to you. If ever you get carried away, as I did just now, do not entrust your thoughts to paper. Letters are intercepted all the time. There are curious eyes everywhere."

Pietro was about to tear up the sheet, when the Cardinal held up his hand.

"Wait. On second thought, place it on the coals in the brazier. Ashes to ashes, as the Bible says."

Pietro did as instructed and followed the prelate out into the courtyard. They mounted their horses and, with the Cardinal's outriders clearing the way for them, rode to the Vatican.

Leaving their horses with the servants in the courtyard, they entered the pope's residence. It was as grand as Pietro had expected. Great works of art and elaborate furnishings met the eye everywhere. The décor was exquisite. Even in the entrance hall there was no shortage of marble and gold leaf ornaments, crystal chandeliers and door panels carved of exotic wood. If the Pope respected the ideal of clerical poverty, he was restricting it to the spiritual kind.

The two men were greeted by the papal chamberlain and admitted to the audience room, where Pope Clement received them clothed in the splendor of his regalia. He was seated on a throne covered in red velvet and edged with gold. The Cardinal doffed his skull cap and took up station by the side of the Holy Father. No one's head remained covered in the presence of the Pope, not even that of a prelate of the Church.

Pietro, following the instructions of the chamberlain, took a step into the chamber, kneeled down and waited for the pope to give him benediction. When the Cardinal motioned for him to come closer, Pietro approached reverently. He stopped half way to kneel again and receive a second benediction before crossing the room to the edge of the carpet laid at the foot of the pope's throne. According to protocol, he kneeled down humbly on both knees. As in a well-rehearsed ballet, the Cardinal stepped forward and slightly lifted the pope's robe to reveal his right foot, shod in a red slipper decorated with a white cross. Now it was Pietro's move again. He slid forward on his knees, bent low and kissed the holy foot. The Cardinal draped the robe over the slipper again, straightened up and introduced Pietro to His Holiness. He explained that the young man was the archivist of the Duke of Ferrara and the author of the essay presented to him — he pointed to the vellum copy now sitting on a small table beside the papal throne.

Pietro had carefully rehearsed the answers to the questions he expected the Pope to ask about his essay, but His Holiness thanked him without saying a word about the booklet or the cause of Ferrara. Instead he offered the kind of admonition one might hear at a Sunday sermon. He exhorted Pietro to be loyal to God and his church and to devote his life to virtue and charity. Pietro responded with a promise to do so, bowing deeply. He received another blessing, and that was the end of the audience. On a sign from the Cardinal, Pietro rose and retreated in the order in which he had entered, going backward, so as not to show the pope his back. At the door, he kneeled for a last benediction and shuffled out the door.

Pietro had expected the audience to be the highlight of his mission to Rome, the culmination of his visit, but it turned out to be no more than an empty ceremony. No doubt his essay, the fruit of his researches, was destined to be stowed away unread. Pietro's shoulders slumped. Fatigue overcame him, as if he had done a day's hard labour working the oars in a galley.

In a little while, the Cardinal joined him in the hall.

"You have acquitted yourself well," he said amiably.

"But to what purpose?" Pietro said. "Do you think His Holiness will deign to read my essay?"

"Ah, you lead me into temptation to speak candidly again," the Cardinal said, "and I am too weak to resist a young man of your parts. To speak the truth, then, I believe His Holiness will ask one of his secretaries to read your work and enter it in the catalogue of documents with a one-line notation describing its contents. — And now you owe me a candid reply in return. How do you like your master, Don Cesare?"

Pietro, however, knew better than to blurt out what he thought of his patron.

"Everyone admires his strong will and determination," he said. "No doubt Don Cesare has the qualities required in a ruler."

"To be feared rather than loved, you mean? — for that is how Machiavelli put it in his manual for princes."

"That was not my meaning," Pietro said. "Nor do I think that popular opinion is the measure of a good ruler."

"Shrewdly answered, my friend. But what you call strong will and determination, I am inclined to call lack of scruples. And I have heard that Don Cesare is apt to play cruel tricks on his enemies."

"Then I shall take great care not get on his wrong side."

"I may not have given you enough credit for prudence, young man. Either that, or you are a fast learner and have absorbed the first rule of diplomacy — discretion."

"Your Eminence is too kind."

The Cardinal eyed him curiously. "I am told that Don Cesare's brother, Alessandro d'Este, has arrived in Rome. Has he been in touch with you?"

This was news to Pietro. "No, I have had no message from him."

"How very odd. You would think he'd contact his brother's emissary. I understood from Don Cesare's letter that his brother will be promoting the cause of Ferrara, continuing your good work, if I may put it that way." The Cardinal gave Pietro an ironic smile, for surely it was a joke to compare the reach of Alessandro d'Este with that of a young archivist.

"And so my mission has run its course," Pietro said, as they walked back through the corridors and down the curved staircase to the main entrance.

The Cardinal was no longer smiling. "Very likely," he said. "But if you find yourself out of a job, which can happen to the worthiest of men, my offer stands, you know. You are welcome to join my household." Once again the Cardinal rested his hand on Pietro's shoulder, kneading it gently.

"You are putting me under a great obligation, Your Eminence," Pietro said stiffly. "I very much regret that I must decline your generous offer for the reasons I mentioned earlier. The affairs of my family require my presence at home."

The Cardinal released his shoulder and walked on. "Then I wish you luck in your endeavours," he said.

Pietro bowed. They reached the courtyard of the papal palace. A servant helped the Cardinal into the saddle, and the great man followed his outriders through the gate, turning around once and raising his hand to Pietro in a genial farewell.

Alessandro d'Este in Rome? Pietro pondered the news as he was riding back to his own lodgings. Alessandro was Leonora's and Cesare's half-brother, born of their father's concubine. He was intended for a career in the church, but he loved pleasure too much. As a youth he led a dissolute life, dressed extravagantly, surrounded himself with a shiftless crowd of loafers, and fathered a number of illegitimate children. Pietro had seen Alessandro only once, at Donna Leonora's wedding feast. He had sown his wild oats, it was said, and buckled down to do his duty, promoting the family interests. Thirty years old, he was a man to be reckoned with in diplomatic circles. He retained his worldly spirit, however, and refused to be ordained, putting off that evil day as long as he could. So far there had been no need to abandon his freedom and be shackled by vows. He was clever enough to maneuver into a position of power and obtain the provostship of the Abbey of Pomposa without taking his vows. The Church bends its rules for the rich and powerful! Pietro thought. And now Alessandro was in Rome, still a layman, still enjoying the life of a bachelor, while lobbying for a cardinal's hat — or so Orazio said. Of course Alessandro was not the first man to hedge his bets and delay his ordination until he was assured of a lucrative career in the church.

Until then he left his options open. If the church could not provide for him, an heiress would. He had the Este name to offer after all. Other men had refused to make a commitment one way or another, and were ordained only after obtaining a cardinal's hat. He was determined to hold out as well. It was all a question of spending money in the right places and cultivate the right connections. He had come to Rome first and foremost to promote his election to the cardinalate, but of course he would also use the occasion to lobby for his brother's succession to the duchy of Ferrara.

In the circumstances, Pietro was surprised that Cesare had not recalled him. There was nothing more for him to do in Rome. His mission was over, and the feeling of uselessness weighed on Pietro's shoulders. Nevertheless he sat down after returning to his lodgings and dutifully wrote a report about his audience with the pope. It was a short letter since there was nothing of substance to report. The audience had followed the usual routine and was therefore of no interest to Cesare. The essay Pietro had considered so incisive a few weeks ago, would be instantly forgotten. What was memorable to him, could not be reported to Cesare: the astonishing candor of the Cardinal when he dictated to him his so-called letter, and the revelation that it had been only a lesson in diplomacy and calculated to make him feel like an inexperienced fool. There was a great deal Pietro suppressed in his own letter to Cesare, including the Cardinal's offer of employment and his reaction to the old man's hand on his shoulder. The very memory of the soft, caressing fingers made him shiver.

The following morning Pietro went to Cigi to have his letter delivered to Cesare and to replenish his supply of ready cash.

The banker took his letter and counted out the money Pietro had asked for.

"I was about to send for you," he said. "This is the last instalment of funds I am holding in your name. I have had a message from the Right Reverend Provost, Alessandro d'Este. He asked me to settle your bill of lodging. He wants you to pack up here and present yourself at the Villa d'Este in Tivoli, where he is staying at the moment."

"I have heard of His Reverend's arrival," Pietro said, "and take it that my assignment is at an end."

"Your assignment in Rome at any rate," Cigi said. The tone of his voice was not quite as hearty as it had been in their earlier conversations.

"I suppose he will send me back to Ferrara."

"He did not say."

"And how am I supposed to get back to Ferrara?"

The banker did not meet Pietro's eyes. "I assume the Reverend Provost will look after you needs," he said in a reserved tone, then added almost as an afterthought: "But you should speak to Messer Amosto before you go."

"I'm afraid that business is over."

"I see," Cigi said and looked at him thoughtfully. He came around his desk and put a fatherly hand on Pietro's shoulder. "Well, I for one like a man who guards his honour and won't allow himself to be bought with a dowry. Integrity is a rare thing in our time, but it doesn't pay. So, let me say: If you find yourself in dire straits, I am willing to make you a small loan. It will have to be a very small sum because I can't expect to be repaid by your master. Cesare is a hard man, you know."

"I do know," Pietro said, "and I appreciate your kindness all the more, Messer Cigi."

The two men shook hands, and Pietro took his leave.

When he arrived at his lodgings, he found the maid folding up his clothes.

"The mistress told me that you are leaving, sir," she said with a dimpled smile. She did not hold out her palm, but it was clear that she expected a tip, and Pietro who had lately felt a great shortness of friendly smiles, obliged. He put a coin into her hand.

"And do I get a kiss of thanks in return?" he said.

She blushed very prettily, stood on her toes and pressed her lips against his cheek. He would have liked to put his arm around her and feel the fullness of her round breasts, but the thought of Livia arrested his hand. He meant to be true to her from now on. Such frivolities would have to stop.

"The ostler wants to know when he should bring around your horse tomorrow morning," the maid said.

"After breakfast."

"After breakfast," she echoed, curtsied and escaped, leaving Pietro to ponder his situation. Why did Alessandro d'Este wish to see him? For a debriefing? Hardly. Pietro was a novice in the game of politics. No doubt the Reverend Provost had his ear to the ground and knew more than Pietro could ever hope to discover. He speculated that Alessandro had an assignment for him. Otherwise, Cesare would simply have recalled him to Ferrara. He wished he was not so completely dependent on the purse of his master! If he was his own man, he would strike out for Gesualdo at once. He wondered whether Livia had received his contrite letter by now. For an impatient lover, a letter was too slow a means of communication. How much better it would be if he could present himself in person, ask Livia's forgiveness on bended knees and be rewarded on the spot with a smile and a kiss. Or not. She may never forgive me for callously sacrificing her to my ambition, he thought. In that case he was not anxious for a fast reply to his letter!

CHAPTER 30

The next morning, Pietro set out earlier. The Villa d'Este was a five-hour ride from Rome. Entering by the main gate leading into the grounds, Pietro was amazed at the grandeur of the building and the intricate design of the garden surrounding it. Standing in the elegant loggia that formed the entrance to the palace, he looked down on the tiered fountains, the white gravel paths crisscrossing the lawn, and the flowerbeds arranged in a semi-circle like a great amphitheatre.

The Provost, he was informed, would receive him in half an hour. In the meantime he was free to roam the grounds. He passed a pair of marble dragons spouting jets of water and a water organ emitting eerie sounds. At the far end of the garden he saw a fashionable couple with a small child. The mother held the little girl up to a vase overflowing with water and allowed her to dip in her little fingers and splash her father. He snatched up her hand and laughed good-naturedly. It looked like a happy family outing to Pietro. As he drew nearer, however, he recognized the gentleman. It was Alessandro d'Este. He had grown a raffish moustache turned up at the ends. The dark curly hair framing his narrow face made his long nose appear even longer.

The scene was too domestic for a man who wanted to be made a cardinal, Pietro thought and retreated. What he had seen was another confirmation that the Church of Rome had sadly declined from the apostolic ideal. He turned back to the Villa and sat in the reception room, already crowded with petitioners seeking an audience with the Provost. He was kept waiting for more than an hour before being called up and conducted to an inner chamber.

There he found Alessandro d'Este sprawled behind his desk in a posture of boredom. He nodded to Pietro and crooked two fingers of his hand to signal the secretary standing behind him. The man leaned forward with a respectful bow.

"Pietro Paci," he read off the list in his hand, "come to take instructions."

"Ah, yes, my brother's emissary," the Provost said with an ironic gleam in his eye. "You are the man who warned us of Cardinal Gesualdo's fall from power." He barely suppressed a derisive laugh. "You told us that the Cardinal will no longer be able to promote the cause of Ferrara. Very perspicacious of you."

"I hope my service has been satisfactory," Pietro said. He was stung by the sarcastic tone of the Provost and afraid of what was to follow. He remembered Cigi's ominous words "if you find yourself in dire straits" — would Cesare leave him stranded? Was his cruelty not sated by sending him on a fool's errand and promoting a marriage that could only shame him?

The Provost cleared his throat. "My brother's trust in you has no limits, it appears. He wants you to go to Naples and give us a report on the Prince of Venosa, who is currently residing in that city."

Pietro's heart began to race and his mind went from dejection to hope. Naples! Livia only a day's ride away! Or perhaps even *in* Naples if her mistress had accompanied the Prince! Although that was unlikely. Leonora must be close to giving birth by now.

"Let's hope you'll bring your perspicacious mind to bear on the situation there and spot the signs," the Provost said.

"I shall do my upmost to justify the trust Don Cesare put in me, but I would be grateful for more detailed instructions. Is there anything in particular I should watch for?"

"I can't imagine why Cesare places such confidence in you if you need everything spelled out," the Provost drawled. "Ingratiate yourself with the Prince and keep your eyes open. They say he is an excellent huntsman and a great lover of music, if I recall correctly. Do you know anything about horses? Do you play any instruments?"

"I am afraid I'm no expert in either field."

"Now I'm really baffled. What was Cesare thinking? Why did he choose you of all people? You must have a charming manner. I hope you do. But what *is* your field of expertise?"

"I am the Duke's archivist. I am a historian."

"And what good is a knowledge of history?"

The answer rose to his lips before he could suppress it. "It allows us to understand the past and to anticipate the future. As Cicero says: History is the teacher of mankind."

It was the wrong answer, of course. The Provost was annoyed.

"Spare me that old chestnut!" he said. "Let me tell you how the Prince of Venosa anticipates the future. He studies magic, not history, or so they say."

"Magic?" Pietro said. "You cannot mean—"

The Provost crimped his mouth. "You are shocked?"

"It is a dangerous subject and forbidden by the Church."

The Provost shrugged. "There is a great deal that is forbidden by the Church and practiced nevertheless," he said.

And you are a prime example of a man flaunting the rules of the Church, Pietro thought. Aloud he said: "And how will I bring myself to the Prince's attention?"

"We shall provide a letter of introduction of course," the Provost said turning his head, so that Pietro was not sure whether he was addressing the words to him or to his secretary.

The man nodded. "Letter of introduction," he murmured and made a notation on his list. Then he bent forward and whispered something into his master's ear.

"Yes, I know," the Provost said. "We are wasting time. There is a line-up of petitioners waiting to speak to me." He waved his hand at Pietro in an impatient farewell. "Come back tomorrow, Messer Paci, and we shall have everything in readiness for you: a gift to present to the Prince and the funds you will need to travel to Naples and back to Ferrara when the time comes to make the return journey." He laughed. It was a negligent, mirthless laugh. "Unless of course you prefer to stay with the Prince. Perhaps he needs an archivist."

Nothing would please me more, Pietro thought — if Livia is willing to give me a second chance. At the same time he resented the Provost's dismissive tone and the implication that he had nothing of value to offer. He took his leave from Alessandro d'Este, determined to prove him wrong and find a patron who would value his services.

It had been a most unsatisfactory conversation. Offering hospitality or arranging for lodgings was not on the secretary's list, as Pietro discovered. He had to find his own lodging and pay for it out of his own shrinking funds. When he returned to the Villa the

195

next morning, he was not even offered the privilege of a second interview with the great man. It was the Provost's secretary who gave him a purse of money, directions to a banker in Naples, and a tightly wrapped parcel, sealed with the Este crest. "A gift to offer to the Prince of Venosa," he said. "To ensure a more gracious reception than you might get otherwise."

"And my letter of introduction?"

The secretary shrugged. "Perhaps it is enclosed in the packet. The only instruction I have is to give it to you and arrange for a berth on board of a ship sailing from Rome to Naples tomorrow — which I've done. Be in the harbor at dawn, and ask for the captain of the Benevento."

And so, Pietro was out of pocket for a second night in an inn. He chose a cheap guesthouse close to the harbour.

It was still dark when the maid knocked on Pietro's door to wake him up. The shadows of the night were barely ebbing. An icy draft blew through the ill-fitting window and rattled its frame as Pietro got out of bed. He pulled on his boots and stowed the parcel containing the gift for the Prince in his saddlebag. As he was doing so, he wondered about the letter of introduction. Was it in the sealed packet as Alessandro's secretary had suggested? It was an awkward arrangement. He might need the letter to obtain an audience with the Prince in the first place. It was his ticket of admission, so to speak. It also occurred to him that the customs men in Naples might ask questions about the contents of the parcel. His baggage had been searched when he entered Rome. No doubt the Spaniards who controlled the territory of Naples had a similar procedure in place. When the secretary handed Pietro the parcel, he had felt square edges and concluded that it contained a book. But what kind of book? Would it cause him difficulties if he was searched? The experience of the last few months had changed Pietro. He had set out from Ferrara, an easy-going, optimistic lad. He had become more cautious, indeed more suspicious of people. His interview with Cesare's brother had not been reassuring. The Provost treated him with contempt, and Cesare himself never meant to do him any favours, as he understood now. Pietro had been imprudent enough to offend him. He had seen Livia after Cesare had warned him off. He had rescued her when Cesare wanted her out of the way. Another man would have shown his anger openly and made him suffer the consequences in short order. But Cesare was devious. He had the cruelty of a cat playing with a mouse, killing his prey slowly. He had put Pietro at risk twice — at the risk of shame and ridicule, serving as bait to a notorious lecher and marrying a disgraced woman. Would he endanger him a third time, aiming to have him arrested or worse, condemned to death? Being caught with a forbidden book could land him in the court of the Inquisition.

A servant came to the door of his room and announced that Pietro's horse was saddled, but he told the man to wait. He was not ready to leave. He had made a bold decision. After barring the door, he reopened his saddle bag, took out the parcel and broke the seal that held down the flap of the cloth wrapper. He had guessed right: it contained a book. But there was no letter of introduction with it. By the light of the candle, Pietro saw that the book was bound in plain pigskin stretched over a wooden board — no clasps, no gold-stamped borders, no gilt edges — hardly a present suitable for a Prince. He opened the book and read the author's name: Giordano Bruno. A man under interrogation by the Roman Inquisition! He blanched when he saw his own signature on the flyleaf under a neatly printed dedication to the Prince of Venosa. The signature made him out the owner of a condemned book, or at any rate the presenter of the book. He held it up to the light of the candle and studied the signature closely. It was an excellent forgery, duplicating his own handwriting. Four lines of poetry were written on the title page below the author's name. They, too, were penned in what looked like Pietro's hand. He read the verses:

Ah, where is thy magic, Bruno?
Where your elixir turning lead to gold,
Your spell so lethal to the object of your anger?
Go forward, cast your foe into the depth of Hades.

Pietro quickly realized that the poem was an adaptation of his love poem for Livia. Someone had copied the words from the sheet he had tucked into the pages of *Polidoro* — the book he had lost in his scuffle with the thief. The book was returned with the plausible explanation that it had been found in the street, but what if the explanation was spurious and the book had been taken from him for a sinister purpose? Someone had imitated his handwriting and used the words of his poem or rather twisted them into a new poem, turning the lament of a lover into an ominous invitation to harm an unnamed enemy. How easy it would be to use those words against Pietro and make him out a follower of Bruno, a heretic and a traitor to the Spanish crown!

197

He leafed through the book written by Bruno and was astonished at the author's daring theories. Bruno spoke of an infinite number of worlds and the transmigration of souls, a philosophy completely at variance with the tenets of the Catholic Church. Pietro's skin crawled when he read another paragraph calling Christ a "magus" and questioning his miracles. Such heresies would be fatal to the bearer of the book. This was a trap to land him before a tribunal and expose him to torture and a fiery death. Pietro tore out the flysheet bearing his name, held it over the lit candle, and watched the flame curl the edges of the paper and devour it. Ashes to ashes, as Cardinal Gesualdo had said, burning his candid letter. Pietro had not expected to apply that lesson so soon.

The stars had begun to pale in the sky when he finally left the inn and set out in the direction of the harbor. In the distance he could make out the black masts of the ships against the night sky. But first he had to rid himself of the treacherous book. He turned off into a narrow lane leading to a lagoon. The ground was muddy, Pietro's breath a cloud of vapour. The windows of the decrepit houses overlooking the lane were dark and empty like the eyes of a blind man. He dismounted at the water's edge, a shallow spot overgrown with reeds. Looking around to make sure there were no witnesses, he tossed the book into the brackish water and watched it sink to the bottom.

CHAPTER 31

Gesualdo Castle, winter 1594

It was five months since Livia had come to Gesualdo with her mistress, and this afternoon, like every other, resembled a set piece in a play, with each of the characters going through the steps and speaking their lines in turn. Life at Gesualdo castle was regulated like clockwork. That is how the Prince liked it. His meals were served punctually three times a day and the dishes removed exactly an hour and a half after the company had sat down at the table. There was a time set for reading, for composing and playing music, for receiving petitioners, discussing business with di Grassi, and going to mass. There was a time also for entertainment, though rarely: a banquet, a dance, an evening of games, a day of hunting when in season. But such entertainments had to be planned in great detail and not without giving the Prince notice a long time ahead of the persons involved and the sequence and duration of events. The least deviation caused him anxiety. He became irritated or, worse, fell into a state of immobility, as if the world was too much for him and he wanted to withdraw his mind from its contemplation. The court was attuned to his peculiarities, and Leonora was content to indulge her husband like a sick child. She had hoped that her loving companionship would ease his anxious mind, but it was clear by now that his mental state had worsened rather than improved, and she feared he would remain an invalid for the rest of his life.

The days passed slowly for Livia. Emmanuele provided the only diversion, the only spontaneous movement in the rut and humdrum of her life. Every morning, at the time of the boy's recess, Livia took her seat in the loggia and through the window watched him dash out of the building on the other side, followed by his kitten which had grown from a ball of fur into a young cat. Then Don Antonio appeared at the door and called after him:

"Please not to run, Emmanuele."

Emmanuele slowed down reluctantly protesting: "But it is recess. It's my free time."

"It does not become a gentleman to move in an undignified manner, whatever the time or occasion. *Festina lente*, as the proverb says. Make haste slowly."

The tutor lingered at the door and watched Emmanuele cross the courtyard, enter the loggia and take his seat on the bench beside Livia. Then he politely bowed to her and turned back into the house. She was glad when the door closed on him, relieving her of his lugubrious sight.

"And how is your day going, Emmanuele?" she asked, turning to the boy whose fresh and eager face cheered her.

He began telling her of his lessons in History and in Latin, but his eyes kept wandering to the open book in her lap. "What are you reading, Donna Livia? A secret message written in cipher?"

She put her arm around him and gave him an amused smile. To think that the son of a renowned composer had never seen a musical score!

"Nothing secret about it. It's a madrigal. This is the way to write music and guide the singer. This particular piece has been composed by your father. Would you like me to sing it for you?"

He nodded eagerly. She moved her fingers along the notes, giving voice to the composition, and he listened with rapt attention, keeping his eyes on the score.

"I see," he said when she came to the end of the piece. "You follow the ups and downs of the notes with your voice."

"That's right," she said. "And do you see these dots and ties?" She pointed them out to him. "They indicate the duration of the sound."

She told him the names of the notes, and he repeated them after her eagerly.

"So you like music, Emmanuele?"

"I like to listen to the sound of the instruments coming from the music room at night," he said. "I wish I were allowed to sit in on the concerts, but my father does not wish to see me. Perhaps I could sneak in without him seeing me. I could sit down in the back after everyone is seated, and duck out before the applause is over."

"I don't think you should do anything behind your father's back."

"And why do you think he doesn't want me to meet Donna Leonora?"

"Because of her delicate condition. Perhaps you father thinks you are too lively and is afraid of over-exciting Donna Leonora."

"No, I tell you what it is," the boy said. "He thinks my mother is looking out through my eyes and harming people, but it can't be true because I've never done any harm to my tutor or to you, and my cat is also doing well."

Livia agreed. "He must be doing well. He is growing fast."

"And he is happy in my company. Have you heard him purring, Donna Livia? That's his way of showing me that he is happy, because animals can't smile, Don Antonio says." His face turned serious as he looked out on the courtyard. "And here he comes to fetch me. I wish recess wasn't so short."

The tutor was crossing the yard in measured step, carefully putting one foot in front of the other, as if he was walking a tightrope.

"Emmanuele," he said, stopping at the entrance to the loggia. "Time to return to the school room. I hope you have not importuned Donna Livia."

"Not at all," she said. "We always find something interesting to talk about, don't we, Emmanuele?"

"Yes," the boy said. "We talked about the fact that animals can't smile."

"And who was the first author to point that out?" the tutor said.

"Aristotle. A Greek philosopher."

"Dates?"

"384 to 322 ante Dominum."

"Very good."

"And Donna Livia sang to me. You should ask her to sing for you, too, Don Antonio. Her voice is very sweet."

"Indeed, I have had the honour of hearing Donna Livia sing in church, and if I may add my praises to Emmanuele's, madam, your voice is very fine indeed." As he spoke the words, he stood at attention like a sentinel, with his hands stiffly by his side, and his lips in a twist meant to pass for a smile. He cut such an awkward figure that Livia pitied him. She would have liked to put him at ease but she was afraid of encouraging him. He took too keen an interest in her, as it was. She could not go into town without "chancing" to meet Antonio there, and the other day when she took a walk in the courtyard, he waylaid her and asked in a trembling voice "May I join you, dear lady?"

He made conversation stiffly at first, then more steadily with his words falling on Livia's ear like rain. It seemed rude to keep entirely silent on her part. She could not forego asking a few polite questions in turn.

"And your family is from Naples?" she asked him.

"Alas, I have no family. I am an orphan and was taken in by the Dominicans as a novice. But even though I grew up in poverty and had seen my share of lawlessness, I was shocked by the godless behaviour I witnessed among the friars. They are shameless womanizers and brawlers in the streets. One of them ripped a gold chain from the neck of a woman at prayer. Another was found to be a burglar. The most notorious member of their order, Giordano Bruno, is being tried for heresy in Rome. The friars have caused such scandal in Naples that the Pope tried to dissolve the order a year ago, but in vain. They could not be dislodged."

"So you left the order?"

"I never took the vows."

"Then you have made your escape and have found a safe harbour here at court."

"I don't know that I am safe," he said. "I worry — and not only about myself." He hesitated. His pale face flushed. It seemed to cost him a great effort to push out the words when he said: "Do you know Aurelia Darrico?"

Livia had taken note of the name when it was first mentioned to her and had made inquiries about the woman. Was she by any chance related to Benito Darrico, the man they had met in the instrument maker's shop at Venice? Yes, she was told, she was Benito's sister and a herbalist.

"I know the woman," she said in answer to Antonio's question.

"Have you heard any complaints about her?"

Livia gave him a surprised look. She had heard that Aurelia was cheeky, and some said, too fond of men, but that was hardly Antonio's business.

"Why are you asking?"

She noticed that his hands trembled. He swallowed, and his voice sounded hoarse when he said: "Aurelia's mother was Maria d'Avalos' maid. She was dismissed together with all the other

202

women in her household. I wonder whether Donna Leonora is aware of the daughter selling herbs here in the castle."

"The Prince has kept you in his employ in spite of the fact that you served Maria d'Avalos. Is there any reason why Aurelia Darrico should not be treated with the same clemency? Why should she be shunned just because her mother was in the service of the late Princess?" Livia spoke sharply because she disliked Antonio's mysterious tone. If the tutor had a complaint against the woman, why not be frank and come out with it instead of asking roundabout questions?

Antonio shrank from Livia's probing eyes. His flush was gone, and he had turned as white as chalk.

"What is your point, Don Antonio?" she demanded to know. "What are you worried about?"

"Only that—" His voice had become a helpless stammer. "Only that—"

"You said that you did not feel safe — in your employ, you mean?"

He pulled himself together, licked his dry lips, and tried to speak again, but his voice had fallen to a whisper.

"Yes, that is what I meant. It's nothing, really," he said. "I am importuning you with my talk, Donna Livia. Please to excuse me."

CHAPTER 32

"Don Antonio is so very formal and serious," Livia said to her mistress later on when they sat in the music room, going through the scores to settle on a programme for that night's concert. Through the window, they could see the tutor marching the boy up and down the gravel path that ran the length of the courtyard. It was the hour allotted to the boy's exercise. Antonio's body was tilted forward, his hands folded behind his back. He stepped deliberately and never lifted his eyes from the ground, as if he was counting the steps. Perhaps he was. From time to time he stopped to give Emmanuele time to catch up with him or to ask him questions. At least that is what it looked like, a series of questions punctuated by a raised finger and a nod when the boy answered correctly or a slashing motion when he did not.

"I agree," Leonora said, watching the scene below. "Don Antonio is too grave for a little motherless boy. He needs a softer hand to guide him." She paused, seeing the Prince coming through the door, and rose to greet him. "We were just talking about Emmanuele," she said and took his arm impulsively, signaling Livia to leave them alone.

The Prince had frowned at the mention of the boy's name. "I have asked you to keep your distance from him, my dear," he said after Livia had left the room.

"And I have obeyed your command, Carlo, but even at a distance I can see that Don Antonio never smiles." She squeezed his arm. "My dear, will you not change your mind and allow the child to join us for a concert — tonight, for example, when we are among ourselves?"

"I am afraid that is not possible," the Prince said. The colour had drained from his face. "I cannot permit Emmanuele to come into your presence, Leonora. He must not lay eyes on you. I have explained my reasons to you, have I not? He has his mother's spirit in him. She will use Emmanuele to harm our unborn child."

"But he is a mere boy! An innocent babe. It seems cruel to banish him thus."

The prince stiffened and withdrew his arm. "Innocent and defenseless against the dark powers, and therefore more vulnerable and likely to fall victim to an evil spirit."

"Dearest Carlo," Leonora said. "I don't mean to do or say anything you would not approve of. But if the boy is indeed subject to evil spirits, would it not be better to counteract that influence by teaching him goodness?"

"I have seen to that already, as I am in duty bound as his father. He does receive moral instruction. The tutor prays with him daily, and the parish priest instructs him in religion."

"Perhaps something more is needed. A gentle influence. Might the boy not be instructed in poetry or music?" Leonora looked up into the Prince's face with beseeching eyes, but he would not meet her gaze. She persisted. "I cannot think of a more sacred aura than that of a room filled with music. If he could listen to you playing the lute, I believe he would be infused with divine light."

The prince hesitated. "I may consider his attendance in future, but I cannot bear to put you at risk now while you are with child."

"Then might Livia read poetry with him or teach him the madrigals you have composed?"

He softened under her gentle persuasion. "I see you won't leave me in peace until I grant your wish. If it will make you happy, my dear, Donna Livia has my permission to instruct the boy in singing."

Leonora was all smiles now.

"Then I'll ask her to speak to the tutor and see how singing will fit into his lesson plan," she said.

"Let her arrange for a time to teach him, but the boy must not come here for his music lessons. I wish him to stay in his own quarters. Donna Livia must teach him in the school room in the other wing. And be sure to tell her: When she returns from those

206

sessions, she must sprinkle her hands and face with holy water before coming into your presence. Those are my instructions."

"They will be followed," Leonora said, agreeing readily to his request. She had grown used to his odd ways.

"And yet...," he said. She could see the misgivings in his eyes and was afraid he would retract the favour granted, but he only sighed. "I shall put my trust in God then," he said. "May it turn out to the best."

Leonora faithfully repeated the Prince's instructions to Livia and made it her first task the next morning to call for the tutor to inform him of their plan.

He appeared before the two ladies, greeting them in his usual, cheerless manner. Leonora could not make up her mind whether to dislike the man or feel sorry for him. He seemed so bleak, so crowlike, and at the same time so meek and timid. Apprehension was written on his face as he listened to the proposed arrangement.

"I am most eager to oblige the Prince," he said, "I only hope my teaching has not in any way incurred His Lordship's displeasure."

He looked anxiously from Leonora to Livia and back again.

"Not at all, Don Antonio," Leonora reassured him. "What I propose is no reflection on your teaching skills. Donna Livia and I have been putting our heads together. We thought the boy needed something to lighten his day. That is all."

Embarrassment replaced the apprehension on the tutor's face. "I have been told that I am too stern and perhaps also too demanding, madam, and I readily admit that I have no ear for pleasantries. It is my training, I suppose. I have been a student of theology for too long."

It has nothing to do with his training, Livia thought. It is in his nature. And his looks aren't inviting either. How unattractive he is, poor fellow! His forehead is too wide for his lean narrow face. His whole face lacks balance: the upper half gentle, almost saintly, the lower half dominated by a severe, unsmiling mouth. She could see that Leonora pitied him as well and was trying to put Antonio at ease by drawing him out.

"And where did you receive your training, Don Antonio?"

"In Naples," he said. "My guardian sent me to the Dominicans, but they are a corrupt lot. Thieves, vagabonds, and heretics." He stopped when he saw the disapproval in Leonora's eyes. She was a pious woman and did not like to hear the church criticized. "Accept my apologies, madam. Indignation has carried me away," he said. "I hope Your Ladyship will forgive my intemperate words, although, alas, I speak the truth. In any case, I left without joining the order and instead entered the service of a noble family. Like many of my station, I depended and am still depending on the good will of a patron to make my living."

"And what family did you serve?"

Antonio hesitated. "It is a name best left unspoken within these walls," he said, keeping his eyes cast on the ground. "It is a name that has brought disgrace on the House of Gesualdo."

Leonora nodded. She understood his meaning. He had been in the service of Maria d'Avalos.

"After the death of my unfortunate mistress," the tutor continued, "the Prince dismissed the members of her household. I was the only one he kept on because, as His Lordship deigned to say, he liked my face which matched the melancholy mood of the house. And, believe me, madam, that was the only time my natural gravity proved to be an asset. As for the rest, society prefers a smiling to a serious man."

"I have nothing against gravity, Don Antonio," Leonora said, "but a little more joy and tenderness is called for when dealing with a child."

The tutor bowed humbly. "I am at your command, Madam, and will do anything in my power to oblige."

Alas, it was obvious that it was not in his power to oblige and learn to smile and speak graciously. It was agreed at any rate that Livia should take charge of the boy for an hour after recess each day and teach him singing and reading musical scores.

CHAPTER 33

Teaching Emmanuele was a pleasant addition to Livia's duties. Yet there were times at the end of the day when she felt melancholy. Alone in her room, she thought "What am I doing here so far from Ferrara?" She leaned on the window sill, looked out at the mountain range thinly veiled in mist, and longed to see the Po valley instead. Or was she longing to see Pietro and hear the sound of his voice? No, she told herself, she was not the kind of woman to indulge in hopeless dreams and in thoughts of what could not be. Her longing was no more than a pang of homesickness, which was natural even if her loyalty was with Leonora and she wanted always to make her home where Leonora was. Besides, Livia was not the only member of the household who had followed her mistress to Gesualdo. There was Leonora's maid Camilla and Monna Alfani, the Mistress of the Wardrobe, as well as Fina the midwife — they had brought a breath of Ferrara with them. And at the end of November, just ahead of the first winter rains, Giulia arrived in all her newly-wed bliss and threw her arms around Livia, enveloping her in a billowing cloud of loving words.

Last summer, when the two women had said farewell in Ferrara, Giulia had been in two minds about encouraging Giovanni di Grassi's courtship. The Prince's majordomo was a very eligible man, but she did not like to make her home so far from all that was dear to her. No one sympathized with her. Not the Duchess who had left her native Mantua for the love of her husband. Not her mother, whose family was from Bologna and who had followed her husband to Ferrara. And there was the example of Livia, who had gone to Gesualdo to serve Donna Leonora. It was a woman's lot to go where she was wanted. Giulia's parents favoured the union with di Grassi and urged her to accept him. He came from a wealthy family in Florence. He had a prestigious position at the court of the Prince. He was a kind man even if he did not smile often. What more could she ask for? Time was running out for Giulia. She had passed her twentieth birthday. Her voluble tongue had discouraged other suitors. Every day she had to listen to the arguments of family and friends urging her to accept di Grassi, until they filled her head and she no longer remembered her own objections. "You've finally come to your senses," her mother said when she accepted the Prince's majordomo as her suitor. "It's all settled then."

Di Grassi, who had gone to Gesualdo with the Prince, returned to Ferrara in the fall to wed Giulia. He stayed on for two weeks to allow his young bride to make her good-byes before taking her on the long journey to Gesualdo. How glad she was to be welcomed at the castle by Livia and be taken under her wing!

Together, the two women inspected the spacious suite prepared for her. The quarters were handsome and well-furnished, as became Di Grassi's position at court.

"I only wish Giovanni had stayed with me in Ferrara for three months, as the Prince did when he married Donna Leonora," Giulia said. "But he was given only four weeks' leave. There was hardly time for me to get ready for the journey, and here I am, my head in a whirlwind. Oh, Livia, I wish you could have been with me!"

"So do I. For your wedding at least."

"Ah, the wedding! It was the most glorious and sumptuous feast, and I'm so sorry you could not be my bridesmaid. But you will be able to admire the gifts I received, the dresses and capes and jewelry. Giovanni himself gave me a magnificent necklace and earrings set with amethysts — to match my eyes, he said."

"Then you must model your new dresses for me," Livia said.

"But they don't quite fit me - yet," Giulia said. "My mother thought they should be loose. In case, you know." She smiled coyly.

Livia understood the hint. Giulia was hoping to be pregnant soon.

"In fact, my flux is late, but that could be on account of the journey. What do you think?"

"I know nothing about such things. You should ask Fina. All I can say is: I hope all your wishes come true and you will have a happy life here in Gesualdo with your husband."

"Oh yes, Giovanni is a dear, dear man. I don't know how I could have gotten through everything without him. The carriage ride, I mean — I am never comfortable on horseback, but the carriage was almost worse. I thought I would not survive it. My poor bones are still all shaken up. I'm sore all over and will be sore for weeks, I'm sure. Those roads! I never saw such rough pathways and such mountains, and someone told me that the woods were full of bandits, so that I was mortally afraid, but Giovanni said, there was no danger because they had all been driven out by an army of the Pope." She fetched a deep sigh as if telling about the journey was as strenuous as the journey itself. "And now I have a special story to tell you, Livia," she continued, perking up. "You will be ever so surprised to hear it. At one of the inns where we stopped, they told us that a young man, a member of the Farnese family, had been captured by bandits and was rescued in a most daring raid, in which several men were killed, or was it several horses that were killed? In any case, a young man rescued him and was celebrated as a great hero, they said, and they named him to us. You will never guess who it was -"

She paused and gave Livia's hand an excited squeeze.

Livia smiled. "No, I will never guess, I'm sure. You will have to tell me, Giulia."

"Your Pietro!" Giulia said with a triumphant crow.

The name flooded Livia's heart with a stinging sweetness.

"What do you mean — *my* Pietro," she said sternly to disguise her agitation.

"Oh, you know what I mean. I just thought you might like to hear -" Giulia stopped mid-sentence. "Oh, dear! Forgive me. I have opened an old wound."

"It's not your fault," Livia said. "It is silly of me to be so affected by the name of a man I should have long forgotten."

"Well, I won't say another word," Giulia said. "I've been talking too much already. Giovanni always says 'half will do, remember that, and you'll be alright' — isn't that clever of him? So I'll stop right here. It's your turn to tell me about your life."

"As much as I would like to tell you all about myself, Giulia, we will have to leave it for another time. It is the hour when I give singing lessons to Emmanuele, the Prince's son."

"Singing lessons! To Emmanuele! Is the child back in his father's favour then? For Giovanni told me-"

211

"It's a complicated story, Giulia. We'll talk about it when we have more time."

She was glad to escape, not from Giulia's prattling which had a soothing quality about it, like running water, but to calm her heart which had started pounding at the sound of Pietro's name. She saw that her attempts to drive him out of her mind had been in vain. She had tried hard to paint him as a villain, a hard-nosed courtier thinking only of his career, and here he was back in her heart, a hero, a white knight who had fought bandits and saved a man's life.

As always, the lesson went well. Emmanuele had a quick mind and a good ear for music. He diligently studied the scores and enjoyed singing along with Livia, adding his boy's treble to her soprano. He even sketched out tunes of his own and played them on his flute.

Teaching Emmanuele would have been pure joy if Don Antonio had not made it a habit to slip into the schoolroom long before the hour was up. Out of the corner of her eye Livia saw the door open silently, just wide enough for the tutor to squeeze through. Emmanuele looked up and stopped tracing the notes on the score before him. He half rose to greet his tutor, but Don Antonio held up his hand as if to say "Take no notice of me" and sat down in the window seat.

They resumed their lesson, but Livia's peace of mind was gone. At the end of the hour, as she put away the score, Antonio approached with measured steps and quizzed Emmanuele: "What have you learned today? Have you been on your best behaviour?" But even as he asked the boy questions, his eyes darted to Livia.

His silent admiration did not sit well with her, and one day she spoke up.

"Don Antonio," she said, "I don't mean to find fault, but it is distracting for Emmanuele if you come in halfway through our lesson."

He faltered. "I didn't mean — I didn't think it would distract him. I am so fond of hearing your voices—" Your voice, he meant to say, for his eyes were on her. "—But of course if you do not wish me to come in, I will wait in the hallway."

"No, no, it would not do to keep you standing in the hallway," she said annoyed at her weakness, but she could not be impolite to a man, who had impeccable manners himself.

He promptly took advantage of her courteous reply.

"Then I will presume on your kindness, Donna Livia, and come in just for the last little while and keep to the very back of the room."

From there on, he tiptoed into the room toward the end of her lesson and shrunk against the back wall, shadow-like, watching them — no, watching Livia— with eyes as dark and profound as a well. He trained them on her face and never let go, not for one moment.

One afternoon, not long after her awkward conversation with Antonio, Livia sat in the veranda with her mistress. Leonora was big with child now. The maid had draped a shawl over her shoulders and placed a brazier near her feet to take the chill out of the air. On sunny days, the glazed windows enclosing the veranda doubled the warmth of the rays and made for a cheerful vista, but today the landscape was drab with rain, and a wintry gust made the treetops sway and the branches shudder.

Livia had put down her embroidery and was watching the rain slanting across the panes when Leonora put a hand on her arm and said:

"We must have a talk, Livia."

Her voice was unusually serious.

"Don Antonio has asked to see me," she said. "Do you know what this is about?"

"I think he is worried about his position," Livia said. "He hinted at something like that the other day, although I couldn't quite make out what he was worried about."

"Carlo has given me no indication that he is dissatisfied with Don Antonio's services. I suppose I can reassure him on that point, but I suspect he wants to speak to me about another matter. I couldn't help noticing that he follows you around like a dog. Perhaps he will ask me to endorse his courtship."

"Oh, no!" Livia said. "If he has failed to notice my lack of interest, he must be blind and deaf."

"Love has that effect, my dear. It makes us blind and deaf and robs us of our rational faculties."

"I hope he hasn't got it into his head to propose to me."

"If he truly has no chance of winning your heart, Livia, you must tell him so gently. Or better still, put the blame on me. He knows you are an orphan and in my charge. You cannot make a decision about your future without my approval. Tell him that I will not give my approval because I have another gentleman in mind for you."

"Or I might point out to him that I have no dowry, and he is a man without means himself."

"That may serve as an excuse, but you cannot think that I'd let you go without a dowry, my dear? I will make provisions for you of course, and the Prince, too, will reward your service with a marriage gift once you find a gentleman to your liking."

"I did find a gentleman to my liking once, but alas-"

"And now you are wondering, why did I not speak up then and tell you that I would provide for you. I wish I could have helped you earlier, my love, but time was against us. I was under Cesare's iron rule then. He kept me on a short leash and would not have permitted me to 'squander' money on your happiness — you know how he despised all talk of love. But my circumstances have changed, and your prospects have changed accordingly. Now that I have my own income and an allowance from Don Carlo, I can afford to be generous to my friends."

Livia pressed her hand. "You are my patron angel, Leonora, and I thank you for having my interests at heart."

Leonora regarded her silently. "Your thanks are rather formal, my dear."

Livia sighed. "Forgive me if I don't sound as elated as I should be and as your generosity deserves, but I doubt I will ever be able to take advantage of your kind offer. In plain truth, I no longer have a desire to marry."

"What! Not marry and never know the love of a husband and the happiness of children? Could it be that a certain someone is still inscribed in your heart, Livia, and will not allow anyone else to take possession of it?"

"How well you know me, Leonora! It is as you say. Love once settled in a woman's bosom is hard to drive out. I cannot stop thinking of Pietro, and I fear I'll become an old maid thinking of him."

"Then I may have a remedy for your ailing heart."

"You are teasing me, surely. What remedy would that be?"

"This!" Leonora said with a triumphant laugh, and flourished a letter she had kept hidden under her shawl.

Livia Prevera, lady-in-waiting at the court of Carlo, Prince of Venosa, at Gesualdo was written on the outside of the folded square, but even before she read the words, Livia had recognized Pietro's hand. He heart gave a violent thump.

"How did this come into your hand?" she asked full of wonder.

"It came this morning, enclosed in a letter from Cesare, but I did not want the past to interfere with your future or with any understanding you might have with Don Antonio. That is why I asked all those questions — so I would know how to answer Don Antonio if he raised the subject of his courtship."

"But how is it that your brother was in possession of a letter addressed to me?"

"Your billet doux has been on a long journey, from Rome to Ferrara and from Ferrara to Gesualdo. Cesare says the letter was delivered to him by mistake, together with another addressed to him."

The two women looked at each other knowingly. It was not likely that the letter had come into Cesare's hands by mistake. It was clearly addressed to Livia, yet the seal had been broken and no effort made to disguise the tampering, as if Cesare wanted to give her a warning.

"I suspect there was no mistake," Livia said, thinking of that other time when Pietro's letters to her had been intercepted. "Someone wished to keep this letter from me."

Leonora nodded. She, too, knew Cesare's reach and his grudge against Livia. He was not a man to let bygones be bygones.

"For all I know, you may be right, but the letter has found you at last, Livia, and you will want to read it in private."

Livia pressed the square to her heart and blew her mistress a grateful kiss before leaving the veranda and running up to her room.

She unfolded the letter as she hurried up the steps. She was so impatient to read the contents that she stopped in the hall to run her eyes over the page. It was a poem. She skipped through the lines and let her eyes wander to the bottom of the page. "Forgive me," she read. "Your ever-loving Pietro."

Livia pushed open the door of her room and dropped on the bed, laughing out loud and wiggling her toes — not for the usual reason, because she was uneasy or in two minds, but because she couldn't keep still in her happiness.

She read and reread the letter. He loved her still. He missed her. He had made a mistake putting his career first, he wrote. If she was content to marry a man who could offer her only a modest living, he in turn was content to share his life with her. He was eagerly awaiting her answer —

Livia wished she could give him an answer this very instant. She looked at the date. The letter was written over a month ago. Pietro asked her to send her reply to Rome, but he also said he did not know how much longer he would remain in the city. What if he was already on his way back to Ferrara? She would consult with Leonora tomorrow.

CHAPTER 34

The next morning, however, Livia's questions had to be put off. Leonora stayed in bed longer than usual. She felt languid.

"I'm worried," she said to Livia. "The child no longer quickens within me."

Livia felt Leonora's forehead. It was cool, thank God. "Shall I call Fina?" she asked.

The midwife came. Her solid body and gentle face were a reassuring sight. She passed her hands over Leonora's distended belly, fingered her sides like someone trying to guess the contents of a wrapped present, and pronounced that the hour of birth was near.

"The child's body is very low and its head pointing downward," she said.

Soon Leonora felt the first contraction, and was taken to the special chamber prepared for the happy event. The verdant frescoes adorning the walls gave it the peaceful aura of a meadow in spring, and the great bed which dominated the room was made up with the finest cotton sheets and a festive red coverlet edged with gold embroidery.

Leonora had asked for her marriage chest to be placed where she could see it from the bed. She thought that the cheerful family scenes painted on the sides would serve as a happy inspiration, and yet she was apprehensive.

"Of course you are worried," Fina said when she saw her anxious looks. "It's only natural. Every woman is afraid but, God willing, you will be a happy mother by this time tomorrow and wondering what you worried about." She plumped up the pillows on the bed, patted Leonora's hand and gave her a motherly smile full of understanding.

But Fina didn't know what weighed on Leonora's mind. It wasn't giving birth, or not *only* giving birth that worried her. She looked across to Livia, and Livia nodded to show that *she* knew about her worries and understood. She felt the same apprehension as her mistress. It wasn't fear of the natural dangers every woman faced when giving birth. It was fear of the unnatural that made them both tremble.

The Prince's warnings against demonic powers were like a drumbeat in Leonora's ears. She leaned back on the pillows. Her dark hair had been tucked into a tight-fitting cap beaded with pearls. The birthing cloak, fixed at her throat with a jeweled floral clasp, was folded back. Her thighs were covered only with a fine woolen chemise. Fina had tied up her own hair with golden netting, as was the tradition in the Este family. The ladies of the court took up their position around the bed like guardian angels, talking softly to Leonora, petting and soothing her.

For a moment her fears were eased by the kindness written in their faces but then her eyes wandered to the corners of the room. She thought she caught a movement just below the ceiling, a vibration in the air, or was it the thin smoke curling up from one of the candles surrounding the holy relics that had been placed at the foot of her bed.

She saw Livia looking up. Her eyes, too, were following the drifting smoke. In the light of the flickering candles her face had a grayish look — the shadow cast by a dead soul? And what was that sound? A murmur rose up from behind the screen which had been set up by the door. She stared at the panel painted with pomegranates, blood-red and spilling their seeds. It seemed a bad omen to think of blood at a time like this, and the murmurs were like whispered incantations. Leonora's womb contracted, and she cried out, pointing to the screen:

"Who is there?"

Camilla, her maid, approached the bed: "Only the witnesses, madam."

She sank back and closed her eyes. Oh yes, the witnesses, to make sure that no other child was smuggled in and substituted for her little prince or princess. But who could keep the devil from sowing his seed in another man's field?

The ladies pressed closer to her, ready to ease their mistress through the hours of labour. Giulia was at her elbow, asking a thousand questions. Of course she would. She was hoping to bear di Grassi healthy children and eager to store everything she saw and heard in her memory. Lucky Giulia. She would be fighting only the forces of nature. Leonora was up against the shadowy power of ghosts. Her fingertips were itching, her palms seemed on fire.

She looked down on her hands and inspected them anxiously. They looked unblemished, but wait, the back of her left hand was mottled. Was it the leprous touch of the devil? She cast an anxious eye at the windows hung with heavy curtains to dampen all noise.

"Livia," she said, wincing as the pain of another contraction rippled through her body. "Are the windows shut tight? I feel a draft."

"I will check," Livia said. She understood Leonora's fear. She had heard Carlo's warning. Every breath of wind could carry evil, he said.

"The windows are all latched," Livia said and gave her mistress a reassuring smile.

The hours went by. The contractions came with greater frequency. Leonora could not repress a groan. She grasped Fina's precious birthing stone in one hand and a talisman the Prince had given her in the other. It was shaped like the head of a marten and made of enameled gold, decorated with garnets, and pearls. It had protected the Prince's mother and grandmother during child labour.

One of Leonora's ladies, who had gone to tell the Prince that her time was near, came back, bearing a note from him. She unfolded it.

"Dearest," he wrote. "I dare not come near the birthing room lest the demons that afflict me seize upon the unborn child. When you read this, I shall be on my way to Naples, drawing the evil spirits away from you, I hope. I kiss your hands, my beloved. I fear the spirits will be jealous if they hear my good wishes. So I write no more and keep my thoughts hidden safely in my heart."

Leonora's head drooped. "He has gone to Naples," she said tonelessly, and the ladies looked at each other in surprise. They were at a loss what to say about the Prince's strange behaviour or how to console their mistress. How could he be so heartless and go away at a time like this! They shook their heads, confirmed in their opinion that he was mad.

To lighten Leonora's mood and divert her mind from the Prince's inexplicable action, Fina asked if she had made the usual bets about the child being a boy or a girl. Leonora blushed a little and said, yes, she had been foolish enough to make an arrangement with a merchant. He would donate a length of silver cloth if she gave birth to a boy, but make her pay double if it was a girl.

"Don't tell my confessor," she said to the women surrounding her bed. "He does not approve of betting."

The ladies laughed knowingly and promised to be discreet.

Soon the contractions became more frequent. Leonora gripped her belly and bit her lips to stop herself from crying out. In an interval of calm between contractions, she turned to Giulia.

"You seem very quiet all of a sudden, my dear. You aren't usually at a loss for words."

"It's just that I don't want to miss anything, my lady," Giulia said. "I have never been present at a child's birth, and −" She hesitated, then pulled out the notebook in which she kept her list of symptoms. "I thought I'd write it all down. It will stand me in good stead when my time comes, and well-" She trailed off.

The ladies surrounding Leonora exchanged meaningful glances. Was this a hint that Giulia was pregnant?

"Is it really the first time you see a child born?" Fina said, smiling. "Then we must make this an easy birth so as not scare you."

"I hope you will make it an easy birth for my own sake," Leonora said. "So you are writing a book about giving birth, Giulia?"

"Not a book, my lady. Just a list of symptoms. I hope you don't mind me. It will be ever so useful when I−, when my hopes−"

"Out with it, Donna Giulia. Say it and it will come true," Fina said. "You hope to be the mother of a healthy boy by this time next year."

"That is what I meant to say, and Fina, dear Fina, you must stay and see me through."

"There are local midwives, too, you know," Fina said.

"That dreadful Darrico woman they have been telling me about?"

Fina silenced her with stern look. To speak of a reputed witch in the presence of a woman about to give birth! Leonora turned pale. A great panic welled up in her chest, but Fina was quick to change the subject.

"Now let's see this booklet of yours, Donna Giulia," she said. "What have you written down so far?"

"Nothing much as yet. I mention the pangs of course—"

The words seemed to have a suggestive effect. Leonora arched her back and moaned. Another contraction, and this time she could not hold back. She screamed out loud.

The time had come. The servants got the birthing stool ready and eased Leonora out of the bed and on to the chair. Camilla sponged her mistress' brow.

"Tip back, my dear," Fina said. She massaged Leonora's belly and quietly rehearsed with her when to push and what to expect next.

In the meantime, Camilla folded back the coverlet of the bed, placed coriander seeds in the hem of Leonora's chemise and rolled it up.

"I'm told this will help with the birth, madam," she said.

The Princess' face was bathed in sweat. Her cries came in quick succession now, matching the contractions. The baby's head appeared between her legs, a sticky tangle of black hair. She strained and pushed and screamed as the midwife eased out the little body and placed the baby into a basin.

"A boy," she said, and the room erupted in victory cries.

"A boy!" the attending ladies exclaimed joyfully.

Leonora sank back into the supporting arms of Livia, her face flushed with the exertion and the weary ecstasy of success. "Let me see him," she said in a trembling voice.

Fina held up the baby. He was perfect.

"My little angel," she breathed. Her eyes met Livia's, who smiled and mouthed "Thanks be to God. Amen."

Meanwhile Giulia wrote in her booklet:

The newborn looks like an old man, grey until he turned pink with his first breath. His body is covered with blood and vernix. They cleansed it with water, adding a spoonful of warm wine, and they put a little sugar into the baby's mouth, to comfort his stomach.

"The redder the wine the healthier looking the child," the midwife said, and Giulia took down everything she said.

The redder the wine the better. It cuts through the phlegm, or else the vapour mounts into the brain. It strengthens the child against epilepsy. Wash not only face, but also armpits, groin, buttocks. Use rose or walnut oil to soften the skin. Swaddle infant tightly into cloth warmed at the fireplace. Place in rocking crib.

Leonora was resting. An exhausted smile played on her lips. Fina had washed her lower body and wrapped her in clean linen bandages. The servants had taken away her blood-soaked chemise and dressed her in a white gown edged with gold. They brought a bowl to wash her hands and face and a plate of food to strengthen the new mother.

Capon, partridge. Nothing too rich. Avoid fruit. Walnut liqueur to repair the blood. Two spoonfuls of olive oil to move the bowels because lying in bed will cause constipation. Other forms of purging too violent. Clean thighs, vagina, buttocks with warm water and concoctions of comfrey root, peach stones, nutmeg, yellow amber and ambergris, crushed and mixed with white wine. Block up private parts with dry cloth to prevent swelling of the womb.

"And what are you going to do with the afterbirth?" she whispered to the servant carrying it away. Fina had drawn it out like a mass of dough and placed it into a pan. "What happens with the placenta?"

"We usually bury it right away, Donna Giulia," the servant said. "That way no harm can come to it, for it's the child's double in a manner of speaking. Only this time I'm going to burn it over glowing coals and bury the ashes. Those were the Prince's instructions."

Giulia followed the servant out of the room, eager not to miss any detail, and saw the long line of well-wishers in the ante-room. The townspeople had come bearing sweetmeats and nut cakes for the new mother. The wealthy among them had brought silver spoons, fork holders, goblets, and lengths of cloth with gold and silver weaves. The members of the household came with votive offerings to be placed on the altar in the chapel: wax candles, an embroidered altar cloth, and money for special masses and prayers on behalf of the child.

Livia, who had left the birthing room earlier, was standing with the housekeeper at a long table. They accepted the presents of the visitors on Leonora's behalf while a secretary noted down the names of the well-wishers and the nature of their gifts.

Giulia stopped at the table and looked over the presents.

"Well, then. Are all your questions answered and have you written down everything you observed?" Livia asked.

"Of course. Every little detail! And what a lesson I have learned today. A lesson from life, which is the best teacher." She took Livia's arm and led her away from the crowd to a window recess.

"I still haven't got the flux," she whispered. "And this morning I couldn't keep anything down."

"That's good news I take it?" Livia said.

Giulia nodded. Her mouth crimped into a secret smile. It was all but certain that she was pregnant, but she didn't want to say it out loud and jinx her luck. "I thank God for sparing me a long wait. But I can tell that I'll suffer! This morning I was so dizzy I couldn't get up and had to ask the maid to bring me a bed pan. I'll spare you the details, Livia, but I've added half a dozen symptoms to my list. Well, I know this isn't exactly an illness, but still. Thank God, my mother had the foresight of provide me with a recipe for an infusion of herbs, which helped a bit, but as I said, I had no appetite at all. And my maid isn't as sympathetic as she ought to be. It's just a foretaste of things to come, she says. The labour pains are ten times as bad as nausea, she says. She has given birth to three healthy sons and so of course she thinks she knows it all. I complained to Giovanni that she was too sassy, but he said I was to blame because I was too familiar with the servants. I must learn to keep my distance and not talk so much. I suppose he is right, but I can't help myself."

"You shouldn't have talked about Aurelia Darrico at any rate," Livia said. "It's very bad luck to speak of a reputed witch to a woman in labour."

"I'm so sorry," Giulia said. "I can't tell you how sorry I am." Repentance was written on her face. "It was inexcusable. Giovanni is right. I must learn to control my tongue. I will apologize to Donna Leonora at the very first opportunity. I hope she'll forgive me."

"I think it will be better not to remind her," Livia said. "But really, it is the most amazing thing, Giulia! You've been with us only a few weeks, and already you seem to know everyone here in

223

Gesualdo, even a woman who dabbles in midwifery and God knows what else."

"That's because Leticia, my maid, has her ear to the ground. Yours, I notice, is innocence personified and doesn't know a thing." She lowered her voice to a conspiratorial whisper even though they were now out of people's earshot. "When I first heard of Aurelia offering her services as midwife and herbalist, I thought she might be able to teach me something about their curative powers, but Leticia warned me off. So then I found out that she isn't a healer at all. She brews love potions, and her decoctions have driven some men mad and caused others to die of excessive love-making. The whole Darrico family is disreputable. Her mother was denounced to the Inquisition as a witch, Leticia told me, but she decamped to Venice and lives with her son there. Her daughter Aurelia —" She stopped when she saw the woman, whose name was on her lips, coming through the door. She was carrying a gift for Leonora: sweets prettily arranged on a white plate with scalloped edges.

Giulia gave her an appraising look as she passed them to join the line of well-wishers. She had to admit: Aurelia was an attractive woman. She had an abundance of glossy brown hair and an enticing smile for the men, who couldn't help ogling her. In her eyes was a banked-up fire, a kind of magnetism.

"No wonder women are jealous of her and accuse her of bewitching their husbands and lovers," Giulia whispered.

Livia sighed. "Please, Giulia," she said. "Let's say no more about that dreadful woman."

"You are right," Giulia said. "Here I go again, talking too much. And I can see you are tired. It's been a long day for you and for all of us. I'd better let you go."

The great event was over. Livia was relieved that the birth had gone well and the Prince's ominous talk of evil spirits had been just that — anxious talk. But she had suffered with Leonora and was as exhausted as if she herself had been in danger.

"I will go to my room and rest a little," she said to Giulia and moved to the door, but she was not allowed to escape. Don Antonio was lingering there, lying in wait for her.

"Donna Livia," he began, stepping into her path.

She held up her hand, warding him off. "Please excuse me, Don Antonio. I am too tired for words."

But he followed her out the door. "I must speak to you, Donna Livia. Please to listen to me. I realize this is not an opportune time, but what I have to say to you is urgent, indeed a matter of life and death."

Livia slowed her pace. His mouth and eyes were lined with suffering. He looked more pallid than ever, too wretched to refuse.

"What is it?" she said coming to a stop.

But he stared past her. The fear of death was in his eyes.

She turned and saw that Aurelia had appeared at the door. She was on her way out after delivering her gift and cast a slanting glance in their direction.

A nervous twitch ran across the tutor's face. He waited until Aurelia had left the courtyard, before he spoke again, but he sounded choked. His voice was so low that Livia was obliged to stand close to hear what he was saying. Anyone observing us, she thought, will think we are lovers.

"I must warn the Prince," Don Antonio said. His breath came in quick gasps. "But he refuses to speak to me or even to accept a letter from me, indeed to accept anything my hand has touched. He considers me polluted because I was in Maria d'Avalos' service and perhaps also because I keep company with his son. Yet I must warn him. His Lordship is in mortal danger, as is his wife. I meant to speak to Donna Leonora in person, but that is impossible now. And to make things worse, the Prince has departed for Naples, I am told, and will not return until the day after the purification ceremony. And so I have no choice and must put everything into a letter. Will you see that it reaches the Prince, Donna Livia? I have no one else I could trust with this task."

"But will I not incur the Prince's wrath if I obtrude a letter on him that comes from you? You say he does not wish to receive anything you have touched. Why don't you just tell me about your fears, and I will see what can be done?"

"The danger of being overheard is too great, Donna Livia, and I cannot trust myself to say the right things here on the spur of the moment. I might get carried away and say what will cause even more trouble. In grave matters like these, a man must choose his words carefully. Believe me, I would not ask you lightly to run the risk of displeasing the Prince, Donna Livia. I admire you too much for that. Let me put what I have to say in writing. You may read my letter, and if you think the contents should be brought to the Prince's attention, as I'm sure you will, do me the favour of copying it out in your own hand and see that the message reaches His Lordship with all due speed."

"I shall make my decision after I have read your letter," Livia said curtly. She wanted to get away from the tutor and the awkward situation he had created. His whispers were attracting attention. "Have the letter ready when I come to the schoolroom later on," she said.

He thanked her profusely. "I knew you would not refuse me, Donna Livia. You are a woman of courage. If my admiration for you could be any greater —"

His desperation was so obvious now that passers-by gave them curious glances.

Livia stepped away from him. "I need to rest before I give Emmanuele his lesson," she said firmly. "Until later then."

"I only hope I'm not too late," he said.

CHAPTER 35

When Livia knocked on the door of the schoolroom later that day, there was no answer. She was puzzled. Where was Don Antonio? Where was his pupil? She opened the door and looked around. The room appeared deserted. Then she saw Emmanuele cowering under his desk. His face was streaked with tears.

"Thank God, it's you, Donna Livia! I thought it was Aurelia coming back for me," he said, crawling out of his hiding place. His voice was high and tremulous with fear.

"My dear boy!" she said, hugging him close. "What happened? Where is your tutor?"

"Aurelia came to fetch him. I watched at the window and saw them go to her house." He beckoned Livia to come to the window and pointed in the direction of the forest which came right up to the northern wall of the castle. "Do you see the cottage in the clearing there, Donna Livia? That's where she took Don Antonio and turned him into a dog."

"Calm down, my dear boy. Your imagination is running away with you."

"I swear I saw it, Donna Livia. He went into the house, and afterwards a large black dog came trotting out. Aurelia is a witch, you know."

"Who says she is a witch?"

"Don Antonio. In his letter."

"Emmanuele, sit down, and start from the beginning. Don Antonio wrote you a letter?"

"Not to me. To my father. It must have been difficult to write because he told me to read my book and be very quiet. He needed to concentrate on what he was doing, he said, and I mustn't interrupt him. Then, when he was halfway down the page, he put it aside, took out a fresh sheet of paper and started over again. Then Aurelia came and told him to come with her. She whispered something into his ear — I thought I caught your name. Don Antonio turned white and looked like he was going to be sick. Then he said: I'll come with you."

Emmanuele's mouth worked as if he was chewing on something tough and sinewy that kept him from saying more.

"And the letter Don Antonio wrote?" Livia said. Perhaps it was the letter he meant to give her, she thought.

The boy swallowed hard. "He handed it to me and said — in a very stern voice as if I had done something wrong: This is your exercise, Emmanuele. Please to read and copy the page. I looked at the heading and saw that it was addressed to you, but I was too scared to say anything."

"And where is the letter now?"

"Aurelia took it from he. She said there was no need to give me an assignment. They wouldn't be long. She snatched the page out of my hands, read it, and said: Just as I thought. Then she crumpled it up and put it in her pocket. I thought Don Antonio would protest, but he said nothing and went away with her. So then I remembered the other page, the one Don Antonio put away when he started on the letter Aurelia got hold of. It was still there on his desk, and I went and read it because I thought it was an assignment. But it wasn't. It was—"

He stopped short. There was fear in his eyes.

"And where is that page now?"

He pulled a sheet of paper out of his jerkin. "I hid it just in case Aurelia would come back."

"You did well," Livia said, taking it from his hands. There were only a few lines on the page:

Donna Livia,

Here is my letter to the Prince: Your Highness will excuse my audacity in writing to you, but it is a matter of the greatest importance. The safety, indeed the very life of the Princess and your newborn son are at stake. Aurelia Darrico, whom you know well, is out to exact revenge. She is a poisoner and a witch like her mother. I overheard her threaten

228

The letter broke off at that point. Livia looked up and saw her own alarm reflected in the boy's eyes. Leonora, sweet Leonora, in mortal danger! Her dearest friend and the innocent babe threatened with death! Fear gripped Livia like an icy hand stifling her breath. But this was no time to give in to weakness. She must act at once.

"I'd better look into this," she said, speaking in an even tone and hoping that her show of steadfastness would reassure the boy as well. "I'll go to Aurelia's house at once."

"And if she turns you into a dog?"

"Emmanuele, that is a figment of your imagination," she said firmly, as much to convince herself as the boy. And even if there was witchcraft involved — she was ready to fight the devil for Leonora!

"Can I come along?" Emmanuele said. He looked up at her with pleading eyes.

"No, this is no business for a child," she said, trying to keep her voice and her mind on a level keel. "Let's see now. Have you had anything to eat since breakfast?"

He shook his head.

"Then go to the kitchen and ask the cook to prepare a meal for you, and by the time you have eaten, I'll be back."

The boy lowered his eyes. "But, Donna Livia," he said. She stopped him mid-sentence.

"No buts, Emmanuele. Be a good boy and do as I say." She waved him through the door, then went to the window and watched him cross the courtyard and enter the kitchen door before setting out on her own errand.

The rain which had come down steadily all morning had stopped, but the sky was ashen, blending in with the stones of the castle wall. Livia pulled her hooded cloak around her shoulders and set out in the direction of Aurelia's cottage. She shivered, from the cold as much as from a sense of foreboding. The footpath leading to the cottage was a narrow track slippery with leaves that deadened the sound of her footsteps. A sensation of dread curled through Livia as she entered the forest.

When she reached the clearing, she stopped and stood under the shelter of the trees, watching the house for a moment. Silence surrounded her. Aurelia's cottage was low-slung with a ragged roof. Thatches of straw hung down over the eaves. It had a neglected appearance. Rank vegetation had grown up around the walls. Cobwebs festooned the windows. The ground below the overhang was strewn with rubbish, splintered pieces of wood and broken tree branches, heaps of twigs and dead leaves, as if someone had piled up kindling and could not be bothered to carry it inside. Livia went up to the door, raised her hand to knock, then changed her mind. Perhaps it was better to act with stealth. She tried the door. It was unlocked. She was about to enter when she heard a low growl. A black mastiff came careening around the corner of the house and lunged at her with his teeth bared. The half-open door saved Livia. It acted like a shield, keeping the beast from jumping her and sinking his fangs into her throat. He caught only the billowing fabric of Livia's cloak and tore it as she slipped into the house and bolted the door against him. Her heart pounded as she listened to his furious barking and scratching. He hurled his body against the door over and over, but it held fast.

Livia looked around the room: a tumbled bedstead, a roughly hewn table and chair, a chest, clothes strewn on the floor and hanging from a hook in the wall. A door at the far end of the room opened to steps leading down — to the kitchen? The place seemed deserted. Livia had meant to creep up on the house, but the screams she let out when she saw the dog must have alerted anyone close by. Yet her cries had gone unanswered. Where was Aurelia and the tutor? When the beast left off clawing at the door and silence returned, Livia made out a low moaning sound. It came from below. She walked down the steps into the kitchen, a foul-smelling dugout half buried in the ground with a single window, barred and stopped up with rags. The fire in the hearth was burning low, leaving the room in murky darkness. Livia groped her way along the wall, guided by the sound of the moans. The walls were damp and sticky with a greasy layer, years old. She bumped into a shelf and upset an earthenware jar. It hit the ground with a crash and broke into pieces. The pungent smell of medicinal herbs filled the air and coated Livia's tongue. It was a smell she had come across before, but where? There was no time to search her memory because she heard the sound of footsteps nearing the kitchen. Or thought she heard steps. She listened with bated breath, but all was silent. The moaning had stopped as well. Instead she heard the gurgling sound of a death rattle. Her foot touched something soft. A body! She bent down and by the glow of the embers saw that it was Don Antonio stretched out on the floor. There was a gash in his throat, a ragged gaping wound that had soaked the front of his shirt with blood.

As Livia knelt beside him, calling him softly by name, the kitchen door banged shut, as if caught by a gust of wind. The wounded man stretched out his arms toward her. They were scored with scratch and bite marks, the broken skin crusted with dried blood.

"Donna Livia," he said. His voice was a hoarse whisper. "Run while you can. She will kill you."

"No, I cannot leave you like that," Livia said. "Let me—" She took off her shawl and wrapped it around Antonio's throat, trying to staunch the blood, but she could see it was no use. It soaked through the thin fabric almost at once, giving it a dark rusty hue. "I'll get help," she said.

"There is no help for me," he said feebly. "I'm dying. The dog —"

"Hush," she said, and stroked his cheek.

His parched lips stretched into the semblance of a smile. He searched for her hand. "Donna Livia," he said with a great effort, but he was too weak to go on. The words died on his lips. He closed his eyes.

For a while she sat with him quietly. Then she gently withdrew her hand and got up. Time was of the essence if she was to save him — if it was possible to save him — but when she tried the kitchen door, she found it bolted from the other side. It wasn't the wind that had banged the door shut. Livia's ears had not deceived her when she heard footsteps. Someone, lurking in the house, had locked her in. The realization made her breath come faster. She rattled the door in vain. She was a prisoner. There was no way out. Even if she managed somehow to break the lock, how could she escape the fangs of the dog guarding the house — a vicious beast that had ripped Antonio's throat! She could not help thinking of that other attack on the road to Gesualdo, the mastiff that had killed Fina's mule, the talk of the guards saying that one of the robbers looked like a woman, the tales spread at the inn that the rider was the devil in disguise and the pine forest a meeting place for witches. Livia had given no credit to those tales at the time and had brushed off Emmanuele's claim that Aurelia was a witch. Now those thoughts came back unbidden, growing like weed, filling her mind with a thicket of confusing ideas. How did it all fit together — the rumours she had heard about Aurelia and the scene she had seen with her own eyes? The vicious dog that killed Fina's mule and the beast that savaged Antonio? The ambush on the road and the trap into which she had fallen now? She was still sorting through her thoughts when she became aware of another danger: the smell of smoke and the rustling sound of fire coming from somewhere close to the window. Panic seized Livia. She tore at the rags which covered the window, blocking the

231

daylight. They seemed coated with oil or pitch and were hot to the touch — singed by flames, she realized when she peered through the iron bars. The kindling she had seen piled against the house was on fire. She could hear the rush and roar of the flames as they rose, whipped by the wind, and licked the straw-thatched roof. Here was certain death. She was fated to burn alive like a heretic, unless the smoke suffocated her first. Already she felt a tightening in her chest.

No sound came from the corner where Antonio was lying. Perhaps a merciful God had delivered him from all cares and spared him the horror of a fiery death. She thought of the letter she had written before going to bed yesterday, a letter to Pietro, full of love and forgiveness. Would someone send it on to him? Would he weep for her? But she was not dead yet and she meant to fight for her life. Pietro's face appeared to her, strong and reassuring like a guardian angel. She took hold of a poker and tried to pry open the door. Pietro, she whispered, as if the name itself could give her strength. Then she reproached herself. Why put her trust in a man? She ought to seek salvation in the name of God and the saints. She called out to St. Florian, protector against fires. She wedged the poker between the frame and the door, but she could not budge it and fell on her knees, pounding the thick planks with her fists and crying desperately. Her breath came ragged now. Her lungs filled up with the smoke drifting through the window now that its path was no longer blocked by rags. Smoke curled from the corners of the room, where the ceiling rafters joined the stone wall. Once the beams of the roof caught on fire, it would not take long for the house to collapse and bury her in a smoldering grave. She leaned her forehead against the locked door and prayed to God for delivery. She thought there was an answering call, the voices of men, or was it only the dog barking and snarling somewhere outside? Then her mind could no longer hold any thought except a vision of Pietro cradling her in his arms, but perhaps it was Death holding her, calming her and taking away all fear.

CHAPTER 36

Naples, December 1594

The ship rounded the peninsula at Bacoli and sailed into the bay of Naples. It passed Saint Elmo's fortress and Castelnuovo, guarded by five massive towers and a wall jutting into the sea.

Standing at the ship's railing, Pietro admired the sight of the city before him. The houses rose in tiers, crowding up against a mountain range. The hills surrounding it were planted with vineyards and olive groves and dotted with mulberry trees — "to feed the silkworms," the man standing beside him explained.

Pietro's fellow passenger had already pointed out the most famous landmark: Mount Vesuvius.

"I was born in Nicolosi," he told him. "When I was eight years old, the volcano erupted. The lava spewing from its mouth swallowed everything in its path and buried our village. There have been five or six eruptions since, but nothing like the one that wiped out Nicolosi. I wouldn't want to live anywhere near the volcano. Almost every day you can hear rumblings and groans coming from its mouth as if it was possessed by evil spirits."

Pietro pointed to a warren of buildings not far from the harbour. "And what kind of settlement is that?"

"The garrison housing the Viceroy's soldiers," the man said. "They are supposed to defend us against pirates, but you want to know the truth? The Viceroy is afraid of a rebellion. That's why he hired soldiers." He spit into the water. When he spoke again, his voice was a growl. "And if he goes on like this, putting the thumbscrews on the common people, he will have his rebellion."

Pietro was glad when they reached the pier and the man moved away. He was dangerous company. Pietro had barely escaped the snare set for him by Cesare who had foisted a dangerous book on him. He had thrown away the book and warded off the charge of possessing the writings of a heretic. He did not want to come under suspicion of keeping company with a rebel next. It sounded as if his fellow passenger favoured the idea of a revolt at any rate. He seemed well informed about the garrison and the mission of the soldiers. Orazio had told him the same thing when he set out for Naples: Count Olivares was recruiting mercenaries because he feared an uprising. Looking at the barracks, Pietro wondered whether his friend was quartered there now. He would make inquiries tomorrow.

The harbour was filled with vessels of all sizes, from little fishing boats with brown homemade sails to large seagoing ships fully-rigged, with foreign names on their sides. There was a bustle of lading and unlading. The docks were crowded with porters. As customs officials searched the passengers' luggage, a mixture of worry and relief flooded Pietro's mind — he had discarded the treacherous "gift" for Prince Carlo, which would have landed him in the court of the Inquisition, but how was he to present himself to the Prince without a gift or a letter of introduction? It would be best to abandon that pseudo mission altogether, but admission to the Prince's court provided the best and perhaps the only chance of seeing Livia again. She had not answered his contrite letter and proposal of marriage, but there might be reasons for her silence other than the one feared most — that she longer cared for him. The letter may not have reached her. Or she may have sent a reply to Rome. Or she had no ready means of sending a reply. There were so many question marks in his life now, not just concerning his letter and Livia's response. Was Cesare's cruelty satisfied at last, or would he continue playing tricks on him to get his revenge? And why was he so implacable? Because Pietro was in love with a woman who had been in Cesare's way — a love that was all but hopeless, even without the obstacles Cesare had thrown into his path?

Even if Pietro made his way into the presence of the Prince Carlo, ingratiated himself with him and was taken into his service, he had no guarantee of succeeding with his courtship. What if Livia was married by now and happy in the arms of another man? Life in Gesualdo would be torture for him then. And even if all went well and Livia forgave him and agreed to become his wife, he was not out of Cesare's reach. The court of his brother-in-law would offer Pietro no protection against Cesare if he was as determined to ruin him as he seemed to be.

Pietro's mind was filled with doubts and anxieties as he made his way to the banker to cash his draft. He took little notice of life around him, the peasants sitting beside their baskets, selling their produce, the poor and sick camped out in the streets even during the rainy winter, the swarm of children and importunate beggars in the slums surrounding the harbour or the ornate coaches and elegant sedan chairs in the more prosperous part of town where the banker carried on his business,.

At the counting house, Pietro obtained a sum of money, enough to cover his immediate needs. He would have to be frugal from now on. He could expect no more money or favours from the court of Ferrara. The face of the young man who served him told him as much. In Rome Cigi had received him personally with a cordial smile. Here he was looked after by a sullen underling, and no arrangements had been made for his lodging.

"There's a place down the street that takes in lodgers," the young man said with a sulky droop of his lip. "It's got a baker's shop on the main floor, you can't miss it."

"Do you recommend it?"

The man shrugged. "My cousin stayed there once. He said the price was the best thing about it. If it's not good enough for you—" He gave him a look that said 'but I think it will do for your kind' and half turned away. "If you want something better, I can't help you. I'm not in the business of recommending lodgings."

Pietro thanked the man curtly and went to the place he had pointed out. The house was not overly clean, but it was affordable, and the landlady seemed friendly enough. Pietro would have liked to allow Cesare to believe that he had fallen into his trap and come to grief and thus put an end to his tricks. But his transaction with the banker would be registered in Ferrara. And if he succeeded in entering the service of Prince Carlo and settled at his court in Gesualdo, Cesare would hear of it as well. He therefore sent a brief message to Alessandro d'Este, informing him of his arrival in Naples and the "regrettable loss of the present meant for the Prince." It had fallen into the hands of a thief, he said. It was better to pretend ignorance and keep up appearances with Cesare's brother in spite of the dirty tricks played on him. Let his enemies attribute his escape to luck!

235

The next morning Pietro rode to the garrison and inquired for Orazio Farnese at the guard house. His friend was indeed quartered there. Soon the two men were sitting in a tavern and catching up on their lives over a pitcher of wine. The tavern was plain, but remarkably clean. The floor was covered with fresh rushes and the rough-hewn tables wiped spotless — unlike many inns Pietro had seen on his travels, where the crumbs and greasy remnants of dinners were swept on the floor, and dogs scavenged among the filthy rushes for discarded bones.

The young woman who served them wore a neat scarf and apron. Her glossy dark hair was woven into tight braids and pinned on top of her head. She had a pleasant face with soulful eyes and full cheeks, but her mien was unusually grave. Pietro caught an exchange of looks between her and Orazio, which he could not interpret. She seemed vexed.

Orazio took a gulp of his wine, as if he needed to quench not only his thirst but also the discontent written on his face. He smoothed his brow, however, when he saw Pietro's searching look, and was quick to shift the attention away from himself.

"And so Cesare d'Este sent you to Naples to report on Prince Carlo?" he said. "He should have done his spying last year, before signing the marriage contract."

"No doubt he did, but the circumstances have changed. As you've pointed out yourself, the Prince's uncle has lost power and can no longer promote the cause of Ferrara."

"And Cesare wants to get out of the contract?"

"He may want to get out, but that will hardly be possible. A marriage can't be cancelled as easily as a contract for a shipment of spices."

"Yet it has been done. There are reasons for dissolving a marriage that are acceptable to the Church."

"In certain conditions, I know — if consent was lacking, if the parties are too closely related, if the marriage hasn't been consummated — but none of these conditions apply. Donna Leonora isn't related to Carlo. She consented to the marriage, and she was pregnant when she left for Gesualdo."

"But there are other reasons for dissolving a marriage, such as a partner's incurable madness or acts of heresy—"

"Heresy!" Pietro said, thinking of the forbidden book Alessandro d'Este had asked him to give to the Prince.

"Does heresy fit the case? Is that the evidence they expect you to dig up?"

"I wonder."

This was a new twist in the story. Pietro thought the trap had been set for him. Perhaps Cesare hoped to kill two birds with one stone and cast suspicion on both the bearer of the book and the recipient.

When Pietro told his friend of Cesare's latest machinations, Orazio's face darkened.

"He is a dangerous man," he said. "You should look for another master."

"I *am* looking for another master. I thought of approaching the Prince, but that might be difficult without a letter of introduction."

"Will you be better off serving him than the Estes?"

"To tell you the truth: I was ready to abandon the courtly life. I've come to realize that I'm not cut out for it. A man has to be unscrupulous to succeed in that game."

"Unscrupulous, glib, devious and striking with lightning speed like a snake. That goes for any courtier anywhere, whether it's the ducal court in Ferrara or the papal court in Rome. Gesualdo will be no different. So why attempt to ingratiate yourself with the Prince?"

"Because there is a young woman in Gesualdo, who has captured my heart. Her name is Livia Prevera, and for her sake, I am willing to persevere and play the courtier a little longer, if that post takes me to Gesualdo and into her presence."

He was going to say more and explain everything to Orazio — the who and where and what for — but he was no longer sure how it all fit together. The story of his love, which had a beginning and end once, was suddenly elastic and malleable, had to be picked apart and put together anew.

"I suppose love warrants patience and suffering," Orazio said. He had put on a smile but it did not cover up the restlessness Pietro had noticed in him earlier.

"Are you speaking from experience?" he asked.

Orazio's hand swept the tabletop in a dismissive gesture. "The short answer is yes, I have suffered and am suffering still. I will spare you a longer answer. The story is too trite: wrong time, wrong place." His eyes wandered to the young woman serving another patron now. "And wrong woman. In short, I have lost my taste for love."

"But you haven't lost your taste for the military?"

"Not for fighting at any rate, not for the clanging of swords and the rush of battle, but I am stuck in the barracks, and I am getting tired of it. I may be holed up here for another year without

237

seeing any action," he said. "And the company is wretched — a pack of ill-bred villains, drunkards, gamblers, and whoremongers who do not know the meaning of discipline. Fortunately, I have made the acquaintance of a few worthy citizens in town. Indeed, I am invited to dine at the house of Councilor Fulvio di Constanza tonight. Why don't you come along? I'll send him a note. He won't mind another guest at table. On the contrary, you can satisfy his thirst for news from Rome. Too bad you can't bring out the story of Alessandro d'Este's intrigue and your narrow escape from the Inquisition. The Councilor would be well entertained by it, but I suppose you must be discreet if you want to be a player in the diplomatic game."

"I can't say I find the story entertaining myself, and it will certainly be wise to keep it to myself. I told you only because I can rely on your discretion. As for the diplomatic game: I wish the Prince would take me into his service and give me another chance at it. Serving him may not protect me from Cesare's ill will — his arm is long — but it would provide me with an independent living. And that is certainly an urgent consideration. I must make a living."

"Let me ask Don Fulvio to intercede with the Prince on your behalf. He knows him well. In fact, he was in charge of investigating the death of his wife and her lover five years ago. If we can get him going on the subject, you may find out some interesting details, and it's always good to know as much as possible about the man you hope to serve."

When they left the tavern, Pietro remarked that the serving girl had been none too friendly and the landlord had not greeted his guests, as was common courtesy.

"The old man doesn't like me or my fellow soldiers," Orazio said. "He is in league with the rebels and supports their cause. But perhaps you have already guessed my reason for patronizing this inn."

"The wrong woman?"

Orazio gave him a look, sullen and hot at heart. "The less said about her and her grandfather the better."

CHAPTER 37

As Orazio had expected, the Councilor extended his invitation to Pietro. When the two young men arrived and sat down to dinner with their host and his wife, they found him in a talkative mood, but what he told them about the Prince's court concerned events more recent than the honour killing five years earlier. Donna Leonora had given birth to a son. The good news was tempered, however, by another, troublesome story.

"The man who tutored the Prince's son by his first wife died in a fire — under suspicious circumstances," the Councilor said.

"The devil was in it, if you ask my opinion," his wife put in.

Don Fulvio cut her off impatiently.

"But I did *not* ask your opinion, my dear."

His wife persisted, however. "The tutor died in Aurelia Darrico's house, they say, and whenever that woman is involved, there is only one conclusion to be drawn. She bewitched the poor man, just as she bewitches all men."

The Councilor's heavy brows contracted. "We shall leave witchcraft to the judgment of the ecclesiastical courts."

"The mere fact that she tried to run away after the fire and wanted to join her mother in Venice, they say—"

The Councilor rapped the table. "That's enough, my dear."

Pietro would have liked to hear more about the fascinating Aurelia, but nothing more was said of her. The tutor's death, however, was a natural lead-in to that earlier event — the scandalous death of Maria d'Avalos.

"I understand that you investigated the crime," Pietro said.

"I took the witness reports," the Councilor said. "But you mustn't call it a crime. The Prince had every right to kill the culprits."

Donna Anna laid her hand on her husband's arm. "You should ask the music master to give us a recital after dinner. He has set a poem to music. It's all about Maria d'Avalos' death, and it's the saddest thing you have ever heard. You know the poem I mean, Fulvio. By Torquato Tasso."

The Councilor nodded savagely. "*On the Death of Two Most Noble Lovers.* No, I will not listen to verses praising a woman who betrayed her husband. A fitting subject for a crazed poet like Torquato Tasso, but not one I will have recited in my house."

Donna Anna blushed under the disapproving eyes of her husband.

"I do not mean to defend Maria d'Avalos' conduct, Fulvio, but she must have suffered a great deal in her brief marriage. The prince was barely twenty years old at the time and already as dry as an old stick. Some people say that his temperament was so cold he had a young man sleep with him to warm his back." She tittered nervously. "Can you imagine?"

"I prefer not to imagine it and recommend you to do the same," Don Fulvio said severely. "Where, may I ask, do you get such information, which is hardly fit for the ears of our company?"

Orazio laughed. "My ears are used to barrack talk and fortified against all assaults," he said.

Donna Anna defended herself. "I had it from a most respectable source. It was Fra Domenico who told me the story."

"That confessor of yours is a disgrace to the Church," the Councilor said.

"But you must admit that the Prince is peculiar."

"I don't know what you mean by peculiar."

"For one thing, his wife — his second wife, I mean — presented him with a son three days ago, or rather could not present the child to him because Don Carlo took off as soon as she went into labour and has announced that he will stay at his residence here until she has been churched and the purification ceremony is over. You must admit that's odd. And Fra Domenico said so, too."

"I don't care what Fra Domenico says. He is worse than an old woman when it comes to retailing gossip. As for Maria d'Avalos—" He turned to Pietro. "If you want to know the truth about her death, don't listen to gossips. Or to poets. Read my report."

Pietro said he would be glad to do so.

"Come back tomorrow, and I'll have the dossier ready for you."

Pietro thanked the Councilor for this opportunity to inform himself of the facts of the case.

"Quite right. The facts. The rest is drivel, you know. It didn't take long for scandal sheets to make their appearance in town. They were sold at every street corner and in every tavern and offered the most scurrilous details about the death of those wretched lovers. That their bodies were left on the stairs of the Palazzo San Severo — the Prince's residence at the time. That their bloodied corpses remained exposed for two days and the entire city came running to view the spectacle." The councilor paused. "If that had been the case, I would have observed it from this very table!"

He glanced toward the window, as if he wanted to check the Palazzo across the street and verify that there were no corpses lying on its steps. Pietro, too, turned his head and looked at the stately building whose carved stone pediments and finely wrought iron balconies were visible through the windows of the dining room. The arched and pillared carriage gate was flanked by two guards. The smooth stone steps leading to the gate were deserted.

"It is true at any rate that the Palazzo is haunted," Donna Anna said. "My own maid told me that she saw the dead princess at the windows of the upper floor and heard her moaning at night."

Fulvio di Constanza waved his hand as if to shy away a fly. "Your maid is a silly woman and talks a great deal of nonsense."

"She is not the only one who saw the ghost. But everybody agrees that Maria d'Avalos could have saved her life if she had heeded the warnings. She knew very well that her affair with the Duke of Gandia was much talked about. Gandia himself thought it was better to abstain from amorous meetings for a time. But Donna Maria goaded him. If his heart was capable of such fear, she said, he was no better than a lackey, and nature had made an error in creating him a nobleman. Naturally her words touched the Duke to the quick, and he hastened to assure her that he would lay down his life for her—"

"And whoever told you that story apparently has a cloak that renders him invisible and allows him to listen in on people's private conversations," the councilor said. "Or else he got it from

241

one of those pamphlets that are a tissue of lies and salacious inventions."

"Including the story that the Duke was found in Donna Maria's bed, wearing a woman's nightgown?" Orazio said, grinning. "I've read those scandal sheets, you know."

"Well, as to that—" the councilor said. "But enough of Donna Maria and her tragic death." He turned to Pietro. "Let us talk about your travels instead. You arrived here from Rome yesterday, Orazio tells me?"

The conversation turned to Pietro's dealings in Rome as far as they could be told, and the unfortunate loss of the present he was to convey to the Prince.

"No traveler is immune to thieves," the Councilor said. "They are a pest."

"It is an unfortunate business," Orazio put in. "The gift was Pietro's letter of introduction, as it were. It is his hope and ambition to serve the Prince."

The Councilor made no reply, but gave Pietro an attentive look as if to measure his suitability for a post at the Prince's court.

After the servants had removed the dessert dishes and Donna Anna excused herself, the men sat a little longer over their glasses. The talk circled back to the death of Maria d'Avalos, and the Councilor who had been so intent on propriety as long as his wife was at the table became more garrulous.

"The law was on the Prince's side of course," he said. "But the rest of the world thinks of him as a murderer. Or a madman even."

It was hard to forget the scene at the Palazzo San Severo, when he was called there to conduct the investigation, the Councilor said.

"The Duke of Gandia was stretched out on the floor of the princess' bedroom, wearing a woman's nightgown — yes, that's a fact, I'm afraid. One sleeve was red with blood. He had been stabbed in the chest repeatedly, and the wounds were gaping open — like little crying mouths, they looked. The left side of the Duke's face was scorched by a shot that went right through his head, so that his brains were oozing out. And Donna Maria — what a wretched sight it was to see that beautiful woman lying on the bed, drenched in blood. Her throat was cut. There were stab wounds to her face and her hands, as if she had tried to ward off her assailant. A shot had gone into her leg and shattered it. You could see the shinbone." He shook his head. "It was a gruesome sight."

Of course the whole bloody tragedy could have been avoided, he said, if the Prince had managed his wife properly. It proved once again that it was best for a man to marry a young girl and surround her with trusted servants to keep a tight watch on her morals and preserve her innocence. Instead the prince had chosen Maria d'Avalos, twice widowed and with a reputation for having a rapacious appetite for sex.

"Don't you wish you had known that woman?" Orazio said, grinning at Pietro. "I can't blame the Prince for taking his chances with her."

"Well, I will say this much in his defense. Everyone was taken in by Donna Maria's angelic looks. That face of hers — as round and as soft as a child's. And her eyes — as large and innocent as a doe's. Go to the Cathedral and look at the painting above the main altar," he said to Pietro. "The artist used her as a model for one of the holy women depicted there. And indeed she looked like a saint. I was taken in myself and charmed by her beauty. It was a great privilege, I thought, to have Donna Maria as a guest or be seated next to her at one of the grand banquets the Prince gave. And what a pleasure it was to listen to her soft voice telling the most amusing stories and to watch her elegant figure—" The councilor cleared his throat. "But she was a viper!"

"The pamphlet I read claimed her first husband died of overindulging in conjugal relations," Orazio said. "And her second husband lasted only half a year before wasting away in her arms."

"For all I know, she poisoned them both. Or rather that old servant of hers did it. Silvia Darrico. My wife is not entirely wrong when she says the devil is in those Darrico women. I know that Silvia's love philters have driven men mad. So, beware, young men."

"Fortunately I have no need of love philters," Orazio said.

"Good for you, and I hope you will never be so foolish as to use them, for the consequences outlast the pleasure they give. The Prince, they say, suffers from ill health as a result of Silvia Darrico's concoctions."

"What is the nature of his illness?" Pietro asked, remembering the incident he himself had witnessed when he attended the marriage negotiations in Gesualdo and was a party to the hunt arranged in honour of Cesare d'Este.

"I believe he has seizures from time to time, but it's all being hushed up. The trouble evil women can cause! Thank God my two daughters have been properly raised and are women of sterling character. Both have been married off to advantage and are living lives that would not supply even half a line to the scribbler of a scandal sheet. As for the Duke, Maria d'Avalos' lover — mark my words. If his wife had been less religious and more accommodating, he might not have looked for satisfaction elsewhere."

"The scandal must have been hard on the Duke's widow," Pietro said.

"She decided to enter a convent. If you ask me, she should have taken vows earlier if she wanted to live like a nun, instead of marrying the Duke and then neglecting her wifely duties and driving him into the arms of another woman — with dire consequences."

"What surprises me it that the families of the two victims did not embark on a vendetta," Pietro said.

"The Prince was afraid of that as well. I counselled him to leave his residence here at once and depart for Gesualdo. He took my advice, hired soldiers and posted sentries on the walls of his castle. He was prepared for an assault, but the affair blew over. The two families preferred oblivion to revenge. They wanted the world to forget the scandal."

Don Fulvio leaned back in his chair. He had come to the end of his tale and cast a benevolent look at Pietro. His good manners and courteous talk had gained his approbation, or else the wine they were drinking had its beneficial effect.

"So you are in need of an introduction to the Prince," he said. "Perhaps I can oblige."

Pietro bowed and expressed his profound gratitude for any help the Councilor might give him.

"Come tomorrow then, and while you read my dossier — for you certainly ought to know the truth about that affair if you mean to enter the Prince's service — I shall have my secretary draw up a letter of introduction. The Prince cannot fail to look with favour on a young man recommended by me."

"Well," Orazio said as they were riding home, "you are all set. I wish the old man could get me out of the barracks, but I'm afraid that will take more than a letter of reference."

"It would take a rebellion, I suppose," Pietro said.

"Right, and I can hardly expect the Councilor to foment a rebellion for me."

CHAPTER 38

When Pietro arrived at Don Fulvio's house the next morning, his host took him to the library.

"Here it is, as promised," he said. The dossier had been laid out for him on a desk. "Read it, and when you are through, ring for my secretary. He will have a letter of reference ready for you. I would have liked to hear your opinion of the affair, but you must excuse me. I have an engagement I cannot put off. I hope we will have an opportunity to talk about the case another time."

The Councilor left, and Pietro settled down to read his report. The library was not designed to foster concentration. The black and white floor tiles were arranged in a swirling pattern. An ornate desk was placed at the centre, where the lines converged in a kind of bull's eye. The curving pattern of the tile had a disquieting effect on Pietro. The murals covering three of the four walls were distracting as well. They had the intrusive quality of a trompe d'oeuil. The scenes, taken from ancient history, depicted philosophers holding forth and seers giving their oracular pronouncements. The figures were painted with such precision and so lifelike that they seemed like visitors from the past ready to draw Pietro into a conversation. He thought with nostalgia of the quiet vaulted room that had been his domain in Ferrara, the white-washed walls, the unadorned shelves stocked with books and ledgers. Thinking of the simple life he had enjoyed there made him sigh, but nostalgia was of no use to him now. He must think of his future. Serving at the court of the Prince offered him the best chance to make a life for himself and see Livia again. Here was an opportunity to gather information about Don Carlo. It would help him to say the right things if he was asked to present himself to the Prince.

He opened the folder Don Fulvio had left for him on the desk and began to read:

Statement of the witness Silvia Darrico, maid in charge of the princess' wardrobe:
"On the night of 16 October, at ten o'clock, Donna Maria prepared to go to bed. I helped her undress and went to my room, which was next to hers, to freshen her petticoat and prepare the clothes for the following day. A little later I heard the Duke of Gandia whistle from below the balcony, as he always did to attract my lady's attention. Then Donna Maria called me and asked for a nightgown because, she said, the one she wore was wet with perspiration. I brought her one with the collar and cuffs embroidered in black silk. After I went back to my room, I lay down on my bed without undressing, thinking Her Ladyship might call for my services again. Then I fell asleep.

Later I woke up with a start when someone entered my room by the connecting door that opens on to a spiral staircase which leads down to Prince Carlo's bedroom. I thought I was dreaming when I saw by the light of the moon three men passing my bed, followed by the Prince himself. One of the men was carrying an arquebus. It was too dark to see whether the others were armed as well. They entered my lady's bedroom, and I heard the Prince say 'There he is, the scoundrel!' and right afterwards 'Whore, I shall kill you!' I heard two shots and a great deal of screaming and commotion. That is when I stopped my ears and hid under the bed and did not come out until the Prince's valet called my name and said. 'Both of them are dead.' I did not have the courage to enter my lady's room until the next morning, when I saw her on the bed, lifeless. On the chair beside the bed were a pair of green breeches, a white doublet, and green silk stockings, and on the floor was the Duke of

246

Gandia dressed in my lady's nightgown and covered with blood."

Asked by the magistrate what happened to the bodies, she said:
"The Marchioness of Vico, Her Ladyship's aunt, came, and we helped her wash and dress my Lady's body and place it into a coffin. I heard it was taken to the church of San Domenico. I don't know what they did with the body of the Duke."

Paolo Bardotti, the Prince's valet was questioned next. He reported:
"On the Tuesday evening, I served supper to the Prince on the mezzanine floor. After supper, I made up his bed, helped him undress and put a coverlet over him, then went to bed myself. Around midnight, the Prince called for a drink of water. I went down to the courtyard to draw water and saw that the street door was open, which was unusual for that time of night. When I brought the glass of water to the Prince, I saw that he was dressed to go out. He told me to fetch him his cloak. When I asked where he was going at this hour, he replied: 'Hunting.' I expressed surprise, and he added: 'You will see the kind of hunting I have in mind.' He took a dagger from the chest by his bed and, armed like that, went up to the apartment of Donna Maria. As I opened the door to the corridor, I saw three men waiting for him, each armed with a dagger and a small arquebus. They rushed up the stairs to Donna Maria's bedroom, with the Prince calling out: 'Kill that scoundrel together with the harlot!' I followed them as far as the maid's room, but stopped when I heard screaming. A little while later the Prince came out, his hands covered with blood. He called out 'Make sure that they are dead.' Then the three armed men joined him, descended the stairs and left on horseback."

Thus the witness reports taken by me. Afterwards I accompanied the Prince to the Viceroy, seeking his advice about the case. He agreed that the laws were on the Prince's side, although perhaps he should not have become personally involved. "What?" the Prince said.

247

"Is it more honourable to hire a knave to kill my wife than go after her myself and have members of my family kill her paramour?" The Viceroy said that was a matter of opinion. Culpability, however, was a matter of the law, and in that respect the Prince had done nothing wrong.

This concludes my investigation into the deaths of Maria d'Avalos and the Duke of Gandia. In witness of the truth thereof, I sign with my own hand: Fulvio di Constanza, Councilor and Judge of the Grand Court.

Pietro closed the folder and sat for a while in contemplation. So these were the bare facts. But did the details contained in the report add up to a whole? There was a great deal missing, he thought, remembering what the Counselor's wife had said the other night at dinner. The record of facts did not tell the reader of Silvia Darrico's sinister arts, or the role she may have played in corrupting her mistress, or the potions that sickened and killed her first two husbands. Nor did the report tell of the Prince's state of mind, and the agony and remorse he must have suffered. Or did the fact that the law permitted the killing satisfy his conscience? And of course the report said nothing of the aftermath, of the tears Maria's motherless child must had shed, the misery of her servants when her household was dissolved, or the havoc Silvia Darrico's concoctions wrought on the Prince's own health. No, the facts fell short of the sum total. Perhaps those scandal sheets which their gruesome details reflected more accurately the horror of the affair.

In the afternoon, Pietro made his way to the Prince's residence to seek an audience. The Councilor had supplied him with a letter of introduction. The palazzo, where the Prince was staying, was not far from San Domenico Maggiore. Pietro passed the church and looked up at the high windowless walls and the crenellated roof. It had the appearance of a fortress. The monastery adjoining the church was where Saint Thomas Aquinas had once lectured. To think that the place which fostered the great saint also brought forth the heretic Giordano Bruno, whose godless book had almost been Pietro's ruin! But God and good fortune had saved him, and he hoped his luck would hold. He came armed with Don Fulvio's letter and was accompanied by the Councilor's servant. The

248

guards at the entrance of the Prince's residence nodded to the man and waved them through into the courtyard. At the palace door, the servant took his leave, well rewarded by Pietro. He had come to understand the value of an attendant who wore the livery of an important magistrate.

He entered and stood in the hall of the palazzo, looking around. A magnificent marble staircase led to the upper story, its gray pattern rippling like a river of ice. On his right he saw a desk where a secretary might screen visitors, but it was unmanned. Perhaps he had come too early. It was barely past the hour of siesta.

He was considering his next step, when a door at the far end of the corridor burst open and the Prince rushed out, followed by Giovanni di Grassi protesting in an urgent voice: "Your horse, sire-"

"Let me be," the Prince shouted, brushing him off impatiently. "I shall walk."

He made for the door leading to the street, but the majordomo stepped in front of him, blocking the Prince bodily.

"My lord, let me accompany you," he pleaded.

"No man shall stand between God and my conscience," the Prince said, shouldered past the anxious man and charged out into the courtyard.

The majordomo leaned against the door, defeated. It was then that he caught sight of Pietro, who had stepped back and was standing in the shadow of the wall.

"Pietro Paci! You here!" he said, dismay showing on his face as he realized that the young man had witnessed the embarrassing scene. "I must say you have a knack for showing up at the most awkward moments."

"That is hardly my fault, sir," Pietro said.

"Well, you kept your mouth shut the last time, and perhaps you can be of help to me now. I fear the Prince is on the brink of another seizure. Run after him. I've done my best and will only aggravate him if I try again. See what you can do."

There was no time to lose. Pietro went after the disturbed man. He could see the Prince moving along the street with jerky steps as if his legs were too stiff to bend at the knees. People were getting out of his way, staring after him, and shaking their heads, thinking perhaps that he was drunk. Pietro caught up with the Prince at the doors of San Domenico. The church was all but deserted at this hour and steeped in the silence of ancient stones. The Prince entered and stood for a moment in the dark nave looking up to the painted ceiling, then turned to a side altar, where he fell on his knees. It was hard to tell whether it was an act of devotion or the move of a man overcome by illness.

Pietro, who had followed him into the church, took up station by one of the pillars and watched the prince closely. He appeared more haggard than the last time he had seen him in Ferrara. His pale face was like marble, his eyes lay deep in their sockets. After a while he got up and stood for a moment dazed. Then he looked around and caught sight of Pietro. To his surprise, the Prince seemed to recognize him and be glad to see him. He stretched out his arms like a supplicant.

"It's him!" he said in a low voice, speaking to himself. "My guardian angel. The face I saw when I came out of my trance." He went up to Pietro and opened his arms as if to embrace him.

"I am no angel, my lord," Pietro said, stepping back in confusion.

"Man or angel, God sent you once to save me from tumbling over the cliff, and has sent you again to save me from peril. So be it. I'll make my confession to you."

"I am a layman, my lord," Pietro said. "I cannot hear your confession. You must seek out a priest."

"A man may confess to another when he is in imminent danger of death, as I am, for the devil has me in the grip. He is clawing at my chest, trying to take my soul from me. Will you hear my confession, whoever you are?"

Pietro resigned himself to the inevitable. "I am Pietro Paci, at your service," he said.

"Pietro — the name of the first apostle. *You are Peter*, the Lord said, *and on this rock I shall build my church, and the Gates of Hell shall not overcome it.*"

The Prince took Pietro's arm and pulled him into the central nave. Their steps echoed under the vast stone arches as they walked up the aisle. The Prince stopped and pointed to a large painting above the main altar.

"You see that woman who poses as a saint? She is Maria d'Avalos, who took me to the Gates of Hell."

Pietro looked at the image of the Prince's first wife described so eloquently by the Councilor the previous night. The painter had made her a woman of great beauty with a wide immaculate forehead, finely arched eyebrows, and a soft mouth. Her hair was covered with a veil of gauze, and the expression of her face, as she regarded the book in her hands, was that of an angel or saint.

"She led me into temptation. She caused me to sin gravely," the Prince said, beginning his confession. Pietro had no desire to hear more. It was good to have a ruler's trust, but knowing too much about his moral lapses was dangerous. Carlo might come to regret his candour and resent Pietro's knowledge of his flaws. Even if there was no danger, it was embarrassing to intrude on a man's intimate thoughts and feelings. Pietro wished he could get away, but the Prince had grasped his arm and would not let him go.

"The period of mourning for her late husband had not yet elapsed when I married her — it was against divine law," he said and gave Pietro the beseeching look of a penitent asking God for forgiveness. "That was my first sin. My marriage was doomed from the beginning. I should have taken the advice of my music teacher and remained celibate. He understood the importance of music for my spiritual well-being. I should have remained true to the Muse, but I married that devilish woman, and she raised in me an unbridled, an unholy desire. Lust debases a man, and I confess to my lust. That was my second sin."

He paused for a moment, expecting perhaps some acknowledgement from his "confessor" but Pietro was too uncomfortable with Carlo's declarations. He could do no more than nod, and the Prince went on breathlessly.

"Then Maria accused me of neglecting her. Her soul fed on love, she said, and I was depriving her of sustenance. Nature had made her a creature of love, she said, but I say she was a creature of the devil who implanted in her an unchaste and libidinous desire for Don Fabricio Carafa, the Duke of Gandia. God said: *The vengeance is mine*. But I took it upon myself and killed Don Fabricio together with my faithless wife. That was my third sin."

Again he paused and waited for an acknowledgement from Pietro.

"Maria d'Avalos has paid for her sins with her life," Pietro said choosing his words carefully. "May her soul rest in peace."

"No, God will not allow her to rest in peace!" the Prince cried. "She roams the world as a ghost and she continues to haunt me, working her mischief through the devil and his minions and through Aurelia Darrico, who has revived my lust. I confess that I had carnal knowledge of her, even after I came to realize that she was a witch and in league with the devil. That is my fourth sin. May God have mercy on my guilty soul. How many times did I drink the potions which the devil helped Aurelia brew, how many times did I lie with her, and would do so still if God had not

251

delivered me from her clutches by sending me a good and gentle wife."

"Then surely that is a sign that your sins have been forgiven," Pietro put in. He was trying to calm and reassure the penitent Prince, but the fear in his eyes only deepened. He let go of Pietro's arm and put his fingers on his lips. "No, don't say so. God may have forgiven me the sin of fornication, but now I have offended him again. I have the loss of another man's life on my conscience. My son's tutor died in the house of Aurelia. God will lay his death at my feet when the day of reckoning comes. Aurelia threatened to harm my wife and newborn child. The tutor meant to warn me and paid with his life. I am responsible for his death. That is my fifth and last sin. I fear it will be my death!"

He swallowed hard and crossed himself. He had come to the end of his litany. "Almighty God," he continued. "I deeply repent of my deeds and ask your forgiveness with all my heart. The taste of remorse is in my mouth, as bitter as cinders. I promise to do penance, any penance you see fit to impose on me. I will do whatever this man, whom you have sent to save me, counsels me to do. Only spare my innocent wife and child and deliver me from all evil. Amen."

He looked humbly at Pietro.

Pietro thought it best to play the role of the confessor imposed on him. He made the sign of the cross and said: "Your sins are forgiven. Go and sin no more."

The Prince slumped forward and leaned heavily against him. A shudder ran through his body. Pietro feared it was the onset of another seizure.

Out of the corner of his eye, he saw a woman enter the church. She looked at Pietro and the man in his arms, clapped a hand over her mouth as if to keep herself from crying out, and ran off.

Pietro half-walked, half-dragged the Prince to the entrance of the church. He reached into the stoop filled with holy water and splashed it on the Prince's face. Either the miraculous power of the water or the cold sprinkle brought him out of his stupor. His eyes snapped open, but his mouth remained a jagged line, frozen in silence.

In the meantime the woman had alerted the friars, and two black-robed figures approached. They recognized the Prince and asked if he was ill.

"He is not himself," Pietro said cautiously.

But the friars knew of the Prince's ailment and understood Pietro's meaning at once. Supporting the sick man between them, they led him to the sacristy and urged him to lie down on a bench. He stretched out but immediately jumped up again and went into a mad dance. His limbs trembled and twitched. His whole body contorted into a crooked shape.

"Make room for him and leave him be," one of the friars whispered. "It is not the first time we see him like this. I wish he did not come here, or at least avoided looking at the painting above the altar. It has a curious effect on him."

By and by the jerking motions of the Prince slowed and changed to languorous twirls and glides. Finally his body crumpled, and he fell to the floor. Once again the friars lifted him up and laid him down on the bench, and this time he lay still. After a while he recovered his wits, looked around, and acknowledged his helpers.

In the meantime the friars had sent a message to di Grassi and he came in a coach to take the sick man home. The Prince rose from the bench with difficulty, took Pietro's hand in silent gratitude and allowed di Grassi to lead him to the waiting coach.

The next morning Pietro presented himself once more at the Prince's palace. The Majordomo received him with a smile of welcome.

"You are a lucky man," he said. "You have won Don Carlo's favour, and that in spite of a letter from his uncle, Cardinal Gesualdo, which wasn't exactly a recommendation. But the Prince saw something positive even in the unflattering picture his uncle drew of you. And now that you have rescued him from despair, or so he tells me, he trusts you implicitly."

"I am glad to hear it," Pietro said, "but what did the Cardinal write about me?" He was taken aback by this latest treachery.

"That's not for me to say. Perhaps the Prince will tell you himself. He is in consultation with the Prefect of San Domenico, but he asked to have you sent in as soon as you arrived."

He nodded to the secretary, who showed Pietro into the audience room.

"Pietro Paci!" The Prince rose from his chair and welcomed his visitor with open arms.

The Prefect, who had been interrupted in mid-sentence by Pietro's entry, gave the newcomer an inquiring look. "Perhaps I should come back at a more opportune moment," he said with a bow to Don Carlo.

"No, stay," the Prince said. "I want this man's opinion on the merit of your proposal."

The Superior's face darkened. "Is that wise, my son? This is a private matter."

"God has sent this man to be my guardian angel," the Prince said. "I intend to take his advice." He took Pietro by the arm and pointed him to a seat next to his own. "The Reverend Father believes that my seizures are caused by evil spirits. He advises me to undergo exorcism. What is your opinion?"

The Prefect saw that he had to persuade not only the Prince but Pietro as well. He addressed himself to the young man who seemed to enjoy Don Carlo's special favour and brought out his proposal once more. "I should add that Fra Lippo, the exorcist I have in mind, is a most devout and holy man," he said. Turning back to the Prince he made another point he hoped would sway Carlo: "And Your Lordship will remember that the rite is not only an act of purification but also an occasion for charity. Surely, God will look with pleasure on the donation Your Lordship so kindly promised us. He will bless Fra Lippo's undertaking."

The Prince ignored the Prefect's appeal and repeated his question to Pietro. "What is your opinion?"

"I hesitate to voice any opinion, my lord," Pietro said. "I hardly know-"

"The alternative would be flagellation," the Dominican said. "It has been shown to be a very effective means of driving out evil spirits." He had come to realize the importance of the young man's opinion and kept his eye on him. When he read disgust on Pietro's face, he changed course at once.

"I do not mean that Your Lordship would have to undergo the rite. It would be sufficient to hire flagellants to perform the act on your behalf, Sire. I have in mind two young postulants, who have provided this service before and are eager to perform it again. You will see the joy in their faces as they suffer under the lash, for they look upon it as an opportunity to show their devotion to God and earn your gratitude besides."

"It seems to me that I should atone for my own sins." the Prince said.

"You would do your part of course, and humble yourself by washing the wounds of the flagellants with wine and cleaning the whips after the ceremony."

"Pietro Paci will make the decision for me," the Prince said, taking the young man's arm, as if to lean on him.

Pietro was reluctant to choose between the alternatives. Exorcism and flagellation were equally abhorrent to him. The whole business smacked of corruption, a scheme for extracting money from the Prince rather than a means of healing him.

The two men looked at Pietro expectantly. He had to make a choice.

"Exorcism seems preferable to flagellation. At least we read about it in the gospels," he began and became convinced by the sound of his own voice. "And we have the example of Christ healing men possessed by demons."

"And they came out into a herd of swine," the Dominican intoned, "*and, behold, the whole herd ran violently down a steep place into the sea.* Matthew 8:32. Yes, the Lord himself showed us the way to cast out evil spirits. And this is a most propitious season, Your Lordship. We are all obliged to do penance during Advent."

"So be it," the Prince said. "I'll undergo exorcism." He dismissed the Prefect with a wave of his hand. "Go and make the necessary arrangements."

When the friar had left, the Prince went to the window and stood there silently for a time, looking at the sturdy tower of San Domenico, deep in thought. When he turned, his face had lost its turbulent aspect. He was a reigning prince once more.

"Tell me," he said to Pietro, "is it true that you were to present me with a book by a condemned author?"

Pietro tried to hide his consternation at this unexpected question.

"I was given a sealed parcel to deliver to Your Lordship," he said, "but it was stolen from me. Alessandro d'Este, who entrusted the parcel to me, said nothing about its contents."

"Then it was the hand of God, who protected me and would not allow you to be the agent of my destruction. My uncle warned me. He said you were a babe in the woods, a fool in the hands of seasoned schemers. The Estes were planning to use you to bring about my ruin, he said, but I wrote back reminding him that *God's foolishness is wiser than human wisdom,* that God had sent you to pull me back from the abyss once, and would not allow you to harm me now. It is well to put your trust in God. He has protected us both."

"I am honoured by your confidence in me, my Lord, but how did your uncle, the Cardinal, come to know what was in the parcel?"

255

"He is well connected. He has a veritable army of informers. The book you were asked to present to me was a work by Giordano Bruno, who has been condemned as a heretic. Cesare d'Este no longer values his connection with the House of Gesualdo. He is plotting my ruin, but I shall defeat his purpose with the help of God and with the loving devotion of my wife."

"I wish your Lordship and Donna Leonora many years of happiness together."

"The letter of introduction Don Fulvio wrote on your behalf mentioned that you wish to enter my service."

"That was indeed my hope, Your Lordship."

"Another sign of God's providence. You are looking for employment. I am looking for a tutor for my son, for a man who can instruct the boy and protect him against evil. I must be vigilant in these unhappy times, not only against my earthly enemies but also against the demonic powers of Aurelia Darrico, a woman in league with the devil and out to harm me and my household."

Aurelia Darrico! The Councilor's wife was not the only one who regarded her as the devil's helpmate!

"God in his mercy has sent you to protect me and my son," the Prince continued. "And the exorcism will purify my soul."

Pietro bowed. "It will be an honour to serve Your Lordship in whatever capacity you wish to employ me."

CHAPTER 39

The Prince was in a hurry to shore up his defenses against the sinister forces he feared were aligned against him. This suited the Dominican prefect as well. He too was in a hurry - to receive the Prince's donation — and he lost no time to arrange for the exorcism.

Two days after his audience with the Prince, he was ready to have the rite performed. He welcomed the Prince, when he arrived at the appointed time with Pietro at his side and led them to the sacristy. A group of Dominicans had assembled there. The walls of the room were lined with the sepulchers of Spanish grandees. Their portraits watched over the room with stony gravity and would bear silent witness to the cleansing of the sinner's soul.

A purse of money discreetly changed hands. The prefect asked the Prince and Pietro, who was to assist in the ceremony, to stand in the centre of the room.

Fra Lippo, the exorcist, robed in black like an executioner, was kneeling before a cross, deep in meditation. The Prefect touched his shoulder and whispered into his ear. He nodded, rose and draped a stole embroidered with biblical quotes over his shoulders. At last he deigned to take notice of the Prince, who was waiting humbly, with his head bent low like a poor petitioner.

"On your knees!" he said harshly as if he was talking to a slave — a slave to sin.

The Prince obeyed and dropped to his knees. On the exorcist's direction, the Prefect wound a strip of linen around the Prince's neck, with the end trailing on the floor.

"These are the sins that tether you to the Devil," the exorcist said in a somber voice. "You are the Devil's dog, but I shall deliver you from your abominable master."

The Prince meekly submitted to the linen being put around his neck. His eyes were full of melancholy.

Pietro was instructed to take the end of the "leash" with one hand and hold a wax figure of the Lamb of Christ in the other.

The exorcist had placed a vessel of holy water on a table that served as a make-shift altar and placed candles on the four corners. They cast fantastic shadows on the sepulchers, as if the bodies of the dead were rising from their graves to watch over the proceedings. Pietro shivered at the ominous sight. He gripped the wax image of the Lamb of Christ more firmly and hoped it would protect him against the evil spirits the exorcist promised to call forth. The Prefect and three of his brethren had taken their places on chairs ranged against the wall. They pulled their hoods up over their heads, concealing their faces in the shadows and burying their hands in the sleeves of their tunics, all but vanishing in the sepulchral darkness.

The exorcist began by reciting prayers and invoking God's mercy. His voice was thin at first, but assumed a darker timbre and a fuller ring when he addressed the devil directly.

"I charge you to quit the body of this man!" he shouted. The walls seemed to cast back a faint echo, but it was only the Prefect and his companions repeating the words in a low murmur.

The exorcist now began to rail against the devil, striking the prince with his fists, dealing him heavy blows on the chest and spitting into his face. The Prince swayed under the assault and made pitiful noises.

When the Prince recovered his balance, the exorcist thundered: "Do you love your Saviour Christ and abhor Satan?"

He replied with a weak "I do."

A groan rose from the brethren as if the devil could not bear to be renounced.

The exorcist bent down low and, bringing his lips close to the sinner's face, screamed again: "Do you love your Saviour Christ and abhor Satan?"

The Prince flinched and mumbled another "I do."

Once again the friars in the corner groaned in a devilish chorus, but the exorcist seemed to require a firmer answer. He shook the Prince's shoulders and asked the question a third time, adding in a threatening voice:

"Speak up and proclaim your love of God and your hatred of Satan in a loud voice. Wake up the sleepers in their sepulchers, call for their help!"

The Prince drew a deep breath, and repeated in a steadier voice: "I love my Saviour and abhor Satan."

The Prefect and his brethren rose with a great shout, walked to the four corners of the room and lifted up their candles, holding them above their heads and making the shadows leap and dance on the painted ceiling.

The exorcist took from the folds of his robe a pyx, a small box containing a consecrated host. He held it against the Prince's cheeks and roared out a litany of saints' names to pit against the spirits possessing the sinner. He did not stop his harangue until the candles had burned low and filled the Sacristy with a haze of smoke.

The Prince's head lolled from side to side. He seemed to be in a trance by the time the exorcist wound up his invocations, sprinkled him with holy water and ordered the Devil, or rather Pietro, to release him from his bonds.

"Rise up and give thanks to God!" he said.

The Prince struggled to his feet with Pietro's help.

"Thanks be to God," he said. His lips quivered when he asked the exorcist in a whisper: "Am I healed now?"

"It was a noxious and obstinate spirit that took possession of you," the man said. "We might have to repeat the procedure to drive him out for good. But let us hope that God has heard our prayers and delivered you from the Evil One."

The Prefect added his assurances: "I saw the shadow of the Evil One rising from Your Lordship's head and hovering above your shoulders until the drops of the Holy Water dissolved it. Aurelia Darrico will have no more power over you."

He looked at Pietro for affirmation and gave him a chagrined look when he seemed unconvinced by the Prefect's claims and remained silent.

He had found the rite theatrical and degrading for the Prince. Surely the devil — if he was the cause of the Prince's ailment—was too cunning to be overcome with such crude methods, he thought.

In the meantime the brethren had lit new candles to illumine the Sacristy. The exorcist took off his stole and with a final blessing led the Prince to the door.

Don Carlo leaned heavily on Pietro's arm as he took the few steps to the sedan chair waiting for him outside. Pietro suspected that he too doubted the efficacy of the rite.

"What do you think of exorcism now?" he said to Pietro who was steadying him. "Is it powerful enough to drive out the devil?"

"I am not wise enough to answer that question, sire," Pietro said.

"God's fool knows more than these wise men," he said, slumping back in his seat, exhausted. "They pretend to holiness, but they are men of the world."

They certainly profited nicely from the rite, Pietro thought. The purse the Prince handed to the Dominican before the ceremony had looked substantial.

That same night Pietro met with Orazio at the tavern near the garrison and told him about the rite he had witnessed.

"Those exorcists are charlatans and swindlers," Orazio said.

"I wouldn't go as far as calling them swindlers," Pietro said. "Perhaps they believe in the rite, but it was an undignified spectacle and did the Prince no good."

"The whole thing did you some good, at any rate. You've been hired to teach the Prince's son. How old is the boy?"

"Nine."

"Then you have a chance to shape the mind of the future Prince of Venosa. Who knows, you may end up as his chief councilor and make your fortune as a courtier after all." There was a hint of amusement in Orazio's eyes.

Pietro fell in with his ironic tone. "You seem to have great expectations of me."

"And why not? The tutor of Emperor Charles became his chancellor and ended up on the papal throne."

"And died a month after he took office!"

"Alright, but let's assume your post in Gesualdo will be less strenuous than the work of the pope and will not give you a heart attack."

"I don't know about that. The last tutor died a premature death."

"Under suspicious circumstances, as Don Fulvio said the other night. Have you heard anything more?"

"Only that Aurelia Darrico is accused of setting the fire and is held responsible for the tutor's death. Don Fulvio's wife isn't the

260

only one who thinks Aurelia is a witch. She will appear before an inquisitorial court on charges of heresy and witchcraft."

"Well, let the judges deal with that sordid story. In the meantime, let's drink to your good fortune — and your prospects of being united with your beloved in Gesualdo."

"Not so fast. I have no guarantee that Livia Prevera still regards me with favour. It's almost a year since I said good-bye to her in Ferrara. I was a fool then and preferred my so-called career to her love. I can't tell you how often I've regretted what I said to her, and even more what I didn't say. I buried my true feelings and gave her the impression that I was resigned to the situation. I thought I would get over my infatuation soon enough, but I haven't. I cannot forget Livia. I missed her every day and finally wrote to ask her forgiveness. That was a month ago. So far she hasn't answered my letter."

"I see." There was no great sympathy in Orazio's eyes. Perhaps he was thinking of his own unhappy love story. "In that case, congratulations may be premature," he said. "But there is another occasion to celebrate. Let's drink to my escape from the boredom of the barracks. I have decided to leave in a month' time, when my present term is up."

Now it was Pietro's turn to tease his friend. "Are you afraid of eternal peace descending on Naples? Have you given up on the rebels?"

"Not at all, but I have a better understanding now who they are. Do you remember the conditions I listed under which I was willing to join battle once more?"

"You said you wanted a worthy enemy. You had enough of fighting bandits."

"And I still hold to that condition. The followers of Tommaso Campanella — the leader of the rebels — are madmen and ignorant peasants armed with shovels and pitchforks."

"You have mentioned Campanella before. Who is this man? Does he really have the power to foment a rebellion?"

"He is an unlikely leader of rebels — a Dominican and a philosopher, whose crazed ideas landed him in the inquisitorial court at Rome. They tortured and imprisoned the man, but it seems they couldn't get a handle on his heresy. In desperation they sent him back to his native village in Calabria, hoping he'd end up buried and forgotten. But instead of lying low, he went around the countryside and preached to anyone who would listen to him. He ranted against the Spanish rule in Naples, promised to overthrow the Viceroy, and with God's help to introduce a popular government where everyone shared alike — the land, the houses, and the women, too. His scheme is more utopian than More's *Utopia*, and yet the peasants embraced it, and he has followers here in Naples, too. If they make a move, the Viceroy will send in the troops, but I don't have the heart to use my sword against that kind of men. There is no glory in mowing down ignorant folk."

He signaled to the serving girl — the handsome young woman who had served them the last time. She came to their table. There was something between those two, Pietro thought, a faint weave connecting them, a tension as between secret lovers. Yet she did not give Orazio so much as a smile. For a moment there was a look in his eyes that reflected only her and excluded all else: Pietro, the other patrons, the smoke that hung thickly under the rafters. Then he became conscious of his surroundings again and said: "Refill our cups, Elena."

As she turned to go, he took hold of her arm. "And perhaps I can get a smile out of you for once when I tell you the good news — I'm leaving Naples."

She quickly lowered her eyes, but not before Pietro had read the regret in them. Orazio had caught it too.

"Don't tell me you are sorry to see me go."

"What I think cannot possibly matter to you," she said, freeing her arm from his grasp and pulling away.

"But it does. Why do you begrudge me a smile, Elena? Have I offended you?"

"No, you have been more civil to me than any of your comrades — as befits the gentleman I take you to be. But what can a gentleman want from a serving girl other than making sport of her?"

"I assure you, Elena, I will always remember-

He was interrupted by the landlord, who had come up and put his hand on the shoulder of his granddaughter.

"While you listen to the assurances of this gentleman, Elena, you are neglecting the other patrons," he said. "And what's this talk about remembering?"

"The gentleman was telling me that he will quit Naples," she said.

"Good riddance and be damned!" the Landlord said. "The devil take you and all your comrades!"

Orazio's face went white with anger. "I see I'll have to give you a lesson in manners, old man," he said. He pushed back his chair violently, seized the landlord by his beard, dragged him

262

down and rubbed his face in the rushes on the floor. "That will teach you to swear at a gentleman!"

The clatter and hubbub in the tavern ceased. All talk stopped, then rose again in a chorus of excitement, as the patrons scraped back their chairs and stood to watch the fight.

The old man bucked and kicked against his assailant's shins, but Orazio held him fast.

"Apologize!" he said, his voice storm-darkened. His fellow soldiers thumped their fists on the tables and echoed his demand. "Apologize, you bastard, you bloody son of a dog."

Orazio was holding the old man down with an iron grip. "Let's hear you say you are sorry you didn't show the respect you owe me."

"And what are you going to do if I don't?" The old man's wheezed under the pressure of Orazio's hold.

"I'll send *you* to the devil, or my name isn't Farnese."

Tears were running down Elena's cheeks as she implored her grandfather to apologize. "I'm begging you, grandfather. Say you are sorry. You have injured the honour of a gentleman."

The old man twisted his neck and, speaking with his mouth full of rushes, declared that he was not going to apologize to anyone for saying what was true. The soldiers were brutes hired to harass good citizens.

Orazio tightened his grip on the man. His fellow soldiers had formed a circle around the pair and cheered him on. "Make the old bear dance," they shouted. "Teach the son of a bitch a lesson he won't forget."

Elena was sobbing now, and Pietro tried to pull his friend off the man on the floor.

"Come, Orazio," he said. "Is it honourable for a young soldier to fight an old man with a lame leg?"

The other patrons urged Orazio on and jeered the landlord. "Break his legs! And his arms while you're at it. Cripple the bastard."

"Spare him for my sake," Elena pleaded.

"Let him go, Orazio," Pietro said quietly. "If you are eager to fight, I'll stand in for the old man. At least then it will be a fair match."

He had calculated his words well. The appeal to honour and fairness was effective. Orazio released the landlord, and said to Pietro: "You are right. This fellow isn't worth getting my hands dirty."

263

The others, who had been raring for a fight, groaned with disappointment, but Orazio pulled out his purse, threw money on the table to pay for their drink and made for the door.

Once outside, he turned to Pietro and said. "I suppose I owe you thanks for bringing me to my senses. I was about to make an ass of myself fighting that peasant."

"Not to speak of distressing the young woman, for whom you professed an interest," Pietro said tersely.

They rode on in silence, but they did not get far before a little boy came running after them, shouting "Gentlemen, gentlemen, hoy there, wait up!"

They stopped.

The boy caught his breath. "Elena says to thank you," he said to Pietro. "And to give you this." He held up a handkerchief wrapped around a mysterious lump. "That's all she has to give you, she says, but she baked it herself, and everyone says she's the best pastry cook around."

The lump turned out to be a large macaroon. Pietro accepted the gift and rewarded the little messenger with a coin.

The boy tugged his forelock and ran back to the tavern.

"Well," Orazio said, "since we are friends, I expect you to share your loot with me."

"Meaning, you want a taste of Elena's sweet gift? I'm not sure you deserve it, my friend."

"Meaning, you can have the macaroon, and I'll take the handkerchief as a keepsake, and so we'll each have our fair share."

"Hardly fair after you showed no consideration for the young lady's feelings," Pietro said, but seeing the longing in Orazio's eyes, he took pity on him and handed over the keepsake. Alas for the woman who loses her heart to a soldier, he thought. The brutal business of war makes them unfit for true love, which requires surrender.

CHAPTER 40

The next morning Pietro made his way to the Prince's residence bright and early. He had what he wanted: a post at Don Carlo's court. It was a stepping-stone to his next goal: winning back Livia. She was in his dreams and in his waking thoughts. He was eager to leave Naples and make his way to Gesualdo, to find Livia and look for the answer to his letter in her eyes. But no one had told him when he was to take up his duties.

After a lengthy wait, the secretary showed him into di Grassi's office. The Majordomo was a busy man and always on the edge of nervous exhaustion, it seemed to Pietro. Not surprising, perhaps, considering that he had a large household to manage and served an unpredictable man. But this morning di Grassi looked more agitated and harassed than ever.

"What can I do for you?" he said, without taking his eyes off the document in front of him.

"I'm sorry to impose on your time, sir," Pietro said, "but I am in an awkward position. I have received no instructions concerning my duties."

Grassi looked up impatiently. "Haven't you read my letter?"

"Your letter?"

"Which I sent to your lodgings this morning."

"This morning? Then I missed your messenger. I spent the morning in your waiting room."

"And that idiot of a secretary didn't show you in at once?"

The "idiot" appeared at the door that very moment with a letter in his hand.

"Sir, you sent a message to Signor Paci this morning, but it couldn't be delivered." He looked at Pietro and shrugged his shoulders as if to say: It's not my fault that you are here when the messenger was there.

"Confound it all," di Grassi said. "What a muddle you've made of this business. Have you got the contract ready at least?"

The secretary bowed. "The papers are ready to be signed by Signor Paci."

"Then get on with the rest of your work," di Grassi said, dismissing him.

"You can sign the papers on your way out," he said to Pietro. "I wrote to tell you that the contract is waiting for you here. It lists your duties and will answer all your questions, I assume."

"And how soon will we depart for Gesualdo?"

"Not soon enough for me. I wish I could go this minute. My wife is very sick, you know."

"I'm sorry to hear it. I hope she is under the care of a good physician."

"The physician is useless. All he can suggest is purging and bleeding, purging and bleeding. And in addition—oh, what's the use of going on about it? I've asked the Prince for leave to go to Gesualdo, but he won't let me off until the trial is over." He saw Pietro's questioning look. "Aurelia Darrico's trial. That was the other reason why I wrote to you." He pointed to the sealed letter the secretary had returned to him. "You and I have been assigned our roles in that play, the final act of the tragedy, I hope. It means that I am stuck here for another week at least."

"And what is my role?" Pietro asked. "I know nothing about this affair except that Aurelia is being held responsible for the late tutor's death."

"It's all in my letter," di Grassi said, "and you can read it at your leisure. Let me just say that Aurelia is accused of a long list of crimes." He listed them off on the fingers of his hand. "Witchcraft, arson, murder."

"The murder of the tutor?"

Di Grassi nodded. "Her dog ripped the man's throat, and she went off and left him to bleed to death on the floor of her witches' den. And she came damn near to killing Livia Prevera, Donna Leonora's lady-in-waiting, who came looking for him."

266

Pietro's heart began to pound as he took in the ghastly news. "Livia Prevera!" he exclaimed, putting his hand to his chest to calm his beating heart.

Di Grassi saw the gesture and the shock written on his face and gave him a curious look.

"You know Donna Livia?"

"I met her at the ducal court in Ferrara," Pietro said, swallowing hard. He was afraid of losing face if he gave away the true state of his feelings. What if Livia no longer cared for him and rejected his offer of marriage? He would look like a fool in the eyes of the Mayordomo. For all he knew, Livia had given her heart to the tutor. Why else would she have gone looking for him?

"How did she end up, coming to the rescue of the tutor — were there no men around to help him?"

"She unwisely decided to investigate when she heard that he had gone missing. Donna Livia has a great deal of pluck, you know, too much for her own good if you ask me. And she almost paid for it with her life. Aurelia trapped her in the house and set fire to it."

A fire was raging also in Pietro's mind.

"And was Donna Livia hurt?"

"She was lucky. The men who came to beat down the flames, found her unconscious, overcome by the smoke. A downpour helped them put out the fire before the roof collapsed. Donna Livia was dazed, but otherwise unhurt. The tutor was beyond help. But really, I don't have time to tell you the whole story. You will hear it soon enough when we are briefed before our appearance in court. Aurelia will be tried for arson and murder. And poisoning may be added to those charges. She brought a plate of sweets as a birthing gift for Donna Leonora. My poor wife, who has a sweet tooth, tasted them and fell ill as a result."

"I can see why you are anxious to return to Gesualdo."

"I wish I could be with her now, but there is Aurelia's trial to be gotten through first, and this is what we need to talk about. The secular court will deal with the charges of murder, but first she will be called before a tribunal of the Inquisition to stand trial on charges of witchcraft. Livia Prevera has already given her deposition and told the inquisitor about the paraphernalia she saw at Aurelia's cottage. They say the woman brewed magic potions there, and the mastiff she kept was her demon lover and the devil incarnate. Other witnesses have come forward and attested to her depravity and signed statements against her. But the deposition of the Prince was a ticklish business."

"What! Did the Prince offer testimony as well?"

267

"Alas, it is common knowledge that Aurelia supplied him with potions. The Prince's legal counsel thought it best to put it all in a written deposition to forestall worse — that he be asked to appear in person. We went over every word in the deposition to make sure there was nothing self-incriminating in his testimony. Of course there is no telling what Aurelia will say about the Prince under cross examination."

He gave Pietro a searching look as if he could read there what Aurelia might say.

"Her testimony might be detrimental to the Prince's good name," Pietro said cautiously, thinking of the confession the Prince had made to him. He had listed carnal relations with her as one of his sins. Pietro assumed that the Majordomo was aware of Carlo's affair with the woman.

"It would have been better to stay clear of the ecclesiastic court," di Grassi said, "and to stick to the murder charges, which are handled by the secular authorities, but someone denounced the woman to the bishop and accused her of witchcraft and set the inquisitorial process in motion."

"What if Aurelia implicates the Prince in her evil practices and says that he took her potions willingly although he knew of her reputation as a witch?"

"You've put your finger on the problem. She may do just that, but the judges will not accept the word of a suspected witch. Three witnesses of good reputation are necessary to convict, and no one will support her accusation. Even so, we do not want even a breath of innuendo to reach the public."

"There can be little danger of that happening. The trial will take place *in camera*, won't it? And the proceedings of the Inquisition are never made public."

"That is correct, but the trial requires the presence of two clergymen and two laymen of good standing. And that is where you and I come in. The Prince has asked the Prefect of San Domenico and the man who performed the exorcism to attend the trial. They will keep their mouths shut in the expectation of his continued patronage. You and I will be invited to attend the proceedings as the lay representatives."

"Me of all people?"

"You have observed the Prince in the throes of convulsion and have been present at the exorcism. He tells me that he has been candid and told you about his involvement with Aurelia. And most importantly: he trusts you to keep silent about the proceedings. And now that he has taken you into his service, you have an obligation to be loyal to the House of Gesualdo. That is understood, I take it."

Pietro bowed. "I will serve the Prince as best I can."

CHAPTER 41

The vaulted chamber in which the inquisitorial trial was held was lit only by the slanted rays of the light coming through a solitary barred window. A long table had been set up on a raised platform. The walls were bare except for a large iron cross behind the Inquisitor's seat, which was distinguished from the rest by a high and ornately carved back. The examiners entered in procession behind two servants bearing torches casting their unquiet light on the gloomy room. The Inquisitor, dressed in a red robe, took his seat at the centre. The others sat down next to him, assessors on the right, observers on the left. Their seating order was determined by rank. The clerical observers — the Prefect and Fra Lippo the exorcist—sat next to the Inquisitor, the two laymen, di Grassi and Pietro, further down. The notary took his seat at separate table, paper and pen at the ready to record the interrogation.

A wooden rail separated the members of the tribunal from the accused.

When Aurelia was led in, there wasn't a man who could resist gaping at her. They were astonished by her beauty and moved by her melting eyes. Her head was crowned with thick hair of the darkest brown. She had a supple figure and moved with the indolent grace of a cat. Her style of dress was demure, but cut in a cunning fashion to reveal her tempting curves.

At a nod from the Inquisitor, the notary placed a bible before her and directed her to repeat after him: I swear to speak the whole truth and nothing but the truth, so help me God.

After she had been sworn in, the Inquisitor rose and began the proceedings in the usual manner, asking her name and that of her parents. Was her father living?

"He died when I was a year old," she said.

"And your mother?"

"She has gone to live with my brother in Venice."

"Is it true that she was accused of witchcraft five years ago?"

"It is true, but she was acquitted. The woman who accused her was motivated by spite."

"But your mother was convicted of blasphemy and had her tongue pierced?"

So far Aurelia had faced the tribunal boldly and with the mysterious authority beauty gives to a woman. There was power in her eyes, even though they lacked the force of character.

"Yes," she said in answer to the Inquisitor's question about her mother, and for a moment she lowered her eyes.

"Is it true that you fled after your house was destroyed by fire and that you attempted to seek refuge with your mother in Venice?"

"I did not *flee*," she said, recovering her poise. "I left after the fire because I was destitute. What else was I supposed to do? I lost my home. I lost my store of medical herbs. They were my livelihood and cannot be replaced easily. It is natural that I should seek refuge with my mother and brother."

The Inquisitor said nothing in reply to her explanation and proceeded to the charges against her.

"Aurelia Darrico, you stand before this court, accused of witchcraft. Is it true that you are in league with the devil and that he helped you brew magic potions?"

She answered him with a hint of defiance. "No. Whoever said that is a liar."

"The witnesses say that you have a dog who is possessed by the devil, and that you admitted as much yourself."

"They misunderstood me. I may have said that he is 'a devil of a dog', but I only meant that he is a vicious beast. I should have gotten rid of him long ago. He attacked Don Antonio and inflicted a lethal wound on him. He tried to jump me too, but I took a burning stick of wood from the fireplace and was able to hold him off. I dropped the stick when I ran away and I may have caused the fire — I don't deny it, Your Honour, but I did it inadvertently.

Those who say that I set the fire on purpose are accusing me wrongly."

"We are not concerned with arson in this court. That is the bailiwick of the secular court. We are concerned only with moral lapses and crimes against faith. So let me ask you: Have you, an unmarried woman, had relations with men?"

"No, Your Honour."

"I remind you that you are under oath and have sworn to speak the truth. Have you had relations with men?"

"No," she repeated firmly.

"The witnesses say that you are leading a wicked life, that you keep company with thieves and robbers, that you have lain with married men and even with priests."

"They are lying, Your Honour!"

The Inquisitor paused and gave her a probing look before he continued on a new tack.

"Have you ever been in the company of the Prince?"

"I have seen him."

"You have been in the company of the Prince, then?"

"I have, but not very often."

"Have you had occasion to be alone with the Prince?"

"No," she said, but there was a hitch in her voice.

"Yet you have been seen in his apartments. What were you doing there?"

"I was talking to the Prince's servants. I know many people in his household, Your Honour. I sell poultry and eggs to the cook, and herbal infusions if anyone asks me for them. That is how I make my living."

"The witnesses say that you sell magic potions."

"Healing potions, Your Honour. Herbal teas and the like."

"Who taught you about the nature and efficacy of herbs?"

"My mother."

"Who has been accused of witchcraft."

Aurelia bit her lip and did not answer.

"Have you given such potions to the Prince?" the Inquisitor continued.

"Never."

"Have you received money or gifts from the Prince?"

She hesitated. "A necklace, once."

"Any other gifts?"

"A dress."

"Were these gifts given in remuneration for a service you provided to the Prince?"

"No, they were gifts freely given."

"I remind you to speak the truth, Aurelia. If you are obstinate, we may have to apply torture. I repeat my question: Did you receive these gifts in remuneration for a service you provided?"

"No."

"Why did the Prince give you gifts then?"

"Because he is kind, I suppose."

"Have you had carnal relations with the Prince?"

"Never." Again there was a ring of defiance in her voice.

"Put the accused to the torture," the Inquisitor said and called in his servants.

Aurelia cringed at the sight of the two burly men. "No!" she screamed, "I beg Your Honour. Don't put me to the torture!"

"Do you wish to change your answer?" he said, but she shook her head, and the servants took her arms roughly and marched her off between them, crying for mercy.

The Inquisitor turned to Fra Lippo. "Go with them and observe the procedure," he said to the Dominican. "Make sure that the accused is completely undressed and her orifices searched. Witches often conceal charms or amulets on their body that make them insensitive to pain. And report to us what the accused says under torture and especially whether she is moved to tears, for that is something to watch for: A witch has no tears."

The Dominican bowed and followed the servants to the torture chamber.

"In the meantime we shall pray for the accused," the Inquisitor said.

They all bowed their heads, as he led them in prayer. They raised their voices to God, but the screams coming from the cellar could be heard over their pious responses. After a while the gruesome noise ceased, and the Dominican appeared at the door.

"She has confessed," he said. "She was stripped and thoroughly searched, but she had no talisman on her body. They tied her hands behind her back and raised her up by the wrists with a pulley. At first they raised her only a few inches and she moaned and promised to confess everything, but when they let her down, she refused to speak. They pulled her up higher, and when her shoulders started to crack, she screamed 'spare me, and I'll confess everything'. They let her down again, and she confessed that she had relations with the Prince and wept copiously."

The Inquisitor nodded. "That's a good sign," he said.

When Aurelia was brought back into the courtroom, held up by the two servants, she was a pitiful sight. Her dress was in disorder, her hair disheveled, her face racked with pain and smeared with tears. When the servants let go of her arms, she collapsed on the stone floor.

The Inquisitor ordered a stool to be brought and motioned the servants to help her up. She slumped on the stool, moaning. The inquisitor resumed the interrogation.

"I am told you have admitted to carnal relations with the Prince," he said.

"I did," she whispered.

"How many times did you have relations with him? Speak up."

"I can't remember." There was no defiance left in her voice. Her will was broken.

"When was the last time you had relations with him?"

"I can't remember. Two years ago, I think. When he left for Ferrara to get married."

"And did you have relations with the Prince after he was married?"

"No, I swear I didn't."

"Is it true that you said"—the Inquisitor consulted the depositions —"that you said 'The Prince has abandoned me. I will get my revenge on him. If he doesn't want to be with me, I don't want him to be with other women.' Did you say words to that effect?"

"No. I was sad that he no longer loved me, but I didn't say any of those things."

"I may have to put you to the torture again."

"No, Your Honour!" she screamed. "Spare me, for God's sake. Don't make me suffer again. I admit it. I said something like that."

The Inquisitor ran his finger down the deposition and found what he was looking for.

"And is it true that you said 'He will be mine from the waist down, so that the Princess can have only kisses.'"

"That was just stupid talk. I didn't mean anything by it."

"And did you also say that you will put a spell on the Prince to make him suffer for leaving you, and that he would not get well until he came back to you?"

"I said nothing about a spell."

"I admonish you to speak the truth. If you confess the truth and repent, you may obtain forgiveness from God and mercy from this court."

She sighed and trembled.

"Confess! Did you put a spell on the Prince?"

"I have no spells, but I confess that I fed him menstrual blood."

"Drinking menstrual blood may lead to a person's death. Did you intend for the Prince to die?"

"No, I swear I didn't mean to harm him. I only wanted to tie him to me, and they say if a man drinks your menstrual blood and if after intercourse you soak a slice of bread with a mixture of his seed and your spittle and place it into your private parts, he will be yours forever. That's why I did it, not to harm him. If that's a sin, I beg God for forgiveness."

"Did you give any potions to the Prince, or do you know of other persons who gave him potions?"

"Maria d'Avalos, his first wife, gave potions to him, at least that's what I heard."

"And where did Maria d'Avalos get them from? Did your mother supply them?"

"I know nothing about that, Your Honour. I swear I never gave him any potions myself."

"Did you use any other magic on him?"

"No."

"I may have to put you to the torture—"

"No, no! Have mercy on me, Your Honour. I'll tell you everything. I made a small statue of clay and stuck nails into it and bound it with hair from the head of a dead man. I buried it outside the castle gate, so that the Prince would have to pass by it. But that's all. And I know now that I did wrong, that it's all a pagan superstition. I repent, Your Honour, I repent! May God have mercy on me." She put her hands up to her face and sobbed.

The Inquisitor observed her closely, as if to make sure that her tears were genuine. At last he said:

"Aurelia Darrico, seeing that you have confessed and expressed contrition for your sins, you will be reconciled with the church. Rise and repeat after me-"

She got up from her seat with great difficulty and stood slumped, with her head hanging low.

"Repeat after me," the Inquisitor said: *I swear that I believe in my heart and profess with my lips that the Lord Jesus Christ, in company with all the Saints, abominates the wicked heresy of witches; and that all who follow or adhere to it will, together with the devil, be punished in the eternal fire of Hell unless they turn their hearts and are reconciled with the Holy Church. And therefore I abjure, renounce, and revoke that heresy of which you, My Lord and your officers hold me suspect.*"

He stopped from time to time to allow Aurelia to catch up and repeat the formula he read out to her, and she did so, raising her head and showing him a penitent face.

When the rite of reconciliation was over, she asked: "And am I free to go now?"

"You have saved your soul, Aurelia, and we rejoice with you on earth, as the angels rejoice in heaven. This court dismisses you, but you will be handed over to the secular court to answer the other accusations brought against you: arson and the murder of Antonio Paulella, and the intended murder of Livia Prevera, whom you kept prisoner in your cottage, and of Leonora d'Este whom you attempted to poison."

When she heard what awaited her, she howled in desperation and fell to the floor like one dead.

"Take her away," the Inquisitor said to one of the guards.

But as the man bent over her, she reared up, snatched the dagger from his belt and plunged it into her heart. For a moment there was stunned silence, then everyone moved at once. They jostled each other in their haste to get to the woman, who had collapsed on the floor in heap, her glossy hair loose and streaming like a black river. They toppled the scribe's chair in their rush. It hit the floor with a thump. Sheets of paper rustled to the floor. What drove them — the desire to help? But Aurelia was beyond help. To watch her die, to pray over her? They stopped and stood in a circle around her, suddenly confused and in awe of her unholy beauty. The guard had wrested the dagger from Aurelia's hand. Blood spurted from the wound in her breast, its smooth white skin and berried nipple visible through the torn dress. They stood still, arrested by the sight, watching the dying woman expel her last breath with a deep sigh. Only then did they come out of their daze. They looked at each other and remembered that they had a role to play, that they were here not merely as human beings who might be permitted to shudder at the sight of death or as men who might be touched by a woman's beauty, but as judges and representatives of the Church. They were the law and had a duty to perform. They recovered their dignity, smoothed down their robes, crossed themselves and spoke of God's will. At the command of the Inquisitor, the servants carried off the corpse and the scribe gathered up his papers and made a final notation: The accused died of her own hand.

Pietro too recovered his bearings, but Aurelia's piercing cries were still ringing in his ears, and the image of her mangled body remained in his mind's eye as he joined di Grassi and returned with him to the palace to inform the Prince of what had happened.

CHAPTER 42

Gesualdo Castle, December 1594

It was late afternoon when Livia crossed the courtyard to Leonora's apartment, but the day was already spinning into darkness, and the wintry light turning to dusk.

"You're just in time to admire little Alfonsino," Leonora said, taking the baby from the wetnurse, a young farmwife whose bountiful breasts offered enough nourishment for her own *and* the princely child. The long consultations that had gone into choosing this fresh-faced woman! Was she healthy? Yes, her energetic step and her glowing cheeks told them so. Was she respectable? Was she of good character? A nurse's sinful disposition could be transmitted to the baby suckling her milk, just like any other disease. Yes, everyone said she was a good and honest woman. And the final question: Was her milk of good quality? Fina inspected it herself. It was white and sweet-tasting. She placed a drop on her fingertip and let it roll off. It was perfect, she said. Not too watery and not to thick. The woman was hired.

"I'll leave him with you then, madam," the wetnurse said, curtsying. "I'll come back for him in a little while."

"Don't be in a hurry," Leonora said. "I feel I don't have enough time with my little angel."

With his hunger stilled and his soft round face in repose, the baby did look angelic. Leonora kissed his little fists.

"I only wish Don Carlo was here and could see him, but I know his great fear of evil spirits. He won't come near me until the priest has performed the ceremony of purification."

Livia thought she detected a subtle shift in Leonora's feelings for her husband, from love to sympathy. He was an invalid, a man of sorrows. Or perhaps what she saw was a natural progression, a levelling that happened in every marriage. Was a gradual decline in the intensity of feelings inevitable? Could it happen to her if she accepted Pietro's offer of marriage? Livia bridled at the thought that her love could wane. In that case, it was better not to marry at all. What was life without passion! Was fondness and affection really all she could expect? No, ten times no! She could not bear the thought of losing the glow of romance and the fire of passion. She would never allow her love for Pietro to fade to mere good will. But then Leonora had always been different, more placid in temperament, more restrained in her longings, gentler in her feelings. Then she recalled her thoughts to the present. Why think of marriage, which was only a distant dream. She had sent off her letter to Pietro, but who could tell when it would reach him. Or if it would reach him. There were so many barriers to their happiness.

"In any case," she said to Leonora, "your wait will soon be over. The churching will take place in less than two weeks, and Don Carlo will return then."

The words of the churching prayer said it all: "Thou hast turned into joy the pains of childbirth." But there were so many details to take care of. The household expected a feast to celebrate the occasion. The Prince had given his consent reluctantly. He disliked large gatherings, but he knew what he owed to tradition and to the honour of the House of Gesualdo. The invitations had gone out, and everyone, from the stable boy to the Mistress of the Wardrobe was in a fever to make the occasion a success. The Prince himself was concerned only about the sacred rite.

"He is anxious to have the ceremony done properly," Leonora said. "In his last letter he pleaded with me to observe every detail minutely — the veil, the lit tapers, the prayer, the offering."

She must kneel at the communion rail during the blessing, he said, rather than sit in the churching pew. Leonora needed no explanation for his preference. Maria d'Avalos had occupied that pew when she was blessed after the birth of Emmanuele, and so it was to be avoided like a thing infected with the plague. The Prince was particular also about the veil Leonora wore for the blessing. It must be of white damask and fringed.

280

"And we still need to decide on the number of tapers and on the votive offering."

"Fina will help you with that."

"With the ritual, yes, but otherwise she is of no help at all. On the contrary. She is full of fearful tales, about fairies attracted to young mothers and snatching away their babes. I know I shouldn't believe in such pagan myths, but after the dreadful events of the past month, I cannot help being afraid."

She opened her arms wide. "Come and let me kiss you, Livia. To think how close I came to losing you to the devilish schemes of that Darrico woman." She embraced her friend fondly. "You risked your life to protect me, not once, but twice — for I know now that you also fended off an intruder in Venice."

"You know about that incident? Who told you?"

"Giulia."

"And how did she find out?" Livia said, nonplussed.

"From her husband. Don Giovanni had the matter investigated and, although he could obtain no solid proof, he is convinced that the intruder was Aurelia's mother and that she meant to harm me or the Prince. She lives with her son in Venice, and your description matched her appearance: an old woman with a dark complexion and reeking of the potions that are her trade. You remember that I had a sense of foreboding when we met her son in the instrument maker's shop — Benito Darrico, I mean."

"You were alarmed, I know, and that is why I was at pains to hush up the incident with the old woman. I did not want to give you further cause for worry. But nothing remains a secret once Giulia has heard about it."

"Poor Giulia! Let's not be hard on her. The poison has taken a dreadful toll on her health, and she suffered a miscarriage. Thank God she is out of danger now. Fina tells me that she took a few spoonfuls of gruel yesterday and a little tea, although she hardly has the strength to swallow."

"She takes the miscarriage harder than everything else —the stomach cramps, the nausea, and the dizziness," Livia said. "But Fina thinks it was a blessing in disguise. She has seen babies born blind and deformed because their mothers ate spoiled food during their pregnancy. Who knows what the poison would have done to the unborn child."

"May God watch over Giulia and restore her to health soon! But we mustn't forget our other patient — Emmanuele, for disturbances of the mind can be as serious as ailments of the body.

The poor child is shaken by the death of Don Antonio. I wish Don Carlo allowed me to comfort him."

"Indeed, Emmanuele needs a mother. I believe you would soon become fond of each other. He is a dear boy and sensitive, but he hides his feelings and is too solemn for his age. I only hope the new tutor is a kind man and will treat him with understanding."

Leonora broke into a smile and pressed Livia's hand. "You will see for yourself in a few hours. The Majordomo is on his way here and will bring the tutor along."

"It did not take long for the Prince to choose a new teacher for his son. Has he told you anything about him, Leonora?"

"I hear he is a most agreeable man. I'm sure you will take a liking to him at once."

Livia was at a loss to explain the sparkle that had appeared in Leonora's eyes. She wouldn't think of match-making, would she? Not after Livia had confessed her enduring love for Pietro, the man whose name was etched in her heart and could never be erased.

"It does not matter whether or not *I* take a liking to the new tutor," she said to Leonora, "as long as he wins Emmanuele's heart. But speaking of the man who has won my heart, I have answered Pietro's letter and sent my reply to Rome. But what if he is no longer in Rome and has already returned to Ferrara? I think I should send another letter there. Will you be kind enough to give it to your courier?"

"Of course," Leonora said, "if you think it's necessary to write again. We'll talk about that tomorrow. Right now I want you to go to Giulia and let her know that Don Giovanni is on his way and expected to arrive tonight. The news will perk her up. The arrival of a loved one is a great restorative."

There was a strange light in Leonora's eyes. If I didn't know better, I'd think she was up to something, Livia thought as she closed the door behind her. But I must be mistaken. It is not like Leonora to play games.

CHAPTER 43

"How is our patient?" Livia asked the maid who was taking her to Giulia's bedroom. "Is she awake?"

"She is, and will be very glad to see you, madam. She takes such comfort in your visits."

Livia went into the room, parted the curtains of the bedstead and bent down to kiss her friend's cheek.

"How are you, my love?" she said.

Giulia's face, once as rosy and smooth as a peach, was pale and haggard, but the sight of her visitor brought a flicker of life to her eyes.

"I'm better," she said. Her voice was no more than a breath.

"I have excellent news for you," Livia said. "Don Giovanni is on his way here."

"When will he arrive?" She spoke so softly Livia had to lean in to hear the question.

"Very soon. Perhaps even within the hour."

"I wish I could sleep away that hour and wake up to see his dear face," Giulia whispered.

"Shall I sing you to sleep?" Livia asked.

"That would be nice."

Livia began to sing softly. Giulia's lips were moving, keeping pace with her, as if she was trying to sing along. Her eyelids fluttered, her hands fingered the coverlet restlessly, but after a while their movement slowed and came to rest. Her lips were still parted, but they no longer moved to the rhythm of Livia's song.

Livia stopped and watched her friend drift into sleep. Her eyes wandered to the bedside table, to Giulia's notebook, her list of symptoms, which was never far from her. It was lying face-down, as if she had been reading it. Livia turned it over and saw the heading on the page: The Poisons.

Was this Giulia's bedside reading? How macabre. But she couldn't help running her eye down the list.

Poisonous champignons: Causes dimness and mist over eyes, giddiness, trembling, and loss of balance, vomiting, palpitations, convulsions.

Belladonna: Absorbed through the skin. If ingested causes dizziness, nausea, palpitations, agitation and breathing difficulties. This is followed by weakness and sleepiness.

Ergot: Constricts blood vessels, causes seizures, nausea, hallucination, and uncontrolled movement. Skin looks burned and blistered.

Adulterated cheese or sweetmeats. Mixed with a potion of red lead, vermillion, and copper dissolved in brandy: stomach cramps, bowel disorder, paralysis, bilious obstruction, anxiety, restlessness.

Livia shuddered and closed the book. She sat at Giulia's bedside a little longer and was saying a silent prayer for her recovery, when she heard the sound of voices in the courtyard and the ring of hooves on the cobblestones. The Majordomo and his company had arrived.

Livia moved to the window and looked down, but night had fallen. The only light came from the open door of the stable, and she could make out nothing except shapes moving in the darkness and horses being led away. Then there were steps in the corridor, and the Majordomo appeared at the door.

Livia put her finger to her lips.

He cast a tender look at his sleeping wife and beckoned Livia out into the corridor.

"How is she?" he said in a low voice. "She looks peaceful at any rate."

"A little better, I believe, but the loss of the child weighs heavily on her."

He nodded, resigned. "I was afraid that God would deprive me of her, too."

They looked at each other silently, thankful for Giulia's escape.

"Well, then," the Majordomo said, straightening up. "I've brought along the new tutor. My servant has taken him to Emmanuele's apartment. Perhaps you should join them and smooth over the first meeting between teacher and pupil."

"I will go at once. I meant to talk to him about Emmanuele's music lessons."

"He seems to be keen on talking to you about Ferrara. He strikes me as the nostalgic type. Not a quality I would want in a tutor. I'd expect him to be more rational."

"He is from Ferrara?"

"I believe you know him. Pietro Paci."

The sound of Pietro's name was like a lick of fire. It melted the words on Livia's tongue. Pietro here! Pietro the new tutor! She had enough strength only to nod. What would Di Grassi think of her confusion? But he was preoccupied with thoughts of his own and had already turned away to go back into the room and take up the vigil at his wife's bedside.

Livia was left behind in the corridor. Now she understood the gleam in Leonora's eye. She was in the know. Livia would have liked to give full rein to her joy, to shout out her happiness. As it was, she skipped down the stairs and danced a pirouette in the entrance hall, making the stone flags ring to the tapping of her heels. Pietro here! A courtyard away. Was *he* as impatient as she was to hold him in her arms, to look into his eyes and say aloud all the loving words she had stored up in her mind and whispered to herself many times?

CHAPTER 44

On the road from Naples to Gesualdo, Pietro had had plenty of time to think of Livia. Idleness opens the floodgate of thoughts. He rehearsed the explanation or rather the apology he would offer her for his callous behaviour, his shameful preference for a career at court over her love. What could he say in his excuse? The betrayal weighed heavily on his conscience. Like a hobgoblin, it had taken up residence in a dark corner of his mind. It popped up at the least provocation and needed to be wrestled down over and over again.

On his arrival in Gesualdo, nothing was more urgent to his mind than to inquire for Livia. But of course Di Grassi had a different agenda for him: He must meet his pupil. He directed a servant to take Pietro to Emmanuele's apartment.

The vestibule leading to the young Prince's rooms was bare except for a row of gilded chairs, and yet it did not look bare because the walls were crowded with painted figures, a mural depicting a parade of solemn-faced saints worshipping the Christ child. The vestibule led to an ornate drawing room.

A large room for a nine-year-old boy, Pietro thought, and of a somber elegance that made no concessions to a child's taste. It opened into a dining room with a table running the whole length, at the head of which Emmanuele sat by himself, dipping his spoon into a bowl of soup.

He put down the spoon, pulled off the napkin which he had tucked into his shirt front, and got up to make a formal bow to Pietro.

"Welcome, Don Pietro. Forgive me for starting my meal without you, but it was past my usual dinner time. My tutor used to stress the importance of keeping to a schedule," he said. He moved and spoke with a gravity unnatural in a child.

He has been bred for succeeding his father and already has the demeanour of a prince, Pietro thought and wondered what kind of a man the late tutor had been, to instill such premature earnestness and such stiff manners in his pupil.

"You were right to keep to your schedule," Pietro said. "I like order myself."

"Then take a seat," Emmanuele said, pointing to the place setting beside him. He turned to the servant who stood at the credenza awaiting his young master's orders. "Serve the first course to Don Pietro, and I shall wait a little to allow him to catch up."

The dinner was a quiet affair. The boy was on his best behaviour, as if to honour the ghost of his dead tutor.

To break the silence which threatened to overtake them, Pietro asked questions about the majolica vases displayed around the room. The little Prince answered him promptly. He was well-informed about the origin of each object.

"And that one over there?" Pietro asked.

"The one with the snake handles? It was made in Turin by a man named Fontana. It is my favourite, although my tutor called it grotesque."

"I recognize your father's portrait," Pietro said, pointing to a dark painting that showed the Prince with his hair slicked back in a widow's peak, his eyes strikingly black and his lips pressed together in a straight line, as if he wanted to keep his whole person a secret.

"Girolamo Imparato painted it," Emmanuele said. "And the matching portrait on the other side of the mirror is my grand-uncle Carlo Borromeo." The painting showed a man in profile, with a prominent nose. He was dressed in the robes of an archbishop.

During the long pauses in their conversation, Pietro's thoughts wandered back to Livia. He had been told she would join them. He was torn between impatience to see her and uneasiness about how she would receive him.

288

He recalled his thoughts to the present, to his host, the strangely grown-up child, who was his responsibility now. The boy was unsmiling and kept his large expressive eyes lowered as if he was afraid — afraid of showing his sorrow, his vulnerable soul? He was so young, and yet he had been scored by fate already and had suffered grievous losses, the violent death of his mother, the alienation of his father, and now the murder of his tutor.

After dinner, Pietro and his precocious pupil retired to the drawing room.

"You have been through a most distressing experience," he said to the boy. "Would you like to talk to me about what happened?"

"No," he said. "It hurts me to think of — of Don Antonio."

It sounded as if the very name of his tutor had left a scar on the soft tissue of his heart.

"Then tell me about your curriculum," Pietro said. "I suppose you have started Latin lessons?"

"I have learned the declensions and conjugations."

"You mentioned that Don Antonio kept you on a strict schedule. What was your routine?"

The boy swallowed hard. It was difficult for him to speak of anything invoking his late tutor.

"We got up at sunrise. 'Make full use of the day,' Don Antonio used to say. *Carpe diem.*" The boy stopped speaking. His silent breath hung in the air. His eyes glistened with a mistiness not far from tears.

Pietro reached out to him. He wanted to put a comforting arm around the boy's shoulders, but he shied away, moved out of Pietro's reach and turned his face, so that his puckered lips and moist eyes would not betray his grief.

"I understand your sadness," Pietro said. "But remember: *Tempus sanat vulnera*. Time heals wounds."

Emmanuele drew a deep breath. "*Tempus sanat vulerna*. Time heals wounds," he repeated. A flicker of courage came into his eyes and he went on telling Pietro of his routine. "After breakfast Don Antonio taught me Latin and history. We stopped at noon, to eat. Then Donna Livia taught me music." The ghost of a smile appeared on his lips. "You will like my music teacher."

"I know Donna Livia from Ferrara. I was told she would join us here in a little while to discuss your curriculum."

"I'm glad she will join us," the boy said. His lips trembled into a smile. After that, their conversation flowed with greater ease.

When the long-awaited knock came, and Livia was shown into the drawing room, Pietro felt the full power of her charms. For a heart-stopping moment, their eyes met. Then she lowered them modestly. She was thinner than he remembered. The gauntness gave her an air of fragility he had never seen in her before. He wished he could take her dear face between his hands and kiss her forehead, her cheeks, her mouth. He listened to her soft, sweet voice greet Emmanuele, then him.

"Welcome to Gesualdo," she said. It was like a benediction. Pietro wanted the room and everything in it to disappear and allow them to be alone in the pure ether of joy, but Emmanuele was there beside him and he had to go on playing the tutor.

With an effort he answered Livia's greeting, forcing himself to look serene. He tried to read his fate in her eyes. He thought he detected love there, but he needed the assurance of tender words. He swallowed the questions he wanted to ask, or rather, he trimmed and shaped his speech to suit the occasion, but it was hard because the room held one too many, and his happiness had to be deferred.

"Donna Livia will tell you about our music lessons," Emmanuele said. "But first let me show you the school room." He was the perfect little host.

Pietro followed Livia and the boy into the vestibule. There was a brief moment when he stepped back to let her pass, admired the delicate lines of her figure, and stole a moment to look into her eyes. Alas, it was too brief a moment to read the complex language of her feelings. They entered the schoolroom, a long, narrow chamber which overlooked the road leading to the castle gate.

Emmanuele pointed to a door at the far end of the room. "Your apartment" — His voice caught on the word "your" and stuttered to a halt. Drawing a long breath to steady himself, he continued: "Your apartment is through that door, Don Pietro."

Pietro guessed that this had been Don Antonio's room. Emmanuele opened the door and stepped back. The chamber was large and simply furnished with a washstand, a bed, a clothes press, and a table with two chairs. It was devoid of elegancies or comforts except for a square of carpet on the floor in front of the bed. The room was as solemn as a monk's cell. Perhaps it reflected Don Antonio's taste, Pietro thought. Or it was the solemnity of a dead man's room.

When he turned back to the school room, Emmanuele was standing at the window, looking out silently as if he was hearing voices in his head.

Livia called to him softly.

He turned. His eyes were bright with tears. She opened her arms to him, and he did not reject her consolation. She looked at Pietro over the boy's heaving shoulders and said:

"Emmanuele saved my life."

"I have heard the story from the Majordomo," Pietro said. His heart contracted at the thought of the mortal danger Livia had faced trapped in a burning house and the despair she must have felt.

"But I was too late to save Don Antonio," the boy sobbed.

"You did all you could," she said, stroking his silken hair. "He stood at this very window and watched me go to Aurelia Darrico's cottage," she said to Pietro. "He waited and watched, and when he saw the house go up in flames, he summoned help. If he had not sounded the alarm, I would have perished." She looked at the boy with hot eyes. "I owe you my life, Emmanuele."

There was a knock at the door. The boy freed himself from Livia's embrace and rubbed his cheeks.

"Come in," he said, his voice still rough with tears.

His valet entered and announced: "The maid has brought the hot water basin, my lord."

"I will be with you directly," Emmanuele said. He turned to his visitors: "It is my bedtime."

"Would you like me to join you for breakfast tomorrow morning?" Pietro asked.

"That would be good. My valet will wake you," he said with a nod to the man waiting on the doorstep.

He bowed to Livia. "Good night, Donna Livia," he said. "Good night, Don Pietro."

The door closed on him.

Pietro and Livia regarded each other in silence. The moment of truth had come. Was Pietro forgiven? He did not dare offer Livia his lips. He hid the desire in his own eyes until he saw it in hers. Only then did he dare to take her in his arms. He drew her close and felt the warmth of her body. A thrill ran through him as he kissed her. The words he had so carefully rehearsed on the road slipped his mind. He closed his eyes and, like a man entering a dream or slipping under water, he felt weightless, floating in a sea of happiness.

It took time for thoughts to return to his mind and words to come to his lips. There was so much to tell her. They sat across from each other on the hard chairs of the school room.

"You said very little in your letter to me," she said.

"Only what mattered most. That I love you, that I want to marry you."

"But the young woman in Rome — I was told that you were willing to marry her because she had a large dowry."

"Never!" he said and believed his own lie because the idea of marrying for money seemed preposterous to him now. How could he have considered marrying anyone but Livia? No, a few months in the school of life had brought about a great change, transforming him from an innocent into a seasoned man, from a fool into a sage, or at least a thinker. Truly Pietro had sloughed off the old man.

"But now you must tell me about your ordeal, Livia. I was told you had a narrow escape."

"A brush with death," she said. "I was saved in the nick of time."

Pietro passed his fingertips over her hair, a tender probing, a confirmation that she was here beside him, alive.

"And poor Giulia," she said. "She fell into the trap set for Leonora and nearly died. I'm glad Aurelia will be tried for witchcraft. She deserves to be burned at the stake! Have you heard anything about the trial? I know she was taken to the prison of the Inquisition in Naples."

"The trial was held two days ago," he said, "and Aurelia is dead."

"Dead! How is it that we have not been told of the judgment or its execution?"

"She died of her own hand when she saw that she could not escape the law. She would have paid for her crimes, no doubt. She was a poisoner, an arsonist, and a murderer, yes, but as for being a witch — I don't know about that."

"Donna Leonora is convinced that she bewitched the Prince and poisoned his health."

Pietro thought of the Prince's confession to him. He had been Aurelia's lover, but there was no need to invoke the devil to explain his sinful actions. Aurelia was a beautiful temptress. She may have used drugs to kindle her lover's passion or strengthen her hold on him, but nature supplied those poisons. She did not need the help of the devil for brewing love potions. But why talk of Aurelia at a time like this? There were other things that concerned them more intimately.

"Let's not talk about poisons and witchcraft, Livia," he said. "Let's talk about us. I wrote you a letter —"

"And I answered it, sending my letter to Rome."

292

"It did not reach me, but you can give me your answer now. I'll be glad to take it from your lips," he said, ready to receive another kiss, but she drew back.

"Then you must ask me the question again, Pietro." A pixie smile curved the corners of her mouth. "On your knees! I must make you suffer a little for deserting me."

He got down on the floor at once and bent his knees to her. "Sweet Livia, my love, will you be my wife?"

"And will you take me without dowry?" A sparkle danced in her eyes.

"Your love is all I want," he said.

"Then I will take you as my husband and promise to love you forever."

He rose, and they kissed solemnly. Slowly, slowly their happiness took on solid shape and their bodies relaxed into a close embrace. Then Livia laughed and pulled him by both ears, like a little boy who had been naughty. Her voice had a thrill in it when she said: "I don't know if you deserve it, Pietro, but Donna Leonora has promised me a dowry and said she will be godmother to our first child, if it is a girl."

He answered her only by tightening his embrace. It seemed the earth could hold no greater happiness. They kissed again, more fondly, more impatiently, pressing up against each other. "Come," he said, and she did not resist when he led her to the bed in his room. They said no more. Their hearts were too full of delight in each other's presence. She guided his hands to her bodice and helped him undo the laces. When she slipped out of her chemise, he had already pulled off his clothes. They embraced with a desire long repressed because they had no reasonable hope. They had kept it alive through sunless days and fulfilled it only in their dreams until now when their dream came true. They made love in a pitching, rolling storm of passion. They drowned in a sea of pleasure, uttering cries of ecstasy. When they had sated their desire and lay in each other's arms exhausted, it was late. The candles casting their light through the open door were burning low, and it was time to part for the night. Reluctantly Pietro released Livia from his embrace. It was not wise to risk her reputation even now that they were pledged to each other.

He kissed her hands. "Will I see you tomorrow?"

"When I come to give Emmanuele his music lesson."

In the vestibule, they found the valet lounging on one of the gilt chairs, his legs stretched out in front of him. When he saw them, he sat up and gave them a sly look.

"I was waiting to lock up, Donna Livia," he said and buried a grin in his weasel face.

He lit the way for her, and she followed him downstairs.

Did he have his ear against the door panel when they were making love? Did he have his eye against the keyhole, when they were in each other's arms? It was an appalling thought, but Livia was too happy to care about what rumours the valet might spread. They could no longer harm her.

CHAPTER 45

A week had gone by since Pietro's return. The morning was crisp and cold, but the sun was out after a long stretch of dreary weather and cast its melting light over the courtyard. Livia and her mistress were taking the air, walking up and down the gravel paths, tightly wrapped in fur-lined cloaks.

"Don't you miss our strolls in the ducal garden?" Leonora said. "I certainly do, and come spring, I'll miss the blossoming fruit trees and the boats on the canal."

The courtyard, though well-designed and pleasant to look at in summer, was no substitute. The square separating the palace proper from the wing that housed the staff and contained the storerooms was designed like a formal garden and had cheered Leonora when they arrived in Gesualdo the previous year. The flowerbeds had been in full bloom then, and orange trees in large planters cast a decorative shadow over the lawn. Now the lawn was bare, and the marble tiles of the terrace, so pleasantly cool in the hot season, were an icy wasteland.

"But to be candid, this is all the exercise we need," Livia said. "Neither you nor I ever enjoyed long walks. We persevered only to get away from prying ears. We wanted to talk where no one could overhear our conversation. But now that Don Carlo has returned from Naples, the length of a courtyard is all the distance you will want between him and you."

The Prince had come back the previous night, earlier than planned. He meant to stay away until after Leonora's churching, but circumstances forced his hand. It was no longer safe to remain in Naples. The people, restless under the iron rule of the Spanish Viceroy, had been roused by the fiery speeches of Campanella. Their resentment reached a boiling point and found its outlet in a violent uprising. The rebels fought the troops of the Viceroy in the streets and in the hills surrounding Naples. As fires raged and gutters ran with the blood of the wounded, those who could, fled the city and sought refuge in the countryside.

The Prince and his retinue had been warned of the impending revolt and made their escape in time.

"You are right," Leonora said Livia. "There is no need here to take the air to avoid eavesdroppers. I no longer have any secrets."

Livia looked at her mistress sideways and gave her an impish smile. "Oh? No secrets at all? Then we must devise an intrigue. Life is dull without secrets, don't you think?"

She looked so droll that Leonora laughed out loud. "I see you have recovered your spirits, Livia. I was afraid you'd turn into one of those tedious, pinch-mouthed spinsters who never laugh and are the bane of all dinner parties. But Pietro is working his miracle on everyone. You are cheerful again, and the Prince has rallied and returned from Naples a happier man, although the occasion that brought him back is anything but happy."

The two ladies reached the terrace at the end of the courtyard. The smile vanished from their lips when they looked at the chaotic scene below. The road was full of refugees from Naples, a long line of stragglers, women carrying children, men weighed down with packs, carts loaded with people and household goods, sheep and pigs herded along. In the distance they saw the remains of Aurelia's cottage. Only the walls were left standing and the scorched beams of the roof. The refugees had turned the ruin into a rudimentary shelter from the wind, stringing up blankets and keeping fires lit for warmth and for preparing meals.

"Someone should tell them to keep away from that cursed place," Leonora said. She had gone very pale. "I wish that poisoner had died in the house fire or been condemned to burn at the stake."

"What difference does it make *how* she died?" Livia said.

"It makes a difference to me," Leonora said. "I wanted her declared a witch. I wanted everyone to witness her death, her body being consumed by fire and turn to ashes. Instead she died reconciled to the church — or so the Prince tells me. It amounts to her being acquitted. I don't know how she was able to pull the wool over the judges' eyes. I truly believe that she had the power to bewitch men. You asked me just now if I still have secrets. There is one thing I kept to myself, and I'll confess it to you now. It was I who sent the denunciation to the bishop."

"You?" Livia asked. The admission caught her by surprise. She had never thought of Leonora as vengeful.

"You are surprised?"

"Because I know your gentle soul. You never wish harm on anyone."

"But I will do anything to protect my beloved Carlo. Only I did not dare tell him or anyone else of my letter to the bishop. I knew he dreaded the sight of Aurelia and I too was afraid she would cast a spell on him and make him ill if she found out about my plan. So I wrote to the bishop privately. Giulia showed me her Book of Symptoms and convinced me that Don Carlo's seizures were the result of poisoning. They were caused by ergot, she said, or belladonna. And Don Carlo himself told me that Aurelia's mother brewed love potions for Maria d'Avalos. I am all but certain that he fell victim to her sinister practices. And Aurelia has followed in her mother's footsteps."

"But Don Carlo had seizures in Ferrara. No one gave him poison there, I am sure."

"The poison has long-term effects, Giulia tells me. The seizures may decrease in frequency as the body filters out the noxious substances, but the Prince may suffer from ill effects for years to come. And then Aurelia attempted to poison me, and you told me yourself of the jars you saw on the shelves of her kitchen and the toxic odour they gave off. I put all that into my deposition, together with the rumours I heard, that Aurelia had the devil's assistance in brewing those poisons. And yet the tribunal acquitted her of the charges of witchcraft. —That much the Prince told me, but he was not present at the trial, and the records are sealed. I would like to know what transpired. If my depositions together with the evidence presented by the witnesses did not suffice to condemn Aurelia, if she was able to trick the Inquisitor and convince him of her penitence, then surely she is in league with the devil."

Livia had never heard her mistress speak in such a peremptory manner and did not like the hard look in her eyes. It was so unlike the woman she knew and the gentleness she loved in her friend.

"Why torment yourself with thoughts of that wretched woman, Leonora?" she said. "Why not be content with the fact that she is dead and that the Prince has returned from Naples in a more settled mood? You say it is Pietro's good influence, and I don't begrudge him the credit for curing the Prince of melancholy. Pietro has certainly brightened *my* life and provided the perfect cure for *my* ailment. But all I needed was love. The Prince suffered from a greater malady — fear of being possessed by evil spirits. If you ask my opinion, Aurelia's death has done more to relieve his anxiety than anything Pietro could have said or done. Whatever the manner of her death, her noxious influence has been removed, and for that we must be grateful."

"I thank God for his mercy — but I cannot rest until I know what happened at Aurelia's trial. Has Pietro given you an account of the hearing? He was present after all."

"He was sworn to silence, and he would not break his oath. The proceedings of the Inquisition are as secret as the sacrament of confession."

Leonora lowered her eyes. "I wonder how much Giulia knows about the trial," she said, almost as if she was talking to herself. "Nothing escapes her notice."

"Her talents lie in that direction," Livia said, "but I wish you'd let the affair rest."

She could tell that her advice was not wanted. Leonora did not let the affair rest. "Don Giovanni was at the hearing together with Pietro," she said. "No doubt, Giulia has cross-examined him already. And no man can stand up to a grilling from Giulia."

Livia shrugged. "Then you must speak to her."

"Or you could speak to her on my behalf," Leonora said. There was embarrassment in her voice.

Livia couldn't suppress a smile. "You want me to do what you don't think is right?"

"You are teasing me," Leonora said, "I think it's quite alright to ask Giulia. And didn't you say you are going to visit her this afternoon? I would come along, but I'm wanted here." She was looking past Livia. The nurse had appeared in the courtyard, holding Alfonsino in her arms. "Nurse is bringing my little angel," she said and hurried off, but after a few steps she stopped and came back, taking Livia's arm.

"Don't tell Giulia I sent you," she said in a confidential whisper.

CHAPTER 46

Giulia looked wan, but she was no longer confined to her bed. She was reclining on a lounge that had been placed near a sunny window. On a table beside her was a plate of macaroons.

"Have one," she said to Livia. "They are heavenly."

Livia helped herself to one of the delicacies on the plate. "I see the cook finally found the magic ingredient to tickle your palate."

"Not her. She has no imagination, but she has hired a new pastry cook, one of those refugees from Naples, who came away with only the clothes on her back. Mind you, Giovanni says it's such a motley crowd, it's hard to tell the genuine refugees from those on the run from the law. But she is genuine. Her grandfather was killed, and his inn burned to the ground."

"And how do you know that her story is true?"

"Because she came recommended by Pietro Paci."

"Pietro? Since when does he take an interest in pastry cooks?"

"Wait until I tell you the whole story. It's unbelievable, really. You remember the young man I heard about on my journey from Ferrara, Orazio Farnese, who was kidnapped by bandits and taken hostage and whom Pietro rescued from certain death?"

"I remember you telling me that story, but what does his rescue have to do with those macaroons — which are indeed delicious."

"He fell in love with the pastry cook."

"Who did?"

"Orazio Farnese. It's the most romantic story I have ever heard, and very sad, because a pastry cook and a member of the Farnese family! What can I say? Their love was doomed from the beginning, and then he is a soldier in the Viceroy's army and she's the granddaughter of a rebel! But he helped her escape, or something like that, and wrote a note to Pietro asking him to do whatever he could for her. And so Pietro recommended her to the cook because he had tasted her macaroons before and knew she was an incomparable baker."

"Her looks had nothing to do with his recommendation?" Livia asked. She meant it as a joke, but the moment the question was out of her mouth, she knew she had made a mistake. Giulia pounced on it at once.

"Livia! You aren't jealous of a pastry cook? Well, for all I know she may be beautiful. It never occurred to me to ask my maid what she looked like. It was Leticia who told me the story, you know, when she brought me the sweets."

"Speaking of beautiful women and sweets, poisonous sweets, that is," Livia said, eager to change the subject and get on with her mission. "Has Don Giovanni talked to you about Aurelia's trial? Pietro has told me absolutely nothing."

"Giovanni wouldn't say anything either. The proceedings of the tribunal are confidential, he said. But, Giovanni! I said. Aurelia tried to poison me, and so I have a right to know what happened, don't I? He kept putting me off. So I knew there was something he wanted to conceal from me, something important, and in the end I winkled it out of him. If I hadn't been so ill and if he hadn't been afraid of upsetting me, I really believe he would have held on to his secret and left me in ignorance."

"And what was the secret you winkled out of him?"

"Swear you won't tell anyone."

"Not even Donna Leonora?"

"Especially not Donna Leonora because — I hardly know how to put it." But of course Giulia never could hold back a secret and blurted it out all at once. "Aurelia confessed that she was the Prince's lover!"

"Oh, dear God!" Livia was appalled. "We must never let Donna Leonora find out about that."

"It would be very distressing, I know. But then again, the Prince has done worse things, and Donna Leonora pardoned him."

"She has a generous heart."

"Or a strong sense of duty. I've been thinking about marital relations lately and have added a whole paragraph to the section on broken hearts in my Book of Symptoms. Do you know what I've observed?" She paused to give weight to her findings. "Married women are not as prone to develop broken hearts as single women."

Livia smiled indulgently. "And what do you ascribe that to?"

"There are two possibilities. Either marriage has a tempering effect on feelings, or motherhood shifts them. A mother's heart is more liable to be broken by her child than by her husband. That's my theory."

"And have you felt the tempering effects of marriage on yourself?"

"Not at all! And I hope Giovanni's feelings for me will always remain the same. I certainly love him as much as on the first day of our marriage. You must understand that my observations are general. I haven't had a chance to refine them. To begin with, one has to make allowance for variants in the human constitution, the humours of the body, the phlegms, the viscosity of the blood, the pulse rate, and so forth. Some people are more hot-blooded than others, as you can tell by looking at their complexion. Donna Leonora isn't the passionate type. I'm sure you'll agree with me on that. There is also the possibility that she has shifted her love from her husband to her child, as I said. In any case, I don't think hearing of the Prince's affair would break her heart. It might distress her at first—"

"But you haven't told anyone about this, have you?"

Giulia hesitated. "Well- I've told you."

"Anyone else?"

"I don't know why you are interrogating me like that, Livia. I am not trying to keep anything from you. I mentioned it to Leticia, if you must know, but it was old news to her. She said all the servants knew about the Prince's affair because Aurelia is a brazen hussy and bragged to everyone about her conquest and showed them the presents the Prince gave her."

"Giulia, this must not reach Donna Leonora's ears," Livia said sternly. "Never mind your theory about broken hearts. I can't have her made unhappy by an ugly rumour-"

"Oh, *she* can't be made unhappy? And what about me? Nobody cares if I'm unhappy!"

Something inside Giulia shattered, and she broke into sobs. "No one cares how unhappy I am about losing my baby. No one even lets me talk about it. They all hush me up and tell me to put it out of my mind, not to think about it, but I can't forget!" She covered her face with her hands and howled in despair.

Livia gently pulled her hands away and looked into her teary eyes. "I'm so sorry, Giulia," she said. "I know you've been through a great deal. You have every right to complain. We all thought it was best to be discreet and talk as little as possible about your loss. But it was the wrong thing to do, I see now. You needed a good cry." She put her arms around Giulia. "Let me kiss your dear face," she said. "Tell me that I am forgiven, and then let's talk about your sorrows."

Giulia leaned into her, exhausted. "I forgive you," she said, "and I promise not to say anything about Aurelia to Donna Leonora. Believe me, I know what it means to be distressed."

The two women settled into a heart-to-heart talk. Giulia sobbed out her grief and shed more tears of anguish until her face cleared and her eyes turned limpid like the sky after rain has purified the air and dispelled the clouds. A faint smile began to pull at the corners of her mouth, as she reached for a macaroon.

CHAPTER 47

In the schoolroom Pietro watched Emmanuele slumping over his desk. The boy's attention wandered. He was doodling in the margin of his exercise book. In a word, he was finally acting like a boy his age and proving the truth of the proverb *Tempus sanat vulnera*, Time heals wounds. He had begun to see the metaphorical meaning of *Carpe diem*. It did not mean that he must be watchful from dawn to dusk. It meant only that he should make use of opportunities as they came his way — opportunities to study, to play his flute and, sometimes, to loaf, play with his pet, or daydream.

Life is taking a turn for the better, Pietro thought — for them all. He and Livia would soon be joined in marriage. His place at court was assured. The Prince was a changed man, well, not entirely changed. He was in better health and therefore in better humour, but he was a stern man and taciturn by nature. Or was that the outcome of being raised a ruler, have people bow and scrape in your presence and fulfil your every wish? And yet you had no friend, no equal with you could be at your ease? Pietro thought of all the ill-tempered men in high places he knew, all the arrogance he had seen at the court of Ferrara, and worse, the cruelty and scheming he had been exposed to. At least the Prince was not cruel, although he stood on ceremony and knew how to keep a man in his place. No doubt he rued the time when he demeaned himself before Pietro under the influence of his illness.

But unlike Cesare, Don Carlo was no schemer. He showed his displeasure openly, if he took offense, and he was fair-minded. He did not seem to hold it against Pietro or di Grassi that they had witnessed the effects of his illness. He trusted their honour.

There was a rap on the door. Emmanuele sat up straight.

The door opened, and the valet appeared. He stood aside and bowed deeply to the Prince, who had followed him into the room.

A look of apprehension came into Emmanuele's eyes. He got up from his desk and shrank against the wall, quailing under his father's imperious eyes.

The Prince nodded to Pietro and turned to the boy.

"Don't cringe like a menial," he said to him in the voice of a ruler. "Remember who you are. Stand up straight and come forward."

Emmanuele obeyed. He stepped up to his father and bowed, but his taut movements betrayed fear.

The Prince chucked him under the chin and looked into his upturned face, then let go and turned to Pietro. "I have shown you the painting in the Church of San Domenico, which portrays Maria d'Avalos. What is your opinion? Does the boy look like his mother?"

"He does, my Lord," Pietro said. "But if you had asked me if he resembled his father, I would have given you the same answer. He seems to combine the features of his parents in equal measure."

"Look me in the eye," Don Carlo said to his son. Emmanuele raised his head with an effort. His arms were tightly pressed against his sides, as if they were glued to his body. The Prince fixed him with a long stare, then asked Pietro: "What do *you* see in his eyes?"

"The boy's native intelligence and his unspoiled character, my lord. He is an excellent student and a promising musician, Donna Livia tells me, for I am no judge in such matters." He turned to Emmanuele. "Why don't you show your book of compositions to His Lordship?"

The boy fetched the book and handed it stiffly to his father.

"He has learned to play the flute," Pietro said, while the Prince leafed through the pages. "Perhaps you would like to hear him play a piece for you, my Lord?"

The Prince nodded. "Play this for me," he said to Emmanuele, pointing to a recent composition of the boy's.

Emmanuele brought out his flute. Unease was written on his face, but he took up position in the middle of the room, faced his father, and began to play, giving a credible performance.

The Prince drew a deep breath. "Do you play any other instruments?" he asked.

"No, sire," the boy said with a polite bow. Playing the flute had given him courage. He had recovered his poise.

"Then you must come to the music room and choose one of my violas. The music master will teach you how to play it."

The boy shot Pietro a questioning look. He did not know how to answer this surprising suggestion. The music room had always been out of bounds for him.

Pietro seized the opportunity and answered on the boy's behalf:

"When shall I bring Emmanuele to the music room, my lord?"

"Bring him tomorrow afternoon. He may stay for the evening concert, and I will use the occasion to introduce him to Donna Leonora."

Pietro thanked the Prince for the invitation. Emmanuele stood in a daze, but after a meaningful glance from his teacher, followed his example, thanked his father and accompanied him to the door, bowing respectfully as he left.

When they were alone again and the meaning of the Prince's visit sank in, the boy finally relaxed and gave a great whoop of joy. The music room had taken on a magic quality in Emmanuele's imagination like a hidden treasure that needed a sorcerer's touch to become visible, or a locked vault that could be opened only with a miraculous key. Indeed, the room was a wonderland for any lover of music. The course of events had not entirely caught Pietro by surprise. He was aware that Livia and her mistress had been urging the Prince for some time now to reconcile with his son. Their labour of love had borne fruit at last. Carlo had overcome his superstitious fear and was ready to allow Emmanuele back into his life.

The next day, there was no room in the boy's head for Latin conjugations. It was crammed with all the wonderful things that awaited him. Pietro put aside the Latin grammar book and switched to the subject of musical instruments. That topic caught the boy's attention at once, but there was nothing new Pietro could teach him. He knew more about musical instruments than his teacher. His interest began to flag again. His fingers drew circles on the table, his eyes wandered to the window. It seemed pointless to go on. Pietro was searching for another subject, when Emmanuele said:

"I would like to give Donna Leonora a welcome present when I am introduced to her this afternoon. May I send my valet to Old Catarina? She embroiders handkerchiefs, you know, and may have something to suit the occasion."

"We might as well go there ourselves," Pietro said. "Lessons seem to be lost on you this morning, my young friend." He tried to look stern, but he understood the boy's excitement and could not hide a smile.

Catarina lived with her husband Fazio just outside the castle walls, in quarters reserved for old servants who had proved their worth and had been unfailing in their devotion to the family. The old couple shared a room there. In spite of the wintry weather, Pietro and his pupil found Fazio sitting in the yard whittling on a piece of wood. He stopped when he saw them coming through the gate and made his obeisance to the young Prince.

"Not too cold out for you, Fazio?" Pietro inquired.

The old man shrugged. "It's alright as long as the morning sun warms my back. I've worked in the fields all my life, sir, and hate to be cooped up inside like an ox in his stable."

Catarina appeared at the door and curtsied to the young Prince.

"What an honour, my lord. What a very great honour," she kept saying as she beckoned him into the room. "To come to our humble home in your own person. What an honour indeed!"

The room was furnished with a table, two chairs, and a straw pallet, all of the plainest sort. The walls were bare. A sewing basket was standing beside a chair at the window. It was filled with the tools of Catarina's trade: needles, spools of thread, and cut-out squares of batiste.

Catarina listened to Emmanuel's request and was eager to display her wares. She had been putting the final touches to an embroidered handkerchief for one of the ladies at court, Donna Sibilla. The monogram was almost done. The lower part of the S was complete, she pointed out, but she could easily continue and turn the flourish around to form the letter L instead. It would take her no more than half an hour. While they waited, she said, they might ask Fazio to carve a bird for the young Prince, or anything else he wished.

"He is a wizard with the carving knife," she said, "and will be pleased to oblige Your Lordship."

"Don't go on like that, woman," the old man said. He had overheard her praise and was too modest to let it go without protest. "It's no wizardry. It's a gift of God, but I'm ready to put my skills at your service, my lord—" He bowed to the young Prince. "Anything you want me to carve, my lord, I'll make it as good as I can."

"I want a cat," Emmanuele said without hesitation. "Can you carve me a cat? It has to be very smooth and round. I mean to give it to my baby brother, so that he too has a pet like mine."

"A cat?" the old man said. "But if you want it smooth and round, my lord, it will be hairless."

Emmanuele was amused by the idea. "Yes, make it a hairless cat!" he said.

Within an hour they had what they wanted: a fine handkerchief with Leonora's initials stitched in the corner, and a toy cat. Next they called on Livia to help them make their gifts presentable. They put the handkerchief, neatly folded and perfumed, into a sandalwood box and wrapped the baby's gift in a piece of lace, which Livia had hunted up.

"The 'cat' looks more like an egg with a whiskered face and a curling tail," Pietro said.

Livia saw Emmanuele's face cloud over. He was having second thoughts about the hairless cat, but she hastened to reassure him: "It's just the thing for a baby's hands to hold on to."

It was, at any rate, a great success with Leonora, who embraced Emmanuele with tears in her eyes, when he was introduced and presented his gifts.

Even the Prince, who had seemed stiff and tense when Pietro and Emmanuele entered the music room, relaxed when he saw the afection with which Leonora greeted his son and his eagerness to please her in turn. Yet he kept a wary distance from the boy and did not embrace him or even put a friendly arm around his shoulder when he showed him the instruments in the room. Would he ever be able to conquer his fear of Maria's ghost?

CHAPTER 48

It was Christmas Eve, and the court walked in procession to the church of Santa Maria delle Grazie to attend high mass and view a painting the Prince had commissioned for the main altar. The church, which stood at the end of a walled road, had a plain stone façade crowned by a belfry. Its nave was unadorned except for the new painting, a majestic piece reaching from the stone floor almost to the lofty ceiling. The lower half was lustrous in the glow of the candelabras illuminating the altar and shining their light on two painted figures, Don Carlo and Leonora kneeling before the Son of God. The painting was called "The Atonement". The artist had given an expression to the Prince's face which Livia recognized at once. It was the face of a man looking inward and listening with great concentration to music, or in this case, to a sound audible only to him, the words of pardon spoken by Christ. The upper reaches of the painting were wrapped in a holy and mysterious darkness. Enthroned on the judgment seat, Christ looked down on the sinner, his right hand raised in a gesture of absolution. The fires of hell separated the Prince from Leonora, but angels hovering above the abyss seemed to form a bridge between them. Both the Prince and his wife wore the garb of penitents, bare of worldly trappings. Leonora's hair was unadorned. No golden earrings, no jeweled necklaces or rings with bezeled gemstones diverted the onlooker from the aura of piety and devotion that suffused the painting. Leonora's face was placid and full of dignity, her hands folded in prayer, her eyes turned on her husband. She regarded him with serenity as if she, too, was absolving him from his sins.

A concert of sacred music had been arranged after mass to celebrate the unveiling of the painting. The ladies and gentlemen of the court were conducted to the whitewashed assembly hall of the Capuchin monastery next door, and in that sober room took their seats on chairs set up for them in a semi-circle. Emmanuele was by his father's side. It was their first public appearance together, and Livia noticed that the courtiers looked at the boy with new respect, with the deference due to the Prince's heir.

As the choir sang Christmas motets, Livia gave her mistress a searching look. How well the painter of The Atonement had captured the serenity of her face! But she also remembered the bliss that had lit up Leonora's eyes when she was a bride, the joyous love with which she had regarded her husband then. There was love in her eyes yet, but it was the caring love of a nurse for an invalid and the pleasure of seeing the patient regain his strength.

When the singing came to an end and the applause died down, the Prince called on Emmanuele to make an announcement to the assembled court.

The boy, dressed like the Prince in somber Spanish black, stood before the audience with the poise of a seasoned performer. Young as he was, he had something of the commanding air of his father and also of the grace and beauty of his mother, which had charmed so many men and fascinated the audience now.

With hardly a glance at the paper in his hand on which he had written out his little speech, he said: "It is with great pleasure that I announce to the court the engagement and forthcoming marriage of my music teacher, Donna Livia Prevera, and my tutor, Don Pietro Paci."

He paused to allow the pair to rise and acknowledge the smiles and congratulatory murmur of the audience.

"To celebrate the occasion," he continued, "I have set to music the verses of the Roman poet Catullus, and shall sing them for you. My father will do me the honour of providing the accompaniment."

The Prince rose and took up the Venetian archlute Leonora had given him. As he played, Emmanuele sang in his clear boy's voice that rang like a bell:

To dream of something dear, in hopeless yearning,
And find the dream come true, is joy complete...

After the last note had sounded, there was a moment of breathless silence as if the audience needed time to awaken from a beautiful dream. Then they rewarded the young composer with prolonged applause, and even after father and son had returned to their seats, there was a murmur of admiration all round. Pietro beamed a smile on his pupil and nodded his head to him in acknowledgment of his performance. Livia too thanked him for his musical present, but as she bent down to Emmanuele she saw a film of tears shimmering in his eyes. Leonora, who sat on his far side, noticed it too. She leaned over and whispered to the boy: "How is it that you look sad in the midst of your triumph?"

"I am sorry that Don Antonio could not hear me," the boy answered in a low voice. "He would have been proud of me."

"Then let me tell you that I too am proud of you," Leonora said, squeezing his hand. "You will be a great musician one day, like your father."

Gentle love filled her voice, and Livia thought: That is Leonora's way. But I want more than gentle love. I want my heart to soar. I want passion in my life. She looked with longing at Pietro and saw an answering light in his eyes.

EPILOGUE

Four years had passed after that blessed Christmas when Pietro received a letter from his friend Orazio.

Ferrara, 31 January, 1598

Dear Pietro,

When I hired on with the Pope last year, I thought I would finally get to fight the war I always wanted to fight. For a worthy cause — for surely Ferrara is a worthy boon for any commander — and under a worthy leader, Cardinal Pietro Aldobrandini, the Pope's nephew. And against a worthy enemy — your old nemesis, Cesare d'Este.

The conditions were promising. Cesare d'Este did what the pope expected him to do. On the day his uncle, Duke Alfonso, died, he occupied the castle and told the pope if he wanted his fief, he would have to take it by main force. The necessary preparations were made in Rome. We marched on Ferrara. I expected to fight hard and win a glorious victory or die a hero's death, but I am an unlucky man, Pietro, and destined to be baulked by fate. In the end it was treason that brought Cesare to his knees. We did not fire a single shot. His commanders betrayed him. His supporters deserted him, and Cesare fled to his castle in Modena. He is holed up there now, awaiting punishment. And I have missed my chance at glory once again.

The pope made his triumphal entry into Ferrara two days ago. You have never seen the likes of it. The pageant must have cost a fortune, but the Pope wanted to drive home a point: No one deprives him of his rights. A thousand people participated in the parade. I counted twenty-seven cardinals among them. Three magistrates presented the key of the city to the Pope. He was surrounded by a hundred Swiss guards and preceded by a float with a golden chalice containing the consecrated host. I am willing to lay a bet that the tiara the pope wore was worth half a million scudi. He was carried on a litter by eight men, under a baldachin of gold brocade held up by eight professors of the Ferrara academy. And I swear the whole city turned out to see the parade and cheer the old fox.

I suppose there is only one hope left for me, one chance to see heroic action: The Turkish war. And if I'm captured by the heathens, I shall immediately convert to their faith, for the Koran promises seventy beautiful maidens to the warrior who dies for Allah.

Write me your news. I know you have little time now that you are in charge of the young prince's establishment. And then there is your own household, which is growing larger every year. I congratulate you on the latest addition, a son — I know you felt outnumbered by the woman folk after your wife presented you with a daughter last year. Well, now you have an ally. May he grow up healthy and worthy like his father.

If there is an opportunity and you are out of Livia's sight, give a fiery kiss on my behalf to the beautiful Elena and tell her, if I knew with certainty that there was among the seventy virgins one as excellent as she

*is, I would not wait for the Turkish war but convert to
the Muslim faith tomorrow.*

*Your friend,
Orazio Farnese*

*PS. Burn this letter at once, or the Inquisitor will come
after me.*

That's Orazio for you, Pietro thought: masking his true
feelings, hiding them under the cover of a joke. There was a time
once when he had envied the scion of the House of Farnese. Now
he would not trade places with him for anything.

ABOUT THE AUTHOR

Erika Rummel has taught history at the University of Toronto and Wilfrid Laurier University, Waterloo. She divides her time between Toronto and Los Angeles and has lived in villages in Argentina, Romania, and Bulgaria. She is the author of more than a dozen books on social history, and has written five novels, *Playing Naomi, Head Games, The Inquisitor's Niece* (winner of the 2019 Evvy Award for Best Historical Fiction), *The Painting on Auerperg's Wall,* and *The Effects of Isolation on the Brain,* an excerpt of which was awarded the Random House Creative Writing Award in 2011. She is the translator of the correspondence between Alfred Nobel and his Viennese mistress, and has also written a novel based on them, *Three Women and Alfred Nobel.*